WICKED GIRLS

HEATHER ATKINSON

Boldwood

First published in Great Britain in 2022 by Boldwood Books Ltd.

Copyright © Heather Atkinson, 2022

Cover Photography: Depositphotos and iStock

A CIP catalogue record for this book is available from the British Library.

Paperback ISBN 978-1-80415-183-9

Large Print ISBN 978-1-80415-179-2

Harback ISBN 978-1-80415-178-5

Ebook ISBN 978-1-80415-176-1

Kindle ISBN 978-1-80415-177-8

Audio CD ISBN 978-1-80415-184-6

MP3 CD ISBN 978-1-80415-181-5

Digital audio download ISBN 978-1-80415-175-4

Boldwood Books Ltd
23 Bowerdean Street
London SW6 3TN
www.boldwoodbooks.com

1

GLASGOW, MAY 1988

Valerie watched her cousin Toni with concern. It was Toni's twelfth birthday and she'd been really looking forward to it, but now her party was in full swing, Toni just looked sad. She was wearing the white dress with the bow on the back her mother had purchased after her daughter had begged and pleaded when she'd spotted it in a clothes shop. Now Toni sat slumped on the floor, not caring that her dress was getting creased and crumpled.

Both Toni and Valerie were involved in a game of 'pass the parcel' with five of Toni's friends and three more of their cousins, as well as Toni's thirteen-year-old brother, Frankie, who wore a gaudy red shell suit that clashed shockingly with his thick mop of ginger hair. Frankie worshipped his sister and never strayed far from her side. Andy, their older brother, sat watching with his mother and stepfather. At sixteen years old, he considered himself too mature for such childish games. The rest of the children were laughing, eyes widening with glee every time the parcel came towards them, while Toni merely accepted it with bored indifference before thrusting it at the girl who sat on her right.

The music stopped just as it again reached the birthday girl, who rolled her eyes.

'Antoinette,' said Moira, Toni's mother and Valerie's aunt. 'Aren't you going to take the paper off?'

Toni didn't reply, attacking the wrapping paper, tearing at it with nails that had been painted pink.

'You won,' commented Valerie when Toni stared impassively down at the pretty pink handbag.

'I don't want it,' pouted Toni before slinging it into Frankie's lap. She got to her feet and stormed out of the room.

'I don't want a fucking handbag,' exclaimed Frankie, chucking the item at the girl sitting beside him.

'Frankie, language,' Moira chided him, pushing back her enormous perm, the fringe of which kept flopping into her eyes, the multi-coloured bangles on her wrist clacking together.

Valerie looked to her Aunty Moira, who was frowning up at her second husband, Eric. Toni and Frankie's real dad had vanished when Toni was only seven years old. The rumours about what had happened to him varied according to who you spoke to, but Valerie had overheard her own parents saying he'd left Moira for another woman.

'I don't know what's wrong with that little madam lately,' commented Moira to her husband. 'Nothing we do pleases her. She's spoilt, that's the problem.'

'I told you no' to give in and buy her that dress,' replied Eric. 'She's had a fortune spent on her lately and does she appreciate it? Course not.'

Valerie got up and followed her cousin through the large, plush house to the kitchen, where she found Toni pouring herself a glass of orange juice.

'Are you okay?' Valerie asked her.

'I'm fine,' she muttered before taking a swig of juice.

'You don't seem it. What's wrong?'

'Nothing.'

'I know that's not true. Please tell me, I might be able to help.'

Toni's laugh was humourless. 'No one can help me.'

'Has someone hurt you? Is that the problem?'

Valerie's worst fears were confirmed when Toni's eyes widened and filled with pain.

'If they have,' she continued, 'you should tell Uncle Roddy. He'll sort them out, he won't let anyone hurt our family.'

Valerie was a little afraid of the fear that filled Toni's intense dark eyes. She was a beautiful girl with waist-length black curls. Her mother spent hours working on her curls, so they resembled a doll's.

'He can't help me,' Toni rasped.

'Why not? Everyone goes to him for help. He's head of this family. If someone's upset you...'

Toni slammed the glass down on the kitchen unit with a shaking hand. 'He can't help me. Leave me alone.'

Valerie was shocked when Toni stormed past her out of the room. They'd been close since they were very young, Toni just eighteen months older than Valerie. They were the best of friends and told each other everything, but suddenly Toni was keeping secrets from her and Valerie couldn't understand why. If their Uncle Roddy couldn't help, then no one could.

Unwilling to let the subject drop and allow her cousin and best friend to continue suffering in silence, Valerie went after Toni, who was making for the stairs. She was stopped by her mother calling, 'Toni, you've got another visitor. He's brought presents.'

The prospect of presents would usually have Toni racing to meet them, but this time, she sighed and hung her head.

'Toni,' snapped her mother, warning in her voice. 'Come and see your guest.'

Valerie watched her cousin slink back towards the living room with her head bowed. She followed and saw it was Uncle Roddy himself, arms laden with gifts for his niece. He was a big man, tall and powerfully built, but ugly, with flabby jowls and pockmarked skin. His greying hair was permanently slicked down with gel.

'There she is,' he beamed at Toni, dumping the presents on the floor and opening his arms to her. 'The beautiful wee birthday girl. Come and give Uncle Roddy a hug.'

'Toni,' said Moira, warning in her voice, when her daughter just stood there. 'Give Uncle Roddy a hug.'

Valerie saw Toni's reluctance to even approach the man, but she could understand that. Uncle Roddy was the most feared man in Glasgow, as well as one of the wealthiest, and he'd done many bad things to get that wealth. Pretty much every member of the family was afraid of him. But Toni had always been able to wrap him around her little finger by giving him one of her cute, dimpled smiles. Now she looked like she didn't want to go anywhere near him.

'Toni,' hissed Eric, who was starting to look a little nervous. 'Give your uncle a hug.'

Unwillingly, the little girl approached Roddy and gave him a brief hug.

'That's better,' smiled Roddy, patting her back before handing Toni her gifts, which Valerie had no doubt would all be very expensive. He always splashed out on Toni, while the rest of the young cousins got cheap, crappy gifts. Roddy might have been wealthy but he was tight with it.

Valerie was confused. Toni loved receiving gifts and normally she would have torn into all the shiny paper and bows by now, but she remained sullen and silent, her lower lip sticking out. Moira and Eric appeared a little nervous.

'Well, open them then,' urged Moira.

With a sigh, Toni picked up one of the gifts and reluctantly removed the paper to reveal a beautiful doll with long black curly hair, just like her own.

'Oh, it's lovely, Roddy,' beamed Moira. 'Isn't it, Toni?'

'Suppose,' muttered the little girl.

'Don't be so ungrateful,' chided Eric. 'Open the rest of the presents.'

Toni rolled her eyes but sat on the floor to open her gifts, ensuring she sat a good distance from Roddy, who looked on with an indulgent smile. Ten minutes later, Toni was surrounded by more dolls, clothes, jewellery, shoes and an enormous stuffed bear while the rest of the children looked on enviously. Any girl would have been delighted by the mountain of presents but Toni just looked sad and angry.

'Say thank you to Uncle Roddy, Toni,' said Eric, who was starting to sweat, glancing at the family patriarch as he spoke.

'Thank you, Uncle Roddy,' said Toni flatly, without looking his way.

'You're very welcome,' he beamed jovially. 'I could murder a bowl of ice cream,' he announced. Roddy was famous for his ice cream addiction. 'Why don't you get me a bowl, Toni?'

'I can do that,' said Moira, getting to her feet.

'No,' barked Roddy, eyes filling with menace. 'Toni will do it.'

When it appeared Moira was going to object again, Roddy's glower became even more ferocious. Moira looked to her husband, who did his best to avoid her gaze, and slowly she retook her seat.

The amiable smile returned to Roddy's face as he got to his feet and held his enormous, calloused hand out to Toni. 'Come on, sweetheart. Let's have some birthday ice cream.'

Toni's eyes met Valerie's and the latter was shocked by the fear in her cousin's gaze. Obediently Toni got to her feet, took Roddy's hand and let him lead her into the kitchen. Valerie moved to follow, wanting to help her cousin, who was obviously in distress.

'No, Valerie,' snapped Eric, making her jump.

She turned to face her uncle. 'I want ice cream too.'

'You'll have to wait until Roddy's finished.'

'Why?' she frowned.

'Because I say so. Just do as you're fucking told.'

Valerie glanced at Frankie, wondering if he knew what was going on, but even though the boy appeared angry that someone had taken his sister away from him, he knew he had to stay put.

'How about a game of musical statues?' said Moira, forcing a smile.

'We can't play games without Toni,' said Valerie. 'It's her party.'

When Valerie glanced at the closed kitchen door and back at her aunt, she saw Moira was practically sweating with tension. What was going on?

'Musical statues it is,' said Eric with forced cheer. 'Come on everyone, up you get.'

He then proceeded to put on some music at an unnecessarily high volume on the hi-fi, making some of the children wince and cover their ears.

Valerie had a really bad feeling, just as she had two years ago when her dog Gracie had been run over and killed in the street. She glanced at the kitchen door again. Her cousin needed her. Was she just going to stand there and do nothing? If their roles had been reversed, Toni would have battered the door down by now.

Just as she'd made up her mind to go in, there was a shriek followed by an odd gurgle from the direction of the kitchen. Valerie had only heard it over the music because she was standing so close to the kitchen door.

'Valerie,' snapped Eric. 'Come away from that door.'

'Come and join in the fun, sweetheart,' said Moira more gently.

'I heard a weird noise,' she began, pointing at the kitchen door.

'I'm sure it's nothing,' said Moira with forced cheer, her perm becoming increasingly frazzled by the second. 'Now come and join in. We've got prizes to give out,' she added as an enticement.

Valerie, convinced something terrible was happening to her cousin, was in the grip of panic. 'We should check on Toni.'

'Leave it,' barked Eric. 'She's fine.'

His words trailed off as the kitchen door was slowly pushed open and out walked Toni. Everyone in the room stopped what they were doing to gape at her. Toni's curls were in disarray and her eyes were dead and empty. Her beautiful white dress was spattered with red, as was her face.

Valerie's first thought was that she'd shaken the ketchup bottle too hard. That had happened to her once and it had covered her in sauce. Valerie realised it wasn't ketchup when she saw the large butcher's knife gripped in Toni's hand, which was covered in what Valerie now realised was blood and something disgusting and slimy that looked like skin. Glancing into the kitchen, she saw Roddy's legs sticking out from behind the kitchen table.

Moira unleashed an appalled scream and she and Eric tore into the kitchen, giving Toni a wide berth as they passed.

'Oh, god, what has she done?' cried Moira when confronted by the body in the kitchen.

Frankie rushed to follow and Valerie heard him say, 'Awesome.'

'This is not awesome,' exclaimed Eric.

'Toni,' said Valerie. 'Toni,' she repeated louder when her cousin stared straight ahead.

Finally she got her attention and Toni's black eyes focused on her.

'What happened?'

'He wanted me to do something horrible. I said no but he tried to make me.' Toni's grip tightened on the knife. 'So I made him stop.'

Something flickered in Toni's eyes, something Valerie had never seen there before. She might have only been young, but Valerie had seen the same look plenty of times in the eyes of her more violent relatives. It was bloodlust. Toni had enjoyed her first kill.

2

SEVEN YEARS LATER

Valerie sighed and glanced at her watch as she waited on the corner of her street for Toni to arrive. Like the majority of the McVay family, Valerie lived in Springburn, a district north of Glasgow city centre, but her street wasn't as nice as those the rest of her family lived on. Her own parents didn't work in the family business, and instead had rigidly stuck to the legitimate side of life, even though they could have really used the money. That hadn't stopped Valerie getting involved in the illegal side of the family's activities. Although their business endeavours weren't anywhere near the calibre of what they were when Roddy had been alive, the McVays were still up to their eyes in nefarious activities and ruled the area they occupied.

Valerie had resisted at first, although she had been involved in many fights, usually thanks to Toni, who was still her best friend, even all these years later. Toni's natural haughtiness and sense of superiority got a lot of people's backs up, but the cousins had become known as a ferocious team and most of the locals were now wary of them. Frankie McVay had only added to this wariness as he'd developed an unnatural interest in his sister and, since becoming famous not only for his savagery but being a downright lunatic, everybody thought it safer to stay out of Toni's way to avoid arousing his wrath. This wasn't always possible, as Frankie McVay used the flimsiest of excuses to commit violence.

A taxi pulled up and the door opened, revealing a long, shapely leg, the foot encased in a black high-heeled shoe. Toni climbed out, her thick black curly hair halfway down her back. She wore a short black skirt, tight white blouse and white fake fur jacket that ended at her waist. From one shoulder hung a black Dior bag. Toni's clothes were all designer, although, so far, all the fur items she owned were fake. Valerie knew Toni was saving up for a real fur coat, to her cousin's disgust.

'Val,' smiled Toni as she tossed back her hair and strode up to her with her usual confidence. 'I'm glad you're already here, I do hate to be kept waiting.'

'That's because you're the one who's late,' replied Valerie flatly. 'I've been standing here for ten minutes.'

'The fresh air will do you good,' said Toni dismissively.

'Yeah, it's a real garden of Eden around here,' said Valerie, taking in all the concrete, cars and council houses.

'Are you ready to do this?'

'Aye, I am. I've been ready for ten minutes.'

Toni sniffed indignantly before striding down the street, her high heels click-clacking off the pavement.

Valerie knew she was an attractive woman with a tall, lean figure, long, dark straight hair that gleamed in the sun and piercing blue eyes men said were fascinating, but compared to her cousin, she felt like a plain Jane. Toni was always dolled up to the nines and constantly needed to be admired and flattered. Despite her outward confidence, Valerie knew that inwardly Toni needed validation from others to feel worthwhile. The little girl she'd once been and who had been so traumatised by Roddy McVay and his disgusting perversions still lived inside Toni.

'I'm looking forward to this,' said Toni as they walked. 'Sandra Jones is a mean old bitch and she deserves a good kicking.'

'She's not old, she's only twenty-nine.'

'That's fucking ancient.'

'You'll be that age one day,' said Valerie, or at least she hoped her cousin would be.

'I won't have let myself go, though. Have you seen her hair? And don't even get me started on her nails.'

'She's also a vicious cow who likes giving her weans a slap and kicking her dog up the arse. That's why I'm helping you with this, no' because she doesn't file her nails.'

'It's worse than that,' said Toni. 'She bites them too.'

'Her weans?'

'No, her nails. It's disgusting. I hate that.'

Valerie just smiled and shook her head. Toni really had her priorities backwards.

They turned onto the street where Sandra Jones lived, or Sandra Thompson as she was before she got married. The Thompsons lived in Possilpark, just a couple of miles from Springburn, and were long-time rivals of the McVays, their feud dating back to Roddy's time when a member of the Thompson clan firebombed a taxi rank owned by Roddy, killing his younger brother. The succeeding generations on both sides had maintained that feud, until Frankie had come along and exacerbated the mutual hatred by attacking Jimmy Thompson, the present head of the family. Leaders of the Thompson family never lasted long, dying either violently or from heart disease, easily explained by the vast amount of fried food and alcohol they consumed on a daily basis. A healthy family they were not.

Sandra Jones, née Thompson, had moved to Springburn when

she'd married a local man and had remained pretty quiet ever since, until she'd incurred Frankie's wrath by mouthing off in the local pubs that her family was going to kill him for constantly telling people he was going to replace Roddy as king of Glasgow. Frankie would have happily smashed Sandra's skull himself, but he was carefully cultivating his hard man image. He thought hammering a woman would make him look like a coward, so he'd sent Toni and Valerie on this errand and promised them £200 each for their trouble. Valerie needed the money to supplement the meagre wage she got from the petrol station she worked at. Toni wanted the money to spend on clothes, make-up and the expensive beauty salons she frequented. This was something they'd done for Frankie many times before, and everyone in the local area dreaded having the McVay cousins turn up on their doorstep.

Toni pushed open the gate leading up to Sandra's home. The rotting wood was clinging on by one rusted hinge and made an ear-piercing shriek as it moved.

'Well, that just announced our arrival,' commented Valerie. 'A cheap but effective alarm.'

'It gets worse,' said Toni. 'Just look at the state of the lawn. I don't think it's been mowed since the Second World War. And the front door looks like it's been kicked in and repaired with gaffer tape.'

In response, said door was pulled open by Sandra Jones herself and Toni's lip curling went into overdrive. Sandra was big and beefy with flabby forearms. Her blonde hair was very thin and lank and hung about her pasty moon face. A cigarette dangled from her thick lips. She wore a white T-shirt with stains down the front and black leggings that were two sizes too small.

'What the fuck are you pair wantin'?' she demanded before taking a drag on her cigarette and blowing the smoke into their faces.

Toni's eyes narrowed as she fought the impulse to cough. 'Frankie sent us to give you a message.'

'Oh, aye?' Sandra replied cheerfully. 'And you two wee weans are gonnae gi'e it to me, are you?'

'We are,' said Toni with pleasure, tilting back her head, eyes flashing.

'You know, I had a feeling you were gonnae pull a stunt like this, so I took precautions.'

Toni arched an eyebrow. 'Precautions?'

'You might wannae look behind you.'

Toni and Valerie turned to see a group of three men and one woman, all Thompsons, walking up the garden path towards them, the man bringing up the rear tripping over the gate as they went.

'Why is nothing ever simple any more?' sighed Valerie as the four people advanced on them. Sandra for her part had closed her front door and was watching from the living room window with a smug smile.

'What weapons have you got on you?' said Toni, not taking her eyes off the approaching group.

Valerie casually checked her pockets. 'My house key and a lighter.'

Toni turned to look at her. 'Did you just say your house key?'

'Aye,' said Valerie, taking it out and inserting it between the index and middle fingers of her right hand. 'See?'

Toni's response was a raised eyebrow.

'No?' said Valerie.

'It is a bit feeble.'

'Not if I jab it into someone's eye.'

'Eyes,' breathed Toni. 'Perhaps it is a good idea.'

It was Valerie's turn to raise an eyebrow. Her cousin's eye obsession was downright disturbing when she recalled that Roddy had been stabbed in both eyes.

Two of the men and the woman lunged at them as one, while the final man hung back, as though waiting to gauge which way the fight would go before committing himself.

Toni side-stepped as one of the men raised his hand to punch her and his fist went straight into the brickwork beside the front door of the house. All the blood drained from his face and he let out an ear-piercing shriek. His obvious agony caused his friends to hesitate and they stared at him in surprise.

The front door was pulled open by Sandra. 'Oy, Mark, you dickhead. Watch my pointing.'

'I think I've broken my hand,' he screeched, cradling the damaged appendage.

'Oh dear, so sad,' said Toni with mock sympathy before head-butting him.

Mark fell onto his backside, where he decided to remain.

'You bitch,' yelled Sandra. 'That's my boyfriend.'

'Then you have my deepest sympathies,' smirked Toni.

'Hold on, I thought you were married?' frowned Valerie.

Sandra turned bright red. 'Aye, well, fuck off,' she retorted. 'Claire, get her.'

The woman who had entered the garden tried to hit Toni, but Toni dodged and punched her in the face. Claire staggered about, stunned, and fell over Sandra's boyfriend.

The second man lunged for Valerie but she jabbed him in the eye with the key. He screamed and clamped a hand over his face, then Valerie kicked him in the crotch and he fell too.

Valerie and Toni looked to the third man, who was staring at them in shock.

'Fuck off,' the cousins yelled at him as one.

The man jumped and raced out of the garden, tripping over the gate, and rushed down the street.

Toni and Valerie turned to face Sandra, who was standing in the doorway, staring at her fallen friends in surprise.

'You just made a very big mistake,' glowered Toni as she and Valerie stalked into the house, closing the door behind them.

* * *

'I can't believe I broke a nail on that bitch's face,' sighed Toni, examining her blood-red talons as they left Sandra's house.

'You'll live,' replied Valerie, who had never painted her nails once in her life, despite how much Toni nagged her to.

'I'll have to redo them all now.'

'Don't make out you're hard done by. Painting your nails is one of your favourite things to do.'

'There is that,' Toni smiled with pleasure. 'And Frankie will be pleased. Sandra will think twice about opening her big mouth about anything ever again.'

'It's always a good day when Frankie's pleased. Do you think he's been getting a wee bit unstable lately?'

'He's always been unstable, right from when he started torturing animals when he was a wee wean.'

'I know, but don't you think it's been getting worse?'

'He's just trying to cultivate his hard man image.'

'He doesn't need to cultivate it, everyone already shites themselves when they see him, especially after what happened when he was fifteen.'

Toni's expression turned stony. 'Don't ever mention that again, Val. Frankie said we've not even to think about it.'

But Valerie couldn't help think about the fact that Frankie was suspected to have committed his first murder at fifteen years old. A local man had been found stabbed to death in an alleyway. He'd hit

Frankie for stealing a jacket and some money from his taxi when he'd parked it outside his own home to nip in for something to eat during his shift. It hadn't even been a hard hit, just a clip around the ear, but it had driven Frankie into a frenzy and he'd sworn revenge, although he'd been very careful to only mention this to his family. Frankie was far from stupid. When the man's body had been found, they'd all known he was responsible, but no one had said a word.

That was the day Moira McVay became terrified of both her children. She'd feared Toni after she'd stabbed Roddy and was afraid her daughter would want to punish her for not protecting her from that monster, but when Frankie became a killer too, Moira felt trapped with two murderers to raise alone. She'd divorced Eric when he'd been imprisoned for attempted rape of a teenage girl. With Roddy's death, the money had dried up and they'd had to move to a smaller house. The family always made sure Moira had enough to maintain her current, cheaper lifestyle, but they would disown her if she walked out on her kids. They would cut off all financial support and she'd be an outcast, forced to leave Glasgow, the only home she'd ever known. Moira was trapped.

'What do you think Frankie will become if he gets all the power he's after?' said Valerie.

'Rich,' smiled Toni with satisfaction.

'I was thinking more of a despot. No one will be safe.'

'Stop talking like this. It's dangerous.'

'It's true and you know it.'

Toni huffed and rounded on her. 'I mean it, Val. I don't want anything to happen to you, so fucking stop it, okay?'

Valerie was well aware that she was one of the very few people Toni cared about and she was afraid of losing her. 'All right, Toni. If that's what you want.'

'It is,' she hissed. Toni sighed, her expression softening. 'Bad things happen to people who criticise Frankie.'

'I know,' Valerie replied equally gently, touched by how worried her cousin was for her. 'Well, let's go and tell him our mission was successful. That'll put us in his good books.'

A relieved Toni smiled and nodded. 'That's the best place to be.'

Frankie had moved into his own house just a couple of streets away from his mother's. After battering a couple of low-level drug dealers and scaring them off, he'd taken over their patches and was doing very well for himself, so well, in fact, that he'd been able to rent a nice terraced house. The McVay family once again ruled Springburn, but they had barely any influence outside their own neighbourhood, which was a big comedown from Roddy's day when they'd ruled the entire city. Frankie could have afforded to buy his home outright, but that kind of money would have drawn the police's attention to him immediately. It was a small house, just a two up, two down, but Frankie was immensely proud of it. Because he was raking in so much cash dealing weed, cocaine and heroin, he'd filled it with only the best furniture. No flat-packed shite that took a whole day to assemble. It was also spotlessly clean, as he paid one of his mother's friends to clean it for him. He rarely had people round, but he didn't mind Toni visiting because he was obsessed with her, and he didn't mind Valerie because she could be trusted not to make a mess.

Toni rang the bell and they waited for it to be answered. Toni became increasingly uncomfortable when the door didn't open but she knew her brother was staring at her through the spyhole, she could practically feel his eyes eating up her body and it made her feel sick.

Finally, the door opened to reveal Frankie, wearing black trousers and a light blue shirt. Since his elevation in the world, he'd taken to wearing only expensive suits. As he was just hanging around the house, he wasn't wearing a tie and suit jacket, but he still liked to look smart, even if he wasn't going anywhere. On his feet, he wore grey slippers. Shoes were not permitted inside his home. Valerie always thought it was funny that the feared Frankie McVay wore granddad slippers, but she never mentioned the fact.

'It's yourselves,' he grinned at them. 'Come away in.'

Frankie's appearance hadn't changed since he was a young boy. He still had his thick red hair and the square, black-framed glasses, only his hair was now a little more styled and never permitted to become unruly.

After leaving their shoes just inside the door, Valerie and Toni were allowed to pad through to the living room, which contained an enormous brown leather sofa, a coffee table made of gleaming oak, an extravagant sideboard of the same material and the newest television and hi-fi money could buy.

'How did it go?' said Frankie. 'Did you sort out that ugly old bitch?'

'We did,' said Toni proudly.

'Did she gi'e you any bother?'

'She tried. Four of her pals were there but we dealt with them easily enough, didn't we, Val?'

'Aye,' she replied. 'Nae bother.'

'Fucking beautiful,' said Frankie. He delved into the drawer of the sideboard and produced two balled-up rolls of notes, tossing one to each of the women. 'Enjoy spending it, you deserve it.'

'Thanks, Frankie,' they replied in unison before slipping the money into their pockets.

'I've got another job for you, if you're up for it?'

'What job?' said Toni.

Valerie warily awaited his response. She was always afraid Frankie would ask them to deal drugs for him. Her conscience had no problem with giving someone a good hiding, but she baulked at the prospect of selling drugs.

'I want you to keep an eye on Stevie Johnson for me,' said Frankie. 'That wee shite is getting too lairy for his own good and I think he might be relaying information about me to the fucking Thompsons.'

'Wee Stevie?' said Toni. 'Are you sure?'

'No, I'm no' sure, that's why I want you to watch the bastard,' he barked.

'Aye, all right then, Frankie, we will,' she said in a soothing tone.

'You got a problem with that, doll?' he asked Valerie.

'Not at all,' she replied in her usual cool, calm way. Valerie knew it annoyed Frankie that she never seemed to be frightened of him. The truth was, she was afraid of him, she just didn't let it show.

'Aye, good,' he said with a sharp nod, eyes flashing at the fact that once again his anger had seemingly failed to intimidate her. 'The problem is, the wee worm's gone to ground, so you'll need to sniff him out first. Do the job right and you'll get double the pay. You might even start earning enough to gi'e up your shitey job at the petrol station.'

'I enjoy that job,' replied Valerie. 'I meet some interesting people.'

'You mean wankers. Well, on you go then, and let me know the moment you find out if Stevie's a treacherous wee prick.'

The two women put their shoes back on and left, Toni

breathing a sigh of relief that she was out of her brother's company.

'We'd better get right on with finding Stevie, I suppose,' said Valerie.

'Definitely,' replied Toni. 'If Frankie tells you to do something, then you do it. If we keep doing so well, soon we'll both be working for him full-time.'

Valerie wasn't sure that was what she wanted, but she wasn't about to tell Toni that. She didn't want to think what Frankie would do if he found out.

3

Stevie Johnson was a small, unpleasant creature with greasy hair, spots and perpetual stains under the armpits of his tracksuit. However, he was popular in the local community because Stevie always knew what was happening – who was having an affair with who, who was up in court, who was in debt with the local loan sharks. If there was something you wanted to know, Stevie Johnson was your man. Naturally Frankie had recruited him to assist him in his rise to power. An information-gatherer of Stevie's calibre was a very valuable asset. But he could be equally damaging if he decided to turn on his master, which was why Frankie needed to find out if he was a traitor asap.

'Why is he sending us out on this?' Valerie asked Toni.

'Because he thinks we can handle it,' she replied.

'Frankie hates traitors, I would have thought he'd want to deal with it himself, or what about his friends Paul and Jamesie? They're his main enforcers.'

'Aye, they are, but they don't have too many brain cells,' said Toni with an amused smile. 'They'd get distracted and end up getting pished in the pub.'

'I'm not so sure, I think there's more to it.'

'You're getting paranoid. Frankie knows we're the best ones for the job, end of story.'

But Valerie's instinct was nagging at her, so she would stay on guard.

They went to Stevie's home but he wasn't there, which meant a trek around every pub, bookies and café in Springburn, but he was nowhere to be found, and everyone they spoke to said they had no idea where he was.

Valerie and Toni stopped in a café to have a cup of tea and go over their options.

'I'll make that wee sod Stevie pay when we do find him,' sighed Toni, slipping off her left shoe and massaging her foot. 'It's his fault my feet are aching.'

'You'd be much more comfortable in trainers,' commented Valerie.

Toni's eyes flashed. 'I have never worn trainers and I'm no' starting now.'

'Actually, I remember you having a blue pair with ET on the heels when you were wee. You loved them and you used to run around thinking if you ran fast enough, you'd take off into the sky like Elliott's bike.'

Toni's eyes narrowed. 'Don't ever mention that again.'

Valerie chuckled and sipped her tea.

'When we do find Stevie,' said Toni, 'I'll kick him right in the baws.'

'He's playing it smart. We just have to be smarter. Where would he hide?'

'With one of his manky pals, probably.'

'But he wouldn't risk letting anyone else know, not with how persuasive Frankie can be.'

'Hmm, good point. Well, we know he doesn't have any second

properties or island hideaways,' said Toni with an amused smile. 'Maybe he's booked into some cheap bed and breakfast?'

'He wouldn't fork out for something like that, he's known for being a miserly git. Every penny's a prisoner with him.'

Toni's eyes gleamed as she finally scented their quarry. 'Then he's somewhere that's free and no one else will be there.'

'Are you thinking the flats on Balgrayhill Road which were abandoned after that fire?'

'That is one possibility.'

'Jeanie Warren's weans have started saying it's haunted and that no one should go near it because the ghost will get angry and follow them home.'

'I wonder if this ghost is five foot eight, smelly and ugly?'

'I think it just might be. What better way to keep the weans away than scare them with a ghost story?'

'Let's check it out.'

They finished their tea and, feeling revived, the two women continued the hunt. The flats were only a few streets away, so Toni's sore feet didn't have to walk far.

'I'll be needing my foot spa tonight,' she announced, grimacing when pain shot through the ball of her foot every time her shoe made contact with the pavement. She soothed herself by thinking of all the tortures she would inflict on wee Stevie for sending her on this merry dance.

The flats were a five-storey dark cream building, relatively modern but made grotesque by being left to decay after the fire. All the windows on the top two floors were boarded up. Some of the windows on the lower floors, which hadn't been as badly damaged by the fire, had been smashed by teenagers using the debris lying on the ground – abandoned bottles, bricks and stones. A window on the first floor had been left open, and the tattered curtain still hanging from the rail flapped in the breeze, making the building a sad parody of the life that had once inhabited it.

All the doors at the front of the building had been boarded up, but they found one at the rear that had been prised open.

Valerie peered through the crack in the door. The interior was gloomy, but she could make out a bare corridor, scorch marks up the wall, graffiti sprayed across it. The tiled floor was bare and chipped but there was no sign of life.

'I can't see anyone,' she whispered to Toni. 'Shall we check it out?'

Quietly they crept through the gap in the door, Toni walking on her tiptoes to avoid making a sound on the tiled floor with her heels. Her lip curled at the smell, which was a mixture of mustiness, urine and smoke.

Together they poked their heads around the first door on the left. The building was split into small, poky flats. This particular flat was entirely bare, the remnants of fire-damaged furniture the only thing it contained. The other three flats on this level were the same, so they made their way up to the first floor, being careful to avoid all the gouges in the concrete steps. It was impossible to keep their approach silent because of Toni's high heels and all the creaks and groans the building made as they moved through it. Valerie was beginning to wonder at the wisdom of venturing inside, especially as signs adorned the exterior of the building warning that it was unsafe.

Just as they reached the top of the stairs, there was a loud banging sound, followed by an eerie groan.

'Get out,' snarled a ferocious voice.

'If that's a ghost,' said Toni, 'then I'm Peter Andre.'

The two women strode down the corridor towards the room where the voice had come from as the groan increased in volume, accompanied by the rattling of chains.

'Seriously?' said Valerie with a raised eyebrow.

'On three?' smiled Toni.

Valerie smiled back and nodded.

They counted down together before kicking the door, which slammed open and hit something before rebounding. There was another groan, only this time it was one of pain.

Valerie and Toni walked in to find a small, sweaty, spotty man moaning on the floor, blood trickling from his nose. Beside him on the floor lay a thick bike chain.

'Oh, look, Val,' said Toni. 'We caught a wee ghost.'

'So it seems,' she replied.

'I think you broke my nose,' whined Stevie.

'So you're the one who's been haunting this building,' said Toni. 'You've got the weans scared.'

'Good. That's what I wanted. Wee sods kept trying to come in to arse about,' he replied, voice pinched and nasal.

'But you didn't want them here, did you, because you were using this place as your hidey-hole after betraying my brother.'

'I didnae betray him,' exclaimed Stevie. 'That's a malicious rumour. Someone's got it in for me, someone who wants to see Frankie fail.'

Toni knelt beside him, produced a small knife from her jacket pocket and brandished it with glee. 'Now who would do that?'

'There's plenty of people who don't want him to succeed.'

'Like who?'

'The Thompsons for one, but I havenae betrayed him, I wouldn't, I swear,' he cried. 'He scares the living shite out of me.'

'I do hope you're not lying to me,' said Toni, pressing the tip of the blade to his lower eyelid, fascinated by the way the eyeball protruded a little when she put pressure on the lid. One day, she'd go all the way and see if she could get someone's eyeball to pop out entirely, but she couldn't do that to Stevie, not without Frankie's permission, anyway.

'Careful, Toni,' said Valerie. 'You'll hurt him. You'd better call Frankie.'

To Valerie's relief, the knife disappeared back into the depths of Toni's coat and her cousin got to her feet.

'You're right, Val. He'll want to handle this personally.' Toni produced a chunky green Nokia phone. 'I hate these fucking things,' she muttered as she tapped at the buttons, sighing when she pressed the wrong one and it beeped. 'Finally, there it is.' She put the phone to her ear and Frankie answered on the second ring. 'We've found him.' After giving Frankie the address, she hung up and looked down at the hapless Stevie. 'He's on his way.'

'He's gonnae fucking kill me and I haven't done anything wrong,' he wailed.

'You made yourself look guilty by going into hiding,' Valerie told him. 'You should have gone to him instead and explained.'

'Explained, to Frankie McVay? He would have slit my throat before I'd said a word because he already thinks I'm guilty, even though I'm no'. You have to help me, please, or I'll die in this shitehole.'

'Then give us more information. What's going on?'

'I don't know.'

'Oh, yes, you do. You always know what's going on, Stevie, and it seems that knowledge has landed you right in it.'

Stevie dragged himself up to a sitting position and sighed. 'The Thompsons are feared that Frankie will become a power, especially after all the bad blood that went on between them and your family when Roddy was alive. They think he'll want revenge. They also know that I'm one of his biggest assets and by setting me up, they're hoping he'll take me out himself, not only weakening him but making him look like a dickhead in the process.'

'Frankie will be the one to judge you,' said Toni.

'He'll kill me,' bawled Stevie, tears shining in his eyes.

Toni shrugged, she couldn't care less.

Valerie felt sorry for Stevie as he remained slumped on the floor, quietly crying. At one point, he tried to make a run for it, but Toni stuck out her foot and tripped him and he fell face down on the dusty floor, where he remained, limp with defeat, until Frankie strode in with his two best friends, Paul and Jamesie. Paul was tall and stocky with round glasses, dark hair and a goatee beard. Jamesie was scrawny-looking with dirty blonde hair that stuck out at odd angles from his head. He looked perpetually rumpled, as though he'd just got out of bed and dressed in a hurry.

Frankie's lip curled with disgust in a way very reminiscent of his sister as he stared down at Stevie pitilessly.

'Stop fucking crying, you big jessie,' he thundered.

Stevie went abruptly silent but remained on the floor with his head bowed, unable to bring himself to look at Frankie.

Frankie, breathing furiously, knelt by Stevie's side, grabbed a handful of his hair and yanked up his head. 'Have you betrayed me to the Thompsons?'

'No, Frankie, I swear. They're lying because they know that I'll only work for you. They tried to get me to go over to their side, but I told them to piss off and this is their revenge.'

Frankie looked to Paul and Jamesie, who shrugged, before he turned back to face Stevie. 'What a load of bollocks,' he spat at him.

'It's the truth,' cried Stevie.

'I don't believe you.'

Frankie's eyes rolled back in his head, a sign that his anger had reached its peak and he could no longer control it. Stevie screamed in fear when Frankie pulled a machete from inside his long black coat and raised it aloft.

'Frankie,' yelled a voice.

The interruption had the desired effect. Frankie's eyes returned to normal and he turned to look at Valerie. 'What?' he barked, the machete still raised.

'I think he's telling the truth.'

'Thank you,' breathed Stevie, tears rolling down his face and his hands shaking uncontrollably.

'This is down to the Thompsons,' said Valerie calmly, ignoring Toni's frantic gestures to stop talking. 'They're stirring things up so you'll take out one of your biggest assets.'

Frankie slowly lowered the machete, his gaze riveted on her. 'You think the Thompsons are smart enough to come up with a plan like that?'

'I do, and I think we should at least check it out before condemning Stevie. He gathers all your intelligence for you. Without him, you'll be blind, which is what the Thompsons want.'

Frankie appeared thoughtful, the mania gone from his eyes. 'That's some good thinking, Val. I won't let the Thompsons manipulate me, the sly bastards. All right, Stevie boy, you've had a reprieve.'

'Thank you,' the man rasped, still shaking uncontrollably.

'But until I know for sure that you're no' a backstabbing wee worm, you'll live in my cellar. That way, I know you cannae dae a runner.'

Stevie was just so relieved all his body parts were still attached that he didn't object to being kept a prisoner.

'I want you two to check it out,' said Frankie, pointing from Valerie to Toni with the machete.

'Us?' said Toni. 'But I thought you'd put Paul and Jamesie on it.'

'This pair of daft wanks? You must be joking. Jamesie cannae find his arse with both hands and Paul walked into the cupboard instead of the cludgy in his own hoose. How do you expect them to deal with something complex like this?'

Neither of Frankie's friends took offence and instead just smiled with amusement, glad they hadn't been given that assignment because it would be a difficult one to get to the bottom of, and Frankie hated failure.

'Don't get sulky,' Frankie barked at his sister. 'I'll pay you a grand each if you find out what's going on.'

'A grand?' said Toni, eyes gleaming as she thought of all the clothes and shoes she could buy with that money. 'All right, we'll do it.'

Valerie scowled at her, but Toni ignored the look.

Frankie wrapped his arm around his sister, causing her to stiffen. 'I knew you wouldnae let me down, sweetheart.'

He planted a wet kiss on her cheek, Toni doing her best not to grimace.

'You two,' said Frankie, releasing Toni and nodding at his friends while slipping the machete back inside his jacket. 'Get that spotty wee prick to my house. Make sure he's locked up nice and tight in my cellar.'

'On it, Frankie,' said Paul, easily hauling Stevie to his feet by one arm. Jamesie took his other arm and between them they escorted him out.

Stevie nodded his thanks at Valerie as he passed her by, and she nodded back.

'I want results and I want them fast,' Frankie told Valerie and Toni so severely they didn't dare object, not after he'd already been denied his fun.

The two women nodded and Frankie left too, complaining about the smell as he went.

'Great,' sighed Valerie. 'Where the hell are we supposed to start?

'Just keep thinking of the money,' said Toni. 'That's what's consoling me.'

'Not me. I just wanted to help Stevie. I couldn't watch him be hacked to pieces in this horrible place.'

'Your problem is you've got too much compassion.'

'Good, because the day I lose it is the day I give up entirely.'

'That's a bit dramatic!'

'I mean it. What will we become if we continue down this road?'

'Rich,' was Toni's response.

'They are many ways to be rich, not just materialistically.'

'Aye, but that's the most fun.' Toni rolled her eyes when Valerie stared at her stonily. 'Fine, we won't do it, but you can tell Frankie. I'm sure he'll find an imaginative way to show you how disappointed he is.'

It was Valerie's turn to sigh. 'We've no choice.'

'Not if we want to stay in one piece, no.'

'Where do we start?'

'We need to find out what the Thompsons know about Frankie's operation. The Thompsons will probably expect him to make a move, but they won't be expecting him to send two women. That gives us the advantage.'

'But they know our faces, they'll see us coming a mile off.'

Toni paused to think before saying, 'Let's go to that club on Queen Street.'

'Not Archaos?' groaned Valerie.

'That's the one. What's wrong with Archaos?'

'I don't like nightclubs at the best of times but that one's mental. They let in anyone, no matter how slaughtered they are.'

'Well, it's where the Thompson brothers like to go, so suck it up, Val. We're taking a walk on the wild side.'

Valerie tutted.

'And dress up a bit, won't you? We'll need to look like we're out on the town, not going for an interview at a building society.'

Valerie looked down at her black trousers, white T-shirt and black blazer. 'Are you saying my clothes are boring?'

'Aye, I am. You're so pretty and you don't make the most of yourself.'

'Because I don't need to rely on my looks. I have other qualities to see me through life.'

'Only ugly people say that and you're not ugly. I'll lend you something of mine.'

Toni's favoured animal prints and fake furs were not to Valerie's taste. 'No need. I've got a nice little black dress I can wear. Will that do you?'

'Don't you have any colours?'

'There's my pink and yellow shell suit.' She smiled at Toni's appalled look. 'My little black dress doesn't seem so bad now, does it?'

4

———

Valerie winced as the hard, fast music pulsated through the huge, circular main room of Archaos, its coloured walls only adding to the bedlam. As usual, the club was hot and packed.

Toni was in her element, preening herself at the admiring looks she was getting in her tight, low-cut white dress that barely covered her bottom, her bare legs long and supple, the outfit completed by a pair of killer black high heels. Even though she felt a plain Jane in comparison to her cousin, Valerie was getting looks too, but she didn't revel in them like Toni did.

'We'll never find them in here,' Valerie told Toni, having to yell in her ear to be heard.

The club was definitely overcrowded. People were bouncing around the room to the music, others had chosen to dance on tables, one of them tipping up and sending the revellers to the floor in a rattle of spilt drinks and broken glasses.

'Let's try upstairs,' replied Toni, gesturing to the gantry above their heads that looked down on the dance floor. 'It'll give us a better view.'

They wove in and out of the revellers towards the stairs, Valerie glaring at one man who pinched her bottom.

At the top of the stairs, they found themselves a spot on the gantry where they could look down on the main dance floor, but it was still a hopeless confusion of people.

'We should try the VIP room,' Toni yelled in Valerie's ear.

'They'll never let us in. They only want footballers, page three girls and actors.'

'It's worth a try.'

'Okay,' sighed Valerie wearily. She didn't have a better suggestion and she wanted to get out of there as quickly as possible.

They climbed more stairs towards the VIP room, which was known as the Sky Bar. At the door, they were stopped by security. Toni stuck out her bosom and flicked back her hair for all she was worth, but nothing would encourage the doormen to allow them to pass.

Both men received the full force of Toni's shark-like black-eyed glare and, despite being hard men, they were unnerved, sensing something wasn't quite right with this beautiful young woman.

'The Thompsons probably aren't in there anyway,' said Valerie, linking her arm through Toni's and encouraging her away before she stuck the small knife she'd secreted in her handbag into one of the men. 'No way would they let them in.'

'I don't give a shite about them,' spat Toni. 'No one stops me from going where I want. Nobody,' she hissed. 'One day, everyone will fear me and they won't dare get in my way. I fucking swear it.'

'I've no doubt they will,' said Valerie gently.

The rage cleared from Toni's eyes. 'Let's try Bonkers on Hope Street. They might be there.'

Valerie sighed. That place was even crazier than Archaos. Every loon in Glasgow frequented that club. It was named Bonkers for a reason.

'Or Destiny?' added Toni, who loved clubbing. 'They're having a foam party tonight.'

'I thought you hated foam parties because they ruin your hair?'

'They do, but they're still fun.'

'If Frankie gets wind that we're enjoying ourselves rather than working, he won't be impressed. Why don't we try the Thompsons' local pub instead? We'll have more chance of spotting them there than a nightclub.'

'Aye, all right.'

On their way to the pub, the two women passed another night-club, one that was known for being a gay club.

Valerie stopped and tugged at Toni's arm.

'What?' frowned Toni.

Valerie pointed sideways at the queue waiting to get into the club and Toni's lips curled with malicious pleasure. 'Well, I wasn't expecting that.'

They stalked up to the man they'd spotted, who was doing his best to look inconspicuous, standing with his shoulders hunched and head bowed.

'Tommy Thompson,' said Toni loudly.

The man jumped and turned to look at them, appalled when he saw two of his family's enemies standing there. 'What the hell are you pair wantin'?' he demanded.

'We just need a quiet word,' said Toni.

'Piss off.'

'If you don't come with us, we'll go to the pub down the road and tell your family you're waiting to get into a gay club.'

Although it was dark, they could still see Tommy pale at the prospect. His family was notoriously homophobic, as well as racist.

'What do you want to talk to me about?' he said, in a voice tight with nerves.

'Not here,' said Toni. 'There's a decent all-night café on the next street. We'll discuss it there.'

Tommy reluctantly left the queue and followed the two women to the café, slinking along behind them with his hands shoved into his pockets, glad it was dark, hoping no one would see him with them. A light drizzle had started, bringing with it a chilly breeze. Valerie was glad she'd decided to wear a jacket over the dress. She looked at Toni, whose body spilled out of her clingy dress, but she was completely unaffected by the cold. It had to be snowing for Toni to notice a chill in the air.

The windows of the café had steamed up from the condensation, which was a relief to Tommy because it reduced the chances of anyone seeing him with a couple of McVays. He hunched at a table in the corner, mumbling an order for a cup of tea when the waitress approached in a stained apron. He was a handsome man of twenty-two with sandy hair and pretty light green eyes.

'What's wrong, Tommy?' said Toni, eyes dancing. 'Afraid of being seen with us in public?'

'Aye,' he muttered. 'My family will fucking kill me.'

'Then answer us truthfully and this excruciating experience will be over quickly. Now, have your family set up poor Stevie Johnson?'

'Set him up?' he frowned. 'How?'

'Put it about that he betrayed Frankie.'

'Betrayed him how?'

'It's me asking the questions, no' you,' growled Toni, pointing a digit at him. 'So has your family set him up?'

'Not that I know of, but they don't tell me anything.'

'Oh, aye? Keep you on the fringes, do they? Are you a bit thick, Tommy?'

'No,' he retorted. 'I'm done with this, I'm out of here.'

'I don't think so,' said Toni, whipping the knife out of her handbag and pressing it to his thigh under the table. 'Not unless you want this shoving into your femoral artery.'

'You wouldn't,' replied Tommy with a nervous laugh. 'No' in a public place. The polis would easily catch you.'

'The problem is, Tommy, that Frankie sent me and Val to get some answers and he's far more scary than any polis. So I will spill your blood all over this nasty stained floor if it gets us the answers we want.'

'She's being serious,' Valerie told Tommy. 'So just tell us what we want to know and we'll be on our way.'

'I really don't know anything.' He winced when the tip of Toni's knife bit into the cloth of his trousers. 'I'm telling the truth,' he rasped. 'You really chose the wrong person to speak to. I don't get involved in all my family's crap. I just want a quiet life. If you want answers, you need to talk to my cousin, Liam. He knows everything that goes on in our family.'

'Where can we find him?' said Valerie.

'In Destiny. He loves that club.'

Toni and Valerie looked at each other and nodded.

'All right, Tommy,' said Toni. 'We'll try Liam, but if you're messing us about, we'll come back and cut your cock off.'

Tommy gasped with relief when Toni retracted the knife. After Toni and Valerie had left, Tommy took out his phone.

'Liam, all right, mate?' he said into the Nokia. 'I've sent a couple of presents your way – Toni McVay and her cousin, Valerie. Aye, have fun,' he added before hanging up.

It was only when the waitress returned to the table with three cups of tea that Tommy realised he'd been stuck with the bill.

* * *

Destiny was as busy as Archaos but things were more orderly here. Toni and Valerie wandered through the club, scanning the area for Liam Thompson before spotting him talking to a couple of friends at the bar. As they watched, he shook his friends' hands and made his way to the exit.

'Is the arsehole leaving already?' said Toni. 'We had to pay a fiver to get in here.'

'Let's get after him before we lose him,' said Valerie.

They followed Liam out of the club. He looked a lot more intimidating than Tommy with his muscles, tattoos and the scar down the left side of his face, just under his eye. Liam paused to light a cigarette before heading down the street, alone.

'I wish you'd wear quieter shoes,' Valerie told Toni as her cousin's high heels clicked off the pavement. 'He's going to spot us at this rate.'

'No, he won't. Look, he's talking on his phone. He'll tell us what we need to know and finally I can go home and soak my feet.'

'Do you know how he got that scar?' said Valerie.

'Why do you want to know?'

'Just curious.'

'You think it's sexy, don't you?' she grinned.

'No. Like I said, just curious.'

Toni and Valerie hesitated when Liam suddenly detoured down an alley.

'I don't think it would be a good idea to follow him down there,' said Valerie.

'He probably just needs to take a piss.'

'Or he heard your high heels and he knows we're following him.'

The two women peered down the darkened mouth of the alley but couldn't hear and see anything.

'Have you got a really bad feeling?' said Valerie.

'I do,' replied Toni.

'Let's get out of here.'

Just as they turned to leave, three men stepped out of the shadows, forming a semi-circle before them.

Liam emerged from the mouth of the alley behind them, chuckling.

'Are you looking for me, ladies?' he said. 'Tommy called to warn me you were coming my way.' His eyes roamed up and down them lasciviously. 'What a nice surprise.'

'We want to ask you something,' said Toni, who was totally unfazed.

'Ask away, sweetheart,' he said with a benevolent smile.

'Did your family set up Stevie Johnson to look like he betrayed my brother?'

'That spotty wee ratbag? Why would we bother?'

'You tell me.'

'I've nae idea what you're talking about. Now, if that's sorted, why don't the three of us go for a drink?'

'No, thanks,' said Toni. 'We have standards and you are way below them.'

'Ooh, cold,' he chuckled. 'But you see, you've no choice in the matter.'

The four men took a step closer to the two women. Valerie's hand slid inside her jacket pocket, the movement unseen in the darkness.

'I wonder what Frankie will say when he finds out I've got his sister and cousin at my mercy,' continued Liam, looking thoroughly pleased with himself.

'So you're saying you know nothing about setting up Stevie?' demanded Toni, determined to get to the bottom of the mystery.

'Will you stop banging on about that twat? He's sod all to do with us.'

'He's a very clever man.'

'You mean he's a gossiping wee prick who sticks his neb where it doesnae belong. If someone's finally given him what he deserves, then it's his own fault. Now, you two are coming with us.'

'I don't think so.'

Valerie turned and pepper sprayed two of the men right in the eyes while kicking the third in the crotch. When Liam made a move, Toni produced her knife and held it out before her, enjoying the shock on his face.

'It's amazing how quickly things can change, isn't it, you fanny?' she sneered at Liam.

'You'd better fuck off before more of my people turn up,' he retorted.

'I don't think anyone else is coming. In your arrogance, you thought you could easily deal with a couple of women. Your tiny pea brain didn't even conceive that we might get the upper hand.' Toni's lips curled back over her teeth. 'You stupid bastard,' she hissed at him.

Valerie recognised that her cousin was on the edge, and she noted how Toni's grip on the knife tightened, how tense her muscles had gone and the malice that filled her eyes.

'Let's get out of here,' said Valerie.

'No' until I've given this shitebag a lesson in manners,' replied Toni, her gaze never leaving a very wary-looking Liam.

'Frankie will want to know what we've found out.'

This had the desired effect and slowly Toni lowered the knife while backing away.

'I will come for you for this, you bitches,' snarled Liam.

'Good luck with that,' sneered Toni.

The two women turned and walked away, as fast as Toni's high heels would allow, leaving the three men on the pavement, while Liam glared at their retreating backs.

'I think he means it,' said Valerie.

'Probably, but who gives a shite about him?' replied Toni. 'He's nothing.'

Valerie didn't think it would be that simple.

* * *

Frankie was in his local haunt, The Admiral, just a few streets from his home. He was surrounded by hangers-on who had been savvy enough to realise that Frankie would one day be a major player. Jamesie and Paul sat either side of him, on bodyguard duty.

Valerie and Toni entered the busy pub, both glad of the warmth.

'What the hell happened to you?' he demanded of his sister when he saw her limping. 'Who the fuck hurt you? I want their name.'

'No one hurt me,' she replied. 'It's my high heels.'

'Well, you will insist on poncing about in those things.'

'I do not ponce about,' announced Toni, eyes flashing.

Frankie kicked the man sitting opposite him at the table in the knee, making him yelp. 'Fuck off, you. Gi'e the ladies a seat.'

The man and his friend hastily got up, vacating their chairs for Valerie and Toni, who gratefully sank into them.

Quietly they related to Frankie what they'd learnt, while he listened with interest, not speaking until they'd finished.

'Cowardly bastards,' he spat. 'Liam couldnae even tackle you on his own, he had to have three of his bum chums with him and he still lost.'

'He said he'll get us back and I think he'll try,' said Valerie.

'Don't worry about that walloper. If tonight's anything to go by, he'll fuck that up too. So you don't think the Thompsons are behind this?'

'No. Liam didn't have a clue what we were talking about and he's pretty clued up on all his family's activities.'

'Back to the fucking drawing board,' sighed Frankie.

'What about the Gordons?' said Toni. 'They've given us almost as much trouble as the Thompsons.'

'Maybe. I'll look into that, although this reeks of the Thompsons.'

'Is Stevie okay?' Valerie asked Frankie. She wasn't sure why she was so concerned with the little weasel, but she was.

'Aye, he's fine. I havenae laid a finger on him. He's all warm and cosy in my cellar watching telly and drinking vodka.'

'Good, because he really is great at what he does.'

'Aye, I know, which is the only reason why his heid's still on his shoulders. You've done some grand work tonight. Take a drink to celebrate.'

Valerie and Toni accepted – it wasn't wise to turn down Frankie's hospitality – before heading home, tired and spent.

'Be careful, Val,' Toni said when they reached her house. 'I think we've kicked off something big tonight. The Thompsons won't take it lying down.'

'And you be careful too.'

'Always,' she smiled. 'Night, Val.'

'Night.'

Toni closed the door behind her and the taxi set off. Valerie sank down in the seat, her mind replaying the night's events. A sense of foreboding had settled over her the moment she'd pepper sprayed those Thompson men. Glasgow had seen its fair share of vendettas and she had the feeling it was going to see another.

5

A few days passed with no retaliation from the Thompsons, but Valerie remained tense, even when she was waiting outside the corner shop for Leo, her boyfriend of three months. Her parents didn't approve of him, so she always arranged to meet him away from home. Leo smoked, took drugs, shoplifted and was a bit of a moron, but he had a car, which had encouraged Valerie to accept when he'd asked her out on a date. Although she could drive thanks to her father taking her out for a few lessons, she had yet to get her licence and had to rely on the bus to get around.

The roar of an engine caught her attention and she glanced down the street to see Leo's bright red Vauxhall Astra tearing down the road towards her far too fast, causing two children on bikes to hastily scoot out of the way.

He slammed on the brakes at the kerb beside her and grinned at her through the open window.

'All right, doll?' he said. 'Hop in, then.'

Valerie hid her annoyance behind a sultry smile. Yes, he was good looking with his styled sandy hair, bright green eyes, winning smile and toned physique, but he was also a bit thick and had no interest in books as she did. Still, things were never boring with him around.

She got into the passenger seat and barely had time to pull her door shut before he set off at speed, jolting her in her seat. Hastily she yanked on her seat belt.

'So, what do you want to do tonight, gorgeous?' he said, his hand slipping to her knee.

'I thought we were going to Toni's? Her mum's gone to stay with her sister in Skye, so she's having a party.'

After the drama with the Thompsons, Toni wanted some fun and relaxation, so she'd arranged this party.

'What's wrong?' said Valerie when Leo pulled a face.

'I like it when it's just us,' he said.

'No, you don't. Most of the time, we're at your friends' houses. We're hardly ever alone.'

Inwardly Valerie sighed when his eyes tick-tocked from side to side as he frantically attempted to come up with a response. It would be nice to meet a man whose brain wasn't powered by a hamster in a wheel.

'That's why I thought tonight it would be great just the two of us,' he said slowly, carefully measuring each word. 'I have a romantic evening planned.'

'No, you don't,' she said flatly.

'Aye, I bloody do,' he pouted.

'It's the same every time I mention Toni. What have you got against her?'

'I've nothing against her, it's just that...'

'Just what?' she said when he trailed off.

'I don't like her, okay?'

'Why, what's wrong with her?'

'She's creepy and she stares at me like she's thinking about cutting my throat.'

'No, she doesn't, that's just your imagination.'

'I am not imagining it. She hates me because she wants you all to herself.'

'She does not. I've had other boyfriends and...'

'And what?' he said when she abruptly went silent.

'Nothing,' she murmured as she recalled every one of her previous boyfriends had suddenly dumped her without warning or explanation. Those men had also had a frantic look in their eyes, like a rabbit caught in the headlights of an oncoming car. But that didn't mean Toni was behind it. 'I said I'd be there and I can't let her down.'

'No, you can't,' he mumbled. 'That wouldn't go well for you.'

'What does that mean?' she frowned.

'It means that something nasty happens to people who upset Toni McVay.'

Valerie didn't bother to deny it because she knew it was true. 'Well, I promised I'd go. You don't have to come. You can just drop me off.'

Leo immediately looked happier. 'Good idea. I'll wait in The Admiral for you.'

'Okay, I'll meet you there when I'm done, or we can meet another time.'

'No, I'll wait. I'd like to spend some time with you today, babe.'

Valerie smiled. Sometimes she felt she was too hard on him because he could be sweet.

* * *

Leo dropped Valerie off outside Toni's house. It was a very nice home but a comedown from the large, plush house they'd had prior to Roddy's murder.

Valerie walked up to the front door and rang the bell, wondering if anyone would be able to hear her over the noise, and then the door was pulled open by Frankie.

'Val,' he exclaimed, throwing his arms wide. 'Ya fucking beauty, in you come.'

'Thanks, Frankie,' she smiled, stepping inside.

He wrapped his arms around her and planted a kiss on her cheek, Valerie grimacing as the frames of his glasses dug into her skin.

Frankie led her into the lounge, which was packed with people drinking, dancing and chatting. Some she recognised, but most she didn't. Toni had friends all over the city.

Toni, as usual, was the centre of attention. She had a natural magnetism that people gravitated to, and her beauty drew them in even more.

'Do you want a drink?' Frankie asked Valerie. 'We've got it all – lager, Bacardi, vodka, wine, Scotch and absinthe.'

'Absinthe?' she replied, eyebrows shooting up.

'Aye. It tastes like shite, but it'll get you steamin'.'

'I'll just have a lager, please, Frankie.'

'You never did have a sense of adventure,' he said before turning and vanishing into the kitchen.

'I didn't think you were coming,' said a husky voice in her ear.

Valerie turned to see Toni standing behind her.

'Where's Leo?' added Toni, eyes darting about the room.

'At the pub,' replied Valerie. 'He said he'd meet some friends.'

'He's always meeting friends when I'm around. I get the feeling he doesn't like me.'

'It's not like that. He just has a lot of friends.'

Toni's black eyes narrowed. 'I didn't think you lied, Val.'

'I don't,' she replied, steadily meeting her cousin's gaze.

'Hmm, well, you're here now. I did hear something interesting about your Leo, though.'

'And what's that?'

'Apparently he's been shagging Tracey Taylor, the daft cow who works in my hairdressers sweeping up hair and making tea.'

'And where did you hear that?'

'Virginia Malcolm told me. She saw them going at it hammer and tongs two nights ago in the park.'

'That's funny because two nights ago he was with me.'

'Then it must have been three nights ago.'

Valerie took this accusation with a pinch of salt. Toni had said similar things about all her boyfriends. Leo hadn't been wrong when he'd said Toni wanted her all to herself, she just hadn't wanted to admit it. 'Maybe,' she shrugged.

'He's a fucking loser. You can do so much better. You should meet my friend, Sebastian.'

Valerie's lips twitched. 'You have a friend called Sebastian?'

Toni nodded. 'He's Regina's friend. Do you remember her? She looks like a horse.'

'Does he look like a horse too?'

'Aye, but he's a fucking stallion. I'll introduce you. Come on.'

Toni grabbed her hand and pulled her over to the other side of the room. Valerie's heart sank when she realised she was being drawn inexorably towards a group of people she didn't know.

'This is my cousin, Val,' smiled Toni, shoving her forward to face the group. Valerie bristled when they all looked her up and down, assessing whether she was good enough to be in their presence. All looked wealthy and extremely well groomed – Toni's favourite sort of people.

'This is Regina – you remember her? Archie, Celia, Megan and...' Toni paused for dramatic effect. 'Sebastian.'

Valerie's eyes widened. Toni hadn't been wrong. Sebastian was a tall, strapping blonde god of a man with a strong jaw and bright blue eyes.

'Hello,' she said, addressing him directly, ignoring his friends.

'Hello,' he replied with a sweet smile. His eyes roamed up and down her but this time, it didn't make her hackles rise. Instead, it was rather sensual.

'Hey, you,' said a voice. 'Here's your lager.'

Frankie unceremoniously dumped a can in Valerie's hand before turning his attention to Celia and giving her his best – and most manic – smile. The wariness in Celia's eyes told Valerie they knew all about Frankie's recent violent and psychotic deeds, and the girl took a step backwards.

Valerie wished she'd asked Frankie for a more elegant drink than a can of lager and she coloured slightly as she stared up into Sebastian's beautiful face.

'Frankie,' said Toni coldly. 'Your pals are here.'

Frankie tore his creepy gaze off an uncomfortable Celia to look at the two men who had just walked in.

'Jamesie, Paul,' grinned Frankie before wandering off to talk to his friends, to Toni and Celia's relief.

'Seb's an amazing tennis player,' Toni told Valerie. 'Everyone calls him Seb, by the way. He hates his full name.'

'I think it's nice,' said Valerie, looking back at the man in question.

'It's a family name,' he explained. 'My great-grandfather and grandfather were lumbered with it. My father managed to escape it, but I wasn't so lucky.'

'I like it. It's strong and noble.' Valerie ignored the laughter of his friends.

'You're the first person to say that,' he replied. 'Your name's very pretty,' he added coyly.

'Thank you.'

When they started chatting, Toni urged the others away, leaving Valerie and Seb alone together. She'd hoped they'd find each other attractive. It was time Valerie realised she could do far better than the losers she usually dated.

Valerie spent most of the evening talking with Seb, completely forgetting about Leo until she glanced at the clock on the wall and saw she should have been at the pub by now. Leo went straight out of her head again when she looked back at Seb. She'd been very pleased to discover he had much more about him than she'd at first assumed. Judging by his appearance, she'd guessed he'd be a sports bore, but he hadn't mentioned the subject once, except to say he enjoyed playing tennis. He was an avid reader of both non-fiction and fiction, mainly the classics, and his favourite book was *The Catcher in the Rye*. Although it wasn't Valerie's favourite, it was one she was fond of and they enjoyed discussing it. Like her, it seemed he didn't get any outlet for his passion for literature.

While the party grew increasingly wild around them, Valerie and Seb remained on the couch together, chatting non-stop. His company was a boon to her because none of her family or friends shared her interests.

They were torn from their discussion by the sound of arguing and they looked round to see Toni locked in a row with two men.

'I'd better see if she needs any help,' Valerie told Seb before getting to her feet.

Before Valerie could reach her cousin, Frankie tore into the room, followed by Paul and Jamesie, and flew at the two men. He elbowed one in the face and grabbed the other by the back of the jacket and dragged the unfortunate man to the floor.

'Frankie, what the hell are you doing?' cried Toni.

'Dealing with these fucking wallopers,' he replied, face set in a snarl.

'There's no need for that, they only complained that the music was shite.'

'What?' he erupted, eyes bulging, red hair standing on end. 'No one calls my music shite,' he shrieked, kicking the man he'd dragged across the floor in the ribs.

Everyone had broken off talking and dancing to watch the show, the only sound coming from the hi-fi in the corner playing 'Insomnia' by Faithless.

Toni grabbed Frankie's arm, forcing him to look at her.

'Please, Frankie,' she said.

Frankie gazed back at his sister, torn between wanting to cause someone serious injury and not wanting to upset Toni, who was one of the very few people he loved.

The song changed to the next track on the CD, Peter Andre's 'Mysterious Girl'.

Frankie released the man he was holding. 'Actually, you're right, pal. This song is shite.' With that, he kicked him up the arse. 'Piss off then, you pair of pricks.'

The two men scrambled to their feet and shot out the door.

Although the fight had stopped before it had gone too far, the atmosphere had been well and truly ruined, so the party began to break up, the guests quietly thanking Toni as they left, afraid of sparking off her unstable brother.

Valerie returned to Seb. 'Sorry about that,' she said, embarrassed by her cousin's behaviour.

'Don't be,' he replied. 'It's not a party unless there's a fight,' he added with his devastating smile. 'The last one I held, my best friend got his nose broken by a wine bottle.'

'Nasty.'

'He was so pissed he didn't feel it until the next morning. I've got to go anyway, I've got to sit an exam in the morning.'

'What subject?'

'Philosophy.'

Valerie realised her smile was soppy, but she couldn't help it. Finally, a man who could think deeply.

'I should be done by one o'clock, though,' he continued. 'If you want to meet me for lunch?'

Valerie beamed at him. Part of her had been afraid the exam had been an excuse to escape her company. 'I'd love to,' she replied.

'Great. Do you know where the University Café is? It's just down the road from the uni.'

'I do.'

'I'll see you there at one.'

'You certainly will.'

When Seb leaned into her, Valerie thought he was going to kiss her, but instead he gave her hand a gentle squeeze.

'See you tomorrow.'

As he left, Toni bustled up to her, looking furious. 'I can't believe Frankie. He ruined my party.'

'At least you don't have to clean anyone's blood off the floor.'

'I suppose there's that to be grateful for, although he scared off Lee Wells just when I was finally making some progress with him after months of trying.' Toni sighed with frustration, her eyes flashing. 'What happened to Seb? Frankie didn't scare him off too, did he?'

'He said he had to go because he's got an exam tomorrow, but he asked me to meet him for lunch.'

'I didn't think you'd go for him.'

'Aye, you did, it's why you introduced us.'

The corner of Toni's mouth lifted into a smile. 'Maybe.'

'And I didn't think I'd go for him either, but he's so interesting.'

Toni took in the way Valerie's eyes shone and smiled. 'I'm glad you've finally set your sights higher than that loser Leo McNulty.'

Valerie's eyes widened. 'Oh, god, I forgot about Leo. I said I'd meet him in the pub. I'd better get over there, he'll be wondering what's happened to me.'

'I don't know why you're still bothering with him now you've met Seb.'

'I need to go, I can't stand him up.'

'I'll come with you.'

'You hate that pub.'

Toni shrugged. 'I fancy a drink.'

'Fine, but play nice. Don't insult anyone.'

'What are they going to do about it if I do? No one dare challenge a member of our family any more, not with Frankie making his presence felt. Everyone shites themselves when they see him.' Toni smiled with satisfaction.

'I'm not sure that's a good thing. All right, let's go before Leo thinks I've abandoned him.'

As the two women made the short walk to the pub, a car full of young men honked its horn as they drove by, the men catcalling at them. Toni tossed back her mane of hair, practically purring with pleasure at the attention. The men went abruptly silent and the car sped away when they realised who they were yelling at. Everyone knew what happened to men who messed with Frankie McVay's sister. He'd given enough demonstrations lately, leaving in his wake a trail of mutilated lotharios.

Toni and Valerie arrived at the pub an hour before it was due to close. Leo was sitting at the bar, drinking and laughing with his cronies.

'He looks drunk,' said Toni disdainfully.

'To be fair, I have made him wait here for three hours,' replied Valerie. 'What else is he going to do in a pub except drink?'

Valerie walked up to Leo and tapped him on the shoulder.

'Hello, doll,' he smiled when he turned to face her. His smile fell when he saw Toni was there too. 'Oh, it's you,' he said.

'In the flesh.' Toni turned her attention to Leo's two friends, gave them a sultry look and stuck out her substantial bosom. 'So, who wants to buy me a drink?'

They both stared at her wide-eyed before scrambling for what money they had left in their pockets and calling to the barman.

'How was the party?' Leo asked Valerie, slinging an arm around her shoulders.

'It was good,' replied Valerie, trying not to think about Seb. She'd done nothing wrong, she'd only talked to him. It wasn't as though she'd kissed him, even though she'd wanted to.

'Good. Did you meet any interesting people?'

He asked this question casually, but she could see how closely he was watching her.

'Not really,' she replied. 'It was just the usual crowd. The party broke up when a fight started.'

'It's not a good night without a fight,' he grinned.

Valerie smiled back, relieved he'd bought her story.

Leo's friends both eagerly held a drink out to Toni. She turned her nose up at the half of lager and accepted the glass of white wine.

Toni sighed when Frankie, along with Paul and Jamesie, strode into the pub with all the swagger of television cowboys entering a saloon. It seemed everywhere she went, he was there too.

The pub went silent, everyone regarding Frankie uncertainly, especially the barman, who was painfully aware that he enjoyed tormenting all the local barmen, usually by throwing glasses at them or bouncing their heads off the bar.

'What the fuck are you doing here?' Frankie demanded of his sister. 'You cannae just walk out of your own party.'

'Valerie was meeting Leo,' retorted Toni with a pout. 'So I thought I'd come in for a drink too.'

'Maw wants you home.'

'She's in Skye.'

'Aye, but she wants you home safe. You also need to tidy up the hoose before she gets back, it's a fucking tip.'

Toni was tempted to snap back that he should do it himself, but not even she dared contradict her brother. 'Fine, I'll just finish my wine first.'

Frankie wasn't so far gone that he wanted to humiliate his little sister in front of all these people, so he nodded before slapping his palm down on the bar. 'Whisky, single malt,' he barked at the barman. 'None of that blended shite.'

The barman swallowed hard and nodded before hastily preparing the drink. Fortunately for him, Frankie was too concerned with a group of three men across the room who were casting him glowers to be interested in him.

'Look at those fucking dobbers,' Frankie said to his friends. 'It's the Gordons. They've been getting in our way the last few months.'

The three Gordon men stared back at them while sipping their pints, challenge in their eyes.

'Don't let them make you angry, Frankie,' said Toni. 'That will make them think they have power over you.'

'Fuck what they think,' he spat.

'They're ugly, meaningless pieces of shite. They're nothing compared to you.'

Frankie smiled and straightened his suit jacket. 'Aye, you're right.' His expression hardened as he leaned into her. 'But don't swear. I don't like it.'

'Whatever you say, Frankie,' replied Toni warily.

His face smoothed out into a smile. 'That's my girl.'

Gently he patted her cheek. Although Toni forced herself not to wince, Valerie saw the unease in her cousin's eyes. Frankie didn't fear Toni, even though she'd already killed someone. The death of Roddy McVay had drastically altered the family's fortunes. They'd been top of the tree but when he'd died, there had been no one suitable to fill the void. His brothers Tam and Stuart were all considerably younger than him and at the time lacking the strength to step into his shoes. Roddy's uncle had tried but he'd been stabbed to death after a stupid argument over a two-grand debt and the McVay family had lost their grip on the illegal businesses, with smaller gangs taking them over while they were unable to fight back.

Roddy's murder had been blamed on an intruder who had come in through the back door and attacked him. No one outside the family knew that it had been Toni who'd stabbed him four times in the torso, twice in the groin and once in each eye, the blade sinking into his brain through the left socket. That had been the killing blow. Two detectives in Roddy's pocket had been put on the case and they'd been more than happy to perpetuate the intruder theory for a big chunk of money. Naturally the case went cold and remained unsolved. Moira and Eric moved house and the family tried to put it all behind them. But everyone who knew what had really happened had regarded Toni with much more wariness after that, all except for Frankie. He was the up-and-coming prince, the one who had shown not only the brutality but the brains to get back what the family had lost when Roddy had died.

No one in the family had so much as chastised Toni for killing the patriarch because they'd felt so guilty for enabling the abuse to occur. And once she'd recovered from the initial shock of what she'd done, Toni had become more confident and self-assured. No one liked to deny her anything in case they too got a knife through the eye. Whereas before she'd sulked if she hadn't got her way, now she just gave them an icy glare that usually led to them giving into her. Frankie was the only one who dared stand up to his sister and she in turn was afraid of him. Now he was the new hope of his family, and he was determined to make the McVay name great again. No one doubted he would achieve his goal, but Valerie was worried about what carnage he'd leave in his wake on his climb to power and what sort of dictator he would become.

6

Valerie was the first to arrive at the café where she and Seb had agreed to meet for lunch. Although she was excited to see him again, she hoped that she looked cool and calm. She sipped a cup of tea while she waited, growing increasingly anxious when one o'clock came and went and he failed to arrive. Her temper grew by the minute as the clock reached 1.30 and he was still a no-show, the pitying looks she received from the waitress only fuelling her anger.

Just as she'd decided to sod the bastard and leave, the door burst open and Seb flew in.

'I'm so sorry,' he panted as he flopped into the chair opposite her. 'The exam ran over, then my friend Dan said he'd give me a lift but he buggered off with his girlfriend, leaving me stranded, so I had to run here.'

The fact that Seb was red-faced and out of breath supported his story, and Valerie's anger was appeased.

'Well, you're here now,' she replied with a sweet smile. 'I expect you'd like a drink?'

'Water, please,' he breathed.

Valerie ordered a glass of water from the waitress, giving her a smug smile that her date had finally arrived.

'How did the exam go?' Valerie asked him.

'Good, I think. I didn't get stuck on anything at least, so fingers crossed.'

'What do you want to do when you leave university?'

'To be honest, I'm not sure. I know I should have some idea by now, but I really don't.'

'What made you take Philosophy?'

'I find it very interesting. I think I'd quite like to teach it. I'd love to turn into one of those dusty old professors who spends the day surrounded by books, smoking a pipe and wearing tweed jackets with patches on the elbows.'

'Sounds peaceful,' she smiled.

'Most people say boring.'

'I'm not most people.'

'I already know that,' he smiled. 'Any cousin of Toni McVay's is going to stand out from the crowd.'

Valerie was struck by the horrible notion that he was just using her to get close to her cousin, but her worrying was interrupted by the waitress bringing his water and taking their order.

Seb gulped down the water and sighed with relief. 'That's better.'

'Just how well do you know Toni?' Valerie said suspiciously.

'Not well at all. She's a friend of a friend. I only met her for the first time last week.'

'She's very pretty.'

'And scary. Too scary for me.'

'So you don't fancy her, then?'

'Fancy her? Nope, not my type at all. I like quieter, thoughtful women who are into books,' he said shyly.

'Me too,' she smiled back. She realised what she'd said and blushed. 'Although I prefer them male.'

'Luckily for me,' he replied with a grin that made her stomach flip over. 'Her brother seems quite the character too.'

'Frankie? Aye, he's... unique.'

'He looks like one of The Proclaimers.'

'Whatever you do, don't say that to him. It sends him doolally.'

'There's nothing wrong with The Proclaimers, I really like them.'

'He doesn't. You do know about my family's reputation, don't you?'

'Aye, course. My friends couldn't wait to tell me all about it before I met Toni for the first time.'

'Doesn't that put you off?'

'Off you? No, why would it?'

'It's put off quite a lot of people in the past.'

'Your family's history is... interesting.'

'And violent.'

'But that doesn't define you. That's why I'm here, because I want to get to know you better.'

'There's plenty of people in this city who wouldn't be seen with me in public because of who my family is.'

'It's not your fault what the rest of your family gets up to and if you're going to ask if it bothers me, it really doesn't. I enjoy your company too much.'

'That's all right, then,' she smiled, pleased.

They enjoyed lunch together, once again chatting about their favourite subject – literature – until Seb confessed something to her.

'You know when I said I wanted to teach?' he began.

'Yes,' replied Valerie.

'Well, actually, I want to do something else, but I was too

embarrassed to tell you. I was afraid you might have ducked out on our date.'

'I wouldn't have done that.'

'You might.'

'Why don't you try me?' Valerie knew, no matter what he said, she wouldn't run out on this man. Already she was smitten.

Seb took a deep breath. 'I want to become a minister.'

'As in church?'

'Yes,' he mumbled, embarrassed. 'I'm actually studying Divinity as well as Philosophy.'

'Oh,' she said, surprised. 'That's not what I expected. So you must be quite a big believer, then?'

'Aye, I always have been. It's always felt right to me. My grandda was a minister too and he had such a happy, fulfilling life. Are you a believer? Don't worry, I won't try to convert you,' he hastily added when her eyes widened. 'I'm just curious, that's all.'

'Well,' she began slowly, having never really thought much about the subject before. 'My family's not at all religious, except my Aunty Moira, Toni's maw. She's always been a big churchgoer but not the rest of us. I've only been to church for weddings and funerals. Our family's had plenty of the latter. I wouldn't say I disbelieve but... I don't know,' she ended, feeling a little stupid for not being able to give a definitive answer.

'There's nothing wrong with that. Spirituality develops over time. It shouldn't be something rigid and inflexible, it should be allowed to change over the course of our life. Anyway, that's all I'm going to say on the matter. I just thought you should know the truth because I'd really like to see more of you.' He cast his eyes down to the table, afraid he'd ruined his chances.

'I'd like that too,' she said with a gentle smile.

Seb looked back up at her, his grin once again making her heart stop. His honesty reminded her that she had a secret of her own she'd been keeping from him and it was time he knew. It was only fair. 'You should know, I'm seeing someone.'

'Oh,' he said, his smile falling.

'I haven't been seeing him for long and it's not serious, but I'm going to break it off.'

'Because of me?'

'Aye. I like you a lot.'

'Great, but I hope he won't be hurt.'

'I don't think he's got the imagination,' she said, lifting her teacup and smiling at Seb over the rim.

* * *

After enjoying lunch together, Seb and Valerie were reluctant to relinquish each other's company, so they decided to take a walk through a nearby park. Valerie loved talking to Seb as they strolled together arm in arm, she felt like she'd known him for years. They shared one of those instant – but very rare – connections. She was disappointed when it came time to leave, but she'd promised her parents she'd be back home to have tea with them and they'd only make a big drama about it if she was late. She said a reluctant goodbye to Seb after arranging to meet up with him the following evening and took the bus home.

She was just in time for tea and sat down to eat at the table with a happy smile. Her family's home wasn't large and luxurious, but it was still very pleasant with nice neighbours, situated on the opposite side of Springburn to Toni. Valerie hoped to get her own place as soon as she'd saved up enough money. Her parents were okay and avoided the violent and illegal activities the majority of their family were involved in, but they weren't the easiest people to live with, especially her mother, who could be overly dramatic.

When her father, Charlie, enquired as to why she looked so

happy, Valerie decided to tell them about Seb. They were always nagging her about her bad choice in boyfriends, so she thought mentioning Seb might get them off her back. Sure enough, they were delighted that she'd met a man who was educated and wanted to settle into a quiet and safe career, although her mother, Janet, did relish reminding her about all the losers and criminals she'd dated.

They were halfway through the meal when the phone rang. Charlie rose to pick up the extension hanging from the kitchen wall.

'It's Toni for you,' he told his daughter, holding the handset out to her with a disapproving purse of the lips.

Toni might have been their niece, but it didn't mean they approved of her ways. All the McVay blood was on Janet's side and Charlie thought himself a cut above them because he came from a law-abiding and, in Valerie's opinion, very boring family. Brown was the perfect surname for them. At least the McVays were a lively bunch.

Valerie took the handset from him and put it to her ear. 'Hello?'

'Val,' replied her cousin. 'I need you to come straight over here.'

'Why?'

'That silly bitch Cassie Cathcart is kicking off again. I'm going to her house to beat the shite out of her and I need you as back-up.'

Valerie was usually up for a fight, but Seb's gentle ways had already rubbed off on her and she was reluctant. 'I'm having tea with my parents.'

'Then hurry up and finish. I'll wait for you,' Toni said before hanging up.

Valerie hung up and turned to her parents, who were regarding her warily.

'What did she want?' asked her mother.

Janet Brown looked rather like Toni, with her curly black hair and dark eyes, but Valerie took after her father with her tall, lean figure, straight brown hair and blue eyes. Janet's gaze could be as haughty as Toni's, just as it was at this moment. It had been a bone of contention between Janet and Moira that the latter had benefited a lot more from Roddy McVay's will, probably because of Toni. When Valerie's mother looked at her, Val often wondered if she wished Roddy had been unnaturally fond of her as well.

'She's got a new dress she wants to get my opinion on,' replied Valerie. Over the years, she'd got used to lying to her parents to spend time with her cousin.

'Oh, well, that's all right then,' smiled Janet. 'Just, please, be careful. You know what she's like.'

'Better than anyone,' replied Valerie before retaking her seat at the table and finishing her meal. She refused to rush out just because Toni demanded it. If you gave her an inch, she'd take a fucking mile.

* * *

By the time Valerie arrived at Toni's house, her cousin was furious about being kept waiting. Valerie headed upstairs to her bedroom to be greeted by cold, black-eyed rage. It was clear Toni was dressed for business because she wore black trousers rather than her traditional skirt or dress, although she still sported high heels.

'What took you so long?' demanded Toni.

'I told you I was having tea with my parents. I couldn't just run out on them.'

'You could have stuck it in the oven to keep warm.'

'They wouldn't have liked it and they would have asked questions.'

'Well, I suppose you did the right thing,' Toni reluctantly

replied. 'I don't want them finding out what I intend to do to that bitch Cassie.'

'What do you intend to do to her?'

Toni smiled, opened the drawer of her bedside cabinet and produced a small knife. 'I'm going to slice that pretty face of hers right up.'

'Oh, no,' said Valerie, folding her arms across her chest and shaking her head. 'I am not going if you're going to use a knife.'

'Don't be boring, Val.'

'It's not boring, it's called being sensible. If you do that, you'll be arrested, we both will. I thought you were going to give her a slap, but I won't be party to assault with a knife. I'm not going to prison for that silly cow, and neither should you.'

Toni considered the wisdom of her words before replacing the knife in the drawer, to Valerie's relief.

'Perhaps you're right,' said Toni. 'I'll just give her a good hiding instead.' Her face creased with annoyance. 'That doesn't offend you, does it?'

'Nope. It sounds like a plan.'

'Fine,' said Toni haughtily. 'Let's go then.'

The two girls left together. Toni called through to Moira – who was back from her holiday and was watching *Hetty Wainthropp Investigates* on the television from her wheelchair in the living room – and Moira told them to have a good time. She never asked her daughter where she was going any more or with whom. She'd long ago learnt not to question her children, especially now she relied on them for everything after the car accident four years ago that had left her paralysed from the waist down. Valerie couldn't help but feel that was penance for allowing Roddy to abuse her daughter.

The cousins strode down the street with purpose, the younger teenagers idling on the pavement hastily moving out of their way, recognising Toni's anger.

'So what's Cassie done this time?' said Valerie.

'She tried it on with my Warren,' hissed Toni.

'Warren?'

'Aye, you know, Warren Campbell.'

'Your ex?'

'He's not my ex, we got back together two days ago.'

'You never said.'

'Because I knew you'd moan at me for it.'

'Aye, I would, because he's a huge loser, even more so than Leo, who you're always having a go at me for dating.'

'Warren is not like Leo,' announced Toni. 'He's absolutely gorgeous and he has prospects.'

'As a petty drug dealer?'

'As an astute businessman.' Toni's eyes narrowed when Val chuckled.

'If you're back with Warren, then why were you trying to get off with Lee Wells at your party?'

Toni smiled and shrugged. 'Well, a girl needs some variety.'

'That's just asking for trouble. Ae you sure Warren's worth the effort of finding Cassie and hammering her?'

'I'm not doing it for him, I'm doing it for myself. I do have a reputation to maintain, and I won't have that cow thinking she's got the better of me.'

They reached Cassie's house, which was a very pleasant but small terraced house with lots of gnomes in the garden. Toni banged on the door but, to Valerie's relief, no one answered. Toni took out her frustration on the gnomes, kicking some over and putting the rest into sexually explicit positions.

'Now what?' said Valerie, hoping Toni would say they should just forget this stupid idea and go home.

'I bet she's hanging around Hannah Dawson's. They're always together. We'll head over there, she only lives down the road.'

Valerie sighed inwardly as she followed her cousin out of the garden and down the street.

'So did you meet Seb today?' said Toni as they walked.

'Aye, I did. We had lunch together, then went for a walk in the park.'

Toni did a double take at her cousin. 'Wow.'

'Wow what?' said Valerie.

'You've got a soppy look in your eyes, one I've never seen before. Whenever you've talked about your boyfriends in the past, you've always looked bored.'

'Maybe, but Seb is not my boyfriend. Leo is, although I've decided to break up with him.'

'Poor Leo,' Toni sniggered.

'I thought you'd be glad?'

'I am, actually. It's about time you realised your own worth. Does Seb know about Leo?'

'Aye, I told him.'

'And what did he say?'

'He couldn't say anything because we were only on our first date, but I did tell him I was going to dump Leo.'

'That's the best thing that could happen to Leo, hopefully from a twenty-storey building.'

'That's not fair, he's quite sweet, actually.'

'Then why are you dumping him for sexy Seb?'

'Because I've got so much in common with Seb. We can talk for hours just about books.'

'Thrilling,' said Toni flatly.

'It is to me. I feel like I've known him all my life.'

'When are you seeing him again?'

'Tomorrow. He's going to take me to a second-hand bookshop he knows. They're having a poetry evening with nibbles.'

'You should be careful, Val. You don't want to wear yourself out with high-adrenaline dates like that.'

'Very funny. I'm looking forward to it.'

'Each to their own, I suppose. I'm just glad you're finally seeing someone decent, for once. When are you going to break the bad news to Leo?'

'Today.'

'Want me to come with you? He might get nasty.'

'I appreciate the offer, but he's not that sort. And you'd probably end up taking the piss out of him.'

'I can't promise that I won't.'

Valerie wondered whether to tell Toni that Seb wanted to be a minister but decided against it. She'd got the impression he'd told very few people, so it was reasonable to suppose that he wanted to keep it quiet.

The conversation ended when they reached Hannah's home. Toni pounded her fist off the door, which was opened by Hannah herself, a pretty, auburn-haired girl with freckles across her nose.

'Toni,' she said, eyes widening.

'Is Cassie here?' Toni demanded.

'No,' said Hannah before attempting to close the door.

Toni and Valerie put their weight against it, sending it crashing back into Hannah, knocking her off her feet. They stalked inside, Valerie closing the door behind them, and headed deeper into the house. They found Cassie sitting on the couch, flicking through a magazine. She was a beautiful woman of twenty with long wavy brown hair, huge dark almond eyes, a tiny waist and large bosom.

'Who was at the door?' said Cassie without looking up from her magazine.

'Your worst nightmare, you bitch,' said Toni.

Cassie slowly looked up, huge eyes impossibly wide. 'Toni,' she breathed.

The two women stared at each other, Cassie with fear and Toni with rage before Cassie tossed aside the magazine and leapt to her feet, running for the back door.

Toni was on her before she could escape the room, grabbing a handful of her long hair and dragging her backwards.

'So you think you can get your badly manicured claws into *my* Warren, do you?' spat Toni.

'I... I thought you'd broken up,' stammered Cassie. 'He told me you had.'

'Liar. You thought you could take what doesn't belong to you, but you fucking can't,' yelled Toni before punching Cassie in the face, knocking her to the floor.

Valerie looked on dispassionately as Toni punched her victim twice more in the face before kicking her in the back. Cassie yelped and then groaned before curling up into a ball and sobbing.

'Go near him again and I'll fucking bury you, you slag,' snarled Toni.

Cassie just sobbed.

'Where's Hannah?' said Toni when they stepped into the hallway to find her gone, the front door standing open.

Valerie and Toni looked at each other quizzically before heading outside. They saw Hannah at the top of the road, frantically talking to two men and pointing down the street at them.

'The cow,' said Toni, hands balling into fists. 'That's Cassie's brother and his best pal.'

'It looks like they don't approve of what you did to Cassie,' said Valerie when the two men stormed down the street towards them, looking furious. Hannah hung back, keeping out of harm's way.

'Oy,' yelled Chris Cathcart as he approached. 'What have you bitches done to my sister?'

'Hmm, he's quite fit, isn't he?' said Toni, eyes appreciatively roaming up and down the tall, broad man with black hair and blue eyes.

'Not bad,' replied Valerie. 'I heard he goes to the gym a lot.'

'I like a man who takes care of himself.'

Chris and his friend came to a halt before the two women.

'Where's my sister?' yelled Chris.

'In there,' replied Toni, gesturing to Hannah's house. 'On the floor, crying.'

'What did you do to her?'

'I just gave her a slap. It's not my fault she's soft.'

'This is because of that loser, Warren Campbell, isn't it?'

'It is,' said Toni, tilting back her head. 'I don't like it when people try to take what's mine.'

'He told her you'd broken up, so you should take it out on him, no' her.'

'He'll feel the force of my wrath too, I promise you that.'

Cassie staggered out of the house, face bruised and swollen. 'She knocked out my front teeth,' wailed Cassie, pointing at Toni.

Chris's fury was turned back on Toni. 'You said you just gave her a slap.'

'I did,' she smiled with satisfaction. 'A very hard one.'

Chris grunted with anger and his hands flexed into fists. 'Someone should give you a hard slap too.'

'What, you?' she laughed. 'Go ahead, but I do wonder what my brother will think about it.'

Chris was thinking this too, which was why he hadn't already knocked Toni to the ground, and they both knew it. He had a reputation as a bit of a hard man, but he certainly wasn't the psychopath everyone knew Frankie McVay to be.

As Chris and Toni stared each other out, Cassie continued to wail in the background.

It was Chris's friend who made the first move. Valerie, who had noted how tense his body had gone, was prepared for his clumsy attempt to strike Toni. She knocked his arm sideways, which sent him off balance, and punched him in the stomach. As he folded in half, she brought up her knee, knocking him onto his backside.

'That has got to be embarrassing.' Toni smiled down at the man, who had pressed a hand to his aching stomach. She looked back at Chris. 'This is women's business and nothing to do with you.'

'So if someone gave you a kicking,' snarled Chris, 'Frankie wouldnae dae anything about it?'

'Of course he would,' Toni purred. 'But that's because he's completely and utterly psychotic and you're not. Now, if you don't want him to come after you, then get out of our way. Although, judging by your friend's performance, I should set Val on you instead, so piss off and take that whining bitch with you.'

Chris cast Toni one last glower before turning his attention to his sister, whose sobs had morphed into little snivels, her face streaked with tears and blood. Gently he helped Cassie to her feet and she clung onto him as she limped up the street. Chris's friend picked himself up off the ground and followed, walking hunched over, arms wrapped around his stomach.

'Well, that was a job well done,' smiled Toni proudly. 'You were superb, as always, Val. Thank you.'

'You're welcome,' she replied.

'You'd make a wonderful bodyguard.'

'That's not what I had in mind for my future,' said Valerie wryly.

'What do you have in mind then?' said Toni as they walked away in the opposite direction to Cassie and the others.

'I've no idea yet.'

'Does your future involve a certain blonde, blue-eyed hunk?'

'He's certainly in my immediate future,' smiled Valerie. 'If that's all you need me for, I'm going to Leo's.'

'To dump him?' said Toni, making no attempt to hide her pleasure.

Valerie sighed and nodded. 'I shouldn't have got with him in the first place. I knew he wasn't for me. Now I have to hurt him.'

'He'll get over it. Sure you don't want me to come with you? I know you think he's a bit harmless, but he could still get vicious.'

'No, thanks,' said Valerie, knowing Toni's presence would only complete Leo's humiliation.

'Well, if you're sure. But take this.'

Toni produced a small knife from her coat pocket and held it out to her.

'I thought you'd left that at home.'

'I did. This is a different one.'

'No, thanks, I don't like knives. What about Neil Gallagher, who got twelve years in Bar-L for wounding someone with a blade?'

'Neil Gallagher's a cretin,' said Toni. 'I'm not and neither are you, so take it because even the most seemingly gentle people can be lunatics.'

'I appreciate your concern, but no, thanks. I'll be fine.'

'You're so stubborn, Val. One day, it may well be your downfall.'

'No, it won't, because I know you've always got my back, just like I've got yours.'

7

The cousins parted ways. Toni headed home and Valerie caught the bus to Leo's house. His street was grey and desolate, the buildings old tenements that had been converted into large modern apartments and would have been lovely had the residents not been the dregs of society who let their homes rot.

Leo lived on the second floor and Val walked into the dirty entryway, and headed up the creaking stairs to the second floor. She knocked on the door and he pulled it open wearing only his jeans, his top half bare, revealing a peely-wally but toned body and lots of poorly designed tattoos.

'All right, doll?' he grinned. 'I wasn't expecting you. Cannae keep away, eh?'

'I just need a quick word.'

'Anything for you, gorgeous. Come on in.'

Valerie followed him inside and closed the door behind her. She'd never liked his flat, which was a mess. Clothes were strewn everywhere, dirty plates and mugs left out. All the furniture was thick with dust, and he hadn't run a vacuum over the carpet in months. The only rooms he ever cleaned were his bedroom and bathroom, otherwise she would have refused to stay.

'No, don't,' she said when he attempted to slide his arms around her waist.

'What's wrong?' he frowned, releasing her.

'I've come here because I think it's time we broke up,' she replied, feeling terrible.

'Why? We're great together.'

'We're just too different.'

His handsome face twisted into a scowl. 'This is Toni, isn't it? She's always hated me.'

'It's nothing to do with her. This is my decision and mine alone.'

'I don't get it. Everything was going well then suddenly you go to that party and...' He trailed off and glared at her with a ferocity she hadn't thought he possessed. 'You met someone there, didn't you?'

'Actually, I did,' she replied casually. 'Someone I have a lot in common with.'

'Like what?' he spat.

'Books, films, everything, really.'

'What's his name?' he thundered in her face. 'I want his fucking name.'

Valerie was beginning to wonder if Toni had been right about Leo's true nature. 'I'm not giving you his name,' she calmly replied.

'You'll give me his fucking name right now. No one steals my bird from me.'

'I don't belong to you.'

To her astonishment, he grabbed her by the shoulders. 'Yes, you fucking do.'

She shoved him away. 'I'm leaving.'

'No, you're not,' he replied, rushing round her and blocking her path to the door.

'Let me leave, Leo,' she said firmly.

'Not until I get some fucking answers. I want the cunt's name right now.'

'No. Nothing's even happened with this man, we've only talked.'

'Like I believe that shite,' he said, squaring up to her.

'It's the truth.'

'You wouldnae know the truth if you fucking fell over it, you bitch.'

'Right, that's it. I'm out of here.'

Valerie stormed past him to the door, but he grabbed her arm and dragged her back, wrapping his arms around her and attempting to kiss her.

'Get off me,' she yelled, moving her face so his lips grazed her cheek instead, leaving a slimy trail.

She slammed her foot into his shin and he released her with a yelp. As she ran for the door, he grabbed a handful of her hair and dragged her back while punching her in the stomach.

Valerie doubled up, the force of the blow winding her. Leo wrapped an arm around her neck and dragged her backwards towards the bedroom.

'You're my bird, no one else's, and I'll fucking prove it,' he yelled.

Valerie was stunned. Leo had always seemed so harmless. Toni had tried to warn her he had a dark side, but she hadn't listened.

Valerie shook herself out of her shock and frantically tried to think her way out of this mess. She made her body go limp, making it harder for him to drag her.

'Come on, you stupid cow,' he said.

When he leaned over her, she reached up and jammed her

thumbs in his eyes. He screeched with pain and dropped her. Valerie scrambled to her feet and rushed for the door, but he ran after her and rugby tackled her to the floor. She landed on her front and he crawled up her body, pinning her down with his weight. Determinedly Valerie brought up her elbow, rammed it sideways into his ribs, and threw him off as she scrambled to her feet for the second time.

As she rushed to the door, it burst open to reveal Toni, knife in hand. The effect on Leo was dramatic. All the anger vanished from his eyes, replaced by fear.

'What are you doing here?' Valerie asked her.

'I knew the shite bag would try something like this,' said Toni, brandishing the knife, which had been polished until it gleamed wickedly. Her lips curled into a smile at the way Leo's eyes widened. She looked to Valerie. 'Like you said, we have each other's backs. Why don't you wait outside, Val?'

'What are you going to do?'

'Just wait outside,' Toni said again before looking back at Leo, who was slowly walking backwards, as though afraid to move too quickly in case it drove her to strike.

'Don't do anything that will get you in trouble,' Valerie told her.

'I won't,' replied Toni before looking back at Leo, malicious pleasure in her black eyes.

Valerie, sore and tired, quietly left without looking at Leo, closing the door behind her. Slowly she plodded down the stairs, glad to be outside in the fresh air. It was starting to get dark and she was just relieved to be out of the flat and that nothing really bad had happened to her.

When her hands started to shake, she shoved them into her jacket pockets. How could she have misjudged someone so badly? Toni hadn't, she'd known what Leo was all along, it was why she'd followed her. What had she picked up on that Valerie herself had missed? What if she'd misjudged Seb too? But Toni had introduced them and she wouldn't have done that if he was anything like Leo. Seb was sensitive and deep, not a brute like Leo.

Toni emerged from the front of the building twenty minutes later, looking very pleased with herself. She was her usual immaculate self, not a strand of hair out of place.

'What happened?' said Valerie.

'Leo's promised never to go near you again,' she replied. 'You don't need to worry about him.'

'That's great, but is he okay?'

'What do you care about that bastard?'

'I don't, but I need to know that you won't get into any trouble.'

'I'll be fine. Honestly,' Toni added when her cousin appeared unconvinced.

Valerie nodded. 'All right. Thanks, Toni. I really appreciate what you did for me.'

'You're very welcome.' Toni was concerned when she saw how Valerie's hands shook. 'Do you fancy going for a drink?'

'Aye, that would be good, actually. I can't go home like this, my parents will start asking questions.'

Toni linked her arm through Valerie's. 'Let's have a few, we deserve it.'

As they walked away, Valerie glanced back over her shoulder. She looked up at Leo's windows, but they were so dirty he could have been standing there watching them and she wouldn't be able to see him.

'How did you know what he was really like?' she asked Toni.

'It was just a feeling,' she replied.

'Instinct?'

'Aye, something like that.'

'I wish my instincts were as sharp as yours. I was convinced he was harmless.'

'A man with his history is never harmless.'

'I suppose you're right.'

'I always am. Anyway, you're well rid of him now and tomorrow you're meeting the lovely Seb. All's right with the world.'

'Aye,' smiled Valerie. 'I'll forget all about that bastard Leo.'

'That's the best thing that could ever happen to him,' said Toni. 'Now let's go and get blethered.'

* * *

Valerie woke the next morning with a headache niggling at her temples. At least her night out with Toni had cured her of the shock Leo had given her. As she lay in bed, attempting to find the will to get up, she gazed at the ceiling, wondering just how far he would have gone. Had his threat been an idle one? Would his rage have wilted or would he have done something terrible to her? Toni had saved her from something horrible, of that she was convinced.

Glancing at the clock, she sighed to see it was 7.30. With a groan, she rolled out of bed and hauled herself into the bathroom. She had to be at work in an hour.

A shower and some breakfast revived her and by the time she stepped out of the door, the headache had gone.

Valerie worked on the till at a local petrol station. She didn't exactly enjoy her work, but the pay wasn't bad and her colleagues were very pleasant. The majority of the public, however, were not and it boggled Valerie's mind how many of them seemed to think she was sub-human just because she was serving them. She would have loved to work in a job she had a passion for, but she wasn't sure how she could manage that, so for now she was happy to work at the petrol station until her path in life revealed itself, as she was convinced it would.

Her shift passed interminably slowly, despite being busy, as she was eager to meet Seb that evening. She was apprehensive that Leo would come in as it was where they'd met in the first place, but he stayed away, so she hoped that Toni's warning had worked. Either that or her cousin had hurt him so much he was unable to leave his flat. She hoped not, for her cousin's sake.

* * *

Valerie enjoyed a lovely evening with Seb. She hadn't thought herself a fan of poetry before but some of it was beautiful, written from the heart. A couple of poems were humorous and had everyone in stitches. She enjoyed glancing at Seb as he listened to the good poetry, his eyes shining with pleasure. It was clear it was a passion for him, and it was fast becoming one for her too.

The owner of the bookshop was a friend of Seb's and was incredibly knowledgeable. Valerie enjoyed talking with him while sipping wine and nibbling vol-au-vents.

After leaving the bookshop, they headed down the road to a quiet pub, where they talked until closing time. Seb's company was a revelation to her, she hadn't thought it possible to have so much in common with another person that you talked non-stop and never ran out of things to say.

It was when they were discussing the work of Edgar Allan Poe that Seb suddenly kissed her. It was so unexpected, especially as she was in mid-sentence, that Val froze with surprise.

'Sorry,' he said, colouring. 'I thought, I mean... I... sorry, I...'

She silenced him with another kiss, before he wrapped his arms around her and pulled her closer.

'Hey,' called a voice.

They broke off the kiss to turn and look at the landlord, who was collecting glasses at the next table.

'You want to act like that, bugger off to a hotel,' he told them.

'We were only kissing,' replied Seb. 'It was our first kiss, actually.'

'Aww, congratulations,' he said sarcastically. 'But don't do it again,' glowered the landlord before stalking back to the bar.

Seb and Valerie looked at each other and laughed while the rest of the customers grinned.

'Maybe it's time we got out of here?' suggested Seb.

'Good idea,' replied Valerie.

They collected their things, got to their feet and headed to the door.

'I've had a great time,' said Seb as they walked down the street together, holding hands. 'Can I see you again?'

'Yes,' she replied immediately. 'When?' Valerie cringed at how eager she sounded.

'Tomorrow? I hope that's not too much, seeing me four days in a row.'

'It's not. I really enjoy spending time with you.'

'Great,' he said with a relieved smile. 'Would you like to go out for a meal?'

'Sounds lovely.'

'What sort of food do you like?'

'Anything, I'm not fussy.'

'There's a nice restaurant I know. The menu's not very exciting but the food is good.'

'That's fine by me.'

'Shall I pick you up?'

Valerie didn't want him going anywhere near her house until she was sure there would be no comeback from Leo, so she arranged to meet him at the restaurant. Seb walked her to the taxi, giving her another kiss before she got into the car. She turned in her seat to keep him in view until the taxi turned a corner and he vanished.

Valerie sank back into the seat, a smile on her face at the end of one of the nicest evenings of her life.

The next morning, Janet quizzed Valerie eagerly about her date and was delighted to hear that she'd had a lovely time and was seeing Seb again that evening. When Valerie reached to switch on the kettle, her sleeve rode up to reveal the bruises on her wrist.

'Did Seb do that?' gasped Janet.

'Course not,' mumbled Valerie, pulling her sleeve back down to hide the bruises. 'Leo got upset when I dumped him.'

'The wee bastard,' her mum seethed.

'He's been put in his place, Maw. Don't worry about it.'

'Don't worry about it? What if he attacks you again?'

'He won't. Toni made sure of it.'

'Toni was there when you dumped him?'

'She followed me there, she knew he would react badly when I didn't have a clue.'

'Well, I'm very grateful to her for protecting you, but how exactly did she make sure he won't bother you again?'

'I don't know, she wouldn't say, and I didn't push the issue.'

'That was very wise of you. Hopefully you'll never see that loser again. I warned you about him, didn't I?' snapped Janet.

'Aye, Maw,' sighed Valerie.

'But you wouldn't listen, you always think you know best, but this proves that you don't.'

Valerie rolled her eyes as her mother continued to chastise her.

'I'd like to meet this Seb,' said Janet when her lecture eventually came to an end. 'He sounds very nice.'

'He is, so sensitive and gentle,' Val said dreamily.

'That'll be a novelty for you, after all the creeps you've dated.'

Valerie ignored the dig. 'If things continue to go well, then I'll bring him round for tea.'

'Great,' smiled Janet, who was pleased her daughter had this nice new man in her life, but a little apprehensive that Leo wasn't done with her. She'd heard about his reputation and knew him to be vicious and vindictive. Hopefully whatever Toni had done to him would be enough to put him off thoughts of vengeance. She wasn't a big fan of her niece, but Toni did have her uses.

8

Valerie's shift passed slowly as she anticipated her next date with Seb.

As she left the petrol station and walked to the bus stop, wishing she could afford a car, she became aware she was being followed.

Glancing over her shoulder, she saw it was Chris Cathcart and two of his friends. It was clear they wanted revenge for what had happened to Cassie but weren't brave enough to take it out on Toni.

Valerie took one look at them and broke into a run as they chased her. But where should she go? Her bus wouldn't be along for another ten minutes, so she couldn't hop onto that. She was on a main road, so hopefully someone driving by would see what was happening and stop to intervene. But every bastard just drove on, even though they could see a lone woman was being pursued by three men.

Across the road, a bus was pulling up. Valerie had no idea where it was going but she didn't care, all she saw was salvation. As the men were gaining on her, she darted into the road, narrowly avoiding an oncoming car, which had to swerve around her. The men tried to follow but were forced to wait to allow a transit van to pass.

Valerie reached the other side of the road safely and was racing towards the bus when the driver – who had clearly seen her running for it – pulled back into the traffic.

'You stupid bastard,' she yelled as it passed her by.

The men had reached the other side of the road now, forcing her to continue running, but they were fast and gaining on her. Valerie had nothing to defend herself with but her fists. She turned to face them and stood her ground. She was a McVay, and her family never went down without a fight.

The men were surprised when she ran at them, hurling her bag at Chris. It hit him in the chest, knocking him off his feet, and he fell into one of his friends, the two of them tumbling to the ground. Valerie tore into the one man still standing, punching him full in the face before kicking him in the stomach. She dodged round him as the other two picked themselves back up, grabbing her bag as she went, and ran back the way she'd come, heading back to the petrol station and safety. Chris and his friend chased after her, leaving the man she'd punched groaning on the pavement.

Then someone finally decided to intervene. An open-backed truck pulled right up onto the pavement between Valerie and the men, allowing her to escape. Two huge, hairy, tattooed men in overalls jumped out and glowered at Chris and his friend.

'Oy,' the biggest of the pair yelled at them. 'You like to pick on women, do you, you fucking cowards?'

Chris and his friend took one look, turned tail and fled, and Valerie breathed a sigh of relief. That was the second time in two days she'd been rescued. Perhaps there was more to Seb's belief in a higher power after all?

* * *

Before heading home, Valerie stopped by Toni's house and was glad to find her in.

'Val, I wasn't expecting you,' she said, wrapped in a silk zebra-print dressing gown, her wet hair hanging down her back. 'I'm just getting ready to go out on a date.'

'Who with this time?'

'Jason McIntyre.'

'After all the trouble you went to over Warren, you're going out with someone else now?' exclaimed Valerie.

'Oh, I didn't want Warren,' said Toni with a dismissive wave of her hand, nails perfectly manicured. 'I just wanted to let Cassie know that she couldn't have him.'

'Well, it's thanks to you that I was chased by her brother and two of his friends when I left work today.'

Toni's eyes flashed. 'What? How fucking dare they?'

'They daren't take it out on you, so they decided to go for me instead.'

'Are you okay? Did they hurt you?'

'They didn't manage to lay a finger on me, thanks to two good Samaritans who saw them off.'

'Bastards,' hissed Toni. 'I'll get them back for this.'

'I don't want to start a feud where we all spend the best years of our lives getting back at each other. I want it over and done with right now.'

'Oh, it will be. I'll tell Frankie. He'll sort them out.'

'You can't tell him. God knows what he'll do. He loves any excuse to commit violence.'

'Then how do you suggest we end it? I am not apologising to that stupid bitch.'

'And I wouldn't expect you to, but I don't want any more violence.'

'Then you shouldn't be in this family. We can never escape violence, it's in our bones.'

Sadly, Valerie knew she was right. 'I don't know what should be done then, but I thought you should know.'

'I'll sort it, don't worry,' said Toni as though it were nothing. 'By the way, how was it last night with Seb?'

'Great. I'm meeting him at a restaurant this evening.'

'Oh,' smiled Toni.

'Oh what?'

'Third date, and you know what they say about third dates.'

'I've no idea what you're talking about,' lied Valerie. 'Have a good evening.'

'I'm sure it won't be half as good as yours with Seb the sex god.'

After enjoying a nice meal together, Valerie and Seb took a walk in a park close to the restaurant that sat on the edge of the River Clyde. The moon was full, casting a glow as they strolled arm in arm. Valerie hadn't told Seb anything about Chris and his friends as she didn't want to spoil their time together. Neither had she mentioned Leo's bad reaction to their break-up. This sweet, gorgeous man seemed a million miles from the ugly lives the majority of her family led and she didn't want to contaminate him.

They stopped walking to lean on the rail and gaze into the black water below. Valerie's heart thudded when Seb took her face in his hands, the way he lightly ran his thumbs up and down her neck, making her tingle with excitement. Just as he was about to press his lips to hers, a voice behind them demanded, 'Give us your fucking money.'

They turned to see two men, all in black, with hoods obscuring their faces. Both brandished knives.

'Are you deaf?' barked one of the men when Seb and Val stared at them in surprise. 'I said give us your fucking money, unless you wannae get stabbed.'

'Get behind me,' Seb told Valerie, his face turning to granite as he regarded the attackers.

But she refused to move and squinted at the mugger's hand that held the knife. Thanks to the moonlight, she could make out the distinctive spider tattoo there.

'Adam, is that you?' she said.

The figure lowered the knife and squinted right back at her. 'Valerie?' he said with surprise.

'Aye, it's me. What the hell do you think you're doing?'

Adam sighed, the knife vanishing into the pocket of his hoodie. 'Cathy's pregnant again and I really need the cash.'

'And you getting thrown in the jail is going to help her, is it? Because that's what'll happen if you keep this up.'

'Aye, I know, but I'm desperate.'

She regarded him sympathetically. 'I can understand that, but this really isn't the way. How would Cathy cope with three weans alone if you got sent to prison?'

'She wouldnae be able to.'

'Exactly. Go and ask my da for a job, he needs some help with his taxi business and I know you're a great driver.'

'Really?' he said hopefully.

'Really. I'll put in a good word for you myself tomorrow.'

'Thanks, Val, I really appreciate that. Sorry about this whole thing.'

'It's all right, no harm done. Now go straight home and don't try to mug anyone else.'

'I won't, not if I know I have the chance of a real job. You won't mention this to Frankie, will you?'

'God, no, he'd go off his heid. That's another reason not to pull a stunt like this again. You're lucky it was me you tried to rob.'

'Aye, I feel shite about that.'

'So you should. Now bugger off before you get up to any more mischief.'

'We will. Come on, Kenny,' he told his friend, who appeared disappointed that no violence was about to ensue.

As the two men walked away, Valerie turned to Seb. 'You okay?'

'I am, thanks to you,' he replied. 'That was... surreal.'

'Sorry about that. Adam's a good lad at heart, he wouldn't really have stabbed us.'

'Are you sure? He seemed rather keen to give it a go.'

'He was just trying to intimidate us.'

'I'm not too proud to admit that it worked.'

She smiled and wrapped her arms around his waist. 'Thank you for putting yourself in front of me. Plenty of men would have thrown me at them and run.'

Seb slid his hands into her hair, sending tingles shooting down her spine. 'Never.'

'Are you sure you don't want to run fast and far from me?'

'Why would I do that?'

'Because one of my cousins just pointed a knife at you.'

'And the fact that you were his cousin meant they didn't hurt us.'

'You're mad,' she smiled.

'About you,' he smiled back.

They kissed again, their movements becoming frantic and passionate.

'Perhaps we should get out of here before someone else comes along with a knife,' breathed Valerie as he kissed her neck.

'Good idea.' Seb raised his head to look at her. 'I don't know how you'd feel about this, but my parents have gone away for a couple of nights, so...'

He trailed off and looked away, embarrassed. Valerie knew he was blushing, even though it was dark.

'That sounds nice,' she replied.

He breathed a sigh of relief and smiled. 'Great.'

They headed back to the main road hand in hand and flagged down a passing taxi. It dropped them off on a street not far from the restaurant they'd eaten at earlier that evening. Seb's house was a well-maintained detached villa with a large drive and good-sized garden on a very respectable estate in Bishopbriggs, which was only a few minutes' drive from Springburn, where Valerie lived.

'Such a pretty house,' said Valerie. 'I love the statue of Artemis in the garden. What?' she added when he did a double take.

'You're the first person who's come to the house who knows who she is. Most people ask who the bird is in the garden with her tits out. You are so sexy,' he smiled.

'And you're the first man I've dated who thinks intelligence is sexy.' Valerie took his hand. 'Are you going to show me inside, then?'

He unlocked the door and they stepped into a spotless hallway. Seb shyly asked her to remove her shoes because his mum went mad if anyone walked on her carpet in shoes and she was happy to oblige. The house was very modern and beautifully furnished by someone with very elegant taste, and the atmosphere was warm and inviting, making Val feel at ease.

Seb retrieved a bottle of white wine from the kitchen and they curled up on the couch together to drink and talk. It wasn't long before the glasses were dumped on the large wooden coffee table and they were frantically kissing.

Seb finally led her upstairs to his bedroom and they lay down together on the crisp sheets of his double bed. All Valerie's past boyfriends had been fast and frantic lovers, determined to get her clothes off in record time, but Seb was gentle and tender, taking the time to kiss and stroke every inch of her. His own body was strong, a result of all the tennis he played, and he gave Valerie her very first shuddering orgasm. Afterwards, he didn't light up a cigarette or head into the kitchen for a can of lager. Instead, he held her in his arms and she rested her head on his chest, enjoying listening to his pounding heartbeat, his skin burning to the touch.

'That was amazing,' she smiled with satisfaction.

'It really was,' he grinned, running his fingertips across her bare shoulder. 'I think we should do that again very soon.'

'How soon?'

'In about twenty minutes,' he replied, making her giggle.

'Fine by me. Your parents definitely won't be back tonight?'

'Definitely. They've gone to stay with friends in Inverness.'

She rolled on top of him. 'Good. Because I haven't even got warmed up yet.'

'What a woman,' he grinned, pulling her down to him.

As Valerie was off work the following day, she stayed with Seb, who didn't have to be in university that day either. They spent the time talking, making love and going through his vast collection of books and discussing them. Valerie called her parents to let them know where she was and that she wouldn't be coming home that night either. While she was on the phone, she remembered to tell her dad that Adam needed a job and Charlie promised to give him a chance. Other than that, they didn't interact with the outside world at all, remaining locked in their own cosy cocoon. To Valerie, it felt like a mini holiday, and she envied Seb his peaceful world full of books and learning and his law-abiding family.

* * *

Valerie was downcast to have to rejoin the outside world the next morning. Seb had university and she had work, so they had no choice.

'I wish we didn't have to leave our cosy nest,' said Seb, pulling her to him.

'Me too,' she replied. 'It's been wonderful.'

'It's my grandmother's eightieth birthday on Saturday and we're having a big family party. Why don't you come?'

'Are you sure you're ready to introduce me to your family?'

'Absolutely. I want to show you off.' He stroked her face. 'You're so beautiful and intelligent.'

Valerie beamed back at him. 'Oh, I've just remembered – Aunty Moira will be out that night and I told Toni I'd keep her company.'

'I remember you telling me about that now. That's a shame,' he said, smile faltering.

'I don't have to go to Toni's, she won't mind.'

'Are you sure?'

'Aye, as long as you're sure your family won't mind me turning up?'

'Course not. I've already told my parents about you and they can't wait to meet you.'

'Do they know who my family are?' she said warily.

'I haven't told them that yet. I want them to be as crazy about you as I am before breaking that news.'

'You don't think they'd take it well?'

'Some of them are very strait-laced and my mum is a defence solicitor, but I know they'll see you're not like your family.'

'I hope so,' said Valerie, who really wanted his parents' approval. If they didn't like her then it could ruin a relationship she had already started to rely on.

9

Valerie's shift passed in a pleasant haze as she relived memories of her time with Seb. She didn't even react when customers were rude to her. She just gave them a serene smile and wished them a happy day. She felt sorry for them that they weren't enjoying her happiness.

Her bubble was burst when, ten minutes after she returned home, there was a knock at the door and Toni stalked in with the demeanour of an angry cat.

'And where have you been?' demanded Toni imperiously. 'I was trying to get hold of you all day yesterday and nothing.'

'I was with Seb.'

Toni arched an eyebrow. 'All day?'

'Aye. I stayed over last night and the night before.' Val sighed dreamily. 'It was wonderful.'

'I'm glad you had a nice time,' said Toni, her voice dripping ice. 'But while you were loving it up with Seb the stallion, the shit really hit the fan.'

'Why, what's happened?'

'Frankie scalped someone in a nightclub the night before last.'

'Scalped?' frowned Valerie. 'What do you mean?'

'I mean he cut off someone's scalp, the top part, hair and all.'

Valerie grimaced. 'Why the hell would he do something so... so sick?'

'Because he is sick. Everyone knows it, but no one wants to say it.'

'And you're sure he actually scalped them?' Val said, not quite believing what she was hearing.

'I saw it, Val. It was...' Toni sighed and closed her eyes as she relived the horror. She took a deep breath and opened them again. 'It's something I'll never forget. The disturbing thing is, no one could find the bit he cut off. I think he kept it as a trophy.'

Valerie's stomach rolled over at the prospect. 'Has he been arrested?'

'No.'

'What? He scalps someone in the middle of a nightclub and he's not arrested?'

'Because no one would tell the polis anything, they're all too scared of Frankie. A lot of the customers left when he started attacking the man and those who didn't leave before the polis arrived said they never saw anything.'

Valerie thought how cowardly people could be, but then again, she knew how dangerous Frankie was. 'Why did he do it?'

'The man was pished and said he looked like one of The Proclaimers.'

'Jeezo, that drives him doolally.'

'I know. He totally lost it. He was in a bad mood to start with because Harry Woodhouse pissed him off again.'

'Who?'

'That new dealer who's been trying to encroach on his territory. Frankie went after him but couldn't get hold of him, again. Frankie hates it when someone outsmarts him and let's face it, there aren't many people who are capable of getting the better of him.'

'Where's Frankie now?'

'Lying low somewhere. No one knows where. He's waiting for it to all blow over.'

'Did he know the man he scalped?'

'No, he was a stranger. He survived, though, because the ambulance arrived so fast. Luckily for him it was down the street at another nightclub attending to someone who'd been glassed in the face.'

'Busy night for them, then. Thank god he survived.'

'And he won't be needing his comb any more.'

'That's not funny, Toni.'

Toni merely shrugged. 'Anyway, I thought you should know because, although no one will tell the polis it was Frankie, everyone knows it was and the McVay name has been dragged through the shite. Again. The guy he scalped has brothers who are low-level dealers and all-round vicious bastards from Parkhead and now they're out for Frankie's blood.'

'That's all we need,' sighed Valerie. 'I can't believe he did that. It's psychotic, even for Frankie.'

'I know,' said Toni grimly. 'He just stepped up a level. Anyway, message delivered. I should be on my way now.'

'You could have phoned to tell me, so why did you come here?'

'You always were astute. Fine. I was curious to find out if you really had spent the night at Seb's.'

'Well, I did and it was lovely.' Valerie wished she was still there rather than locked in another horror of her family's creation.

'I'm glad to hear it. And he treated you nicely?'

'Very. He was the perfect gentleman.'

'And he knows what he's doing?' said Toni, mischief lighting up her eyes.

'Oh, aye.'

'Finally you've met a decent man.' Toni stood there, hand on hip, awaiting the credit.

'And it's all down to you,' said Valerie flatly.

'I suppose it is,' Toni smiled with satisfaction. 'Well, must go. I'm working at the nail bar today. See you around, Val.'

'Bye, Toni,' said Valerie, seeing her out and closing the door behind her.

Valerie sighed, wondering what the hell Seb's family would think of her when word inevitably spread through the city about this latest atrocity. They wouldn't want their sweet son anywhere near her and who could blame them? She wondered if dating Seb was selfish, but she was falling for him hard and fast and was loath to give him up. Judging by the fact that he wanted her to meet his parents, he was feeling the same about her. She refused to give up the first good thing that had come her way because of the unhinged actions of her relatives.

Frankie's antics had big repercussions in the local Glaswegian underworld. His victim was called Robbie Slater and his brothers determined to get revenge for him, so they started to hunt Frankie down, offering bribes for information as to his whereabouts. When that failed, they resorted to threats and violence, but all their efforts were in vain and Frankie remained in hiding. Several McVays were ambushed by the Slaters and battered into submission, but no one could tell them anything.

Valerie spent her time either at work or with Seb, well away from Slater and McVay territory. She expected the Cathcarts to make another attempt on her, but they appeared to have given up, perhaps realising they were taking their revenge on the wrong person.

* * *

Valerie attended Seb's grandmother's birthday party, which was held in the function room of a beautiful four-star hotel in the west end of the city. Euphemia Robertson was a short, frail-looking woman with beautiful silver hair pulled back into an elegant bun, and sparkling blue eyes, like her grandson's. She greeted Valerie pleasantly and shook her hand with her own tiny hand. Although Euphemia looked like a strong breeze could blow her over, there was a strength about her, as well as a good humour. Valerie got the feeling she was the one her family turned to in times of strife for guidance.

'Gran,' said Seb. 'This is my girlfriend, Valerie.'

'Valerie,' said Euphemia. 'What a lovely name. What's your last name?'

'Brown,' replied Valerie. It wasn't the first time in her life she was relieved McVay blood was on her mother's side.

'My, aren't you pretty, Valerie Brown?' Euphemia beamed. 'And I hear you're a very intelligent girl. In fact, I'd say you're the first intelligent girl Seb has dated.'

'That's true,' he grinned.

'You're also the first he's invited to a family function,' continued the old woman. 'So I'd say he's rather smitten.'

'Gran,' blushed Seb.

'Your grandson's a wonderful man,' Valerie told her.

'That's very sweet of you.' Euphemia's blue eyes studied Valerie closely. 'And I think you really do mean that.'

'I certainly do.'

Euphemia's gentle smile lit up her face and she patted Valerie's hand.

Other family members came up to speak to the birthday girl, who was clearly beloved by everyone. Valerie thought of her own family, the majority of whom had been complicit in child abuse just because they were afraid of Roddy, had committed violent or illegal acts and, despite putting on a united front, all bitched about each other behind their backs. There was none of the closeness and genuine love the Robertsons shared. How wonderful it would be to be part of this family.

Valerie told herself not to think such things. She'd only been dating Seb for a week and she might well find herself shut out of the Robertson family when they discovered who she was related to. The news about the scalping in the nightclub had been in all the local newspapers, but thankfully they hadn't mentioned that Frankie had been responsible. Every witness was doing a good job of keeping that to themselves, so her family hadn't publicly been linked to the crime. Still, the McVay family history was bloody and infamous. Valerie had no doubt these good people would go to great lengths to keep their son away from her.

'It doesn't matter to me who your family are,' Seb told Valerie after she expertly evaded enquiries about her own family from his relatives.

'I know,' she said, smiling up at him fondly. 'But it will matter to your family and believe me, that's no judgement on them. My lot are a nightmare. You've already met Adam and he's one of the better ones.'

She was introduced to his parents next, Laura and Jeffrey. His mother was tall, blonde-haired and blue-eyed, while Jeffrey was short, dark-haired, red-faced and extremely round. Both were very pleasant and said they were pleased to meet her.

Seb introduced her to various aunts, uncles and cousins, and didn't leave Valerie's side all evening, until his cute twelve-year-old cousin, who had a huge crush on him, shyly asked him for a dance.

'It's okay,' Valerie told Seb when he turned to her. 'I don't mind.'

The girl took his hand and determinedly led him onto the dance floor and Euphemia, Laura, Laura's sister Deborah and Seb's younger sister Emily waved Valerie over to their table.

Nervously, Valerie took a seat at the table and smiled at them coyly. Not wanting to disgrace herself, she'd purposefully gone easy on the wine, but now she was wishing she hadn't as she really could have used some Dutch courage.

'It's all right, dear,' Euphemia smiled at her. 'We don't bite.'

'So, tell us about yourself, Valerie,' said Deborah.

Valerie looked to Laura, who smiled encouragingly.

'Well,' she began slowly. 'I work at a petrol station, but I'm only doing that until I figure out what I want to do with my life,' she hastily added. 'I live with my parents but I'm saving for my own place. My maw's a librarian and my da owns his own taxi rank and he's a great mechanic too.'

'It's always useful to know a mechanic,' smiled Deborah.

'He's really good, too, there's nothing he can't fix and I don't just mean cars – toasters, microwaves, stereos, the lot.'

'He sounds very handy to have about the house,' smiled Laura. 'I wish Jeffrey was the same. He can't even change a light bulb.'

'But we all know you wouldn't be without him,' said Euphemia, patting her arm.

Laura's smile was filled with fondness. 'That's true.'

Valerie discovered that Emily was also at university and wanted to become a doctor. Deborah was an accountant and Laura a criminal lawyer. It seemed driven career women were a trademark of the Robertson family and Valerie found herself being immensely inspired by them. Talk turned to what she'd like to do, and she explained she wanted to find a career helping people. It turned out alcohol wasn't required to relax in their company after all, as they were all so friendly and interesting.

Seb joined them at the table after his cousin eventually relinquished his company. He took the seat on Valerie's left and held her hand.

'I hope you haven't been relentlessly interrogating Valerie?' he asked his family.

'Of course not,' said Laura sweetly. 'We've had a very nice conversation, haven't we, Valerie?'

'Absolutely,' she replied before looking to Seb. 'The women in your family are very inspiring.'

'I don't think we've ever been called that before,' smiled Emily.

'And it's more than you can say for the men,' said Deborah, glancing over at a group of Robertson males of varying ages and levels of intoxication. One of them told a dirty joke and they all brayed like donkeys.

'Oh, thanks,' said Seb.

'Every Robertson male has their... eccentricity, shall we call it?' replied Euphemia with a knowing look her grandson's way.

'What about the rest of your family?' Laura asked Valerie. 'What do they do?'

Seb knew how uncomfortable this would make Valerie and so he intervened. 'I think that's enough with the inquisition for now. Let's have a dance,' he told her.

'Sounds lovely,' she smiled gratefully.

He led her onto the dance floor and took her in his arms.

'Thanks for saving me,' Valerie told him.

'I hope they didn't go too hard on you.'

'No, they were really nice, actually. Your family's lovely. You're so lucky. I wish my family was like yours,' she sighed. 'At my family celebrations, a fight breaks out in the first ten minutes. At my uncle's fiftieth birthday party, the manager of the social club called the polis because everyone started smashing up the place.'

'At least it was a memorable day.'

'Not really, it was just like all the other family parties.'

'If it's any consolation, my Uncle Jake got so drunk at my cousin's wedding reception that he ended up peeing in the chocolate fountain.'

Valerie laughed. 'I don't think even my family's done that.'

'No family's perfect. We all have our black sheep. We're far more than our blood relatives. Yes, we're a part of them and they're a part of us, but that's not all we are.'

Valerie smiled. 'Thanks, that does make me feel better.' She wrapped her arms around his neck. 'You're so wise. You take after your gran.'

'She is pretty special. She's seen things, strange things no one can explain.'

'Like what?'

'Ghosts. Does that sound crazy?'

'Er, I don't think so,' she said slowly.

'She's seen the ghosts of friends and family before she found out they'd passed, poltergeists, phantom battles.'

'Battles?'

'Aye, quite a few. This country has a bloody history.'

'You obviously believe in the afterlife?'

'Absolutely. I always have, right from being young. It just makes sense to me. I think the universe is far more exciting than what we see here. I can't believe the pinnacle of creation is working like a hamster in a wheel all week and going to the pub at the weekend. I also think that just the experience of being human proves there's a lot more going on than we can even fathom. Love, for instance. Some people will argue that romantic love is just a means to perpetuate the species, but I've never seen a couple more in love than my Aunt Jane and Uncle Wilf and they never even wanted kids. I've been thinking about love a lot lately. Valerie, I've fallen in love with you.'

Valerie beamed with delight. 'You have?'

'Yes, hard and fast.' He blushed adorably. 'I... I hope I've not come on too heavy.'

'Not at all,' she smiled, a lump forming in her throat. 'Because I love you too.'

Even though Seb's parents were home, Valerie was invited to spend the night at their house, an invitation she eagerly accepted. She and Seb made silent love in his bed, accompanied by the sound of Jeffrey's loud snoring.

Valerie went straight to work from Seb's house the following morning, feeling wonderful, but wishing she was still with him. She couldn't believe a man like Seb loved her. He was absolutely perfect and already she was wondering what the duties of a minister's wife were. What a nice, peaceful life that would be. Hopefully they'd get a lovely country parish, away from the city and her family. They would have their own personal library, packed floor to ceiling with old books, and they would spend their evenings together before the fire, talking about philosophy, history and literature. She would help arrange jumble sales and events at the church hall while he tended to his flock, all of whom would adore him. Best of all, they would both be in a position to help people. It would be a beautiful life.

Until her family brought her back down to earth with a thump.

10

Valerie was halfway through her shift at the petrol station when two uniformed police officers came in. At first, she assumed they were there to buy petrol and snacks, which was nothing unusual, but when they approached the counter and flashed their warrant cards, she knew it was much more.

'Has someone been hurt?' she demanded when they said they needed to talk to her in private. 'Is it my parents?'

'It's nothing like that,' said the older of the two kindly. 'We just need a quiet word.'

'You can talk in my office,' the manager said hastily, swooping in before her petrol station got a bad reputation.

Valerie led the two men through to the office and made the mistake of taking the only chair, meaning the two officers – both of whom were tall and strapping – loomed over her.

'We're here to discuss your cousin,' began the older officer, a sergeant.

Valerie was so convinced they were going to say Frankie's name that it came as a total shock when they said 'Antoinette McVay.'

Valerie blinked at him. 'Toni, why?'

'We've had a report of an assault that you were allegedly present at.'

'Assault on who?' she said, expecting to hear Cassie's name.

'William Lundy.'

Once again, Valerie was taken by surprise. 'Do you mean the man who works in the newsagents not far from Toni's house?'

'The very same,' replied the sergeant, taking in her obvious surprise.

'Is he all right?'

'He sustained a broken arm, nose and ribs. He's been left very traumatised.'

'Poor William. He's such a nice man. When was he attacked?'

'Last night at about 8.30. We've been informed that you and Antoinette McVay turned up at his shop and assaulted him with crowbars.'

'Crowbars? This is ridiculous. It's all lies and I can prove it. I was at my boyfriend's grandma's birthday party last night. I arrived at seven o'clock and didn't leave until just before eleven. There were fifty guests there, all of whom can back up my alibi.'

The younger officer scribbled in his notebook as she related the details of the hotel while the sergeant nodded. 'We're going to need the contact number of your boyfriend and his family.'

Valerie's stomach plummeted. 'His family? Do you really have to talk to them?'

'The more people who can back up your alibi, the better.'

'But Seb – that's my boyfriend – and the hotel staff will be able to do that. Is it really necessary to ask anyone else?'

'I'm afraid so.'

'But... they don't know I'm a McVay. I mean, Seb does, of course, but I haven't told his family yet.'

'Why not?'

'Wouldn't you keep it quiet if you were a McVay?'

The sergeant smiled and nodded. 'I can understand that. Well, we'll talk to Seb and the hotel staff and if they can back up your alibi, then hopefully there'll be no need to ask anyone else.'

'Thank you, I appreciate you trying,' she said miserably.

'You have no history of assault and if you're telling the truth about your alibi, it means someone's trying to set you up. Can you think of anyone who'd do that?'

'No,' she replied, trying not to think about Cassie and Chris Cathcart. 'I've no idea at all.'

The sergeant was no fool. This was the first thing she'd said that he didn't believe.

'Have you spoken to Toni yet?' said Valerie.

'No. She was first on our list to talk to but we've been unable to locate her. Have you any idea where we can find her?'

'I assume you've tried her home and the nail bar where she works?'

The sergeant nodded.

'Then she's probably out shopping. It's her favourite thing to do. She's usually back by mid-afternoon.'

After a few more questions about her family, the two police officers left.

Valerie sighed with relief and followed them out of the office, almost bumping into her manager, who was eagerly hanging around outside the door.

'Is everything okay?' she asked Valerie.

'Fine. They wondered if I might have witnessed an incident, but I didn't.'

'Oh,' replied the older woman, not entirely convinced by that explanation, but she let the subject drop and Valerie got back to work.

Valerie was annoyed. She'd been in a great mood and now it had been destroyed thanks to her family, again. Hopefully that would be the last she heard about the matter, but somehow she didn't think so. Thank god she had a strong alibi, but that meant someone had lied. The sergeant was right – she was being framed. The obvious answer was the Cathcart family, but she didn't think that was their style. But if not them, then who? Toni had been implicated too. Either she had assaulted poor William, who had never hurt anyone in his life, and she'd taken along someone for back-up, or she was nothing to do with it either and they were both being set up. She was eager to talk to Toni, but she wouldn't be able to until her shift had finished.

The clock ticked by interminably slowly but finally four o'clock came around, meaning she could leave. She caught the bus home and was relieved to find her parents were still out, meaning she could call Toni in peace. She dialled her mobile phone but there was no answer, so she tried her home number instead. Her Aunty Moira told her Toni wasn't home. Perhaps Toni had heard that the police wanted to speak to her and was holed up with Frankie? If that was the case, then at least she'd been warned.

Deciding she couldn't just hang about the house, Valerie decided to go out and search for Toni. She tried the local pubs, cafés and Toni's friends, but no one had seen her.

Dejected, she returned home to find her cousin sitting on her couch, talking with Valerie's parents.

'Where have you been?' Janet asked her daughter.

'Out looking for Toni,' she replied.

'Oh, have you?' said her cousin cheerfully. 'I'm sorry, I had no idea. I've been out shopping. I've just been showing your maw what I bought – silk scarves and jewellery...'

'Aye, that's great. Toni, a word,' said Valerie before stalking upstairs to her bedroom.

'Oh dear, looks like I'm in trouble,' Toni smiled at Janet before following her cousin, leaving her shopping bags to take up the majority of the floor space in the living room.

'Have the polis spoken to you?' Valerie demanded of Toni once they were in her bedroom, the door firmly closed so her parents wouldn't hear.

'Polis, no. Why would they want to speak to me?'

Toni appeared to be genuinely puzzled, but Valerie knew she was a good actress. 'William Lundy.'

Toni's brow creased. 'You mean that wee fanny who works in the newsagents?'

'The very same.'

'What about him?'

'He had the shite battered out of him, apparently by me and you.'

'What? Why would I waste my time on that prick? I wouldnae risk chipping a nail for him.'

'Someone told the polis we did it. Fortunately, I was at Seb's gran's birthday party when it happened last night at half eight, so I have an alibi. Where were you?'

'Me?' Toni said innocently. 'I was at home with my maw. We were watching a film.'

Valerie's eyes narrowed suspiciously. 'You hate spending time with your maw. What film did you watch?'

'*Titanic*. I just love Leonardo DiCaprio,' she breathed.

'What time did the film start?'

'What are you, the fucking polis?'

'They'll ask much tougher questions than that and you need to have your answers ready.'

'I do have my answers ready but not because I'm guilty.' Toni sighed when Valerie continued to stare at her suspiciously. 'Look, I hate the old bitch who birthed me and we both know why, but

Frankie worships the ground she walks on. He asked me to keep her company while he's away and when Frankie asks you to do something, you do it.'

'All right,' said Valerie. 'I believe you.'

'I'm so honoured,' glowered Toni.

'Neither of us battered William, meaning someone else did and is trying to pin the blame on us.'

'Isn't it obvious? It's that pathetic wee shite, Chris Cathcart.'

'He's the first person I thought of, but that family doesn't go to the polis. They hate the polis.'

'Hmm, you have a point, but I can't think of anyone else.'

'Could this be revenge for the scalping?'

'Why go after us and not Frankie?'

'Because they can't find him.'

'Perhaps, perhaps not. I need time to think. Right, I'm going home to await the inevitable visit from the polis.'

Valerie sighed. 'Let me know how you get on.'

'Will do,' replied Toni before leaving.

Valerie remained in her room, listening to the sound of her cousin saying goodbye to her parents. She watched Toni leave from the window, laden down with shopping bags, heading to the bus stop at the end of the road.

Glancing at the clock, she realised it was 6.30.

'Shit,' she said, yanking the curtains closed.

Valerie changed into smart trousers and a black blouse, dragged a brush through her hair, applied some make-up and tore downstairs.

'Could you give me a lift please, Da?' she said. 'I'm late meeting Seb.'

He smiled indulgently. 'Not a problem, sweetheart.' He and Janet were both determined to encourage this new relationship their daughter had started.

'Thanks,' she breathed with relief.

'Why don't you invite him round for tea?' said Janet. 'Any night except Saturday. Me and your da are off to that pub quiz.'

'I will. Thanks, Maw.' Valerie was pleased. He was the first of her boyfriends her parents had permitted in their home.

'You're welcome. Have a nice time.'

Valerie didn't always see eye to eye with her parents, but thank god they were nothing like Moira McVay.

* * *

Seb was waiting for Valerie outside the restaurant, looking a little worried. He smiled with relief when he saw her waving from the car.

'Good-looking lad,' commented her father. 'He dresses well too. No ripped jeans or leather jackets.'

'I've seen photos of you when you were a teenager, Da,' she replied wryly. 'And in every picture, you wore a leather jacket.'

'Aye, but at least I had no holes in my clothes,' he smiled.

Valerie kissed his cheek. 'Thanks, Da.'

'You're welcome, have a nice time.'

'I will,' she replied before getting out of the car.

She rushed up to Seb, who pulled her to him and kissed her.

'You had me worried there,' he said. 'I thought I'd been stood up.'

'I'm sorry, but I had a mini crisis.'

'Is everything okay?'

'I'll explain inside. I'm starving. Why didn't you wait inside for me? It's pretty chilly out.'

'They stuck me at the table furthest from the window, so I thought I'd come out and see if I could see you.'

'That is so sweet,' she said, linking her arm through his as they went inside and took a table in the far corner. Seb had been right – the only way they could have been seated further from the windows was if they'd been put in the kitchen.

After ordering, Valerie related to Seb the visit from the police and her conversation with Toni.

'I hope this doesn't change anything for you,' she said when she'd finished, afraid he'd run out on her.

'No way. Nothing could do that.'

'And how many of your exes have been interviewed by the police?'

'Two. I dated a girl called Samantha for a few months. It turned out her favourite hobby was shoplifting, even though her family was rich. Before her, I dated Libby, who was always getting into cat fights in nightclubs. She ended up being arrested twice for assault.'

'Well, I don't feel so bad any more.'

'Good, because you shouldn't. You clearly didn't do it and neither did Toni, so it's nothing to worry about. Now let's have a nice meal and relax.'

'Sounds good,' Valerie replied, feeling the stress draining out of her. Just talking it over with Seb had made her feel infinitely better. 'By the way, my maw invited you to come to ours for tea one day. I hope that doesn't freak you out.'

'Not at all.' He suddenly looked unsure of himself. 'As long as it doesn't freak you out.'

'Nope. You're the first boyfriend I've had that my parents want to meet.'

Valerie's eyes flickered and her stomach lurched. Why hadn't she thought of it earlier? Was Leo the one who beat up William Lundy? It was just the sort of pathetic, vicious thing he'd do, and it would explain why she and Toni had been blamed. What should she do? Tell Toni and risk her cousin doing something horrible to

Leo or tell the police? But McVays didn't go to the police for anything.

* * *

On the way home after work the next day, Valerie stopped by Toni's house and was relieved to find her in, reclining on the couch watching television in all her finery eating grapes, looking like a Roman empress. Moira was out.

Toni waved at the opposite couch for Valerie to take a seat.

'Any update on what happened to William?' she asked Toni.

'Two polis did stop by last night but left disappointed when Maw alibied me, as did the next door neighbour, who popped in while we were watching the film.'

'You never mentioned the neighbour to me yesterday.'

'That's because Carla is very easy to forget. Why are you staring at me?'

'Like I said, it's strange you didn't mention her sooner.'

'Sorry, I didn't realise you were investigating the case too,' said Toni, arching an eyebrow.

'I'm just worried that I'm being dragged into a mess you've created.'

'It was nothing to do with me,' snapped Toni, eyes flashing.

'All right, take it easy. I did have a thought about who could be responsible for attacking William and one name did spring to mind...'

'Leo?'

'Aye,' she sighed. 'Well, you just stole my thunder.'

'I thought of him the moment you told me about what happened. Has it only just occurred to you?' said Toni with an amused smile.

'Actually, it occurred to me when I was having dinner with Seb, but I've only just had the chance to tell you.'

'I went round to his flat to make sure the shitebag was behaving himself, but he wasn't there. His landlord said he cleared out yesterday owing £400 in rent. Why anyone would pay a single pound for that flea pit is beyond me. He didn't leave a forwarding address. I spoke to his neighbours, none of whom knew where he'd gone and all of whom agreed he's a fucking loser.'

'It sounds like you've been doing an investigation of your own.'

'I've put some feelers out, so hopefully he'll be found soon.'

'It makes sense that it's him.'

'It was also a stupid plan. He completely failed to consider that we might have alibis.'

'Although we can't be certain William didn't just misidentify us. I mean, it would be understandable after the hammering he took.'

'You mean the polis didn't tell you?'

'Tell me what?'

'That it wasn't William who identified us. He didn't have a clue who attacked him because whoever did it was a fucking coward who snuck up on him from behind. It was a customer in the shop who said it was you and me.'

'What customer?'

'They wouldn't tell me, probably because they knew their witness would have the living shite battered out of them. We'll only know what's going on when we find the witness.'

'Please don't start a witch hunt,' sighed Valerie. 'Not with the polis sticking their noses in.'

'We've got to get to the bottom of this and I don't trust the polis to do it properly. And whoever this witness is, they're trying to fuck with us, and they've got to learn that they can't do that.'

'Did they mention Frankie at all?'

'Aye. They wanted to know where he was, but I said I had no idea. Did they ask you?'

Valerie nodded. 'And I said the same thing. Do you know how he's doing?'

'I haven't heard a word from him.'

'Are you sure he's okay?'

'He's fine. Frankie's always fine.'

'I hope so, but I really think we should sit tight and not do anything. For all we know, we're being watched by the polis.'

'Well, I'm not. I would know if I was.'

'How can you possibly know that?'

'Because it wouldn't be the first time this house has been watched and I always spot them. I can practically smell a polis. They're not like other people,' said Toni with a contemptuous curl of the lip.

'Well, hopefully the whole thing will soon blow over.'

'Doubtful. William is thought of highly in the local community and people are demanding answers. Even some wanker of a local councillor is getting involved. This isn't going to go away, Val.'

'I was afraid you'd say that.'

'You might be content to sit on your arse and do nothing, but not me. When I'm in trouble, I help myself, because I learnt long ago that no one else will.'

When Toni's eyes flashed, Valerie knew she was thinking back to the abuse she'd suffered at Roddy's hands and Toni had defended herself the only way she'd known how.

'I understand,' said Valerie gently. 'But sometimes we can be so busy trying to escape something that we end up running right into it.'

'What's that supposed to mean?'

'It means that by interfering, you might get us all in trouble.'

'What a load of pish. Are you going to help me or not?'

Valerie blinked at her. 'Have you heard a word I've said?'

'I have and it sounds like a load of arse-covering shite. Someone's trying to set us up and we need to stop the bastard before they try again. Next time, they might actually be successful.'

'I don't want to get involved.'

'Too late, you already are involved. This isn't like you, Val. Has the fire in your belly gone out? You used to love a good scrap.'

'I just don't want all the drama any more.'

'Why, what's changed? Oh, I see. It's Seb, isn't it?'

Valerie nodded. 'He's so sweet and gentle and so is his family. I'm afraid of dragging him into my world.'

'And what's wrong with your world?' demanded Toni, her eyes turning blacker.

'It's violent, that's what's wrong with it,' retorted Valerie who was one of the few people not intimidated by Toni's shark-eyed glare.

'Violent maybe, but you forgot to say exciting too.'

'I used to think that, but not any more. Now I want a quiet life.'

'Perhaps I was wrong about Seb, I thought he was worthy of you, but maybe he's making you think you're too good for your own family.'

'He's doing nothing of the sort. I've never heard him say a bad word about anyone. I'm just afraid of involving him in something that may hurt him.' Valerie did not want Toni turning against Seb because she would go out of her way to split them up.

'I see,' said Toni icily. 'But if you hadn't noticed, he's a very big boy who can no doubt take care of himself.'

'He's sweet and innocent and our worlds are poles apart. He really has no idea.'

'And you're afraid of his good, clean family finding out.'

'I am, I won't deny it. At his gran's party, he told me he loved me.'

Toni once again arched an eyebrow. 'Really? That is quick. And what did you say?'

'I told him I loved him too.'

'And you meant it?'

'Of course I did, I would never say something like that without meaning it wholeheartedly.'

'Well, perhaps I should start a new career as a matchmaker,' said Toni before popping a grape into her mouth.

Valerie frowned. How like her cousin to make it all about herself. 'So I hope you understand why I don't want to risk this relationship. I've never loved a man before and I don't want anything to come between me and Seb. I really think he could be the one.'

Toni sat up straighter. 'In that case, leave this situation in my hands. I'll sort everything out and I'll make sure you don't get involved.'

'You're not angry?' said Valerie, suspicious of a trick.

'Why would I be angry? All I've ever wanted is for you to be happy with a man deserving of you and now, finally, you are.'

'Thanks, Toni,' said Valerie fondly.

'See, I'm not all bad.'

'I know that.'

'I've just had a thought – the cottage is free. Why don't you and lover boy spend a romantic weekend there?'

'You mean the one near Slamannan?'

'No, that's having some work done to it. I mean the one at Lochwinnoch. It's perfect, you can be totally alone, which must be difficult when you both live with your parents.'

'And Aunty Moira won't mind?'

'Course not. She's not been there in years, but she does pay someone to clean and maintain it. I can give them a call and make sure it's all spick and span for you.'

'Thanks, Toni, that would be great.'

'You're welcome. You look like you could do with a break.'

'I could and I'm not working Monday, so we could have a long weekend. Thanks, Toni, I appreciate it,' said Valerie before leaping to her feet and rushing to the door. She stopped before going through it. 'This isn't some ploy to get me out of the way so you can track down whoever set us up?'

'Me?' said Toni innocently. 'Never.'

11

When she got home, Valerie was dismayed to find the police waiting for her in her living room. Her parents were there too, quiet and tense. It wasn't the two officers who had spoken to her about the assault on William and she wasn't sure if that was a good thing or not.

'Valerie,' said Janet, maintaining a forced smile. 'Finally, you're home. These two officers want to speak to you about Frankie.'

'Frankie?' she frowned, remaining standing in the doorway. 'Why?'

'We need to talk to him about a couple of matters,' replied one of the constables.

'What matters?'

'I'm afraid that's between us and him,' he replied.

Valerie thought this pair seemed a lot less friendly than their colleagues. 'So why are you here if you want to talk to him?'

'We're having trouble locating him and thought you might know where he is.'

'No idea. Why would I?'

'Because you're cousins and, by all accounts, good friends.'

'Well, we're friends. I'm closer to his sister Toni than I am to him.'

'So can you tell us where he is?'

'No, I've no idea.'

The two officers studied her carefully, their expressions stern.

'You do realise that lying to the police is a very serious offence?'

'I do, so it's fortunate that I'm not lying. Is that it?'

'For now,' replied the officer as they both got to their feet. 'Thank you for your time,' he added before they left.

Valerie sighed and sank onto the couch.

'What on earth is going on?' said Janet. 'Why are the polis asking about Frankie? What has he done now?'

'I've no idea.'

'It must be bad if they're looking for him. And you really don't know where he is? Because if you do, you must tell them.'

'I don't, honestly. I don't think anyone does.'

'That boy's always made me nervous, but I do hate to think of anything nasty happening to him.'

'It's his problem, not ours,' said Charlie.

'I'll give Moira a ring later, see what she knows. Are you all right?' said Janet when Valerie sighed and pressed a hand to her forehead. 'Did walking in to find two polis here give you a shock?'

'Aye, it did a bit.'

Janet's expression became shrewish. 'That's what you get for hanging around with Toni and Frankie. They've always been trouble, dragging our family's reputation through the mud...'

'Because the McVays have always been considered such respectable people,' said Valerie sarcastically.

'They'll never change. One day, you might learn your lesson. I just hope you don't suffer for it.'

Charlie, seeing the irritation flicker in his daughter's eyes, decided to change the subject. 'How did your date with Seb go?' he hastily asked Valerie.

'Great. He said he'd love to come for tea.'

'Lovely,' said Janet. 'How about Friday?'

'Actually, that won't work. Toni said we could use the cottage at Lochwinnoch.'

'Oh, I see. A romantic weekend. That's very kind of Toni,' said Janet, suspicion in her eyes.

'Isn't it? You don't mind me going there with Seb, do you?'

'You're a grown woman now, Valerie, you can do what you like, just stay in touch, won't you?'

'I will,' said Valerie, smiling at Janet, despite the fact that she'd annoyed her with her nagging. It seemed Seb was even improving her relationship with her mother. His goodness was affecting every facet of her life.

* * *

Seb loved the idea of the cottage in the countryside and they agreed to leave on Friday, in three days' time, after Valerie had finished her shift at the petrol station. He was going to borrow his mother's car and they could drive straight there when she'd finished. If she just kept her head down and went from home to work and back again, hopefully she could make it to Friday without anything else happening.

She made it two days.

Valerie didn't want to go to Toni's house in case she got dragged into another crazy situation, but she had no choice, as she had to collect the key for the cottage.

She walked into Toni's front room to find her sitting with her mother – and Frankie.

'You're back,' said Valerie, glad he was safe but unsure what his return meant.

'Too fucking right I am, sweetheart,' he grinned, reclining back into the couch and clasping his hands behind his head with all the swagger of a visiting king. 'And with a bang, too. I'm now working for Duncan Blackwood.'

'The drug dealer?'

'I think you mean the local businessman,' he smirked. 'He has a lot of clout around here and he's seen my potential. He's also managed to smooth things over with the polis, meaning I can come home again.'

'I didn't think he had that much clout.'

'Well, he does, and I start working for him tomorrow.'

Valerie knew better than to ask doing what. 'That's great, Frankie. Congratulations.'

'I'm going to drag this family back into the fucking big time. That arsehole Roddy will look like a fly pitcher compared to me. This family's on the fucking up,' he exclaimed with glee.

'I'm sure we are,' smiled Moira, reaching out to pat his hand before retracting her own. Frankie didn't like anyone touching him, unless they were a beautiful young woman.

'He's gonnae help me finally put the fucking Thompson family in their place and take down that dick, Harry Woodhouse.' His expression turned dark. 'Just wait till I get my hands on him. I've special tortures all worked out for that prick so vicious they'd make Lucifer cry.'

Silence filled the room.

'So, can I have the key for the cottage?' said Valerie, keen to get out of there.

'It's in the kitchen drawer,' said Toni. 'I'll get it.'

Valerie noticed Frankie's eyes follow his sister as she left the room.

Frankie had always had an unnatural attachment to Toni, but it only seemed to be spiralling. It would break Valerie's heart if her cousin had to endure from her own brother what Roddy had forced upon her.

'Thanks,' said Valerie when Toni returned and handed her the key.

'I called Brenda who looks after the place and got her to give it a good going over and warm it through,' Toni told her. 'The cold won't do much for Seb's libido,' she winked.

'Cheers, Toni.'

'You're welcome. Now go and have fun. You deserve it.'

Toni could be violent and vicious, but she also had a kind side. Valerie herself was one of the very few people she genuinely cared about and sometimes it felt like a privilege.

After Valerie had left, Moira said to her son, 'Why didn't you tell Valerie about your big plan? I thought you wanted her to be part of it. She's always proved to be very useful before.'

'I hear she's changed since she met Seb,' he replied. 'Got up her own arse a wee bit. She's becoming ashamed of this family, afraid lover boy's family won't approve of her. I bet they don't even know she's a McVay.'

'That's shite, Frankie,' Toni told him. 'Val knows the meaning of loyalty.'

'Let's hope she does, for her sake.'

This comment chilled Toni to the bone. She knew Valerie's life would be in danger if she didn't bow down to Frankie's plans, but she also knew that her cousin was one of the few people with the guts to stand up to him. Valerie had been given a glimpse of a different life to the one she would inevitably fall into if she continued on the same path and she was going to go for it full tilt. That stubbornness could be her downfall. But then again, Valerie was just as smart as Frankie, and Toni had the feeling Frankie would have a harder fight on his hands than he thought.

* * *

'Wow, pretty,' smiled Seb as they pulled up outside the isolated cottage in the Renfrewshire countryside. The building was a small one-storey stone cottage with ivy climbing up the walls, a smooth, tarmacked driveway leading up to it.

'Uncle Roddy bought it years ago,' explained Valerie.

'As a little country hideaway?'

'Hideaway being the right word. He used this place to lie low whenever the polis were looking for him or his enemies were out for his blood. That's why it's so secluded. No one ever found him here. He had a few places like this dotted about the Scottish countryside to use as safe houses.'

'I'm glad it's so secluded. It means we won't be interrupted,' he said with a wink that made her stomach flip over.

While Seb got their bags out of the boot, Valerie unlocked the heavy oak front door and pushed it open. Inside the cottage was all oak beams and warm tartan furniture with an open log fire. She smiled as she imagined the cosy, intimate nights she and Seb would spend here together. A bottle of Bollinger, two glasses and a bunch of red roses had been arranged on the coffee table.

'Nice,' smiled Seb as he dumped the bags on the floor. 'We'll be very comfy here. Does it have a bath?'

She smiled at the twinkle in his eyes. 'It does,' she replied. 'A large roll-top one.'

'I brought candles and bubbles.'

Valerie giggled. 'And what will I be doing while you're soaking away?'

He pulled her to him. 'You'll be in the bath with me, wet and soapy.'

'I can't wait.'

'I have absolutely no intention of waiting,' he breathed, brushing her lips with a kiss.

* * *

Valerie couldn't remember when she'd last experienced such bliss, not just physically but emotionally and intellectually too. She felt so comfortable with Seb in every single way. Not only was she not afraid to be completely naked around him but she could be herself too. He didn't sneer when she wanted to talk about books or history. On the contrary, Seb joined in these conversations with glee. He didn't tell her she was too fat or too skinny. Despite her weight remaining steady and being a very trim size ten, she'd been called both by previous boyfriends, for whom she was never enough. Seb loved her body and he was constantly touching her, whether that be holding her hand or something more erotic. They remained locked together in their own little bubble, only stepping outside for a breath of fresh air and to walk the pretty garden surrounding the cottage before retreating back inside to curl up together on the couch, cook delicious fresh food or make love. This precious time confirmed that Seb was absolutely the one for her. Already her old life of violence and working for Frankie was falling away. She was now looking to the future of being a minister's wife, and felt like Seb had saved her from a path that would have led to nothing but prison or a young death, because she had no doubt one of those would be Frankie's fate and possibly Toni's too if she wasn't careful.

On their last evening at the cottage, they were curled up together on the couch, drinking red wine, when Seb produced a small black box from his jeans pocket. Valerie's heart thudded with anticipation, but she tried not to get her hopes up.

'I hope you don't think this is too quick,' began Seb, voice croaky with nerves. 'We've not been together long, but I know in my heart this is right, so I don't see the point in waiting any longer.'

'Yes?' she said encouragingly when he paused and swallowed hard.

'I love you so much, Valerie. You're the most beautiful, fun and intelligent woman I've ever met. I feel like I've met the other half of me, like I'm finally complete and I don't want to risk losing you. So...' He paused again to take a deep breath. 'Will you marry me?'

'Of course I will,' she cried before flinging her arms around his neck.

'Thank god,' he breathed, holding her close and kissing her hair.

Valerie's hands shook and her eyes filled with tears as he slipped the ring onto her engagement finger. It was a pretty solitaire, not at all expensive, but she didn't care about that. It meant so much more to her than money.

'I love you so much,' he said, taking her face in his hands.

'I love you too,' she replied, kissing him hard.

'And you're okay with being a minister's wife? It won't be too boring for you?'

'I wouldn't have said yes if that was the case. That's the life I want, with you.'

'I could get a nice country parish, far from the city,' he replied, knowing she would never be fully out of her old life unless she was away from her family.

Valerie gazed at him, her heart swelling with love. 'Sounds perfect.'

He brushed her cheek with his fingertips. 'No, you're perfect.'

They beamed at each other before kissing hard, falling back into the couch together.

* * *

That night, Valerie woke with a start. In the delight of Seb's proposal, she hadn't thought through the consequences. Now the prospect of those consequences had caused her to jump awake at 2.30 in the morning. What would Seb's family think when they now inevitably found out she was a McVay? They might object to the engagement and try to split them up.

She looked at Seb asleep beside her, such a kind, innocent soul, and she was afraid being connected to her family would taint him. At least her parents weren't involved with the illegal side of the family, so she could maintain a relationship with them, but she knew this new life would mean cutting herself off from the rest of the family. The thought of not having Toni in her life was painful, it had always been them against the world. Toni would see her as a traitor, but her cousin was going down a road that she couldn't follow. Valerie had to decide what was more important – her relationship with her family or her future with Seb. She smiled at his serene, sleeping form. There was no contest.

* * *

After locking up the cottage, Seb drove them back to Valerie's house. It was early evening, so her parents would be in, and they were eager to share their big news.

'Hello, sweetheart,' smiled Janet when her daughter walked in. 'Did you have a nice time?' Her eyes widened when Seb followed Valerie in.

'Seb, this is my maw, Janet,' beamed Valerie, holding his hand.

'Pleased to meet you,' he said with a smile Janet's way that made her blush.

'And my da, Charlie,' added Valerie.

'Hello, sir,' said Seb, shaking his hand.

'Sir,' smiled Charlie. 'I've not been called that for a while.'

'It's lovely to finally meet you, Seb,' said Janet. 'We've heard so much about you from Valerie, we feel we know you already.'

'I could say the same about you,' he replied with a charming smile. 'Valerie talks about you a lot.' It wasn't true, but he thought it was the polite thing to say.

'We have some news,' said Valerie excitedly.

'Oh, yes?' said Janet, smile faltering, worried she wouldn't like what her daughter had to say.

'We're engaged,' smiled Valerie, holding out her hand so her parents could see the ring.

Janet and Charlie glanced at each other before looking back at their daughter.

'Well,' said Janet, who was just relieved Valerie hadn't said she was pregnant. 'That's... unexpected.'

'I know we haven't been seeing each other long, but it feels so right,' said Valerie when she saw the doubt in her parents' eyes. 'And we're not going to get married straightaway. Seb wants to be a minister in the Church of Scotland. He's finishing his bachelor's degree in Divinity and Philosophy and he hopes to get his own parish in the country.'

'And that's the life you want, as a minister's wife?'

'It is. I'll get to help people and we can spend our free time together studying literature and history. It's perfect for me.'

When Janet looked to her husband, he raised his eyebrows at her. 'Well,' she said slowly. 'That is quite the announcement and we've only just met Seb. Are you sure you aren't rushing into this?'

'No. It feels right,' said Valerie firmly.

Janet didn't like how fast this engagement had happened. The first flush of a new relationship could overwhelm young people, they didn't realise that feelings could fade. Either it would turn into something deeper, more intimate, or the relationship would collapse. But her daughter had a good head on her shoulders, so she was willing to give Seb a chance. 'You promised we could get to know Seb properly over a meal, so now's the perfect time. I've got a chicken in the oven. Would you like to stay for tea, Seb, or do you have to get home?'

'I can stay,' he quickly replied, relieved he wasn't being shown the door.

'Lovely. Well, take a seat, it won't be long.'

The couple sat on the couch together while Charlie fussed around them with drinks. He was pleased when Seb declined the can of lager he offered him and said he'd have an orange juice instead. That was a test set by Charlie, one all of Valerie's previous boyfriends would have failed.

When the four of them were gathered around the dining table together, Janet fired a series of questions at Seb about his family, his past and how he intended to support a wife. Seb answered all her questions politely and unhesitatingly, leaving Janet and Charlie with little choice but to endorse the engagement. Besides, they both liked him and could see how much he cared for their daughter, it positively shone out of his eyes every time he looked at Valerie. Very wisely, the couple had decided to wait a year to get married, until they were properly settled. Hopefully by then, Seb would have his own parish and he could take Valerie away from Glasgow. Despite what Valerie thought, her parents knew she had worked for Frankie and they would much rather she was a minister's wife than a criminal. This man could be the answer to their prayers.

'Well,' said Janet as they all reclined in their chairs after enjoying chicken casserole followed by apple pie and custard, 'you both certainly have it all worked out. You have our blessing.'

'Really?' beamed Valerie. 'You don't think we're rushing into it?'

'I do think this engagement has happened quickly, but you're being sensible and not rushing into marriage. I also think the future you've mapped out is a very nice one.'

'Thanks,' she smiled gratefully. 'Da?'

'I agree with your maw,' said Charlie. 'Seb, you seem a very nice man with a bright future. You have my blessing too.'

Valerie leapt to her feet to hug her father and then her mother, while Seb stood to shake their hands.

'Now we need to go and tell Seb's family,' said Valerie. 'I haven't told them I'm a McVay. I know that was wrong, but I didn't want anything coming between us.'

'We understand,' said Janet. 'I did the same thing myself when me and Charlie got engaged, but you know what – his family realised who I really was, so it didn't matter to them and I'm sure it won't matter to Seb's family either.'

'That's very true,' said Seb. He turned to gaze at his fiancée. 'They'll be fine because it's impossible not to love you.'

Seb and Valerie left to break the news to his parents.

'That went far better than I thought it would,' said Valerie as he drove. 'I thought they'd say we're moving too fast.'

'So did I, but they came round to the idea and so will my family.'

'We have to tell them I'm a McVay.'

'Not yet. We'll let them get used to the idea of our engagement first and then, when they're in love with you as much as I am, your surname won't matter to them. It'll all work out,' he said, patting her hand.

Seb's parents weren't quite as enthusiastic as Valerie's had been, casting each other sideways glances when they revealed their big news, but they politely congratulated them. Like Valerie's parents, Seb's were relieved they weren't rushing into a wedding, so they seemed content to let the relationship take its course.

Valerie had already decided that the only people she was going to tell about her engagement were her parents, so she wore the ring only when she was at home. The rest of the time, she carried it in her pocket. She didn't want the pressure of the family knowing because she was so afraid of them trying to drag Seb into their world. Frankie might see him as someone else he could rope into working for him. It would be much better if she could keep him apart from her family until he could get his parish and they could leave. But a year was a long time to keep him safe, and she prayed she had it in her.

12

Valerie's happy bubble was burst the following day when Liam Thompson walked into the petrol station and did a double take when he saw who was serving him.

'Oh, interesting,' he said, a smile spreading across his face. 'I didn't know you worked here.'

'I don't work here,' replied Valerie flatly. 'I couldn't afford to pay for my petrol, so I'm working off my debt.'

'I've been meaning to pay you back for pepper spraying my friends.'

'And kicking one in the baws. Don't forget that.'

'I haven't and I don't think he will either.' His brow creased with interest and he studied her thoughtfully. 'You're not afraid of me, are you?'

'It's amusing that you think I would be.'

'Most people are.'

'I'm not most people.'

'I'm starting to realise that.' The hostility vanished from his eyes. 'Do you want to come out for a drink with me?'

'Are you actually asking me out on a date?'

'Aye, I am.'

'But... that's crazy.'

'Why? You're really pretty and you're fucking fearless. I like that.'

'Because our families are enemies.'

'I don't know about you, but that only makes it more exciting.'

'Sorry, I can't. I'm seeing someone.'

'So am I, but I don't care.'

'And that's another reason why I wouldn't go out with you. So, if you could please pay for your petrol, there's a queue building.'

'They'll wait,' he said, leaning on the counter.

Valerie was very grateful for the Perspex screen dividing them.

The manager bustled up to her. 'Valerie, is something wrong?'

'Nothing's wrong. I'm just waiting for this *gentleman* to pay for his petrol.'

'Then please allow me,' said Liam, producing his wallet with a flourish, counting out the money and placing it on the counter. 'Want my phone number with that too?'

'No, thank you,' said Valerie. 'The money will do just fine.'

She snatched it up before he could take it back and continue toying with her. She gave Liam his change and he said he'd see her around before finally leaving.

'Is something wrong with him?' the manager asked Valerie.

'Plenty of things, I should think,' she replied before turning to serve the next customer.

She glanced out of the window onto the forecourt and saw Liam standing by his car, watching her, an odd smile on his face. She was alarmed when he took out a packet of cigarettes and a lighter. Quickly she got onto the microphone beside the till.

'Please don't light a cigarette, sir,' she said into it, voice echoing out onto the forecourt, causing everyone except Liam to jump. 'Petrol is highly flammable.'

Realising all eyes had turned his way, Liam merely smiled, replaced the packet of cigarettes and lighter into his pocket and gave her a sardonic bow before getting into his car and driving off.

'That man's a prick,' commented the woman Valerie was serving.

'Aye,' Valerie murmured to herself. 'An extremely dangerous one.'

Valerie decided not to mention Liam's antics at the petrol station to Toni and Frankie, it would only rile them. She wanted to keep the peace as much as she could, just until she and Seb could leave the area. There was no reason why they had to wait until he found a parish, they could leave Glasgow once he'd finished his exams, and the thought of being away from the city and all the violence lifted a weight off her shoulders.

Toni turned up at Valerie's house that evening to get all the gossip on how her weekend had gone with Seb. Janet and Charlie had already been instructed not to mention the engagement to anyone, so they were being careful to keep it to themselves.

Valerie led Toni up to her bedroom.

'So how did it go?' said Toni, kicking off her shoes and reclining on the bed, leaving Valerie to take the stool at the dressing table.

'It was lovely,' beamed Valerie. 'We had a wonderful time.'

'And lots of sex, I hope?'

'Aye, loads. Here's the key for the cottage, by the way,' she said, fishing it out of her jacket pocket and handing it to Toni, who took it from her and slipped it into her handbag.

'I'm glad to hear Seb's a stallion and not a wet fish,' said Toni.

'Most definitely a stallion,' replied Valerie.

'Good, because judging by my own experience, there are far too many wet fish about.'

'Like Warren Campbell, yet still you beat up Cassie Cathcart over him. I'm still waiting for her brother to kick off again about it.'

'That prick knows when to toe the line. He won't do anything.'

'Let's hope, because, if he does, it'll be me he goes after.'

'Stop worrying, will you? Frankie's reputation is only on the up and up, especially after he got away with the whole scalping thing. And Duncan's put it about that he works for him, so no one dare touch a member of our family now.'

'There's always someone mental enough not to give a shite about things like that and Duncan won't matter to the Thompsons.'

'If they try anything, we'll make them regret it. What is it?' she said when Valerie sighed.

'I'm sick of all the violence.'

'Why? It's fun and you're so good at it.'

'I used to feel like that but not any more.'

Toni's black eyes turned even blacker. 'This is because of Seb, isn't it?'

'Well, aye, it is, in a way. He's made me see there's a different life open to me, one that doesn't involve so much violence. We battered the hell out of Sandra Jones on Frankie's order. Kicking the shite out of people on my cousin's say-so is not how I imagine my future.'

'Sandra's a nasty old slag who hits her kids. Still think she deserves your sympathy?'

'That's not the point. I don't want to be beholden to Frankie my entire life, having to do horrible things to other people just because he orders it. It's only a matter of time before he's telling us to kill people.'

'Now you listen to me, Val – Frankie is the new head of this family and, if we toe the line and do as he says, he'll make us very rich and comfortable. He's already raking in the cash working for Duncan Blackwood and one day soon, Duncan will be out and Frankie will be the big man.'

'You mean he's already plotting to take out his mentor? Charming.'

'Duncan's a prick who deserves it.'

'What I'm trying to say,' sighed Valerie, 'is that I don't want this future, I want something more.'

'Like what? A boring little house with Seb, slogging your guts out in that petrol station and breathing in those manky fumes all day?'

'No, not that. I don't know exactly what. All I know is that I want a future free of all this brutality. How many people leave work and end up being chased down the road by three men because you were in on battering someone they care about? How many women have to go around nightclubs searching for violent creeps and then end up pepper spraying two men in the face? Not many, I can tell you.'

'And that's a good thing. Who wants to be like all those dull farts out there, desperately working every hour God sends just to pay the bills? That will not be me. My future will be filled with luxury and comfort.'

'Maybe I don't care about luxury and comfort,' muttered Valerie, folding her arms across her chest.

Toni's eyes sharpened. 'Perhaps I made a mistake introducing you to Seb? Perhaps it's time your relationship ended?'

'Our relationship is not ending.'

Toni tilted back her head in a challenge but didn't speak.

'I mean it, Toni,' said Valerie. 'You're my best friend and I love you, but we will seriously fall out if you interfere in the best thing that ever happened to me.'

The two women stared at each other. Most people couldn't tolerate Toni's ferocious stare for long, but it had never bothered Valerie, who returned her gaze steadily.

Finally, Toni smiled and shrugged. 'Fine, I won't interfere, but you'll be the one missing out. I might throw a few quid your way when you come to my mansion, begging for some cash to put some credit on the electricity meter.'

'I'll take my chances.'

'Good for you,' she said sarcastically. Toni lithely got to her feet, leaving the bed creased and rumpled. 'Well, as pleasant as this is, I must be going,' she said, voice dripping ice.

'Thanks for coming.'

Toni just arched an eyebrow before stalking out. Valerie listened to the sound of her high heels descending the stairs before she swept out without saying goodbye to her aunt and uncle, slamming the front door shut behind her.

Valerie sighed and shook her head. Toni would sulk for a couple of days before they picked back up where they'd left off. At least, Valerie hoped that was how it would go. She should have just kept her big mouth shut. Toni could be incredibly vindictive when she wanted to be. She was a clever manipulator and didn't like to lose. Valerie knew how much Toni relied on her and if she thought she might lose her then the consequences didn't bear thinking about.

If she could just ride it out for another year, then everything would be okay.

But McVays didn't get happy endings.

* * *

The inevitable call from Frankie came four days later. Valerie had just been starting to relax and think that maybe he'd decided not to use her again. She was to be rudely disabused of that notion.

After receiving the summons, Valerie arrived at Frankie's house an hour later to find Toni, who said hello cordially but coolly. Frankie greeted her like a king talking to his subject. She half-expected him to hold out his hand so she could kiss it. Valerie was disturbed to see Uncle Tam, Moira's older brother, was there too. Tam was a short, tubby man with an egg-shaped head on which sat thin, badly dyed black hair. He had a square jaw that jutted out to one side, and Valerie had never liked him. Like Frankie, he was a psychopath. Most of the McVay family were psychopaths, but Tam was one of the worst. Valerie supposed it was inevitable Tam was brought in on Frankie's burgeoning business – after all, they were two peas in a pod, but she didn't think he would help Frankie's violent streak. On the contrary, he would only encourage it.

'All right, Tam?' she said with a nod his way.

Tam nodded his egg-shaped head, his beady eyes cold.

'So, what's this about?' said Valerie, turning her attention to Frankie.

'I've got a wee job for you and my sister,' he replied.

'What is it this time?' she said flatly, hoping it would be something minor.

'Stevie's still in my cellar. I want you two to take him home.'

Valerie frowned. 'But neither of us have a car.'

'You don't need a car, you can walk. He doesnae live far.'

'Then why ask us? Why not ask Paul and Jamesie?'

Annoyance flickered through Frankie's eyes. 'Because they're fucking busy. I need someone to do the job and you two are the only ones available, so just do it, eh, sweetheart?' he glowered.

Valerie looked to Toni, whose expression gave nothing away.

Toni had an excellent poker face. 'Have you found that he's inno-cent, then?'

'Maybe,' he said enigmatically.

'Okay, Frankie,' said Valerie reluctantly when it appeared that was going to be his only answer. 'If you insist.'

'Oh, I fucking insist,' he snapped. 'Well, don't look so down about it. It's not a big imposition is it, asking you to escort a total prick back to his hoose?'

'I suppose not, as long as there aren't any complications.'

'Like what? He might want to stop at the shop for some sweet-ies?' retorted Frankie with a bark of laughter.

Tam released his odd, creepy giggle. 'That's pure funny, Frankie.'

'Aye, I fucking know. On you go then, Val. Stevie will be getting impatient. I think he's had his fill of my hospitality.' He rummaged around in the pocket of his suit jacket, retrieved another roll of notes and tossed it to Valerie, who caught it with one hand. 'There's a couple of hundred quid to stop you whining.'

'I have to go down to the cellar for him?' said Valerie, pocketing the money. Every spare pound she could get would go towards her escape from Glasgow.

'Aye, ya dae. He'll need a wee hand.'

Valerie looked at Toni, wondering if she was going down the cellar with her, but she made no move to get up. Unease rippled up and down Valerie's spine as the three of them watched her leave the room in silence.

'Well, that was weird,' she whispered to herself once she was outside the room.

She stared at the door to the cellar, which was set into the side of the staircase. This entire situation felt wrong. Could she end up being locked up down there too? Had Toni told Frankie about her plans to leave and he didn't want her going anywhere knowing his secrets? The weight of her mobile phone in one pocket and her pepper spray in the other was reassuring.

Taking a deep breath, she opened the door to the cellar to reveal a black void. Her hand frantically groped for the light switch and she breathed a sigh of relief when it burst into life, lighting up the staircase.

Leaving the door at the top of the stairs open and keeping her hand on the pepper spray in her pocket, she began to descend the stairs. The sound of movement below caused her to hesitate. Was it just Stevie down there or some of Frankie's men waiting to ambush her, perhaps Paul and Jamesie themselves, which would explain why they weren't upstairs with Frankie? They were rarely absent from his side.

As she reached the bottom step, she yanked the pepper spray entirely from her pocket and held it out ready, but the only person there was poor Stevie, perched on the edge of the bed, face white with fear.

'It's you,' he breathed with relief. 'I thought it might be Frankie. He said he was thinking of hacking my legs off with an axe because he could hear my snoring all the way upstairs in his bedroom.'

'That's some snore you've got.'

'Aye, it is. It's cost me plenty of girlfriends.' He frowned at her sceptically raised eyebrow. 'I've had girlfriends.'

'I'm not in the least bit concerned. I've to take you home.'

'Really?' he said, hope lighting up his eyes. 'Thank god, I'm starting to get prison pallor because of the lack of daylight.'

Now she knew she wasn't about to be attacked, Valerie could take in his prison in more detail. The floor was carpeted. There was a toilet and sink at one end of the room beside the bed. At the foot of the bed was a television and a set of shelves holding books, magazines and videos. Everything was spotlessly clean. As prisons went, it wasn't too bad.

'Do you know where the key is?' she said, indicating the chain and padlock tethering his right ankle to the bedframe.

'Over there,' he replied, pointing to a hook embedded in the wall on the other side of the room, from which hung a shiny silver key.

Valerie retrieved it and unlocked his shackle.

'God, that's better,' he said, slowly getting to his feet and stretching. 'I was afraid I'd never get out of here.'

'Do you know why Frankie's suddenly decided to let you go?'

'I assumed because he's found out that I didn't betray him.' Stevie noted her doubtful look and his eyes filled with worry. 'Hasn't he?'

'I don't know, he didn't say. Anyway, let's get you out of here before he changes his mind.'

Stevie pulled on his shoes and jacket and they hastily ascended the stairs, Valerie as anxious about being trapped down there as he was. She led the way, pushing the door open at the top, expecting to see Frankie, Toni and Tam standing there, but the hallway was empty. The sound of Frankie talking emanated from the living room.

'Let's go,' whispered Valerie.

They both rushed to the front door, Valerie turning the handle, panicking when the door refused to open.

'Why won't it open?' whispered Stevie, panic in his voice.

'I don't know,' she whispered back.

13

The living room door opened and Frankie walked out, followed by Tam and Toni. Valerie didn't like the smug look in Toni's black eyes.

'We're trying to get out but the door's locked,' said Valerie.

'That's because I locked it,' replied Frankie. 'You know, security and that.'

'Could you open it so I can take Stevie home?'

There was a tense moment as Frankie just stared back at her. The smirks on Toni and Tam's faces said they knew something she didn't.

Just as Valerie was considering getting out her pepper spray, Toni stepped forward.

'Unlock the door, Frankie, so we can all get on with our lives,' she told her brother. 'Stevie needs to get home.'

'Aye, all right then,' he replied, producing the key from his pocket.

Valerie had to force herself not to yank the door open and run down the street after Frankie had opened it. Instead, she left with her head held high, followed by Stevie, Toni bringing up the rear. Glancing over her shoulder, she saw Frankie and Tam watching them from the doorway. It was a relief when they turned the corner and the creepy sods vanished from view. She wanted to demand answers from Toni but didn't want to have that discussion in front of Stevie, so they walked in silence, Stevie between the two women, all the time panicked thoughts frantically swirling through Valerie's mind. She had the horrible feeling her family wouldn't let her go.

They turned onto Stevie's street, which was a very respectable row of semi-detached houses with garages and nice lawns, not the sort of place you'd associate a scruff like Stevie with. He breathed a sigh of relief when he saw his home was within sight and knew he had Valerie to thank for his safe return. If it hadn't been for her intervention, he was quite sure Frankie would have given in to his rage back in the abandoned tenement and hacked his head off his shoulders.

When they were just a couple of hundred feet from Stevie's home, a group of four men appeared at the top of the street.

'It's the Thompsons,' said Valerie. Liam was among their number.

Movement drew Toni's attention back the way they'd come and she saw another four men striding up to them from that direction. 'And Chris Cathcart and three friends,' she said.

Valerie's head whipped from left to right, assessing the men. They all looked pumped up with aggression and ready for a fight. She frowned at Toni, who appeared unfazed by this turn of events, unlike Stevie, who was quaking in his boots.

'You knew this was going to happen, didn't you?' she demanded of Toni.

Toni's response was an enigmatic smile that told Valerie everything she needed to know.

'Quick, let's get inside,' said Stevie, racing for his house while tugging his keys from his pocket.

In response, the Thompsons, who were closer, reached the house before he could. Valerie grabbed him by the scruff of the jacket and yanked him backwards before they could snatch him.

'Just hand him over, doll,' Liam told Valerie. 'I would hate to break that pretty face, but I will if I have to.'

'Why do you want him?' she demanded.

'Because he can tell us everything Frankie's been up to. We've been waiting for him to be released.'

'So have we,' announced Toni.

Liam looked to her and didn't like the triumph shining out of her eyes. 'What?'

Stevie and Valerie jumped when half a dozen men leapt out of the gardens of the surrounding houses and charged at the Thompsons. Chris and his friends lost their bottle immediately and scattered while the Thompsons charged into the fray.

'Get inside,' Valerie told Stevie, dragging him towards the house as the violence erupted around them.

Toni tottered after them on her high heels up to the front door.

'Hurry up,' Valerie told Stevie as his shaking hands refused to cooperate and put the key in the lock.

'Hey, sexy,' yelled a voice.

The three of them looked round to see Liam rushing up the garden path, holding a baseball bat.

'Oh, Christ,' exclaimed Stevie, dropping his keys in fright.

'Do not call me sexy,' Toni spat at Liam, her eyes flashing.

'I wasnae talking to you,' he retorted, gaze locked on Valerie.

Toni was offended that any man would prefer her cousin and she drew her knife. 'Fuck off.'

'Put that away, doll, before you get hurt,' he told her while still looking at Valerie, which infuriated Toni.

'Will you get the bloody door open?' Valerie hissed at Stevie, who had bent over to retrieve the keys. 'Give them here,' she said, snatching them from his hand. 'Which one is it?'

'The Yale one.'

Valerie jammed the key into the lock and turned it. Stevie charged past her and inside. Valerie looked to Toni and saw her cousin was keeping Liam at bay with her knife. Everyone knew Toni was skilled with a blade and it wasn't wise to take her on.

'Toni, come on,' she called.

Her cousin backed up the two steps towards the front door, glaring at Liam, knife pointed his way. Liam was paying her no attention and was staring at Valerie.

'See you soon, sweetheart,' he winked at her.

Toni stepped inside and Valerie slammed the door shut and locked it. 'Is the back door locked?' she asked a pale Stevie.

'Aye, course,' he replied.

Valerie rounded on Toni. 'This was a set-up, wasn't it? You knew they'd be waiting.'

'Well, of course,' she replied smoothly, slipping the knife back into her pocket. 'We just weren't sure whether it would be the Gordons or Thompsons who turned up. Now we know for sure who set up Stevie.'

'Thank Christ you've finally realised that,' sighed Stevie with relief.

'Frankie realised it ages ago,' sniffed Toni. 'He just didn't want to take the chance of you changing sides and running to that lot with his secrets.'

'Like I'd ever dae that. Jesus, I'm much more feared of him than I am of the sodding Thompsons.'

'Wise man,' said Toni with a satisfied smile.

'You could have at least warned me,' said Valerie.

'You made it clear you wanted nothing to do with the violent side of the business any more, so how could I?'

'That's ridiculous. Of course I'd want to know if I was walking into a trap. And how is this keeping me out of it?'

'Have you had to fight anyone today?'

'No, but I might have if I hadn't managed to get the front door open. Liam looked like he was ready to attack.'

'He wouldn't have attacked you. Apparently he's been talking about you non-stop. It seems he's developed a little crush on you after you pepper sprayed his people. That's why Frankie wanted you here today. He knew your presence would tempt him out.'

'I still say you should have warned me.'

Toni shrugged. 'Frankie thought it better not to.' She went to the window to peer out. 'Looks like our people have the upper hand.'

'Of course they do,' said Valerie flatly. 'There's more of them since Chris Cathcart and his friends did a runner.'

'Yes, they were pathetic, weren't they? Liam made a mistake joining forces with them.'

Valerie joined her cousin at the window to watch the action. Two Thompson men were battered and bleeding on the ground, while Liam and a fourth man ran off down the street, hotly pursued by three of Frankie's men.

'Looks like lover boy escaped,' commented Toni.

'He's nothing to do with me,' retorted Valerie.

Toni turned from the window to look at Stevie, who physically jumped at the malevolence shining from her eyes. 'I hope you realise which is the smart side to be on?'

'I've always known that, Toni. I swear I would never betray Frankie.'

Toni studied him with her black shark's eyes, making him squirm. Eventually, she said, 'Good. Let's go, Val.'

'Take care of yourself, Stevie,' Valerie told him before following her cousin out.

The street had gone quiet. If any of the neighbours had witnessed the fight, they'd done nothing about it because there was no sign of any police cars on the horizon. All of Frankie's people had gone, although two of the Thompson men lay on the ground, battered and bruised. Toni stepped on the hand of one of the men in her high heels, making him screech with pain. She smiled with satisfaction as she and Valerie continued on down the street.

'Well, that went well,' commented Toni. She rolled her eyes at Valerie's sullen look. 'Oh, don't sulk, I hate it when you sulk.'

'I'm not sulking, I'm really pissed off. You should have warned me.'

'Take it up with Frankie, it was his idea.'

'Did you tell him what I said about not wanting to get involved any more?'

'No.'

'Are you sure about that?'

'Aye, I'm sure.' Toni sighed when Valerie just stared at her. 'All right, fine. I may have hinted that you're getting a little disillusioned with it all, but that's it.'

'Did you mention Seb to him?'

'No. I just said you were seeking a different path in life.'

Valerie wasn't sure Toni was giving her the whole truth, but she'd never accused her cousin of being a liar before and she wasn't about to start now. 'I'd appreciate it if you'd keep it to yourself until I've got things worked out. I hope you realise how important this is to me?'

'So you keep saying,' said Toni, examining the nails of her right hand with a bored look. 'Now, if you've finished with the lecture, shall we go and visit Karen McMillan?'

'Why, what's she done?'

'She's been talking shite about me and David Mortimer.'

'Not another one. How many women do we have to beat up because they've said something about one of your exes?'

'She's been saying she was shagging him while he was with me.'

'So what? Everyone knows she's a lying cow. No one will believe her.'

'I can't take that chance. Frankie's reputation must be protected, it keeps us all safe. And if anyone starts making out that I'm a soft touch then it reflects badly on Frankie.'

'He's told you to do it, hasn't he?'

'Aye, he has, and you're coming with me.'

'No, I'm not. I told you, I'm not getting involved in the violence any more.'

'I need you to watch my back. Karen's sisters are nasty bitches.'

'They're certainly tougher than Chris Cathcart but I mean it, Toni, I'm out of this way of life. You do have other cousins, why don't you take Angela instead?'

'Because she's not as handy as you.'

'She's more than capable of dealing with Karen McMillan and her sisters.' Valerie stopped and turned to face Toni. 'We've been best pals all our lives and you mean so much to me. I've always backed you up, but now it's my turn to ask something of you – please don't keep involving me in this stuff. It's not what I want.'

'You're really serious, aren't you?'

'I am.'

'But Frankie had marked you out as a pivotal member in the new family business. He knows how strong and smart you are and that you'll be an asset to his crew.'

'Frankie thinks women should stay at home and cook and clean.'

'Not all women. He's promised to train me up and he knows you're different to other women.'

'I'll choose to take that as a compliment, but it's not what I want.'

'That might not matter to Frankie.'

'I don't care. I'm out.'

With that, Valerie stalked off down the street, hands shoved into her jacket pockets to protect them against the chill in the air. She glanced back over her shoulder at Toni, who was watching her go with a mixture of sadness and malice in her eyes. Valerie just hoped her cousins didn't start to see her as a traitor.

* * *

'Seb, I really should get going,' giggled Valerie.

She kissed Seb and when she tried to get up off the bed, he wrapped a strong arm around her waist and pulled her back down.

'Just five more minutes,' he said, kissing her neck.

'You said that ten minutes ago. I have to go or I'll be late for my shift.'

'Fine,' he sighed, releasing her. 'I just don't want you to leave.'

'I don't want to leave, but I have to. I want to earn as much as I can so we can get our own place together.'

'With a king-size bed.'

'That will be the first thing on the list to buy.'

Valerie indulged in one last kiss before tearing herself out of bed. It was one o'clock in the afternoon and she started work at two. As Seb had a free study session, they'd decided to sneak to his house to enjoy some time together while his parents were out.

As they were pulling on their clothes, they heard the front door open below.

'I thought your parents would be out all afternoon?' said Valerie.

'They said they would be. It sounds like my maw and Aunty Sarah.'

After hastily dressing and running their fingers through their hair, they hurried downstairs, Seb leading the way, to find Laura and a woman who looked very similar to her chatting and laughing.

'Hello, sweetheart,' smiled Laura when she saw her son. 'I hope you've been taking advantage of this study period to get some work done.' Her smiled faltered when a sheepish Valerie followed her in. 'I see that you have,' she added, raising an eyebrow.

'Hi, Mrs Robertson,' said Valerie awkwardly.

'Hello, Valerie. You remember my sister Sarah from Euphemia's party?'

'Aye, I do. Hi, Sarah.'

Sarah nodded with a tight-lipped smile.

No one in Seb's family agreed with their very quick engagement and Valerie couldn't blame them for that. 'I'm just off to work,' she told them.

'I don't envy you, dealing with the general public all day,' said Sarah, not unkindly.

'They can be a nightmare but there are some nice customers,' she replied, following this up with a nervous giggle. What the hell was wrong with her? All her life, Valerie had been calm and self-assured, but that deserted her when she was in the company of Seb's family. She supposed it was because she wanted their approval so badly.

'Well,' she continued when no one else spoke. 'I'll get out of your hair.'

'Can I borrow your car, Maw, to give her a lift into work?' said Seb.

'You have studying to do and I'm guessing you've done precious little of that today,' replied Laura.

'It's okay,' Valerie told Seb. 'I can get the bus. The stop's just down the road.'

'If you're sure?' he said.

'I am.'

'All right. I'll see you out,' he said, taking her hand.

Valerie gave Laura and Sarah a nervous smile. 'It was nice to see you again.'

'You too,' said Laura while Sarah remained silent.

Valerie gratefully walked to the front door and Laura and Sarah's chatter resumed.

Seb closed the porch door behind him so he and Valerie could say goodbye in private.

'They hate me,' said Valerie.

'No, they don't,' he replied, pulling her to him. 'They're just a little surprised by how quickly we got engaged. They'll come round. Don't worry, it'll all be fine.'

She gazed up at this beautiful, kind man. 'Are you sure you want to marry me? What if someone better comes along?'

He smiled and ran his fingers through her hair. 'No one can be better than you.'

She smiled back and kissed him, having to tear herself away when she saw her bus appear at the top of the street.

'Got to go,' she told him. He smiled as he watched her race down the street with the agility of a gazelle.

Valerie made it to the stop on time and hopped onto the bus, taking a seat by the window and smiling to herself as she thought about Seb.

'I knew you couldn't stay away from me,' whispered a voice in her ear.

She jumped and turned in her seat to see Liam Thompson sitting behind her.

'Not you again,' she sighed. 'You're turning into a stalker, do you know that?'

'It's no' my fault you got on my bus.'

'Does it belong to you?' she said with a raised eyebrow.

'It's the bus I take to work.'

'Why do you take a bus when you have a car? You drove it into the petrol station, remember?'

'That was my brother's car. I'd borrowed it for the day.'

'You know what? I don't believe you. You're following me.'

He rested his arms on the back of her seat, and she leaned further away from him. 'It's because I like you.'

'Then you admit it, you are following me.' Panic shot through her. 'How did you know where I was?'

'I've made it my business to know,' he said, leaning in even closer.

Valerie grimaced and hastily moved to the seat on the other side of the bus, but he followed, only this time he sat right beside her. She looked around at the other passengers but there were only two elderly women at the front having a good gossip.

'Will you piss off?' Valerie told Liam.

'I will when you agree to come out with me.'

'I'm going nowhere with you. Our families are enemies and I'm seeing someone.'

'That big soft blonde pup? He's no' right for you. You need a real man.'

'It's none of your bloody business,' she told him. 'So bugger off and leave me alone. This is my stop.'

She gave him a hard look and he sighed and moved so she could get up.

'I know where you work and where your boyfriend lives,' he whispered in her ear. 'Now I just need to find out where you live.'

'Don't push me,' she whispered back. 'Or it'll be the last thing you ever do.'

His smile was wicked. 'You just get better and better, gorgeous.'

'I wish I could say the same,' she replied haughtily.

Valerie hopped off the bus, Liam staring at her through the window, the intensity of that stare making her shiver. That was all she needed with everything else going on – a stalker. She needed to find a way to deal with Liam Thompson and fast before he became an even bigger problem. The bugger of it was she thought she might need Toni to help her handle him and she had the feeling her cousin wouldn't be that eager.

* * *

Toni was absent from Valerie's life for weeks. She didn't call her or pop by for a visit, and Valerie missed her, but she refused to give in and contact her first. Clearly Toni was sulking at her for not wanting to join her and Frankie in the family business and perhaps that was for the best, it would only make it easier for her to extricate herself when the time came for her to leave. Valerie would have liked to share her plans for her future with her best friend but that wasn't possible because Toni might tell her brother. Valerie couldn't risk word getting back to Frankie.

14

The day Valerie had been dreading finally came around – Toni's twentieth birthday. She couldn't let that pass by unnoticed, so she bought a blouse she thought Toni might like. As she was working the late shift, she took it round to Toni's house on her way in to work. The door was opened by Toni herself wearing a leopard-print silk robe, her hair wrapped in a towel.

'Well, look who it is,' said Toni with a sly smile. 'Long time no see, Val. And to what do I owe this honour?'

Valerie held out the gift bag containing the blouse. 'Happy birthday, Toni.'

'Oh, how sweet,' Toni said, snatching the bag from her hand. 'You'd better come in, then.'

'Thanks,' said Valerie, stepping inside and closing the door. That had been a much warmer reception than she'd anticipated.

Thankfully Frankie wasn't there but Moira was, sitting on the couch watching television. Every time Valerie saw her aunt, she looked more diminished and beaten down with life. There was a sadness in her eyes that made her look haunted. Valerie wondered if it was because of Frankie's increasingly violent and erratic behaviour or whether Toni was making her suffer for serving her up to Roddy all those years ago. Frankie adored his maw, but Toni maintained an air of cold indifference towards her. Whereas Frankie's anger was quick and volatile, Toni could happily nurse a grudge and drag her vengeance out over years. It was that control over her emotions that made Toni more dangerous than her brother.

'Hi, Aunty Moira,' said Valerie.

'Hello, Val,' she replied in a tired, meek voice before turning her attention back to the television screen.

The room was filled with flowers and birthday cards and there was a bin bag full of discarded wrapping paper in the corner of the room.

'I see the family gift train has already passed through,' commented Valerie.

'People have been coming to the door all morning with presents,' announced Toni.

Valerie had to hide a smile. Toni made her relatives sound like subjects coming to bestow offerings upon their adored monarch. 'That's nice.'

'I suppose I should open this one too,' sighed Toni, removing the neatly wrapped gift from its bag and tearing open the paper. 'Oh, that's nice. Thanks,' she said before casually tossing the blouse onto the couch and letting the gift bag drop to the floor.

Valerie bit her tongue. She was trying to build bridges here. 'What else did you get?'

Toni took great delight in showing her the perfume, handbags, clothes and make-up she'd been given, although she contemptuously tossed aside the handkerchiefs with embroidered flowers an old aunt had given her.

'I thought I'd wear this tonight,' said Toni, holding up a beautiful scarlet dress.

'You should, you'll look gorgeous,' said Valerie.

Toni had always been a sucker for a compliment. 'Frankie's arranged a party for me at The Admiral. We've got the whole pub to ourselves. You should come.'

Toni was holding out an olive branch and Valerie was more than willing to accept it. 'Sounds great, thanks. What time?'

'Half seven. Bring that hunky boyfriend of yours. Frankie's invited some of his pals and we need as many good-looking men as we can get to balance out the ugly ones.' Toni's lip curled. 'I do hate ugly people.'

'Aye, so you've said, but I'll have to check if he's free. I think he might have plans with his family tonight.'

'Then he can come along after. The party will go on into the wee hours.'

'Like I said, I'm not sure if he'll be able to make it.'

'You're not ashamed of me, are you?'

'God, no.'

'Well, it's certainly starting to sound like it,' pouted Toni.

'It's not that at all, it's just that it's short notice. Look, I'll ask him. That's all I can say.'

Toni's smile returned. 'And that's all I can ask.'

Valerie was glad she'd been invited to Toni's party. She'd never missed one of her cousin's birthdays before and she didn't intend to start now, but she wasn't sure how she felt about Seb coming. What if a fight broke out and someone got glassed in the face? To anyone else, that would be horrific, but to the McVay family, it was just another celebration. Still, she'd made Toni a promise and she would keep it.

* * *

To Valerie's chagrin, Seb was more than happy to go to Toni's party.

'Why do you sound so down about it?' he asked her over the phone.

'My family can be quite full on and that's putting it mildly.'

'If we're going to be married, I should get to know them. I get the feeling it would be better for us both if they liked and accepted me.'

They arranged for Seb to come over to Valerie's house so they could go to the pub together. She didn't like the thought of Seb arriving before she did, like a sheep in a den of wolves. He really had no idea what he was letting himself in for marrying a McVay and she feared this party would give him a good idea. However, he knew Toni before he'd even met her and, if he could deal with her formidable cousin, he should be able to deal with the others. She hoped.

* * *

Valerie smoothed down her hair and took a deep breath.

'Are you all right?' said Seb. 'You look like you're preparing to go into battle.'

'Standard procedure before a McVay celebration,' she replied.

They were standing outside the pub, and judging by the noise emanating from inside, the party was in full swing. The sound of music, laughter and chatter was spilling out onto the street through the door, which had been left ajar to let out some of the heat and smoke.

Seb took Valerie's hand. 'It'll be fine. We'll have a few laughs and some drinks and, most importantly, we'll relax.'

'Or we could go to a hotel for the night?'

'Don't tempt me,' he replied with his devastating smile.

'Let's just get it over with,' she said before they stepped inside together.

The noise hit them immediately. The pub was packed full of McVays from all over the city and they were all eagerly enjoying the reunion. The room was decorated with a huge banner that said *Happy Birthday Toni* alongside pink and silver balloons. Uncle Tam and another uncle, Sam, were knocking back shots to the cheers of their gaggle of friends. Judging by how red their faces were and how they staggered from side to side, the competition had been going on for a while. There was a gaggle of McVay women cackling loudly on the other side of the room, all knocking back pints and smoking. Another of Val's many uncles walked across the room carrying a tray of drinks, fighting to walk in a straight line. The tray made it safely to the table, but he didn't. After putting it down, he tripped over a stool and landed on his face. Two teenagers were frantically kissing against a wall. A McVay male grabbed the boy by the ear and dragged him away, making him wince.

'Get off my daughter, you fucking pervert,' he growled before shoving the boy into a fruit machine with such force it almost tipped over.

'Oh, god,' sighed Valerie.

'They're a lively bunch, aren't they?' grinned Seb.

'That's an understatement, and this is just the calm before the storm.'

'I can see this is going to be a very interesting evening.'

Toni bustled up to them in her figure-hugging red dress, her bosom wobbling and threatening to burst out of her clothes as usual. She looked very pretty with her curly hair piled atop her head and diamond earrings decorating her ears. In one hand, she carried a glass of champagne.

'Val,' she beamed, hugging her with her free hand. 'I'm so glad you made it. Hello, Seb,' she smiled up at him, going on tiptoes to kiss his cheek.

'Happy birthday, Toni,' he replied, handing her the bottle of red wine he carried.

'Ooh, my favourite,' she smiled, accepting it from him. 'Well, feel free to mingle. There's some nibbles in the back room but they haven't really been touched. Our family prefers a liquid diet,' she added with a wink at Seb. 'There's free champers at the bar, so help yourself to that too.'

When more guests arrived, Toni moved to greet them. After retrieving their glasses of champagne, Val ushered Seb to the side of the room, where they could safely watch the proceedings. Tam won the drinking competition when Sam tottered backwards three paces before falling onto his bottom, causing their cronies to cheer. Valerie was relieved that Frankie didn't appear to be present, although she had no doubt he would show his face at some point.

'Aren't your parents coming?' Seb asked Valerie.

'No. They like to avoid these gatherings. The last one they came to was five years ago and Uncle Tam punched out my da. They've refused to come to another family celebration since.'

While Seb looked on, fascinated, Valerie inwardly cringed as her family became increasingly raucous and drunk. Plenty of people came up to talk to them, a lot of the women cooing over Seb, who blushed at the attention.

'You're quite the hit,' said Valerie, after Seb patiently endured being petted by three middle-aged aunts.

'That's a relief,' he replied. 'Are all these people your aunts and uncles?'

'Not biologically. Some are second cousins or old family friends who I've grown up calling aunty and uncle.'

'Toni mentioned once that she and Frankie have an older brother, but she wouldn't say anything else about him.'

'Aye, Andy. He was always embarrassed about being a McVay and left Glasgow when he was eighteen. He lives a very respectable life in Edinburgh as an estate agent and rarely visits. Toni thinks he's a traitor, so he won't be coming tonight. We only really see him at Christmas.'

'It's a shame when families are divided. Who's the woman in the wheelchair? She looks so sad.'

'That's Aunty Moira, Toni's maw.'

'Where's her da?'

'He ran off with another woman years ago. Moira was devastated. She did marry again, a man called Eric, but he got banged up in Bar-L for attempting to rape a seventeen-year-old girl, so she divorced him. She's avoided men ever since.' Valerie decided that Seb had had enough of her family's craziness for one day, so she didn't add that she suspected Tam had killed Moira's first husband out of revenge for cheating on his sister. These little revelations could come slowly over their years together.

'Why is she in the wheelchair?' said Seb.

'She was in a car accident four years ago which left her paralysed from the waist down.'

'Poor woman. No wonder she looks so sad.'

'Aye,' was all Valerie replied; she had zero sympathy for Moira McVay. You reaped what you sowed in this life.

Despite all the noise and chaos, everyone noticed when Frankie entered, flanked by Paul and Jamesie. Tam suddenly became all seriousness and bustled up to his nephew to shake his hand, as did some of the other men. Already Frankie was being treated like the big man around here, despite his youth. Valerie knew it wouldn't be long before he was as powerful as Roddy. She just hoped she and Seb were far away by then because he would be even more of a nightmare than he already was.

After shaking hands with his admirers, Frankie strode over to

Seb, who didn't really understand who he was. He just thought he was Valerie's cousin and Toni's brother.

'All right, pal?' said Frankie, shaking Seb's hand and clapping him on the shoulder. 'How's it hanging?'

'Er, it's hanging fine,' Seb replied.

'I bet Val's glad to hear that,' Frankie quipped before bursting out laughing, his hangers-on all laughing too. 'Glad you could come. You're the first one of Val's boyfriends Toni's ever invited to one of her parties, so hopefully that means you're no' a total loser like they were.'

Frankie glanced at Valerie as he spoke, and she watched him through narrowed eyes, suspicious of all this bonhomie.

'I'm not,' Seb hastened to assure him.

'Toni said you're at uni. What are you studying?'

'Philosophy.' He hesitated before adding, 'And Divinity.' He didn't know why, but Seb got the strong impression that lying to this man wouldn't be good for his relationship with Valerie.

'Divinity?' frowned Frankie. 'What the fuck's that?'

'It's the study of Christian theology.'

Frankie stared at him like he had two heads. He glanced at Paul and Jamesie, who shrugged before he turned back to Seb. 'Why the hell would you want to dae that?'

'Because I find it interesting.'

'Why?'

'It speaks to my soul.'

Frankie looked at Tam. 'Have you been slipping the Harpic into his drink?'

'No' me, Frankie boy,' replied Tam. 'I havenae been near him.'

'What's the point in all that then?' Frankie asked Seb, looking genuinely curious.

Valerie's heart went out to her fiancé. She knew he wanted to keep his dream quiet.

'I want to be a minister,' he told him.

'Minister as in preaching in a church and that?' said Frankie.

'Aye,' replied Seb.

Frankie, Paul, Jamesie and Tam all gaped at him before bursting out laughing.

'It's not funny,' Valerie hissed at them.

'That's no' why we're laughing,' grinned Frankie.

'It's not?' said Jamesie, looking puzzled.

Frankie scowled at him before clipping him around the back of the head. 'I was thinking that with a God-botherer hanging around, we'll all burst into flames any moment,' he quipped.

Valerie rolled her eyes and flashed Seb an apologetic look.

'So it doesnae stop you drinking then?' said Frankie, pointing to the champagne glass Seb held.

'No, I do drink,' he replied. 'Although not a lot.'

'Don't say you don't believe in sex before marriage? Poor old Val. No wonder she looks so uptight.'

'Er, I do believe in that, actually,' Seb mumbled, embarrassed.

'All the better for you, eh, sweetheart?' said Frankie, clapping Valerie on the shoulder, nearly knocking her over.

'Val,' exclaimed Toni, rushing up to her. 'Come and look at what Aunty Mima bought me.'

'Aunty Mima's here?' Val replied, craning her head to look.

'Aye, course.'

'Great,' smiled Valerie.

Mima was her mother's youngest sister and the whole family adored her, even Toni and Frankie. She was the kindest McVay, with a quiet inner strength and dignity. She was also extremely wise and they all went to her for advice. She was like a younger version of Seb's grandmother, Euphemia. Valerie wanted Seb to come with her, but Tam and Frankie were already leading him over to a group of McVay men for a drinking game.

'He'll be fine,' Toni told her, linking her arm through hers and practically dragging her across the room. 'They won't strip him naked and tie him to a lamp post. They'll save that for his stag night.'

Valerie glanced at Toni, wondering if she knew about their engagement, but Toni would have been unable to resist letting her know she'd discovered her secret because she always had to be the smartest person in the room.

'Hi, Aunty Mima,' said Val when she was pulled before her.

Mima had the typical female McVay looks, with her voluptuous figure and thick black curly hair. However, her temperament was much sweeter, and kindness shone from her dark eyes.

'Valerie,' smiled Mima, getting to her feet to hug her.

Mima was only in her mid-forties but could pass for ten years younger. Valerie was quite sure that was because she let nothing bother her and treated life as something to be enjoyed rather than endured.

'It's been a while since I last saw you,' twinkled Mima. 'You're looking very well.'

'Thanks. Aye, sorry about that. I've been so busy.'

'I can guess doing what,' she smiled, glancing at Seb, who was knocking back a whisky shot to the cheers of the McVay males. 'I didn't think a man could be beautiful, but he is.'

'Aye, he's lovely,' she beamed.

'What's his name?'

'Seb.'

'Short for Sebastian?'

'Aye, but he hates that name.'

'I see. Well, sit down and tell me what you've been up to.'

'He's fine, for god's sake,' sighed Toni when Valerie glanced at Seb again. 'The worst that will happen to him is he'll throw up.'

'I suppose,' she said before reluctantly taking a chair at Mima's table.

She forced herself to turn her attention to Mima. She loved her aunt and Toni was right, Seb would be fine, although she couldn't resist glancing over at him occasionally. He drank one McVay man under the table, to the cheers of the rest of the men as his vanquished opponent slid to the floor. Seb himself was very flushed, making his blonde hair look even blonder, but he was standing upright, not wobbling about like most of the other men.

After twenty minutes of this, Valerie decided to rescue him. She excused herself and when Toni attempted to stop her cousin, Mima tapped her arm and waggled her finger at her. There were only two people Toni McVay obeyed – her brother and her Aunty Mima, so she left Valerie to hurry over to her boyfriend.

'All right, boys,' smiled Valerie, taking Seb's hand. 'Give him a wee break, eh?'

'Break?' exclaimed Sam, who was back on his feet after his defeat by Tam. 'The lad's no' a jessie. He can take more.'

'Maybe later,' she said, leading him away before they could drag him back into their drinking games.

Valerie directed Seb to the chair beside her own. Toni grinned when he sat down and almost missed, only managing to right himself at the last moment.

'Your family really knows how to enjoy themselves,' he mumbled, eyes hazy.

'What you need is some champagne,' said Toni.

'No,' exclaimed Valerie. 'I'll get him some water.'

She hurried to the bar and ordered a jug of iced water, anxiously looking back over her shoulder at Seb, relieved when she saw he was talking to Aunty Mima. She'd look after him until she could get back over there.

While Valerie waited for her order, Frankie sidled up to her. He was the only man who wasn't actually drinking. He always liked to be in control of himself. Well, as much as he could be with such an ungovernable temper.

'He's no' bad is Seb,' said Frankie.

Coming from him, that was praise indeed. 'He's a lot more than that,' replied Valerie.

'I don't know what use he'll be to you tonight,' he laughed. 'Unless he sobers up quickly.'

'That is none of your business.'

'Ooh, well, excuse me,' he retorted. 'We're only trying to welcome him into the family, seeing how you seem so serious about him.'

Valerie knew Frankie didn't do anyone a favour unless it benefited him, so this made her suspicious. 'I appreciate that,' she replied, deciding it would be wise not to give voice to her suspicions.

'Don't go getting blethered because there's a job I want you to do tomorrow.'

'No way. You sent me into a trap on the last job I did for you.'

'And you were fine. I dinnae ken what you're getting so uptight about.' Frankie's eyes narrowed. 'You've changed since you started going out with Seb. I hope he's no' making you think you're too good for this family?'

'Of course not, but I want a future with him and all this violence is not part of that.'

'Future as a bloody minister's wife. How fucking boring, all jumble sales and cups of tea.'

'Sounds nice to me.'

'You're wasting yourself, Val. I really want you in on the business. You could go far and you'd rake in a fortune.'

'I thought you didn't agree with women working in the business?'

'I'm making an exception for you because you're an asset to me.'

'So's Toni.'

'She's good at giving someone a slap but she isnae like you.'

'No, she's smarter. She was born for that life.'

Frankie's eyes flickered. 'I don't want her working in it. In fact, I don't want her working at all. She'll have everything she could ever want but no sister of mine works.'

'She would be so good.'

'So fucking what?' he hissed. 'She's no' working and that's an end to the matter.'

Valerie wondered if Toni knew that her brother had already mapped out her life for her, but that wasn't her fight. 'Please understand, Frankie, it's not what I want.'

'Just think, you could pack in your job at the petrol station right now and you'd never have to worry about money again,' he said, like the devil on her shoulder.

Valerie looked over at her angel and smiled. 'There's something I want more than money.'

'That's a stupid fucking decision.'

'You don't need me. You'll go straight to the top, Frankie. I've no doubt about it and you'll have good people at your side.'

There was a loud cheer from the pocket of drunken men and they both looked round to see Paul frantically patting out his beard after trying to drink a flaming sambuca.

'You sure about that?' said Frankie with a raised eyebrow. He grimaced and sniffed the air. 'There's nothing like the smell of singed face fur. Well, you know where to find me when you change your mind.'

'I won't.'

His smile was sly. 'We'll see about that,' he said, before

wandering off to take the piss out of Paul for setting fire to his own face.

Val picked up the tray holding the jug of water and glasses the barman had placed on the bar and returned to her table.

'Get that down you,' she told Seb, pouring out a glass of water and handing it to him.

He accepted it from her gratefully and glugged it down. 'Thanks,' he said. 'That's better.'

'Keep drinking,' she told him when he still appeared hazy and flushed.

'Your conversation with Frankie looked rather intense,' said Toni curiously.

'Did it?' said Valerie, sipping her water, avoiding her cousin's gaze, which made Toni even more suspicious.

Valerie had never been more grateful for one of her family's fights to break out. To their left, two McVays in their mid-sixties were kicking off. One of them shoved over the table they were sitting at and lunged for the man sitting opposite him, grabbing him by the front of the shirt and dragging him to his feet. The man being dragged punched his attacker in the face and they started to fight. Their wives attempted to pull them apart but when that failed, they turned on each other instead. Everyone looked to Frankie, wondering if he was going to intervene, but it seemed he was content with watching, surrounded by his cronies, all of them laughing.

'I would love one family gathering where there isn't a fight,' sighed Mima, getting to her feet.

'Er, should we help her?' slurred Seb as Mima rolled up her sleeves and marched into the fray.

'No need,' shrugged Toni. 'She can handle it.'

Seb was impressed when Mima grabbed one of the struggling women by the back of the blouse, pulled her away from her opponent and slapped her hard across the face. The woman stared at her in shock, putting a hand to her reddening cheek. Mima glared at the second woman, who held up her hands and backed off.

Next, Mima turned her attention to the two men. Fearlessly she put herself between them, the men immediately wilting at her furious look and lowering their fists.

'Spoilsport,' Tam called to Mima, who ignored him.

Seb had to marvel at the rest of the family, who had carried on talking and drinking as though nothing were happening. Valerie hadn't been exaggerating when she'd said it wasn't a McVay celebration without a fight and they'd all become completely indifferent to it.

'Are all the McVay women so tough?' he said.

'We are,' said Toni. 'Especially Val. She's the fiercest of us all.'

'Really?' he grinned at his fiancée.

'I think that honour belongs to Toni,' said Valerie.

'Give over, Val,' Toni replied. 'We both know it's you. That's why Frankie wants you to work for him.'

Seb looked questioningly at Valerie.

'But it's never going to happen,' Valerie told Toni with a hard look, knowing she'd said that in front of Seb on purpose.

'You sure about that?' she smirked.

'I am,' Val replied in a hard voice. 'And Frankie knows it.'

'Frankie's not someone who takes no for an answer.'

'He's not?' said Seb with a worried look.

'Nope. In fact, it tends to make him psychotically angry.'

'I'll be back in a minute,' Valerie told Seb before taking Toni's arm and encouraging her out of her seat. 'I just need a word with my cousin.'

'You're hurting me,' Toni hissed at Valerie as she led her towards the toilets.

'You'll be fine,' Valerie told her stonily.

They burst into the toilets and Valerie finally released her cousin. Toni's eyes flashed with indignation as she assessed her appearance in the mirror. 'You messed up my dress,' she said, adjusting the straps.

'How could I? There's hardly anything to mess up. You said that on purpose in front of Seb. You're trying to come between us.'

'You're getting paranoid,' said Toni, still checking her appearance in the mirror.

'Oh, no, I'm not. Frankie collared me at the bar, trying to persuade me to join him in the business, but I said no. What was the plan for this evening, scare Seb with drinking competitions and fights and talk about illegal activities to get him to dump me?'

Toni sighed and turned to face her. 'Why do you have to make everything about you? This is my birthday party. Every McVay party there are fights and drinking competitions.'

Valerie started to feel unsure of herself. Maybe she was becoming paranoid?

'And if Frankie did try to convince you to join him in the business,' continued Toni, 'then take it as the compliment it is. You know what I think this is really about – you're terrified of Seb seeing the real Valerie Brown, who gets a high from battering the shite out of people. That Valerie will still exist even if she does settle down to be a minister's wife and she'll quickly get bored of sermons and craft fairs.'

'No, I won't. I could never get bored with Seb.'

'I hope you're right,' said Toni, her gaze still focused on her reflection in the mirror. 'As much as you hate to admit it, Val, you have a dark side and it needs to be let out once in a while or it'll explode all over everyone. I should know because I have one myself.'

'The difference is that you let yours out a lot more than I do mine. I haven't seen hide nor hair of Leo since you cornered him. What did you do to him?'

Toni finished faffing with her hair and, finally satisfied with her appearance, she turned to face Valerie. 'No doubt you'll find out soon enough. Now, if we're done here, I need to get back to my guests.'

Toni strode out with a pleased smile, Valerie slinking after her. She exited the toilet and her stomach dropped when she saw Seb still sitting at the table, only now he was talking to Frankie and Tam. Mima was at the other side of the room talking to Moira, so he'd been left alone. While Toni went to chat to a couple of friends, Valerie rushed over to her fiancé's side.

'All right, babe?' she said, sitting beside him and taking his hand.

'Aye, I'm great,' he smiled. 'Just having a nice wee chat.'

'What about?' she replied, hoping she sounded casual.

'This and that,' said Frankie. 'He's fucking clever is Seb.'

'He certainly is,' she replied, praying Frankie wasn't going to try and rope this innocent into his nefarious activities. Frankie hadn't been innocent since he was five years old and had started setting fire to things and punching other children.

'We're going on a lads' day out to Largs next week,' said Tam. 'It's a traditional family piss-up. You should come along, Seb.'

'Aye, sounds good,' he smiled.

Valerie's heart ached at how pleased he was by this invitation, thinking it meant he'd been accepted by her family, when she knew Frankie and Tam were only trying to use him in some way.

'Seb's very busy,' she said. 'He's got exams.'

'All the more reason for him to enjoy a day out by the coast,' said Frankie. 'It's next Saturday, Seb. Think you can make it?'

'Aye, nae bother.'

'Good man,' said Frankie, clapping him on the shoulder. He

rolled his eyes when another fight broke out at the other side of the room, this time between two younger cousins. 'I cannae leave Aunty Mima to sort out all the violence. I suppose it's my turn now. Come on, Tam.'

'Right behind you, Frankie, son,' said the round little man, getting up to follow.

'It was nice of them to invite me to Largs, wasn't it?' said Seb, smile faltering at Valerie's severe expression. 'What's wrong?'

Valerie glanced around to make sure no one was listening before leaning into him. 'Frankie never does anything nice for anyone. He always has an ulterior motive. I'm worried he'll rope you into something dangerous.'

'You don't need to worry about that. I'm no' daft.'

'I know, but he has a way of getting people to do what he wants. If he doesn't manage to persuade them, then he threatens them into doing it.'

'Look at that lot he has around him,' said Seb, nodding at all the scarred and aggressive McVay men. 'What use could he have for me?'

'I don't know, but he'll have something in mind. He doesn't miss a trick.'

Seb realised how agitated she was. 'I won't go to Largs with them if it makes you so uneasy. I'll come up with some excuse.'

'Thank you,' she smiled. 'Because I don't trust them an inch. Oh, I don't know if I'm doing the right thing getting you wrapped up with my family.'

'Don't talk like that. You're the best thing that ever happened to me.'

'And you're the best thing that ever happened to me, but I'm afraid my family will ruin everything.'

'Now I understand why you're so keen to move away.'

'If I don't, we'll both end up on a bad path.'

'The rest of your family do all right, though, don't they? I mean, Frankie hasn't involved them all in his world?'

'No, but he wants young blood and you're big, strong and smart. He will try to recruit you, mark my words.'

'Perhaps we could bring forward our plans to move away, if it's going to upset you so much? We don't have to wait until I get a parish.'

'That's a great idea. I've already started saving every spare penny I have.'

'I'll do the same. We'll soon have enough to start again somewhere else.'

'Like where?'

Seb smiled at the eagerness in her eyes. 'Wherever you want.'

'How about Aberdeenshire? It's beautiful up there and a safe enough distance from Glasgow but still close enough to visit.'

'Sounds good to me. I've been on a couple of holidays up there and it's lovely.'

'Then it's agreed. As soon as we have enough money, we'll leave.'

Seb smiled and nodded, and Valerie felt like she could breathe a little easier now they had a plan.

15

When a third fight broke out, Valerie decided it was time she and Seb left Toni's party. They didn't say goodbye to anyone, they just quietly slipped out the door, Valerie inhaling the fresh air with relief. She stopped in her tracks. Outside the door were four members of the Thompson family, who had frozen with surprise to see them. Two of the men held petrol bombs.

Valerie reacted on instinct.

'Tell Frankie,' she screamed at Seb, before lunging for the closest man holding one of the bombs.

She charged into the man and knocked him against the wall. He dropped the bomb and it smashed on the pavement.

'Get off her,' yelled Seb when another man grabbed Valerie around the waist. He wrapped an arm around the man's neck and dragged him backwards, forcing him to release her.

The other two men frantically attempted to light the rag sticking out of the top of the second petrol bomb, but it was a breezy, drizzly night and the wind blew out the flame on the lighter.

Valerie snatched up a crumpled traffic cone sitting at the kerb and swung it at the man holding the bomb, hitting him in the arm. He dropped the object, smashing it. She hit his friend in the chest with the cone and he fell back against the wall. Next, she turned her attention to Seb, who hurled the man he was holding into a bin, knocking it over, spilling rubbish into the street.

'Are you okay?' he asked her.

'Fine,' she replied. 'You?'

'Aye, good. God, that was exciting,' he grinned.

Valerie flung open the pub doors and yelled, 'The Thompsons are outside. They tried to petrol bomb the pub.'

Frankie and his men, who were standing near the door, tore outside, Valerie leaping backwards to avoid being flattened in the stampede. The four men were just picking themselves up and, seeing their foes, their eyes widened with fright and they tore off down the street. Frankie and his men raced after them, vanishing into the night.

'Someone needs to do something about that spilt petrol,' said Seb.

'Frankie will sort that out,' said Valerie, taking his hand. 'Let's get out of here.'

Her heart was racing and her hands shook, not because of the adrenaline of the fight but because Seb and her family could have been hurt. They were fortunate the four Thompson men had been so inept. It could have been so much worse.

'Where are we going?' he said when she hurried him away from the pub, leaving behind the noise and chaos.

'As far from my family as possible,' she replied.

'Valerie, stop,' he said, gently taking her by the shoulders and turning her to face him.

They were on a quiet street lined by shops, the pub left far behind. It had been raining while they were inside and the orange glow from the street lights and the light from a takeaway, the only thing still open, reflected off the wet pavement. The smell of cooking kebabs emanating from the takeaway made Valerie's stomach churn.

'Talk to me,' he said gently.

Valerie thought what a wonderful minister he would make. That soft, deep voice and those beautiful blue eyes just encouraged you to open up. 'You could have been hurt because of me,' she blurted out.

'But I wasn't. I'm fine.'

'If we hadn't left the pub when we did, then we would have been inside when those petrol bombs came through the window and god only knows what could have happened.'

'Everything's fine. We were protected.'

'By God?' she said with a raised eyebrow.

'Who else?' he smiled. 'Just trust and believe that everything will be okay, as I do.'

'I'm so scared you'll be dragged off the path you want to take because of me and my family. Our relationship could do you more harm than good.'

'Our relationship makes me happier than I've ever been, so how can that be a bad thing?'

Valerie's eyes filled with tears. 'I don't know, I've never felt like this before. All my other boyfriends were already in the world my family are in and I knew they could handle it, but you're so good and I don't think you really understand who the McVays are.'

'They're people, just like everyone else.'

'We're rotten,' she said, eyes full of distress. 'I wish I could have been born into a good, honest family like yours.'

'No one is all good or all bad. Everyone is a mixture of both. My family have had their bad moments. One of my uncles turned out to be a paedophile.'

'Really?' she said, unable to believe anyone related to Seb could have a bad bone in their body.

'Aye, and my grandfather was horribly abusive to my grandmother and my mother. It was a relief to everyone when he died. And I bet there are members of your family who never committed a crime in their life?'

Valerie nodded.

'See? There's good and bad in every single person and every family. Yes, your family is definitely livelier than most, but tonight I also saw a lot of love there. You and Toni obviously adore your Aunty Mima.'

'We do. She's the best of us all.'

'And a lot of the family showed so much care for Moira, fetching her drinks and food and ensuring she had everything she needed. That's good.'

Valerie slowly nodded as she considered his words.

'Then there's you,' he said, so gently his voice was just a breath on the air. 'You tackled those men without a thought for your own safety because you were far more concerned with protecting those you love. You're amazing and I feel privileged to be engaged to you. So please, stop worrying. This relationship is right, and we both know it.'

'Oh, Seb,' she rasped, tears spilling down her face.

They kissed, their movements growing frantic as the adrenaline of the fight still coursed through their veins.

'I want you right now,' he whispered in her ear, sending tingles shooting down her spine.

'Seriously?' she said, looking up and down the darkened street, which was quiet.

'Yes,' he said, eyes filling with mischief.

Together they sneaked around the corner down a deserted back street. They kissed hard, Seb pulling up her skirt while

Valerie unfastened his trousers, biting her lip to keep in her ecstatic moans as he entered her. They made love fast and furiously, the darkness shielding them. Valerie threw back her head as they came together, forcing herself to contain the cry wanting to burst from her lips. Her senses were heightened and she was able to feel the hard stone of the wall she was pressed up against, as well as the drip of water on her head as it started to rain. As the pleasure reached a crescendo, Valerie had never felt so alive.

'I've never done anything like that before,' gasped Seb as they clung onto each other, enjoying the aftershocks running through their bodies.

'It's a first for me too,' she replied, resting her head on his shoulder.

They kissed and he gently put her down so they could adjust their clothing.

'My life has become ten times more exciting since you came into it,' he beamed at her.

'Don't go mentioning this moment when you apply to become a minister,' she smiled back.

'I won't, but I'll enjoy reliving the memory again and again.' Seb slung an arm around her shoulders. 'Fancy coming back to mine tonight?' he asked her.

'Mmm, yes, please,' she said, leaning into him as they returned to the main street, relieved to see the only person in sight was just coming around the corner at the other end of the road. It seemed they'd got away with it.

Valerie felt better. That had been just what she'd needed. Perhaps Seb was right and a higher force was watching over them? The thought gave her a lot of comfort.

* * *

Valerie had taken to cautiously peering around the corner of the building before leaving work, just to make sure no one was waiting for her. She hadn't heard what fate the Thompson men who had attacked them two nights ago at the pub had suffered, but she had no doubt that they had suffered.

Today the only person waiting for her outside work was Toni, who was idly flicking through one of her celebrity magazines.

'Finally,' said Toni when she saw Valerie, casually tossing the magazine into a bin. 'I've been waiting for ages. I thought you finished at four on Mondays?'

'Sharon was a bit late, so I said I'd stay on until she arrived.'

'Silly cow. Not you, Sharon,' she added when Valerie frowned.

'I take it you want to talk to me?'

'No, I just thought I'd hang around here breathing in the petrol fumes,' Toni said sarcastically. 'I don't know how you put up with it, it's giving me a headache.'

'You get used to it.'

They set off down the street together, Toni grateful to leave the petrol station behind.

'I thought I'd come and let you know what happened with the Thompsons. It's the least I can do after you and Seb basically saved all our lives.'

'I assume Frankie and the others dealt with them severely. You don't need to give me the details.'

'You're right, and they won't be bothering anyone again for a long time, mainly because they've all got broken arms and legs.'

When Toni lapsed into silence, Valerie glanced at her. 'What is it?'

'Nothing. You said you didn't want the details.'

'You look disturbed, and I know there's not much that can disturb you.'

Toni sighed. 'All right, I'll tell you – Frankie cut off one of their fingers and kept it as a trophy.'

'To go with the scalp he kept?'

'Aye. He said he's building his own trophy room, like safari hunters have but instead of antelope and lion's heads, his will have human body parts. He actually put the finger in one of my maw's plastic tubs to keep it fresh.'

'Now I hope you understand why I don't want to work for him?'

'Of course I understand, I always have. Anyway, you don't need to worry. Those men won't be bothering the family again.'

'What about the rest of the Thompsons? They'll retaliate. Again.'

'That's why Frankie's started taking his trophies, to put people off retaliating.'

'It won't work. This has been going on between our families for years and Frankie cutting off someone's finger won't stop it. Roddy did far worse and it only exacerbated matters. Sorry,' she said when Toni winced at the mention of Roddy's name.

'It's okay,' mumbled Toni. 'The bastard's rotting away in the ground, where he belongs.'

'I can't believe they were going to petrol bomb the pub with so many people inside. I suppose it put a dampener on your party?'

'It takes a lot more than four pricks with bottles of petrol to do that. I pulled Craig last night, finally.'

'Craig, as in our cousin?'

'Everyone in bloody Glasgow seems to be our cousin but aye, him. I've fancied him for years and finally he gave in to me in the storeroom at the back of the pub. It was very satisfying,' Toni purred.

'Doesn't it bother you that he's your first cousin?'

'No, why should it?'

'I don't know,' said Valerie, not wanting to be drawn into that conversation. 'Are you seeing him again?'

'God, no,' she laughed. 'He's hot but he's a bit thick. I just wanted to make him a notch on my bedpost. I hope last night didn't scare off Seb?'

'Nope. He said it was exciting, god help him.'

'Well, that is a surprise. I thought he would have run away screaming.'

'Not a bit of it. But he was a fish out of water,' Val added hastily. 'He pulled one of the Thompsons off me and threw him into a bin.'

'So he's the one to blame for that. Jack, the landlord, was raging about all the mess on the street outside his pub. He said he'd cut the baws off whoever did it, so naturally everyone's blaming the Thompsons. But it sounds like Seb wasn't so much a fish out of water.'

'Tell me honestly, Toni – is Frankie trying to recruit him?'

'He wants to get to know him. That's all I know. But I think any thoughts Frankie may have had about recruiting him, if he had any at all, were destroyed when Seb said he wants to be a minister.'

'It's not funny,' said Valerie when Toni sniggered.

'I always thought you'd fall for some bad boy in leathers with tattoos and piercings and a motorbike, not a big soft – but admittedly hot – pup who wants to spend his days preaching the Bible.'

'He's intelligent and he loves books. That's my sort of man, not meatheads like Leo. Anyway, you're the one who set me up with Seb.'

'That was before I knew he was a God-botherer.'

'He's not, he's just got his mind on the higher things. And no smutty comments from you, thank you,' she added, when Toni's eyes danced with amusement.

'Me? Never,' Toni said with mock shock. 'Are you seeing him today?'

'No, he's got another exam tomorrow morning, so he's study-ing. I have been distracting him a lot lately.' She glanced sideways at her cousin. 'Did you go after Karen McMillan?'

'Me and Angela went round to her house but she wasn't in, which is typical of the silly cow. We could head over there now.'

'No. I'm sure you can go another time with Angela. Oh, hell,' Val sighed.

'What is it?'

Valerie nodded at an approaching figure. 'Liam Thompson. You don't need that,' she added when Toni pulled her knife. 'Remember, we're on a main road.'

'Suppose,' she said, slipping the blade back into her jacket pocket.

'I bet you think you're fucking clever, don't you?' spat Liam.

'Always,' replied Toni with a smug smile.

Liam ignored her, his attention on Valerie. 'Three of my cousins and my best pal are laid up with broken limbs.'

'Are we supposed to feel sorry for them after they tried to set fire to a building with our family inside?' retorted Valerie.

'That's bollocks. They were just there to throw a few bricks through the windows.'

'They had petrol bombs and you know it.'

'No, they fucking didn't,' he snarled, body throbbing with unspent rage. 'They had a couple of bricks and your lot went way over the top. There was no need to dae that to them.'

'Aye, there was,' retorted a furious Valerie. 'I walked out of the pub to find two of them holding petrol bombs, which they were about to throw through the windows with all of us inside. If you don't believe me, go and ask Jack, the landlord. I know you respect him and he's no reason to lie to you. He's pissed off though as he had to get rid of all the spilt petrol.'

'Bollocks, they wouldnae go against my orders.'

'Well, they fucking did, so maybe you should be taking it out on them rather than us. What were we supposed to do, stand back and let them roast our entire family alive? If that had happened, guess where the polis's first stop would have been? You. Thanks to your moronic henchmen, you could have been banged up for life.'

Valerie was practically yelling in his face, her words muffled by the noise from the passing traffic.

Both she and Toni were nonplussed when Liam smiled.

'You're so sexy,' he told her. 'When are you gonnae gi'e in and come out with me?'

'What?' said Toni. 'This creep has asked you out on a date?' she demanded of her cousin.

'Several times,' replied Valerie while Liam continued to smile at her. 'I keep telling him to piss off, but he won't listen.'

'McVays and Thompsons don't mix,' Toni told Liam. 'It would be much better for your health if you got that through your thick skull.'

Once again, he ignored her, and Toni growled with rage and stamped her foot.

'I might be encouraged to call off my foot soldiers if you come out on a date with me,' Liam told Valerie.

'I don't respond to blackmail,' she replied. 'And I would never go out with you or any member of your family. Now, we're leaving.'

Liam stood aside and watched them go.

'He is such a freak,' said Valerie as the girls walked down the road together.

'And totally into you,' said Toni. 'That's not an insult,' she added when Valerie frowned at her.

'I just want him to leave me alone.'

'He's been hassling you?'

'Aye. Everywhere I turn, he seems to be there. He's come into the petrol station, he was on the bus that I caught outside Seb's. He said he knows where my boyfriend lives and he's going to find out where I live next.'

'Why didn't you say anything?' exclaimed Toni. 'You're being stalked.'

'I don't think it's that bad. He just has a wee thing for me and I didn't say anything because things are tense enough between us and that family. I didn't want to make them worse.'

'You have to tell Frankie.'

'Frankie's got enough on his plate,' Valerie said as they came to a halt at the bus stop.

They spent an anxious five minutes waiting for the bus to arrive, expecting Liam to show up again, but he didn't, all the while Toni trying to convince Valerie to tell Frankie about Liam's unwanted attentions and Valerie stubbornly refusing. Frankie was itching for an excuse to commit bloody carnage just to show Duncan Blackwood what he could really do and she refused to be that excuse.

Thankfully, Toni dropped the conversation once they were on the bus.

'I'll get off with you at your stop,' Toni told Valerie. 'Make sure you get home safely.'

'You don't need to,' she replied. 'I'm sure I'll be fine.'

'It's obvious Liam wants to retaliate, so we can't take any chances.'

'And who will see you home safely?'

'I'm hoping your da will give me a lift. He should be home by now.'

'Aye, he should,' said Valerie, glancing at her watch, which said it was 6.30 in the evening.

They got off the bus and started the two-minute walk to Valerie's house. As they reached the end of the street, and the bus vanished from view, a white transit van pulled up alongside them.

It did it slowly and casually, as though the driver was arriving home from a hard day's work. While the cousins were distracted, bickering over telling Frankie about Liam – a subject Toni had decided to bring up again – the side door was yanked open and two large figures leapt out, clamping their hands over the women's mouths and dragging them into the van. The men jumped in after them, the door was pulled closed and the van set off.

16

'What the fuck?' cried an astonished Toni, squinting at the figures hunched over her in the darkness. As there were no windows in the back of the van and it was separated from the front cab by a dividing panel, it was almost pitch black. 'Val, are you okay?'

'Aye,' she replied, feeling a little dazed from the shock.

When Valerie felt someone trying to pin her hands behind her back in the darkness, she threw herself backwards, knocking them over. From Toni's direction, she heard a male voice cry out in pain.

'How do you like that, you bastard?' cried Toni's triumphant voice.

But there were too many of them for the two women to overcome, especially in the darkness. Valerie herself counted at least four shadows. She and Toni were shoved to the floor and their hands taped behind their backs. Valerie, although she was scared, decided to take this with quiet dignity, while Toni hissed and spat and declared bloody vengeance for this outrage. She even bit one of them, earning herself a slap across the face.

They were pinned to the floor of the van and held there until it eventually rolled to a halt.

'As soon as you let me go,' said Toni, 'I'm going to rip your baws off.'

'Good luck with your hands tied behind your back,' said one of the men, dragging her to her feet.

'I never said I'd use my hands,' she retorted.

The moment she was on her feet, Toni drove her knee into his crotch and headbutted the man beside him.

Valerie threw herself sideways, knocking the man holding her into the side of the van with a resounding clang.

Before the fourth man in the van could react, the door was pulled open, the daylight momentarily dazzling them all.

'Toni, don't,' cried Valerie.

With a war cry, Toni leapt out of the van, landing on the man who'd opened the door, knocking him onto his back. As her hands were still tied behind her, she was unable to get herself upright, so she was forced to lie there with the indignity of her skirt halfway up her bottom.

'Get that silly cow up,' said a voice.

'Liam,' said Valerie flatly. 'I might have known.'

'Sorry for the harsh treatment,' he said, gently taking her by the arm to assist her down from the van. 'I hope they didn't hurt you.'

'No, but we hurt them,' Val replied, allowing him to help her. She didn't want to end up face down on the ground like Toni, who had been hauled upright by another two Thompson men.

'So I see,' grinned Liam when one of his men hopped out of the van nursing the side of his head and another got out while trying to stem the blood pouring from his nose. The third remained on his side, tenderly cupping his aching groin. 'Looks like we got two for one,' continued Liam. 'They were only supposed to snatch you. I had another van waiting near Toni's house for her, but we've been saved the trouble.'

'How convenient,' said Valerie sardonically. She paused to take in her surroundings. They were outside a manky old garage on a gravelled road riddled with potholes. 'Where are we?'

'You're safe. That's all you need to know.'

'Why are you doing this?'

'Because Frankie's gone on the rampage and we need some leverage to calm him down a bit.'

'Rampage? What are you talking about?'

'Not only did he take one of my cousin's fingers, but he's gone and battered the shite out of my younger brother and his best pals. He then went after my uncle and attacked him with a crowbar. He's currently in hospital with practically every bone broken in his body.'

'It's your own fault, you fucking prick,' yelled Toni, still struggling against the two men holding her. 'If you hadn't set up that attack at the pub, they'd all be fine now.'

'Tie her up and gag her,' Liam called after his men as Toni was dragged inside. 'God, she's annoying,' he sighed.

'Well, that will only make things worse,' Valerie told him.

'Instead of blaming me, blame Frankie. He keeps pushing my family, so we've been left with no choice. There's been a lot more going on than you or that noisy cow know about,' he replied, gesturing to Toni, whose loud voice echoed out of the garage. 'Want to come inside and listen reasonably?'

'That depends on what you're going to do to me and Toni.'

'I don't want to hurt you, if that's what you're worried about. Especially not you,' he said, brushing her face with his fingertips, causing Valerie to jerk her head backwards, catching the man holding her on the bridge of the nose.

'Never mind about him,' said Liam, taking her arm while his friend pressed a tissue to his bleeding nose. 'I'll take personal care of you.'

'This crush of yours will get you into trouble.'

'I hope so. I live for trouble.'

The garage was spacious but it appeared to be old, with oil stains on the floor. At least, Valerie hoped they were oil stains. Workbenches lined the walls, the tops covered in tools that had been idly abandoned. There were no vehicles in to be fixed, but it felt like the garage was used a lot. For what purpose remained to be seen.

Two chairs awaited the women, along with two more men armed with rope. Toni was tied to her chair first and gaffer tape slapped over her mouth, silencing her cries, although she still attempted to yell, black eyes flashing furiously above the top of the tape.

'Thank Christ for that,' said Liam, glad Toni had been silenced. He turned to Valerie and indicated the second chair with a sweep of the hand. 'If you'd be so kind.'

Valerie took the chair and calmly allowed herself to be tied to it. The rope was wrapped around her arms and torso, tethering her to the back of the chair. For good measure, her ankles were tied to the legs.

'Such dignity and grace,' said Liam with an admiring smile at Valerie. He scowled at Toni. 'You could learn a lot from her.'

Toni glared at him ferociously.

Liam turned back to Valerie. 'Now, I hope we can talk reasonably.'

Valerie nodded. 'I'm listening.'

'Good. I definitely gagged the right cousin.'

'I thought you'd have Chris Cathcart helping you.'

'That useless fanny? No' after he did a runner outside Stevie's house. He's bloody useless. He buggered off down south like the coward he is when he heard I wanted to pull his spine out.'

'It's so hard to get good help these days.'

'Tell me about it.' Liam looked to his men. 'Did you take their phones?'

'Aye, pal,' said one of the men.

'Great.' He turned back to Valerie. 'Now I'm going to call Frankie and tell him I've got you both and he'll want to speak to you for proof. Can I trust you to tell him you're okay?'

Valerie nodded.

'That's my girl,' he smiled. 'I knew I could rely on you. I'll tell him that if he wants to keep you both safe and well, he needs to come here alone. I take it he won't listen to that?'

'Course not. He'll come but he certainly won't be alone.'

'Just as I thought. I'll arrange to meet him somewhere else.'

'What's your plan? Because you know nothing will stop him from doing what he wants. Whether you hurt us or not, Frankie will just carry on regardless.' Her eyes narrowed. 'Unless this is an assassination attempt and you intend to kill him?'

Toni's eyes widened but she didn't make a noise, desperate to hear the rest of Liam's plan.

'That would only be a last resort,' said Liam. 'Murder's messy and pisses off the polis, but I'm willing to do it if he doesn't back off.'

'This feud between our families has gone on for years, it's become second nature for us all. This won't stop it. You're only going to make it worse. If you let us go, we won't tell Frankie about this.'

'Nice try, doll, but no can do. We both know she at least will go straight to him,' said Liam, pointing at Toni. 'Besides, I've finally got the advantage and I'm reluctant to give it up now. This feud has to stop.'

'I agree, but this isn't the way. You're only going to piss him off even more. I don't want anyone to get hurt, whether they be McVay or Thompson.'

'Believe it or not, I do know what I'm doing.' Liam straightened up and held out his hand to one of his men for Toni's phone.

He dialled and they all waited in tense silence.

'Frankie,' he smiled when the call was answered. 'Guess who?' His smile dropped. 'No, it's no' Homer Simpson.'

Toni cackled into her gag.

'It's Liam Thompson. Good question, Frankie. I got this number off your sister or, to be more precise, her phone. I've got her and your cousin Valerie right in front of me, trussed up like turkeys.' He winced and held the phone away from his ear at the tirade of filth Frankie spat down the line. When it ended, he put the phone back to his ear. 'Oh, you want proof, do you?' He held the phone out to Valerie. 'Speak.'

'Frankie, it's Val,' she said. 'We're both okay, we haven't been hurt. We're in an old garage...'

Liam snatched the phone away and put it back to his ear. 'Satisfied, Frankie? Aye, all right.' He looked to the man standing by Toni's side. 'Take her gag off.'

The man tore it off, making her wince and glare up at him.

'I'll rip your fucking lips off for that, you wee prick,' she snarled.

'Never mind that and talk to your brother,' said Liam, holding out the phone.

'Frankie,' she yelled. 'We're giving these bastards hell. We've already battered most of them. Don't give the sod what he wants.'

'All right, gag her again,' said Liam.

Toni's cries were muffled by fresh tape being slapped over her mouth. She was purple with fury, curls wild and in disarray, clothes for once rumpled.

'If you want to keep your sister and cousin alive and in one piece,' Liam told Frankie, 'then do exactly what I say. You will meet me in one hour at the address I'm gonnae text you and you'll come alone and unarmed. Any deviation from that and you'll never see either of them again. Got it?'

A sound echoed through the room and Valerie's eyes widened. 'I can hear a boat horn, Frankie,' she yelled. 'We're by the water.'

Liam hung up and frowned at her. 'I thought I could trust you to behave yourself.'

'Wouldn't you take advantage of every opportunity if you were in my position?' she replied.

'I suppose I would. Besides, the information you gave him is useless. We could be anywhere along the Clyde.'

She shrugged. 'It was worth a try.'

'Make it your last try. I meant it when I said I don't want to hurt you.'

Valerie was surprised to realise that she believed him.

Liam knelt before her and took her face in his hands. Toni screeched with outrage into her gag that he dare touch her cousin, but Valerie just stared back at him impassively.

'Can I trust you to behave yourselves while me and my pals go out?' he said.

'You do know we're no' seven years old?' said Valerie.

'Aye, I'm well aware of that,' he said, eyes eagerly roaming up and down her. 'But I need you to behave for me.'

'Why should we do anything to make life easier for you after you kidnapped us?'

'Because I'm hoping that, when this is over, we can see more of each other.'

'I already told you, I'm seeing someone.'

'Aye, the big blonde Labrador, I know. But soon you'll realise that he's no' right for you.'

'And you are?'

His response was a smile and he straightened up. 'Let's go. Callum, Caesar, stay and watch over them.'

'Caesar?' said Valerie.

'Terrible name, isn't it?' said Liam. 'A fucking tragedy.'

'It was a tragedy to Shakespeare too,' said Valerie.

Liam frowned. 'Are you all right there, doll? Did my men hit you hard in the heid?'

'No. I mean Shakespeare wrote a play about Julius Caesar and it was a tragedy.'

'Why, was it crap?'

'No. It's a tragedy because Caesar died.'

'So what? He was a walloper.'

Valerie sighed. 'Never mind.'

'Well, I must love you and leave you. Behave yourselves for Caesar and Callum. They don't like being pissed about. In fact, it makes them very angry.' He looked to the two guards. 'Gi'e the ladies some water and something to eat, we need to look after them, but I'm no' averse to you giving that one a slap if she gets out of line,' he said, pointing to Toni. 'But no' this one,' he continued, his digit moving round to Valerie. 'Got it?'

The two men nodded.

'Good. Right, let's get going.'

The rest of the men departed, and both Valerie and Toni turned to study their jailers. The one Liam had referred to as Callum was about their own age. He looked a bit of a mess in his creased jacket and jeans, dark hair uncombed, spots on his cheeks. The one called Caesar was a little older, probably in his late twenties, with jaw-length black hair. His eyes were sharp and intelligent and he was tall and athletic. He too wore jeans and a jacket, but his clothes were crisp and smart. Most striking were the twin scars starting at each corner of his mouth and cutting into his cheeks. Obviously someone had attempted to make him eat a knife sideways at some point in his life. The wounds had healed but there was a redness about them, indicating they had been inflicted recently. Valerie decided that he was definitely the more dangerous of the two.

'Fetch the water, Cal,' Caesar told his underling.

Callum nodded and retrieved two bottles from the workbench. He handed one to Caesar while unscrewing the top of the other and holding it Valerie's lips to drink, which she did eagerly.

Caesar knelt before Toni. 'Are you gonnae behave yourself, doll?' he asked her.

She stared back at him furiously but nodded her head.

'Good,' he said. 'Because I'd hate to gi'e that pretty face a slap.'

Gently he removed the tape from her mouth and held the bottle to her lips. As Toni drank, she kept her gaze on Caesar. When she'd finished drinking, she ran her tongue around the rim of the bottle, causing the corner of his mouth to lift. He straightened up, put the top back on the bottle and dumped it on the workbench.

'Do you really need to put that back on?' said Toni in her breathy purr when he picked up the tape he'd removed from her mouth. 'It really hurts.'

'I won't need to, as long as you don't start shouting again.'

'I won't. Promise,' she said with a wicked grin.

'Aye, all right then, but if you break your promise then it goes straight back on.'

'I understand,' she said sweetly. 'Is it me or is it warm in here?' she added, tossing back her head.

'Feels cold to me,' said Caesar.

'Not to me. I feel so hot.'

'That's what you get for going about in fake fur coats.'

'I wasn't expecting to be tied to a chair in a manky old garage.' Toni leaned back in her chair and stuck out her chest, drawing the eyes of the two men. She strained the cloth of her blouse so much the top button pinged off, the blouse popping open to reveal even more cleavage. Despite the situation they were in, Valerie had to stop herself from laughing as she was reminded of the Hulk getting angry. Callum's eyes bulged out of his head as he stared back at Toni, who winked at him.

'That's some party trick, hen,' chuckled Caesar.

'That's nothing compared to what else I can do. Why don't you untie this rope so we can really have some fun together?'

'Sorry, I've got orders.'

'You don't seem like a man who does as he's told.'

'I do when I'm being paid well.'

'And how much is Liam paying you to watch over two helpless females?'

'You're no' helpless, sweetheart. You're trouble.'

'Why, thank you,' she smiled. 'So, you're not a Thompson, then?'

'Nope. I'm just a pal of Liam's. We've known each other a long time. Now that's all the sharing I'm doing with you, so put a sock in it, eh?'

'What the fuck do you think you're doing?' Toni demanded of Callum when he shoved his hand down her top.

'Get your hand out of there,' Caesar growled at him.

'What's the problem?' said Callum, retracting said hand. 'We've got two gorgeous lassies tied up. We can do what we like,' he leered.

Caesar backhanded him across the face, knocking him off his feet.

'You fucking perv,' roared Caesar. 'Try that again and I'll cut your fucking hand off.'

'Why, Caesar,' purred Toni. 'That was very impressive.'

'I hate twats like that,' he replied, glowering at Callum, who was picking himself up off the floor. 'It's so fucking cowardly. You don't treat women like that,' he spat at his colleague.

'All right, man, take it easy,' he whined. 'I didnae mean any offence.'

Toni was growing genuinely interested in Caesar by the minute. She loved a strong, powerful man, especially one with a protective streak. After what she'd been through with Roddy, that meant a lot to her.

'Stand over there,' Caesar told him, pointing to the back of the room. 'Well away from the lassies.'

Callum sighed, stuffed his hands into his jeans pockets and did as he was told.

'Further,' said Caesar, warning in his voice.

With a roll of his eyes, Callum moved to stand in the furthest possible corner.

'Wonderful,' laughed Toni. 'You really are a man, Caesar.'

'In more ways than one,' he replied, eyes twinkling.

The two of them continued to flirt madly with each other, leaving Valerie to wonder if Toni was doing this as part of an escape plan or whether she genuinely liked Caesar. Probably a bit of both. Toni's eyes were often cold, but they sparkled with warmth when she looked at Caesar. If they could get him on their side, they might just get themselves out of this sticky situation.

Caesar leaned into Toni and whispered something in her ear that made her giggle, his eyes continually slipping down to her chest. He might have morals about not touching helpless women, but he certainly had no qualms about ogling them. Toni had noticed this and was sticking out her chest so far Valerie feared she would do herself an injury.

While Toni distracted Caesar and Callum sulked in the corner, Valerie assessed their prison. There was only one way in and out and she knew the door was locked. Her ropes were thick and tied tightly, so she couldn't exactly slip out of them. There was a small hacksaw lying on the workbench close to her, but she wouldn't have a chance of reaching it without drawing attention to herself.

Instead, she turned her attention to listening, attempting to glean more information about where they were. The boat horn sounded at regular intervals and once or twice she heard the passing of an engine, but there were no voices or footsteps outside, no one they could call to for help. It seemed everything rested on her cousin and her formidable charms.

'These ropes are really digging in,' grimaced Toni after twenty minutes of sweet-talking Caesar. 'It hurts,' she added in her best little-girl-lost voice, throwing in a pout for good measure.

'Sorry, doll,' replied Caesar. 'But they need to stay on.'

'Surely you can loosen them a little bit? I promise I won't be naughty. Why would I want to escape when I'm enjoying your company so much?' she winked.

'Liam won't be happy with either of us if I loosen them.'

'What do you care about that? You're your own man who lets no one tell him what to do.'

'Liam's my pal and I promised I'd help him out after he helped me out.'

'And how did he help you?'

'He helped me deal with those bastard McLaren brothers. Do you know them?'

'No, I've never heard of them.'

'They're a couple of arrogant pains in the arse who unfortunately have a lot of pals who kept trying to target me. It took eight of them to pin me down and do this to my face,' he said, gesturing to his scars. 'I got my own back and battered the shite out of several of them, but I needed some back-up to sort them out once and for all.' He spoke with the air of a man who was far above petty crooks like the McLaren brothers and for whom they were just a mere pest. It was clear he was trying to impress Toni.

'And what did you do to them?' purred Toni. 'I bet whatever it was, it was painful.'

'Aye, it was. Davey McLaren now knows what it's like to be shagged by a crowbar.'

'Oooh, nasty,' said Toni. 'I like it.'

'And I popped his brother's left eyeball right out of his fucking heid.'

Valerie was quite sure that was the moment Caesar completely won over her cousin.

'You took his eye?' breathed Toni. 'What did you do with it?'

'I threw it down a drain.'

This appeared to disappoint Toni a little, but the fact that he'd done something she longed to do still impressed her hugely and Toni was not a woman who was easily impressed.

'Tell me, Caesar,' said Toni. 'What will Liam do to us if Frankie doesn't play ball, which I can guarantee he won't? I know my brother very well.'

Caesar's smile fell. 'Well, he said no' to hurt her,' he said, nodding at Valerie. 'But you...'

'I'm a big girl, I can take it,' she said when he trailed off.

'He said we've to cut off your fingers and slice up your face.'

Toni took this news stoically and tilted her chin. 'Thank you for being honest.'

'Nae bother,' he said, looking troubled. 'If it's any consolation, I think it would be a bastarding shame to ruin that gorgeous face.'

'I totally agree. Perhaps we could come to some arrangement where you don't do that to me?'

'I'd love to, doll, but I always repay my debts.'

'You wanted Liam to help you sort out a couple of nasty bastards who hurt you. The scars, by the way, are incredibly sexy and make you look hard and dangerous. He in turn wants you to hurt a helpless woman tied to a chair. It's hardly the same thing, is it?'

'No, it's no',' he replied in a way that indicated this had already occurred to him too.

'He wants me maimed for the rest of my life because of his vendetta against my brother. That's not fair.'

Caesar nodded, grinding the palms of his hands together, as an internal struggle raged.

'So why don't you let us go?' said Toni. 'You could work for my brother, he'd be very grateful to anyone who saved his sister and cousin. He's raking in the cash and he'd pay you really well.'

Hope rose inside Valerie when Caesar appeared to be sorely tempted by the offer.

'Hey,' said a whiny voice.

They all turned to look at Callum, who they'd forgotten was there.

'Don't you fucking dare, mate,' he told Caesar. 'No one betrays the Thompsons.'

'What are you talking about, you daftie?' replied Caesar. 'People do it all the time.'

'Aye, well, that's no reason for you to dae it too. You owe Liam. If it wasnae for him, the McLarens would have killed you by now.'

Caesar turned to Toni almost apologetically. 'I really do owe him.'

'And how will your conscience cope with being responsible for my mutilation?' demanded Toni.

'I'll fucking hate it, but I have to pay my debts.' He appeared to be genuinely stricken by this, but for now, he was sticking to his guns.

17

They all looked to the door when there came the sound of it being unlocked. The door burst open and in charged three men, one of whom was Liam. Their clothing was torn and they had scratches all over their faces and arms.

'What the hell happened?' said Caesar.

'Her fucking brother happened,' exclaimed Liam, waving a hand at Toni. 'He only brought with him three pitbulls, two Alsatians and a fucking Dobermann and set the bastards on us. Then he and his thick bastard friends stood there laughing while they tried to tear us to shreds.'

'Where are the rest of your men?'

'Fuck knows. The last time I saw them, they were running away to avoid being fucking eaten.'

Valerie had to bite her lower lip so she wouldn't laugh. She was glad Toni hadn't laughed out loud, although her eyes danced with mirth because Valerie was quite sure her cousin would be the one to suffer for this.

'Right, you,' said Liam, storming over to Toni. 'Time to pay for your brother's huge mistake.' He held his hand out to Caesar. 'Knife.'

Toni glanced at Caesar, who appeared torn, but still produced the knife from inside his jacket and handed it to Liam.

'Why the fuck are you standing in the corner like a stupid wean?' Liam demanded of Callum.

'He told me to, man,' he whined back, pointing at Caesar.

'Why?'

'Because he started groping the prisoners,' replied Caesar.

'Not Valerie?' he yelled, making Callum cringe.

'No, Toni.'

'Oh,' he said, simmering down again. 'Who hasnae groped her?'

'Piss off, you cheeky bastard,' yelled Toni.

Liam sighed. 'Put the tape back over her massive gob, will you?'

Caesar gave Toni an apologetic look as he tore off a strip of tape with his teeth and gently smoothed it down over her mouth.

'Frankie had his chance and he fucked it up,' said Liam. 'Now he's gonnae get his sister back in pieces. We'll start with her right little finger. Don't make things harder,' he snapped when Toni screwed both hands up into fists.

She snarled abuse at him into the tape and her eyes said she'd like to murder him.

'Have it your own way,' yelled Liam when she still refused to extend her fingers. 'I'll just cut your whole fucking hand off instead.'

'Stop,' cried Valerie. 'There's no need for this.'

'There's every need,' retorted Liam, rounding on her, so furious his hair appeared to stand on end. 'I warned you what would happen if Frankie didn't behave himself and he fucking didn't. If you want someone to blame, blame him.'

'No,' screamed Valerie when he grabbed Toni's left arm – her fingers still determinedly wrapped up into a ball – and positioned the blade over her wrist.

Toni once more gazed pleadingly up at Caesar, whose eyes were wide with sadness, but he made no move to intervene.

'Do you hear that?' said one of Liam's men, who had scratches on his face and bite marks on both forearms.

'Hear what?' said Liam, holding Toni's arm firmly.

'Barking.'

Liam paled, released Toni and whipped round, eyes darting left and right as he listened. 'I hear it,' he rasped. 'Frankie's here.'

Valerie screamed when Liam raised the knife. The blade flashed but rather than remove Toni's hand, he cut her bonds instead. 'Take her to the car,' he told Caesar. 'We'll need a hostage.'

Toni screamed into the gag as she was hauled upright by Caesar. When she attempted to go to her cousin, Caesar dragged her to the door.

'I'll be fine,' Valerie called to her. 'Don't worry about me.'

Liam had decided that Toni was more valuable to Frankie, making Valerie disposable, despite his feelings for her. Frantically she writhed as Liam used the knife to saw through the rope binding her to the chair, but her hands were still tied behind her back. He held her before him.

'So I'm a human shield now, am I?' snapped Valerie. 'You really know how to treat a lady.'

'Sorry, but I'm no' getting bitten again.'

At least he hadn't pressed the knife he still held to her throat. That was something.

The sound of barking grew louder, as did the shouts and cries from outside before the sounds died away.

Now in the silence, the three men and Callum all regarded each other quizzically. They all looked expectantly at the door, but no one charged through it, and they all started to sweat, grips on the knives tightening as they waited for the inevitable storm to descend.

'Maybe they've gone?' said Callum hopefully.

'Frankie doesnae give in that easily,' said Liam grimly, keeping a tight hold of the back of Valerie's neck. 'Take a look,' he told Callum.

'Me?' he exclaimed.

'Aye, you. What the fuck's the matter with you? Are you scared or something?' he yelled when Callum just stood there.

'I'm no' feared of Frankie but I am of vicious dogs. I was bitten when I was wee.'

'If you don't go and look,' said Liam, gathering all the formidable menace at his disposal, 'I'll stick this knife right up your hole.'

Callum sighed, knowing he had little choice. Slowly he crept to the door, eyes riveted to it.

'Hurry up,' Liam hissed at him.

Callum ignored this and continued to slowly approach the door. He reached out a shaking hand for the handle, grasped it and took a deep breath, everyone else holding their own breath in anticipation.

He flung the garage door upwards and simultaneously leapt aside to avoid the pack of savage dogs he felt sure was waiting for him on the other side, but there wasn't a dog or ginger psychopath in sight.

'What the fuck?' frowned Liam. His eyes widened. 'He must have spotted Toni and Caesar and gone after them.'

'Thank Christ for that,' sighed one of his friends, who'd also been scratched and bitten.

'Where's your car?' Liam asked him.

'On the other side of the building.'

'Let's move. We'll head back to mine and take it from there. You're coming with us, sweetheart,' he told Valerie.

'What joy,' she retorted.

Liam propelled her forwards, his hand still firmly on the back of her neck. She was tempted to try to escape, but these men were all armed and on the edge, so she didn't think it wise to annoy them. They might just lash out first and think later, so she allowed Liam to propel her out of the garage and around the side of the building, where she could see that she was indeed by the edge of the river, but whereabouts on that 106-mile stretch of water she had no idea. Boats were passing by, but they were too far away to help her. Frantically she looked around, hoping to see her relatives waiting to free her, but no one was there. Liam was right, they must have gone after Toni, leaving her behind. At least her cousin was safe, that was one less thing to worry about. Now she could concentrate on escaping.

She was ushered towards a light green Honda Insight and shoved into the back, pinned between Liam and Callum while the other two men got into the front seats.

'Fucking drive, Rob,' Liam bawled at the owner of the car.

Rob nodded, started the engine and sped off.

'Well, that went tits up,' exclaimed the man in the passenger seat.

'Aye, thank you, Tommy, we know that,' retorted Liam.

'We've got Frankie's cousin. We need to use her to make him back off,' Tommy practically shrieked.

'Will you shut the fuck up?' Liam yelled at him. 'I cannae hear myself think.' Liam looked at Valerie curiously. 'What do you think Frankie will do now?'

'He's completely unpredictable,' she replied. 'So, I can only give you my best guess.'

'Go on then.'

'Right now, if he hasn't got Toni back already, then he will be trying to do that and he'll succeed. Caesar seemed smart and tough, but he can't stand up to Frankie, his pals and a pack of vicious dogs alone.'

'Frankie can keep that daft cow, she did my heid in. But will he come for you?'

'Aye, because he has to. I don't mean as much to him as Toni does, but you took someone close to him and he can't take that lying down.'

'How will he do that?'

'Who knows? Like I said, he's unpredictable. I never thought he'd use dogs because he doesn't like them. He doesn't like any animal, in fact. He's also extremely imaginative, especially when it comes to causing other people pain, so god only knows what's running through his mind. But he won't hit you immediately, he'll make you wait. He'll enjoy thinking about you worrying when he's going to strike.'

'Like he worries me,' said Liam, puffing up with bravado.

'He should worry you. Everyone, no matter how tough they are, should worry if Frankie's got them in his sights because he is a genuine lunatic who will stop at nothing to get his own way. He might even tear straight through me to get to you if he's determined enough. Toni will tell him she wants me back safely, but he could blame anything that happens to me on you and she'd be none the wiser, so don't think my presence will keep you safe.'

'I'm no' wantin' you to keep me safe. I want to use you to set a trap.'

'That's what I would do in your shoes.'

'How about you switch sides and start working for me? Help me trap the bastard and finish him off and you'll be a key player in my operation.'

'No, thanks. People who betray Frankie end up dead.'

'It won't matter if I kill him.'

'You won't. Frankie will be the next king around here and you would have been much better off making peace with him, but that will be impossible after this. He has to retaliate in a big way to maintain his reputation and Frankie's reputation means the world to him. You're going to die, Liam.'

'Not today,' he growled determinedly.

Valerie shrugged. 'Perhaps not today, but he will get to you and there's nothing you can do about it.'

Valerie groaned with pain when Callum slammed his elbow into her stomach.

'What the fuck did you do that for?' exclaimed Liam, reaching over Valerie, who had doubled over with pain, to smack him across the head.

'She was winding you up, man,' he replied. 'Making you doubt yourself, and that is something we don't need right now.'

'He's right,' said Tommy from the front seat.

'I asked her a question and she gave me a straight answer.'

'That bird's got into your heid,' said Tommy. 'You need to ditch her fast.'

'She's our leverage,' Liam retorted.

'You mean you don't want to let her go. Boot her arse oot the car right now.'

'No. She's the only advantage we have over Frankie.'

The argument was stopped by Valerie slamming her forehead into the side of Callum's face, bouncing his head off the window, the blood that spurted from his nose smearing across the glass.

'You wee sod,' yelled Valerie.

Callum groaned, dazed. Valerie managed to bring up her legs and turn, so her back was against Liam's side, and started frantically kicking at Callum with such force the door popped open.

'Stop,' cried Liam, grabbing her and pulling her back, but the car drove on with the door flapping open, a semi-conscious Callum hanging out of it. 'Pull over, ya choob,' Liam told Rob.

Rob pulled the car up at the kerb while Valerie screamed her head off for help.

Liam started to panic when passers-by stopped and stared. They pointed at the car, wondering if they should intervene.

Rob and Tommy leapt out and between them picked up Callum, whose head lolled, and he groaned in pain.

'Get the fuck off me,' Valerie yelled at Liam, but he held her fast.

Callum was poured into the front passenger seat by Tommy and Rob. When Tommy attempted to get into the back seat, Valerie lashed out with her legs, keeping him at bay.

'Hurry up and get in,' Rob told him.

'I cannae, this mad bitch won't let me.'

'Help,' Valerie screamed at the top of her lungs. 'I've been kidnapped.'

Some of the passers-by, men and women alike, started to jog up to the car.

'We have to ditch her before someone calls the polis,' Tommy desperately told Liam.

'No,' snarled Liam, holding her tighter.

'Kidnap,' screamed Valerie, still thrashing, her voice muffled by Liam clamping his hand down over her mouth.

'Drive,' Liam told Rob.

Rob, who was panicking with all the people approaching the car, nodded and hit the accelerator, steering the car back into the traffic, the rear door still flapping open, leaving Tommy behind.

Looking out of the back window, Valerie saw Tommy race off, pursued by four men.

'Callum,' cried Liam, kicking the back of his seat. 'Wake up, you daft bastard, and close the fucking door.'

When he wouldn't wake, Rob was forced to pull up on the next street, hop out and close it before jumping back into the driver's seat and speeding off. Valerie continued to struggle in Liam's arms. He grimaced when she bit his finger and writhed in his grip but he was too strong and she couldn't free herself.

'Tommy's gonnae be so pissed off at us for leaving him behind,' commented Rob.

'He'll be fine, he's a fast runner,' said Liam dismissively. 'Callum,' he yelled, this time managing to elicit a response in the form of a groan. 'Have you still got the tape?'

'Aye,' he mumbled, fishing it out of his jacket pocket.

'We need to gag her.'

'I think she broke my nose,' Callum replied, his voice sounding even more whiny and nasal than usual.

'You'll be fine,' snapped Liam. 'Now help.'

Callum climbed into the back seat. Valerie continued to struggle but the two men finally gagged her and bound her ankles together.

'Now do you realise why I want her working for us?' Liam asked his friends. 'You see what she can do?'

'You should dump her in the fucking Clyde,' replied Callum. 'After tying an anvil to her.'

'Shut it and get back into the front seat.'

'With pleasure,' he mumbled, climbing back over into the front. 'I don't want to get headbutted again.'

'Calm down,' Liam told Valerie. 'I don't want to hurt you, but I will if I have to.'

She narrowed her eyes at him over the top of the tape.

Valerie saw the panic in his eyes and recognised that she was pushing him to his limit and that it would probably be wise not to push him any further. Still, she'd tried and she had the bruises to prove it. Frankie couldn't ask for more.

'Where are we going?' said Rob.

'Let's head to Bill's,' replied Liam. 'He'll know what to do.'

Valerie knew Liam's stepfather was called Bill and assumed that was who he was referring to. This wasn't good, as Bill had a reputation as a vicious brute who hated her family. He would not be impressed with a McVay being brought into his home.

'I'll call Caesar and tell him to meet us there,' added Liam, producing his phone.

Something cold crept down Liam's spine when he was unable to get hold of his friend on the phone. Instead, he sent Caesar a text message, he could do nothing else.

Liam kept a tight hold of Valerie the entire journey into Govan, but she made no move to escape, feeling tired and sore and knowing her efforts would be futile. Perhaps there would be a moment when they got her out of the car? Perhaps she could draw someone's attention?

This hope was crushed when they headed up the driveway of a private bungalow, shielded from view of the road by trees and high hedges, which was probably why Liam had elected to come here. Judging by his home, Bill was pretty well off.

As they pulled up, the front door opened and a short, bald, muscular man stepped outside, watching the car grimly as it rolled to a halt. At his heels obediently sat two Rottweilers. Valerie was starting to see why Liam had decided to come here. Maybe he was hoping Bill's Rottweilers could beat Frankie's savage pack?

'Wit the hell's this?' demanded Bill when Liam got out of the car, dragging Valerie with him.

'She's a McVay,' he replied.

Bill's round face turned purple, the livid colour shooting up into his bald scalp. 'You brought a fucking McVay to my hoose? Wit are you thinking, ya prick? Get rid of it right now or I'll be washing the stink out of my carpet for weeks.'

'Take it easy, Bill,' said Liam. 'There is method to my madness.'

'Aye, that'll be a fucking first. So which one's this?'

'Valerie, Frankie's cousin.'

'Where's the sister? You said you were gonnae get her.'

'Caesar hasnae turned up with her?'

'No, no one has, and why have you brought this one here? You were supposed to take her to your garage.'

'Aye, I did, but Frankie found us there, we think, anyway.'

'You don't know?' exclaimed Bill. 'And why are your clothes all torn up?'

'Can we come in?' said Liam wearily. 'I'd rather talk inside.'

'Fine. I suppose I'll have to put up with a McVay wench in my home,' said Bill, frowning at Valerie.

Liam took Valerie by the arm and led her inside, Callum and Rob following. Bill and his dogs brought up the rear. Valerie felt she was being led inside to her doom.

18

Bill's house was large and very well maintained, with expensive furniture and thick carpets, but it was ruined by the stink of dog. The place looked spotless but the smell of fur had seeped into everything and Valerie wrinkled her nose. She'd never liked the smell of dogs.

'Sit there and behave,' Liam told her, pushing her onto the couch.

'I'll have to have the couch deep cleaned now,' commented Bill, regarding her with distaste.

Valerie gave him a haughty look. She would have loved to tell him what she thought of him, but the tape prevented it.

Liam appeared distinctly nervous when both Rottweilers began to growl at him, baring their teeth.

'What's wrong with them?' he demanded of his stepfather.

'They think you're the enemy because you stink of dog,' replied Bill. 'You bloody reek of it, actually. In fact, it looks like you lost a fight with one. Down,' he yelled at the animals.

The two dogs stopped growling, but continued to stare hungrily at Liam.

Bill sank into an armchair, the dogs sitting either side of him at his feet. 'What the fuck happened?'

Liam relayed the entire episode, and when his stepson had finished, Bill sighed deeply.

'Have you got some ice for my face, man?' Callum asked Bill. 'It's fucking aching.'

Bill's face turned purple again, starting from the neck up, and he leapt to his feet. 'How fucking stupid can you get?' he roared, causing the dogs' ears to prick up.

'I only want a wee bit of ice,' whined Callum.

'I'm no' talking about the ice. I'm talking about this almighty fuck-up. Why the hell did you send Caesar away with Toni? She was our biggest bargaining chip and she's probably back with Frankie now.'

'I thought if I split up the hostages, I'd divide Frankie's men,' replied Liam.

'Do yourself a favour, son, and never think again. Everyone knows he's possessive over his sister and would do nothing to risk hurting her. You should have sent this one off with Caesar and kept Toni.'

'He's got a thing for this one,' said Rob, nodding at Liam, who glowered back at him.

'A thing for a McVay?' exclaimed Bill. 'What sort of fucking bad taste is that?'

'I don't have a thing for her,' replied Liam. 'I had seconds to make a call and I made the right one.'

'The shite you did,' snarled Bill. 'Toni would have been much more valuable.'

'Valerie isnae any old cousin, she works for Frankie. She's battered plenty of people on his say-so.'

'Has she now?' said Bill more thoughtfully. 'All right, maybe not as big a fuck-up as I thought. Take her gag off, Rob.'

Rob obeyed and hastily took a step back, not wanting to be kicked or headbutted by Valerie.

'She's quite pretty without the gag,' commented Bill.

'Don't get too close,' said Rob when Bill stood before her. 'She did that to Callum's face.'

'You wouldnae be so stupid as to try and hurt me, would you, sweetheart?' Bill asked Valerie in a patronising tone.

'I'm making no promises,' she replied stonily.

'What work do you do for Frankie?'

'Like Liam said, I batter people for him.'

'Why does Frankie need a woman to do his dirty work? Cannae he dae it himself?'

'Of course he can and he's usually more than happy to, but Frankie doesn't like battering women.'

'I didnae think he had any morals.'

'Hitting women won't help Frankie build his reputation as a hard man, so me and Toni do it for him.'

'Toni gets her hands dirty too, does she? I thought she'd be too afraid of chipping a nail.'

'She enjoys a good scrap and she's really handy too.'

'What else do you do for Frankie?'

'That's it.'

'You expect me to believe that?'

'It doesn't matter what you believe because it's still the truth.'

'You deal for him, don't you?'

'No. I would never touch drugs, whether that's selling them or taking them.'

'Bollocks. If you tell us all about his operation, then you might just get out of this house alive.'

Valerie's heart was pounding. She was being held hostage and not even Liam's crush on her could protect her from this bald, angry beast of a man, who it appeared had a lot more power in his family than she'd thought.

'I can't tell you what I don't know,' she told Bill. 'Ask around and you'll see I've never gone near the drugs side of Frankie's operation.'

'You expect me to believe that ginger prick uses you, a woman, to do his heavy work?'

'Aye, he does, because I'm good at it.'

Bill laughed. The sound was so unexpected and full of humour that the dogs turned their heads to look at him.

'This is the biggest load of shite I've ever heard in my life,' he said. 'If you don't tell me all about Frankie's operation, then we'll start getting medieval on you. Do you know what that means, doll?'

'Torture?'

'Aye, well done. So, start talking. I don't want to torture you, but I will if I have to.'

Valerie took a deep breath to steady the frantic beat of her heart. 'I don't know anything. Frankie plays his cards close to his chest. I bet the only other person who knows the full extent of his operation – other than Frankie himself – is Duncan Blackwood.'

'That wee fanny is no' the big man everyone thinks he is. He likes to make out that he's Don Corleone when in fact he's a fucking window licker from Partick. I bet he won't be around for much longer now he's got that ginger viper in his nest. Now fucking talk,' he barked. Valerie glared back at him defiantly. 'Right, that's it. Rob, get my blowtorch,' he ordered, his gaze locked on Valerie.

'Er,' said Rob, glancing at his friends. 'Where is it?'

'In my shed.'

'In the garden?'

'Aye, course it's in the garden. Where else do you think I'd put my fucking shed, in the downstairs cludgy?'

'Oh, right. Back in a sec.'

As he left the room, Liam said, 'There's no need for this, Bill. We're not psychos.'

'Needs must, son. You'll never be the big dog unless you're willing to do the unpleasant things.'

'But she's a woman.'

'So? She's up to her neck in drugs and violence.'

'Not in the drugs,' sighed Valerie.

'She chose this life,' continued Bill, ignoring her. 'So she should be prepared to deal with the consequences.'

'It doesn't matter what you do to me,' said Valerie, who was clinging onto her composure by her fingernails. 'I can't tell you anything.'

'You'll soon start talking when you smell your skin cooking.'

'I don't think...' began Liam.

'Where is that fucking dingbat with my blowtorch?' yelled Bill, so loudly he agitated the dogs. 'Oh, finally,' he said when Rob ambled in, looking confused.

'I found the blowtorch,' he told Bill. 'But I couldnae find any gas canisters to go with it.'

'They were right there with the torch.'

'No, they weren't. I looked.'

'Then you didnae look hard enough.'

'My maw has a wee blowtorch she uses when she makes crème brûlées,' said Callum. 'I could ask her if you could borrow it?'

Bill's eyebrows shot up. 'Crème brûlées, are you serious? You're making us look like proper pricks in front of our prisoner. Forget the blowtorch, get me the pliers.'

'Where are they?' said Rob.

Bill grunted with rage. 'In the fucking shed,' he exploded, making the dogs whine and paw at the carpet.

Rob sighed and shuffled back out, taking the useless blowtorch with him.

'It looks like your organisation isn't very organised,' Valerie told Bill.

'It's all these fucking young pups, they havenae got a clue. Anyway, while we're waiting, you can tell me what you do know.'

'Well,' she said thoughtfully.

Bill's eyes lit up with hope that she was finally opening up.

'Frankie did have his appendix removed a couple of years ago.'

The slap to her face knocked her back into the couch.

'Don't get smart with me, you bitch,' Bill shouted.

'There's no need for that,' said Liam, helping Valerie to sit back upright, her left cheek bright red.

'Was Rob right?' growled Bill. 'Do you have a thing for her? If you're going soft over a fucking McVay bird, then my foot will be having a quiet word with your arse.'

'I'm no' going soft over her,' he exclaimed. 'I just don't like hurting women.'

'Since when? You were quite happy to give Denise Michaels a whack in the face.'

'Because she came at me with a bread knife. I was only defending myself.'

'And why did she dae that? Because you were shagging her best friend.'

'That's no' important. I think this is a mistake.'

'You brought her here because you need my help. Well, this is my help, so get onboard or fuck off.'

'I thought we'd be coming up with a plan to use her to lure Frankie into a trap, no' torturing her.'

'If we're to lure him into a trap, we need to learn everything we can about him and she can tell us. Ah, finally,' said Bill when Rob returned. 'And he's managed to find a pair of pliers. So he does have a fucking use after all.'

'There's no need to be rude,' sniffed Rob.

'Shut yer geggy, ya whining wee lassie,' said Bill, snatching the pliers off him. 'Right, now we're getting somewhere.' He turned back to Valerie. 'Start talking or I'll pull out all your fingernails. Then I'll start on your teeth.'

'Could you go for the teeth first?' she replied. 'I've got one at the back that's been giving me a bit of gyp.'

'You've got baws, hen, I'll gi'e you that. No wonder Frankie employs you. I'll gi'e you one last chance – what do you know about Frankie's operation and I'm no' talking about his appendix?'

'Nothing and that's the truth.'

'Fine. Untie her hands,' he told Liam.

His stepson sighed, produced his knife and cut the tape binding her. As he cut, Valerie looked up at him beseechingly, just as Toni had done with Caesar earlier, but just like Caesar, he didn't intervene to help her.

'Hold out your hands,' Bill told her.

'No,' said Valerie, hiding them behind her back.

'Why does every woman have to do things the hard way?' he sighed. 'Boys.'

Callum and Rob leapt forward to grab her hands. Her forehead once again connected with Callum's nose and he dropped like a stone, out cold, causing Bill to bark with laughter. He was a little alarmed when she kicked Rob in the crotch and he fell to his knees. She swiftly followed this up with a kick to Rob's face, knocking him flat onto his back.

'I'm starting to see what you mean, Liam,' said Bill, dropping the pliers and rushing to restrain her. 'Stop it, you bitch,' he yelled, slamming his fist into her stomach.

This blow was much harder than the one Callum had given her and she gasped before going limp, all the air pushed from her body, pain throbbing in her abdomen.

'That's got her,' grinned Bill.

He dragged Valerie up off the couch and threw her to the floor, face down. Using his knees to pin down her upper back, he grabbed her right hand and stretched out her index finger.

'Talk or I'll rip out your fucking nail,' he growled.

'Go for it,' she panted, her breath slowly coming back to her. 'Then Toni won't be able to nag me about painting them.'

'Have it your own way,' said Bill, grasping the edge of the nail with the pliers.

'Wait,' exclaimed Liam. 'I've got a better idea. I know where her boyfriend lives. She'd talk to save him.'

'No,' cried Valerie. 'You'll leave him alone.'

'Looks like you touched a nerve there, son,' smiled Bill. 'That's defrosted the ice queen.'

'She'll do anything to protect that soft lump of shite,' said Liam.

'Does he work for Frankie too?' Bill asked Liam.

'No, he doesn't,' yelled Valerie. 'He's sweet and honest and nothing to do with your sordid little world.'

'Oh, you think so, do you?' said Liam. 'Then why has he been seen in the local clubs lately, dealing?'

'You're lying. Seb would never go anywhere near drugs.'

'You really don't know, do you?'

'About him dealing? No, I don't because it's not true.'

'He was seen in Archaos and Bonkers, dealing coke.'

'They don't allow that sort of thing in those clubs.'

'I didnae think a McVay could sound naïve,' laughed Bill. 'There are ways to get around club security, sweetheart,' he told her.

'You're both full of shit,' she spat.

'Go get her boyfriend,' Bill told Liam. 'Finally, she's talking. Imagine what she'll say when I'm pulling out his teeth.'

'No,' Valerie screamed, frantically writhing in an attempt to free herself. 'You so much as touch him and I swear to almighty God, I'll kill you all.'

'Wow, this one's got claws,' grinned Bill, who was having to press down harder to restrain her.

Under the couch she was lying beside, Valerie spotted a dog ball. She grabbed it and hurled it over the couch. The two Rottweilers leapt as one for it, knocking over their owner in their eagerness.

'Argh, you silly bastards,' cried Bill as he toppled sideways.

Valerie leapt to her feet and ran for the front door.

'Someone stop her,' yelled Bill.

As Liam was the only one on his feet, he lunged for her.

Her breath coming out in frantic bursts, Valerie grabbed the front door handle, yanked it open and charged outside. Liam grabbed her arm and tried to pull her back inside but she turned and swung her fist, striking him in the solar plexus. Liam was winded and he released her but he kept moving, throwing himself forward and tackling her to the ground, refusing to allow his only hold over Frankie McVay to escape.

'Help, help,' screamed Valerie. 'Fire,' she added, recalling that was the thing to shout if you needed help as people were more likely to respond to it. 'Fire!'

As she yelled, she fought against Liam, who had hold of her right leg and was attempting to drag her towards him. She kicked him in the face but still he held on. As Bill ran out of the house, she managed to flip herself onto her back. She'd fallen beside a small rockery and as Bill ran to assist his stepson, she snatched up a small pottery figure of a snail and hurled it at him. The snail struck Bill in the chest, making him halt in his tracks. Desperately she delivered a kick to Liam's arm and this time he released her with a grimace of pain.

Valerie scrambled to her feet and charged up the driveway.

'Satan, Lucifer, attack,' Bill yelled at his dogs.

The two Rottweilers charged out of the house and launched themselves at Liam, delighted to finally be able to tackle the person who had offended them from the moment he'd come through the door stinking of rival dogs. With a cry, Liam fell to the ground, covering his head with his hands as the dogs tore at his clothes.

'Not him, you fucking idiots,' Bill bellowed at the dogs. 'I mean her.'

The Rottweilers paid no attention to their master and continued to savage Liam.

Valerie glanced back over her shoulder at the circus and laughed, her heart lifting as she was so close to freedom...

She was knocked off her feet by the small red car pulling onto the drive, a young, startled blonde woman behind the wheel. Valerie hit the bonnet and rolled off with a groan, landing on the tarmac.

'Fucking hell, Caroline,' grinned Bill, who once more had his dogs under control, holding them firmly by their collars while Liam lay on the ground in a daze. 'For once, your shitty driving came in handy.'

'Oh, my god,' said Caroline, getting out of the car. 'I didn't see her. Where did she come from?' She knelt beside Valerie, hands fluttering with agitation. 'Are you all right? I'm so, so sorry. I'll call an ambulance.'

'You're no' calling anyone,' said Bill. 'Just get inside, babe, and don't worry about it. You did good.'

'How can I have done good? I ran someone over.'

'You mean you stopped her from escaping.'

'Escaping? Bill, what is going on?'

Caroline squeaked with shock when Valerie grabbed her arm and used her to drag herself upright before kicking her in the back, knocking her into the two men.

'Sorry, Caroline,' Valerie called after her as she leapt into her car. 'You seem really nice. You can do better than that arsehole.'

Valerie was delighted to see the keys were still in the ignition. She pulled the door shut and locked it, wincing at the pain in her ribs, grinning through the window as Liam and Bill charged after her, the unfortunate Caroline shoved aside.

Valerie backed the car out onto the road and sped off, leaving the Thompson men far behind. She laughed out loud, unable to believe she'd managed to escape and with all her fingernails still attached. Adrenaline pounded through her body and her hands shook. She had to force herself to slow down, not wanting to get pulled over. Although she'd had driving lessons, she still didn't have her licence. On the bright side, she couldn't imagine anyone calling the police to complain about the car being stolen by a fleeing kidnap victim.

19

Valerie drove straight to Seb's house. The clock on the dashboard told her it was just before eight o'clock in the evening and it was starting to get dark. She knocked several times on Seb's front door but, to her frustration, no one answered. The house was dark and silent. She'd thought Seb was studying tonight, so he should be in. Her blood ran cold as she recalled what Liam had said. Had he been telling the truth after all?

Fury coursed through her and she jumped back into the car and drove to Frankie's house to find all the lights burning. She banged on the door with her fist.

'Open up, Frankie,' she yelled.

The door was pulled open by Jamesie, whose eyes widened. 'Val,' he beamed. 'Hey, she's here,' he called over his shoulder.

'Get out of my way,' she said, shoving him aside as she stalked into the house.

'Are you on your period or something?' he retorted as he closed the door.

Valerie found Frankie sitting on the couch in the front room of his home. Tam, Paul and, to her surprise, Caesar were also present.

Toni stood in the middle of the room, face streaked with tears and mascara, her curls in disarray.

'Val,' she cried, rushing up to her cousin and flinging her arms around her. 'Thank Christ, I've been so worried about you.'

'Are you okay?' Valerie asked her.

'I'm fine, but what about you?' She leaned back to look her cousin in the face. 'They hit you, you've got a bruise on your face. The total bastards,' she yelled, face creasing with anger. 'What is it?' she added when Valerie winced.

'My ribs are sore.'

'Sit down, take the weight off,' said Toni, leading her to the opposite couch. 'Oy, give her space,' she snapped at Jamesie when he sat down beside Valerie.

'So-rry,' he said, holding up his hands and sliding further up the couch.

'Did they beat you up?' Toni anxiously asked her. 'Do you need to go to hospital?'

'No on both counts,' replied Valerie. 'I was hit by a car.'

'What?' exclaimed Toni.

'Luckily it was going slowly at the time. That was an accident, actually. I was escaping from Bill Thompson's house and a woman I assume is his girlfriend turned onto the drive. It wasn't her fault, she didn't realise I was there.'

'Bill Thompson's?' said Frankie. 'That's where they took you?'

Valerie nodded.

'I told you we should check there but you said he was nothing to do with that side of the family business,' said Toni, rounding on her brother.

Frankie merely shrugged and held up his hands.

'We've been tearing this city apart looking for you,' Toni told Valerie. 'We haven't just been sat here on our arses.'

'I know, it's fine,' said Valerie. 'I'm just glad you're okay, I've been really worried.'

'Oh, I'm fine, thanks to Caesar.'

'He helped you escape?'

'Aye, he did,' said Toni with a seductive smile Caesar's way. 'There were two of Liam's men waiting outside the garage. They had orders to take me to another manky garage of Liam's, only this one contained a table many people have been strapped to and tortured.'

'That's what he was going to do to you?'

Toni nodded grimly. 'Until Caesar decided that wasn't going to happen, twatted the other two men and brought me here.' She gazed adoringly at Caesar, who smiled back at her. 'My hero.'

'Thank you for doing that for her, Caesar,' said Valerie.

He nodded in response.

'So what happened to you?' Toni asked her.

'Before I reply to that,' she said, looking to Frankie, 'I need an answer to a very important question – is Seb dealing drugs for you?'

'What?' laughed Toni. 'A wannabe minister, really?'

'That's what Liam Thompson told me,' Valerie replied, her gaze on Frankie, whose expression was giving nothing away. 'He told me Seb's been dealing at Bonkers and Archaos.'

'He was lying,' said Toni with a dismissive wave of the hand. 'No way would preacher boy get wrapped up in anything like that.' She frowned when her brother was still quiet. 'Would he?' she added uncertainly.

'That's the question, isn't it, Frankie?' said Valerie.

Frankie wasn't used to people meeting his gaze so steadily, but Valerie did. In fact, she always had. She'd never seemed afraid of him like everyone else. On the one hand, this infuriated him because he wanted everyone to fear him, but on the other, it had made him respect her, which was why he decided to give her an honest answer.

'He is working for me,' he said.

Valerie inhaled sharply and a lump formed in her throat. 'I knew it.'

'But he's no' dealing drugs. He refused to do anything like that. All he's doing is delivering a few messages for me.'

'In nightclubs?' she said sceptically.

'Aye. You see, I don't communicate with my street dealers directly, that way the polis can never tie me to them. I have intermediaries who do all that for me.'

'And who take the risk for you too.'

'They know what they're getting into when they take on the job, but the risk is pretty low. The messages are coded, so if anyone did get hold of them, they wouldnae know what they meant. There's no law against passing on notes.'

'That depends on what the note says.'

'It's a pure clever set-up,' said Tam, looking proudly at his nephew. 'Frankie thought of it all on his own too. Duncan fucking Blackwood could never come up with such a smart scheme.'

The way the men sneered disdainfully at Duncan's name told Valerie he would probably very soon mysteriously vanish and Frankie would take over entirely.

'To anyone not in the know, the message will just look like a load of shite,' continued Frankie.

'How long has he been working for you?' said Valerie.

Frankie shrugged, the belligerence in the gesture making her grit her teeth. 'Just a couple of days.'

'You recruited him at Toni's birthday party, didn't you?'

'I talked to him about it, told him he could make some serious money. He called me the next morning to accept my very kind offer.'

'And he didn't tell you?' a shocked Toni asked Valerie.

Angrily she shook her head. 'No, he didn't.'

'Oh, dear,' sniggered Frankie. 'No' a good basis for a relationship.'

The fact that he found it funny made her furious. 'How much are you paying him?'

'Two hundred quid per message. He's doing it because he wants to get the money together so you can move away. Apparently that's your big dream,' he frowned at her.

Valerie turned cold. Seb, in his innocence, had told Frankie their plans without realising it was a secret. 'And you used that to punish me, didn't you, Frankie? No one leaves without your permission.'

Frankie just glowered back at her.

'Where is he?'

'Archaos.'

'Where are you going?' said Toni when Valerie got to her feet.

'To get Seb before something bad happens to him. The Thompsons know he's working for Frankie and the fact that they knew this before I did fucking pisses me off, by the way,' she said with a glare Frankie's way before looking back at Toni. 'And they might decide to target him now they've lost me and you.'

'God, you're right. I'll come with you.'

'Toni,' barked Frankie when she made for the door with Valerie. 'You're staying here.'

'But Val needs help,' she said, rounding on her brother. 'And after everything she's been through, she deserves it.'

'She can go, but you stay.'

Toni tilted back her head. 'No. If you want me to stay then you'll have to lock me up in the cellar.'

'Don't fucking tempt me.'

Caesar walked to the door. 'Let's go, doll,' he said to Toni.

'What the hell do you think you're doing?' yelled Frankie, leaping to his feet.

'The lassies are gonnae need some muscle and it looks like you're no' gonnae gi'e it, so someone has to.'

'If you want to stay on my right side – which is the sensible place to be – you'll stay right where you fucking are.' Frankie smiled with triumph when Caesar hesitated.

'Let's go,' said Caesar.

Frankie's smile dropped and a murderous rage came into his eyes, but he allowed the three of them to leave unhurt.

'Cheeky fucking bastard,' commented Tam when they'd gone. 'That twat's already far too up his own arse. He has to go.'

'I'm no' so sure,' said Frankie. 'His loyalty's to Toni, that's obvious, meaning he'll go all out to protect her and I don't want anyone taking my sister again.'

'You mean you're gonnae make him her bodyguard?' chuckled Tam.

'Aye, how no'? The Thompsons snatching Toni and Valerie gave my reputation a good gubbing. Now I need to make sure it's protected and he can help me dae that.'

'You surprise me, Frankie, son. I felt sure his heid would end up with your other trophies.'

'No, it won't. Not yet, anyway. He'll live as long as he's useful to me.'

'What about Val? She's getting a bit fucking mouthy.'

'Now Seb's in, she'll have no choice but to work for me too.'

'Why are you so set on having her working with us? Do you have a thing for her or something?'

'God, no,' he laughed. 'She's far too uptight for me, but she escaped from the Thompsons all on her own. How many men do you know who could manage that, never mind women?'

'No' many,' agreed Paul, who'd always been rather fond of Valerie.

'Exactly,' said Frankie. 'Tonight's just made me even more certain she'll be an asset.'

'She's a stubborn cow,' said Tam. 'Always was, right from being wee. It won't be that easy. And she wants to leave Glesga.'

'She won't leave.' Frankie's expression darkened. 'I'll make sure of it.'

* * *

'Thanks for this, Caesar,' said Valerie from the back seat as he drove the three of them to Archaos. They were in the BMW 5 series Toni had been put in after Liam had ordered him to take her away, which turned out to be Caesar's own car.

'Nae bother,' he replied as he drove.

'Caesar is very obliging,' purred Toni, who was in the front passenger seat, resting her hand on his thigh.

He looked at her and winked.

'The Thompsons will be furious,' Valerie told him. 'It'll be dangerous for you if they spot you.'

He shrugged. 'I'll take my chances.'

'That's very brave,' Toni told him admiringly.

'I've never shied away from a fight in my life and I'm no' starting now. Who is this Seb anyway?'

'My boyfriend,' said Valerie. 'He's so innocent. Frankie never should have dragged him into his world.'

'Frankie looked pretty pissed off about us disobeying him,' said Toni.

'Aye, well, fuck him,' muttered Valerie. 'We were kidnapped today because of him and he's roped my boyfriend into a world he is not able to cope with. God, I hope we get to him in time,' she said, shifting in her seat with agitation.

Caesar found a space to park further down the street from Archaos and the three of them got out and ran towards the front of the club.

'Jeezo, look at the queue to get in,' groaned Valerie.

'One of the doormen's a pal of mine,' said Caesar. 'He'll let us in.'

They bypassed the queue and rushed to the front. Sure enough, Caesar's friend waved the three of them inside and they entered, ignoring the protests of those still shivering outside in the cold.

'Should we split up to look for him?' said Toni as they hurried inside after paying the entrance fee. The sound of Coolio's 'Gangsta's Paradise' rang out loud and clear.

'No,' said Caesar. 'The Thompsons could be here and we don't want anyone getting kidnapped again.'

'Very true,' said Toni, leaning into him, resting her hand on his chest. 'I feel so safe with you here to protect us.'

'Concentrate, Toni,' said Valerie, eyes scanning the room.

She couldn't see Seb anywhere in the main room, so they hurried up to the next level, but he was nowhere in sight.

'There's only the Sky Bar to check,' said Valerie. 'I don't suppose you're pals with the doormen on there too?' she asked Caesar.

'I am, actually,' he replied.

'Thank god. Let's go.'

They were once again waved through and Toni smiled with satisfaction as she finally got to enter the VIP area, all thanks to this man who had come into her life seemingly out of nowhere and who not only protected her but, most importantly, stood up to her brother. She only hoped it wouldn't cost Caesar his head.

'There he is,' breathed Valerie with relief, charging over to the far side of the room where she found Seb talking with two men of similar age who looked to be very bad news. Outwardly they were respectable in smart shirts and trousers, hair neatly cut, but viciousness shone out of their eyes. Valerie should know, she'd seen it plenty of times in her own relatives' eyes.

'Valerie,' said Seb, a mixture of joy and apprehension in his eyes. 'What are you doing here?'

'I could ask you the same thing,' she retorted. 'What the hell do you think you're doing?'

He looked to the two men and said, 'Excuse me,' before gently taking her by the arm and leading her away from them, Toni and Caesar following.

'I know you're working for Frankie,' Valerie hissed, shrugging her arm free and rounding on him. 'He's already admitted it. Why the hell would you do this?'

'What happened to your face?' he asked with concern.

'Never mind that. You'd better start giving me some answers right now before I throw your ring right back in your face.' Toni and Caesar were standing a little way off to give them some privacy, so they couldn't overhear, especially not over the thump of the music.

'Please don't do that,' he said quickly. 'I was only trying to earn us some extra money so we could leave sooner.'

'So let me get this straight – you're trying to earn money so we can leave and escape Frankie, who you've started working for?'

'I know it sounds stupid...'

'That is an understatement.'

'...but it was the only way I could think of to get hold of some good money fast. He's paying me really well.'

'Of course he is because you're taking a risk so he doesn't have to.'

'It's only messages, it's no' drugs. I refused to touch them.'

'It doesn't matter. You're still working for a drug operation. You want to be a church minister, for god's sake, and you'll throw all that away if you get caught. What were you thinking?'

'That I want to start my life with you as quickly as possible. That's even more important to me than being a minister.'

'Oh, Seb,' she said, heart swelling with love. 'I really appreciate that, but you've gone about it in completely the wrong way. Now Frankie's reeled you in, he'll never let you go, not now you know some of how his operation works.'

'But it's okay,' he smiled, taking her hands. 'He's already promised he will. Once I've worked for him for a month, we can leave together.'

He was so naïve Valerie's heart almost broke. 'Frankie doesn't know the meaning of a promise. When he was seventeen, he promised a man called Arthur Johnson that he'd help him get more disability money, so Frankie broke his kneecaps, crippling him for life. I shudder to think of the way Frankie will keep his promise to you. Oh, god, what have you done?' she breathed.

'It'll all work out, it will. I've only one exam left.'

'Which you should have been at home, studying for.'

'I've got a week left to study, I'll be fine.'

'Once you've sat that exam, we should just leave. We need to get out of Frankie's grip.'

'Okay, if you think that's best.'

'I really do,' she said, leaning into him. 'I've got such a horrible feeling.'

'Everything will work out, it always does. We've got the divine on our side.'

Valerie had never really got used to this sort of talk. Part of her always cringed but part of her hoped he had a point. 'Aye,' she said, forcing a smile. 'I'm sure it'll all be fine, but please be careful.'

'I've already got some money put aside thanks to Frankie and my savings. My professor's told me he can get me a work placement with a congregation up in Aberdeen. I'll have to do that for fifteen months before I can get my own parish.'

'Sounds good,' she said, taking a deep breath, his calm, reasonable tone soothing her and making her think they might just pull it off after all.

'Now are you going to tell me what happened to your face?'

In all the panic about finding out her fiancé was working for Frankie, she'd momentarily forgotten all about that. 'I will, but we need to get out of here. Have you done what you need to do?'

'Aye, but I said I'd go back to Colin and Gary.'

'Forget them. We need to leave before the Thompsons get here. They know you're working for Frankie and now they've lost me and Toni, they might come for you.'

'What do you mean they lost you and Toni? What's happened?'

'I will tell you, I promise, but we need to go right now,' she said, taking his hand and leading him towards the door.

Valerie nodded at Toni and Caesar, who were standing close to the door, and they all made their way towards the exit. Valerie was pleased with how closely Caesar stuck to Toni and how alert he was. She was glad her cousin would have someone fighting her corner when she'd left for Aberdeen.

As they exited the Sky Bar, Caesar, who was leading the way, came to a sudden halt.

'What is it?' said Toni, who had narrowly avoided walking into his back.

He nodded at some figures approaching the entrance to the VIP bar.

'It's Liam and Bill Thompson,' said Toni, turning to warn Valerie.

'Let's go out this way,' said Caesar, leading them back into the

Sky Bar, pausing to say something to the doorman, which was inaudible to his companions over the music.

The doorman nodded and resumed his stern posture at the door while they rushed back inside. They hurried across the room towards a door at the side of the bar. The four of them rushed through it and down a set of well-lit stairs, the music muffled here, to Valerie's relief.

At the bottom of the stairs, there was a corridor with various doors leading off it, but Caesar took them through the fire exit that led into a back alley.

'Urgh, my shoes are getting ruined,' grumbled Toni as they rushed through dirty puddles of water and dropped litter.

At the end of the alley, Caesar waved at them to stay back before peering around the corner.

'Can you see anyone?' whispered Toni.

'No, it looks all clear,' he replied. 'Let's move.'

They left the shelter of the alley and raced down the road, slowing to a halt when they saw the gang of Thompson men hanging around Caesar's car.

'Oh, shite,' he sighed.

'You should have got a different motor,' called Tommy, who it seemed had escaped the lynch mob. 'You treacherous prick.'

'Quick, in here,' said Caesar, gesturing to the pub they'd stopped outside.

The four of them ran inside the busy pub. All the tables were taken and many customers had been left standing. Caesar had to practically shove a path through the crowd, eliciting plenty of complaints as he made for the fire exit at the rear of the premises.

'Oy, what do you think you're doing?' yelled the landlord.

All four of them ignored him, and the landlord's attention was drawn off them towards the Thompsons charging in, who also roughly shoved customers out of their way in order to reach their quarry.

'Stop it, ya wee bastards,' he yelled at them. 'Or I'll call the polis.'

'Away and raffle yerself, ya prick,' Bill snarled at him so savagely the landlord decided it would be best to allow these people to run through his premises, which it seemed they were intent on doing.

Caesar burst onto the back street first, followed by Toni, Valerie and then Seb.

'Look, there's a taxi,' cried Toni, pointing down the street.

The four of them ran on ahead while the Thompsons raced out of the pub behind them.

'Oh, no, you don't,' growled Caesar when he saw a young couple approaching the waiting taxi.

He sprinted on ahead and reached it just as the man politely opened the rear door of the taxi for his date. Caesar grabbed him by the scruff of the jacket and dragged him backwards.

'Hey, what are you doing?' screeched the woman before starting to whack Caesar with her handbag.

'Get off him, you silly cow,' said Toni, backhanding her across the face, knocking her over.

Caesar threw the woman's boyfriend to the ground beside her and the four of them got into the car, Caesar in the front, Toni, Valerie and Seb in the back.

'What did you do that for?' the driver demanded of Caesar. 'Get out of my car right now.'

'Drive, wee man, before I rip out your tongue,' Caesar snarled back at him.

The driver's eyes widened. He nodded, started the engine and set off.

'We've lost them,' Toni breathed with relief as she watched the

Thompsons standing impotently on the pavement, watching them go.

'Thank you, Caesar,' said Valerie.

'You're welcome, doll,' he replied.

'So that's why you were in such a hurry,' said the driver. 'You were running from someone.'

'Just drive and mind your own bloody business,' said Caesar.

'I will, but I need to know where I'm going.'

'We should go to Frankie's and let him know what's happened,' said Toni.

'I'm not sure that's wise,' replied Valerie.

'He's the only one who can make the Thompsons stop.'

'Okay, fine, but we're dropping Seb off at home first.'

'No way,' he protested. 'I refuse to sit at home doing nothing while you lot sort it out.'

'I don't want to drag you into this any more than you already have been,' said Valerie.

'I dragged myself into it. You warned me and I didn't listen, so now I should sort it out.'

'Let him come, Val,' said Toni impatiently. 'He's a grown man, you should stop treating him like a wean.'

'All right, fine, you can come,' she told Seb.

'Everything will work out,' he smiled, taking his fiancée's hand. 'You'll see.'

Valerie thought that would be a bloody miracle.

20

Frankie received them with a cold, imperious glare. Tam, Jamesie and Paul were still with him. *Ground Force* was on the television and Tam in particular seemed rapt by it.

'You left without my permission,' Frankie told Toni, Valerie and Caesar.

'Because we're grown-ups who can come and go as we please,' retorted Valerie.

'Only if I say so. I'm head of this family now. You'd do well to remember that.'

'Or what? You'll scalp me too?'

'Scalp?' frowned Seb. His eyes widened as he recalled all the horrifying news articles he'd read about that incident, but he decided it was safer to stay quiet.

'I hope you passed on the message before they dragged you out the club?' Frankie asked Seb.

'Aye, I did. It's all sorted.'

'Good because if you hadn't, it would have cost me a fortune.' He sighed with annoyance and glanced at Tam. 'Would you shut that rammy up?' he snapped, gesturing to the television.

'But I pure love this show, it's my favourite.'

'You don't even have a garden.'

'It's no' the gardening I like, it's that bird Charlie Dimmock. And what a pair of Dimmocks she has, eh, lads?' he winked at Paul and Jamesie, who grinned and nodded.

'You've recorded it on the video, you can watch it later. Turn the bloody thing off.'

Tam tutted but he complied and switched off the video player and the television.

'It's lucky we did go, Frankie,' Toni told her brother. 'The Thompsons turned up at the club and it was clear they were after Seb. If they'd got hold of him, they might have learnt some of your secrets.'

Everyone regarded Frankie warily when his left eye twitched but he didn't speak.

'They need sorting out,' said Valerie. 'Because now that plan failed, god only knows what they'll do. They're getting desperate.'

'I think she has a point, Frankie, son,' said Tam. 'We do need to sort those bastards out once and for all. They're bad for business.'

'You'll never be able to expand properly while they're sticking their oar in,' Toni told her brother. 'They'll cause you too much disruption.'

Frankie glanced at Paul and Jamesie, who nodded in agreement.

'All right, fine,' sighed Frankie in a way that said he was doing the whole world a favour. 'I'll sort out the Thompsons.'

'Great,' smiled Toni.

'That's a pure good decision,' said Tam, who was as usual kissing his nephew's arse.

'And you'll let Seb off running errands for you,' said Valerie.

The entire room filled with a tense silence as Frankie regarded his cousin.

'You fucking what?' he said, arching a ginger eyebrow.

'You don't need him. Plenty of people want to work for you.'

Frankie's eyes glimmered dangerously. 'I want Seb doing it because he's no' some useless fanny with a criminal record a mile long. He comes from a good family, no previous run-ins with the polis and he's studying to be a minister. No one would ever believe he's running messages for me, so he can fly under the polis's radar.'

'But this could ruin his life. If it ever came out what he's been doing, then it could spoil any chance of him getting a parish.'

'Have I missed something here? I thought Seb was a grown fucking man. What are you, his maw or something? He can speak for himself, can't he?' The way Frankie snapped at her indicated he was rapidly losing his patience. His feral gaze was turned on Seb. 'Well?' he barked. 'What the fuck have you got to say for yourself?'

Seb glanced at Valerie, who took his hand and nodded encouragingly. He took a deep breath and looked back at Frankie, seeing the real man for the very first time. Frankie had always been so affable and friendly towards him. Now Seb finally understood why Valerie had warned him against her cousin.

'I want out,' he said.

When Frankie's face twisted into a snarl, Paul, Jamesie and Tam all smiled with relish at the prospect of the violence they felt sure was about to ensue.

It was the sound of voices outside the window that drew Caesar's attention and he peered through the curtains.

'Oh, shite,' he said.

'What is it now?' demanded Frankie.

'It's the Thompsons and there's loads of them.'

'How many?'

'It's hard to tell because it's dark but about a dozen, I reckon.'

'Paul, Jamesie,' said Frankie. 'Check all the doors and windows are locked.'

They nodded, leapt to their feet and rushed off to obey.

'Tam, call the boys.'

His uncle likewise nodded and took out his new mobile phone, tongue sticking out of the side of his mouth as he attempted to operate it.

'Down,' yelled Caesar, grabbing Toni and pulling her to the floor, shielding her with his body while the rest of them threw themselves down.

A brick landed on the coffee table, cracking it.

'Bastards,' hissed Frankie, eyes bulging at the damage.

Paul and Jamesie ran back into the room to see what had caused the alarming noise. 'What was that?' said the latter.

'What the fuck do you think it was, you thick twat?' yelled Frankie, gesturing to the brick and split wood. 'That table cost me a grand,' he sighed.

Frankie's eyes rolled back in his head, such was the strength of his rage before he recovered himself. Shoving the damaged table aside, he pulled back the rug it had been sitting on to reveal a square cut into the carpet. He tore that up to reveal the floor-boards, which lifted up to reveal a hoard of weapons – knives, hatchets, a baseball bat, crowbar, even a pair of nunchucks.

'Help yourselves,' he said before grabbing one of the hatchets.

Seb watched in horror while the others lunged for the weapons. Tam grabbed a crowbar, Paul, Jamesie and Toni took a knife each and Caesar also went for a hatchet while Valerie went for the nunchucks. She had no idea why she selected that weapon, never having used a pair of nunchucks before, but for some reason she was drawn to them.

'I hope you can play baseball, Seb,' laughed Frankie, snatching the bat out of the hole and tossing it to him.

Seb caught it with one hand and stared at it, appalled.

'Look at his face,' laughed Paul, pointing at Seb. 'Just so you know,' he told him, 'we're no' going out there for a game of rounders.'

'You okay?' Valerie asked her fiancé, taking pity on how lost he looked.

Seb forced a smile, not wanting her to worry. 'Fine.'

'What's that?' demanded an alarmed Valerie when Frankie fished a small round grey object out of the hole.

'A flash bang,' he replied. 'It'll disorientate the bastards.'

'Thank god for that. I thought it was a hand grenade.'

'If I had one of those bastards, I would have lobbed it oot the window by now and blown the fuckers to bits. Tam,' barked Frankie. 'Are the boys on their way?'

'Aye, but it'll take them five or ten minutes to get here,' he replied.

'Fucking useless. We'll have to handle this ourselves.'

When a figure attempted to climb through the window, Frankie leapt to his feet and raised the hatchet in the air, a scream of fury bellowing from his lungs. The would-be invader squeaked with horror and leapt back out, narrowly avoiding having his leg taken off by Frankie's hatchet, which embedded itself in the windowsill.

'Can we get out the back way?' said Valerie.

'No, doll,' said Paul. 'I saw more of the sods, but the kitchen door's locked.'

'We cannae just sit here like a bunch of scared wee lassies, waiting for them to come in,' said Frankie. 'Let's get out there and tear them apart.'

'We're with you, Frankie boy,' said Tam, leaping to his feet and holding his crowbar aloft, hastily ducking when more bricks came through the window.

'Look after my sister,' Frankie told Caesar, who nodded.

Frankie was pushed beyond the limit of his rage when one brick struck the television, smashing the screen.

'Oh, you pricks are gonnae pay for that,' he roared before leaping through the broken window into the night.

'Frankie,' cried Toni.

'I've got your back, Frankie boy,' yelled Tam before likewise leaping outside.

Paul and Jamesie quickly followed suit.

'What should we do?' exclaimed Seb, eyes wide with panic.

There was the sound of a hammering at the back door.

'Looks like that's being decided for us,' said Valerie before rushing through to the kitchen, the others following.

As she entered the kitchen, the door was kicked in by an enormous Thompson thug, who grinned maliciously to see her standing there.

Valerie gripped the nunchucks by one handle and swung the weapon at his head. The free handle smashed into the man's face and he fell backwards into his friends, knocking them over. She kicked the door shut and pressed herself against it, holding it closed. When hammering started up on the other side, Toni helped her keep it shut.

'Grab this fridge, Seb,' said Caesar.

Seb nodded and unplugged it so the two of them could manoeuvre it in front of the door, the women hastily leaping out of the way.

'There,' said Seb with satisfaction. 'That should hold them.'

They all ducked when a couple of bricks came in through the kitchen window. Toni snatched up a frying pan that was soaking in the sink and whacked the man who attempted to enter through it in the face and he fell back outside with a groan. Caesar pulled the blind when a second man attempted to climb inside. The man's head went right through the slats, as did his hands, and he found himself entangled in the blind.

'Genius,' grinned Toni, before giving Caesar her most flirtatious look.

'Looks like we have to go out the front,' said Caesar when they saw more people pouring into the backyard.

The four of them ran back through the house down the hallway towards the front door, Caesar leading the way. When a man lunged at him from the living room doorway, Caesar grabbed his arm with which he held the crowbar, twisted it, punched him in the face and headbutted him, wrenching the weapon from his hand as he fell.

Toni gazed at him adoringly. 'You just get better and better.'

Caesar smiled back at her before yanking her towards him with his free arm and grinding his mouth against hers. Toni moaned as he kissed her, sliding her fingers through his hair.

'Er,' said Valerie when their kiss started to become even more passionate. 'Could you save that until people aren't trying to attack us?'

Caesar tore himself away from Toni. 'Sorry,' he said.

'Don't be,' purred a flushed Toni. 'It was wonderful.'

He winked at her before pulling the door open a crack and peering outside.

'Jeezo, it's chaos out there,' he said.

'How many are there?' Toni asked him.

'It's hard to tell because it's dark, but Frankie and the others are outnumbered.'

'Then let's get out there and help them,' she exclaimed.

'No' so fast, doll. Frankie told me to protect you.'

'My brother needs help and I'm going to help him,' she said firmly.

Caesar sighed at the determination in her eyes. 'All right, but stay by my side.'

It was Toni's turn to wink. 'I can't think of a better place to be.'

He grinned at her before they charged outside into the fray together, clutching their knives.

'Stay here,' Valerie told Seb before following them out.

'What, no?' he exclaimed before determinedly chasing after her, halting in his tracks when he saw her smash one would-be attacker in the face with the nunchucks. 'Wow,' he gasped in admiration. His eyes widened when a skinny man with a beard lunged at him and he raised the bat to block the man's arm when he tried to punch him. The man screeched with pain when his fist connected with the wood.

Valerie turned just in time to see Seb smash the bat into the side of his assailant's face. Seb looked over to her, his eyes bright with excitement and adrenaline. Then he lunged towards her, grasping the man who'd been sneaking up on her by the throat and throwing him aside. While the man was down, Valerie kicked him hard in the crotch, ensuring he wouldn't be rejoining the fight.

Valerie got caught up facing off against a Thompson woman, who put up a much better fight than her male relatives, and Valerie got a fist in the face that knocked her sideways. Fortunately she managed to keep hold of the nunchucks and whacked the woman in the left leg with them, making her scream and stagger backwards before dropping onto her backside on the pavement.

Breathing hard and with her face aching, Valerie hauled herself to her feet and frantically scanned the area for Seb. The moon was shining brightly, casting an ethereal glow on the carnage. She spotted Frankie first, his red hair lit up by a street light, frenzy in his eyes as he tore through his opponents, Tam, Jamesie and Paul sticking close to him. She could see a bit of blood on the side of Paul's head, but the injury hadn't slowed him down at all. The men Frankie had called had arrived, so the numbers had been evened up. Caesar and Toni were fighting back to back, ensuring no one could sneak up on them. Valerie got the feeling a beautiful friendship had been formed.

It was then in all the chaos she spotted Seb and her heart dropped when she saw he was fighting Liam Thompson. To her amazement, he was giving as good as he got. Somehow he'd lost his bat and the two large, powerful males were fighting with their fists. The punch Seb delivered to the side of Liam's face was impressive – she hadn't known he had it in him – but desperation was spurring him. Seb sent Liam reeling sideways and the breath caught in Valerie's throat when she saw the glint of steel.

'He's got a knife,' she called to Seb.

But he couldn't hear her. As he lunged at his opponent, Liam whipped round with the blade. Seb spotted the danger and moved to one side and the knife missed his chest, sinking into his left shoulder instead.

The scream rose up from Valerie's belly, charged up her throat and erupted from her mouth. The red stain that bloomed on Seb's shirt and rapidly started to spread froze her own blood in her veins.

'No,' she cried, racing over to him, dodging around everyone who attempted to get in her way, eyes riveted to him as he collapsed to the ground, all the colour draining from his face, his eyes full of astonishment.

She threw herself down by his side, her eyes already full of unshed tears, and cradled him. Liam loomed over him, the bloodied knife still clutched in his hand.

'Get out of the way, Valerie,' he growled, eyes lit up with blood lust.

'You want to stab him again then you have to go through me,' she told him before turning her attention back to Seb, pressing down on his wound to try to stem the blood flow. 'Toni,' she screamed. 'Call an ambulance.'

Toni punched her opponent in the face and turned to look at her cousin, eyes widening when she saw what was happening. Frantically she scrambled for the phone in her pocket. Caesar stood firm, defending her against everyone who came her way so she could make the call.

'Just hold on, Seb,' said Valerie, tears rolling down her cheeks. 'The ambulance will be here soon.'

Liam was still standing over them.

'Get out of the fucking way,' he yelled at her.

Valerie slipped her hand into her jacket pocket and covertly produced the pepper spray. Raising her arm, she sprayed him while turning her head and shielding Seb with her body.

Liam cried out in pain and dropped the knife, hands automatically going to his eyes, and Valerie kicked the weapon away from him.

'The polis are coming,' yelled one Thompson man when they heard the sound of approaching sirens. 'Do one.'

The Thompsons all scattered, Bill grabbing Liam by the arm and dragging him away, leaving the McVays behind.

'Caesar, get Toni out of here,' Valerie told him.

'No, I'm staying,' she said firmly. 'Hey,' cried Toni when Caesar flung her over his shoulder and ran down a back street.

'You three should go too,' Frankie told Paul, Jamesie and his uncle. 'The fewer of us who get caught up in it, the better.'

'You should come too,' Tam told him.

'It's my fucking hoose,' he replied. 'And I've got an idea. Go on, piss off.'

The three men melted into the night, so when the police car did turn onto the street, only Frankie, Valerie and Seb remained.

'Stay awake,' she yelled at her fiancé when his eyes slid shut. 'Please.'

Seb's eyes snapped open, but she was dismayed by the few

seconds it took him to focus on her. When he did, a gentle smile creased his lips. He tried to raise his hand to touch her face but he lacked the strength, so she lifted his hand for him and cradled it to her cheek. Frankie stared down at them impassively, untouched by the scene before him.

While they waited, Frankie recited to her the story they would give the police and she just nodded. Right now, that was the last thing on her mind.

The police car screeched to a halt at the kerb and two officers jumped out. Both appeared uneasy when they saw Frankie McVay. He had a formidable reputation, and they were reluctant to tackle him.

'Turn around and put your hands on the car,' yelled one officer as he and his colleague drew their batons.

'All right, don't shite your knickers,' Frankie told them. 'I'm unarmed.'

He held up his hands to show they were empty.

'He's been stabbed,' cried Valerie. 'Help him, please.'

The two officers rushed to Seb's side to assess his injuries.

'Is an ambulance coming?' she demanded of them.

'One's on the way,' replied one of the officers sympathetically. 'It shouldnae be long.'

There wasn't much they could do for him except stem the blood flow while asking who did this.

'I don't know,' said Valerie, her instincts kicking in, making it easy to give Frankie's fabricated story to the police. 'We were attacked by a bunch of people, I don't know who they were. Luckily they scarpered when they heard the sirens.'

The officers appeared sceptical, but Seb was their priority and they managed to keep him conscious until the ambulance arrived four minutes later.

'I want to go with him,' she told the officers. 'I'm his fiancée.'

'All right, but we will need to speak to you at the hospital,' replied one of them.

'I'll be there. I'm not going anywhere else,' she said, the tears still rolling down her cheeks.

Frankie said he wanted to go too, but the officers refused and kept him behind to answer some questions.

21

At the hospital, Seb was taken straight in to be treated, leaving Valerie to call his family. She could barely get the words out as she explained in a raspy voice that Seb had been injured. When his mum asked how, she made an excuse and hung up, unable to put it into words.

Laura, Jeffrey and Emily arrived at the hospital together in a panic, all pale-faced and scared. They'd just thrown their coats on over their pyjamas.

'Valerie,' said Laura, hugging her.

Valerie could feel her shaking as she clung onto her.

'Where is he? What's happened?'

'He was stabbed,' she rasped.

'Oh, my god,' said Laura before bursting into tears.

Jeffrey put his arm around his wife. 'How the hell did he get stabbed?'

Once again, Valerie recited Frankie's watered-down version of events. 'We were visiting my cousin when his house was attacked.'

'Who by?'

'I don't know,' she said, hoping she looked clueless. 'It was dark

and it happened so fast. Someone came at Seb with a knife and...
he... he was stabbed.'

'How many times was he stabbed?' said Emily.

'Once, in the shoulder.'

'At least it wasn't his chest or stomach, that would have been so
much worse.'

'But I don't understand,' murmured Jeffrey, looking lost. 'How
could someone just come along and stab him and why did they
attack your cousin?'

'I really don't know,' said Valerie. 'The police are investigating,
so hopefully they'll find out soon.'

'Did you see the person's face?'

'No. Like I said, it was dark.'

'But I thought you were in a house? Surely you had the
lights on?'

'The attack started with a brick being thrown through the
window. We went out to look and were attacked.' Valerie felt awful
about lying to these good people, but she had no choice. She was
also determined that Liam would pay for what he'd done. The
need for vengeance burned inside her.

Jeffrey regarded her with a quizzical look while Laura and
Emily cried and comforted each other. He wasn't stupid, he knew
more was going on than she was saying, but Valerie was saved from
any more questions by a police officer asking to interview her. She
agreed to go with him once Laura had assured her they would let
her know the second they heard how Seb was.

The constable drove her to the police station to be interviewed
by Detective Sergeant Baillie. Valerie gave the tired-looking, cyni-
cal, middle-aged officer the same story she'd given Seb's family. He
was clearly sceptical and when he pressed her for more information, she put on her helpless, distraught female act and he eventu-

ally said she could return to the hospital, although the look he gave her said he wasn't finished with her yet.

She arrived back at the hospital and found Seb's parents and sister sitting together waiting for news in one of the relatives' rooms, holding hands in quiet, scared solidarity. Valerie had never felt so alone. Clearly, they'd been discussing her role in what had happened to Seb in her absence and had already decided that she wasn't telling them everything she knew. Their looks said it all, they'd closed ranks, so Valerie took a seat at the opposite side of the room to wait for news. Valerie wanted to call Toni, but she didn't dare. Frankie wouldn't appreciate his sister being dragged into the spotlight, so she decided to wait it out, quietly sitting with her head bowed.

An hour later, after waiting in awkward silence, a doctor finally came in to update them. She introduced herself as a senior registrar and was neat, crisp and efficient, just the sort of doctor you'd want in a life-threatening emergency.

'Sebastian's doing well,' she told them.

'Thank god,' breathed Valerie, burying her face in her hands while Jeffrey and Emily gasped with relief.

'The wound itself wasn't too serious,' continued the surgeon. 'But he lost quite a bit of blood. He's had a transfusion, but this can lead to complications, only rarely you understand, so he's been taken to intensive care where we can keep an eye on him.'

'Intensive care?' breathed Laura.

'It's just a precaution. I anticipate he'll recover very well with no lasting effects.'

'Can we see him?'

'Yes, but I'm afraid only three of you can go, especially as it's not actually visiting time.'

'We'll go,' said Laura, pointing from herself to her husband and daughter.

'All right. You may wait here until it's your turn,' the surgeon kindly told Valerie, who just nodded.

None of the Robertsons even looked back at Valerie as they left the room with the surgeon. She slumped into a chair, buried her face in her hands and cried.

* * *

Valerie was kept waiting an hour in the relatives' room until she could contain her impatience no longer. She got to her feet and strode through the hospital towards intensive care.

She had to press a buzzer to be allowed in, only to be told by a nurse that there were already enough people gathered around the patient's bedside. She hung around outside the ward, and when a doctor entered using his swipe card, she sneaked in behind him and frantically scanned the rooms, searching for Seb while ignoring the nurse who intercepted her and said she couldn't be here.

She quickly found his room and entered to find his family still gathered around his bedside. Seb himself was asleep on the bed, looking frighteningly pale, left arm held in a sling.

'What are you doing here?' demanded Laura.

'Has he woken up yet?' replied Valerie, ignoring the question.

'He's opened his eyes a couple of times, but he went back off again. I thought you were waiting in the relatives' room?'

'I was, for an hour,' she told her with an accusing look. 'I couldn't wait any longer, I had to see him.'

The door opened and the nurse who had attempted to intercept her entered. 'I'm sorry, I'm afraid you can't be here,' she told Valerie.

'Please, can I have some time with him?' she asked Seb's family.

'No,' said Jeffrey with surprising coldness. 'We don't want you here.'

'But I'm his fiancée,' she said, a lump forming in her throat.

'You know more than you're letting on about his stabbing and until you start telling the truth, you won't go anywhere near him. For all we know, you did it.'

Horrible realisation dawned on Valerie. They actually suspected her of doing this to Seb. 'It wasn't me, I could never ever hurt him. I love him.'

'We'll just have to wait and see what Seb says when he wakes up. Until then, we've informed the hospital staff that you can't go near him, not until we're sure you're not a threat to him.'

'Of course I'm not a threat,' she exclaimed.

They all turned their backs on her.

'Please,' she wailed louder.

'I really must ask you to leave,' said the nurse sternly. 'We have a lot of sick patients on this ward. Don't make me call security.'

Valerie sighed with defeat and nodded. 'All right, there's no need for that. I'm going.'

As she turned to leave, she rushed over to Seb's bed and planted a kiss on his lips.

'I love you,' she told him, but he didn't stir.

'Get out,' thundered Jeffrey, getting to his feet.

Valerie ignored him, keeping her gaze locked on Seb, praying he'd open his eyes and tell everyone she was innocent, but he continued to sleep on, so she left the room escorted by the nurse, who walked her right out into the corridor. The nurse stood sentinel at the door with a stern look on her face, watching Valerie wander down the corridor, lost and dejected.

* * *

Valerie caught a taxi from the hospital to go to Toni's house. Caesar opened the door and led her into the front room, where she found her cousin was still up. It appeared Aunty Moira had been awoken because she was sitting in her wheelchair wearing her slippers and dressing gown, her hair mussed up from sleep.

'Val,' said Toni, flinging her arms around her neck.

'I am honoured,' said Valerie with a weak smile. 'Two Toni hugs in one night.'

'How's Seb?' said Toni, releasing her.

'His surgeon thinks he'll be okay, but he lost quite a bit of blood, so we'll have to wait and see,' she replied, just the memory of him unconscious in his hospital bed, so helpless and vulnerable, bringing fresh tears to her eyes.

'Thank god,' breathed Toni. 'And how are you?'

'Absolutely shite,' she said miserably. 'Seb's parents won't let me near him because they think I was the one who stabbed him.'

'What? That's crazy.'

'I can't blame them because the story I gave them was so vague they were instantly suspicious.'

'Have the polis spoken to you?'

'Aye, and they didn't believe me either. Where's Frankie?'

'Being interviewed at the polis station too but Duncan Blackwood sent his fancy lawyer down there, so they won't be holding him for much longer. What did you tell them?'

'That me and Seb were visiting Frankie's house when it was attacked and that I'd no idea who was responsible because it was dark. I didn't mention anyone else, I don't want you all dragged into it. So far, the polis only think me, Seb and Frankie were there and that's the way it's going to stay.'

'I appreciate you keeping us out of it, but I thought you'd want Liam punished for what he's done?'

'I do, but I'm no' a grass and I'll deal with him personally,' she said, a storm gathering in her eyes.

'Now you're talking. I'll help you.'

'You really don't want to get involved – I'm going to fucking destroy him.'

'Are you kidding? That's just my sort of gig. There's nothing like bloody revenge, believe me, I know,' murmured Toni, eyes turning black and shark-like as she relived memories of killing Roddy.

'I'll help too,' said Caesar.

'I thought Liam was your pal?' said Valerie.

'He was, but Toni's the one I'm loyal to now.'

'Liam seemed really focused on hurting Seb,' said Toni thoughtfully.

'Aye, and he's gonnae fucking pay for it,' snapped Valerie.

'But why? I know he has a crush on you, but that doesn't seem enough reason.'

'You think there's more going on than we know?'

'It's possible. We'll make him talk, have no fear about that.'

'We will, but we can't do anything tonight, not with the polis sniffing about, and I want to speak to Frankie first.'

'He'll go to war with the Thompsons over this, he has to if he's to protect his reputation, and his retribution will be very bloody,' said Toni with pleasure in her eyes.

'I've no doubt about it.' Valerie glanced at Moira, wondering if she was going to comment on the activities of her children, but she said nothing, staring down at the floor. It seemed she'd given up long ago, or she was just too afraid to intervene.

'Why don't you stay here tonight?' said Toni. 'You shouldn't be on your own and you can be here when Frankie gets back.'

Valerie's limbs felt like lead, and she wanted to be around Toni because she understood. If she went home, she'd have to explain to her parents what had happened and endure their questions and told-you-so looks and she wasn't sure she had the stamina for that. For the first time in her life, Valerie felt fragile.

'Aye, all right,' she said.

'Great. You can share my bed, top and tail like we used to when we were wee.'

'That sounds really nice,' Valerie said, choking up. 'Thanks.'

'Everything will be all right,' said Toni, wrapping an arm around her. 'You'll see.'

Valerie just nodded, not trusting herself to speak without bursting into tears.

Valerie was rudely awoken by the sound of shouting. For a moment, she was tempted to ignore it, she was so warm and comfortable. She turned onto her side and hoped the noisy bastard making all that racket would soon shut up. Then it struck her that the voice was Frankie's and all the horror of the previous night came screaming back.

She sat bolt upright and saw she was alone in Toni's bed wearing one of her cousin's zebra-print nighties. Frankie was ranting and raving about the police and how stupid and inept they were, his language colourful and littered with F-bombs.

Squinting at the clock, she saw it was 8.30 in the morning. She'd only got four hours' sleep, but she was amazed she'd managed to get any at all. She'd expected to lie awake with recent events swirling through her mind and tormenting her, but she'd been out like a light the moment her head had hit the pillow.

Valerie got up and changed back into her clothes before padding downstairs. Frankie for once appeared rumpled, his clothes creased and hair dishevelled. It was clear he hadn't got any sleep. Toni was up, fully dressed in one of her figure-hugging, cleavage-revealing outfits, hair and make-up immaculate, making Valerie feel like a mess, as usual. Moira was also there in her wheelchair, wearing her dressing gown and pyjamas, but there was no sign of Caesar.

'Thank goodness you're back, Frankie,' said Valerie.

'What the fuck did you tell the polis?' he demanded, pointing a finger at her.

'What we agreed – that a bunch of people attacked your house when me and Seb were visiting, and we didn't see who they were because it was dark.'

'Well, they suspect it was the fucking Thompsons and they've hauled in Tam, Jamesie and Paul too. Did you fucking grass?'

'No, I did not,' retorted Valerie, swelling with indignation. 'How fucking dare you? After everything I've been through, you accuse me of that? I could punch you right in the face.'

Toni and Moira's jaws dropped open at her nerve. No one threatened Frankie, not without losing a vital part of their anatomy, and he glowered at her, lips drawing back over his teeth, as though he were about to bite. But instead of launching into the expected frenzy, he threw back his head and barked with laughter.

'So last night didnae break you, then,' he said. 'I was afraid it would.'

'You must be joking,' said Valerie. 'I want to track down Liam Thompson and pull his spine out.'

'And we will, the Thompsons are fucking done. Duncan's already given me the go-ahead but we have to be patient and wait until the polis stop sticking their fucking beaks in.'

'I thought Duncan would be able to make that happen?'

'He's working on it. Until then, we have to wait,' he said, looking furious about the fact.

Valerie thought it would be good for Frankie to learn some patience, but she was keen to get her hands on Liam and make him feel a lot of pain. 'Why did you accuse me of grassing? Has someone said something?'

'Aye, they have. The polis know there was a big fucking battle in the street. Right now, they're interviewing my nosy bastard neighbours.'

'It was probably one of the neighbours who grassed. All they would have had to do was stick their heid out the window to see what was going on.'

'Aye, maybe,' he said, simmering down a little. 'Where the fuck's Caesar?'

The way his eyes narrowed with suspicion said Caesar was one of his main suspects for grassing.

'He went to his brother's house to warn him because he's worried the Thompsons will take it out on him,' replied Toni.

'And you're sure he no' made a stop at the polis station on his way to his brother's?'

It was Toni's turn to be indignant. 'Quite sure. He's no' a fucking grass either.'

'All right, sweetheart, simmer down,' he told her.

'Caesar saved my life last night, so show some bloody gratitude.'

'I am grateful, okay?' he yelled back at her.

'Good,' sniffed Toni, folding her arms across her chest.

'How's Seb?' said Frankie, turning to Valerie.

It seemed Seb was way down his list of priorities but at least he'd asked, eventually. 'Stable. He got through the surgery, but he lost a lot of blood, so he's not out of the woods yet. His family won't let me see him because they think I stabbed him,' she said miserably.

'The fucking dicks. Don't worry, Seb will set them straight.'

'If he wakes up.' Valerie almost added that they'd also find out that she was a McVay but thought Frankie wouldn't take kindly to finding out she'd kept that a secret, he took enormous pride in his lineage.

'Why don't you call the hospital and find out how he is?' Toni asked her.

'They won't tell me anything. Seb's parents will have told them not to give me any information.'

'You don't need to tell them who you are. Say you're someone else.'

'I could say I'm his Aunty Sarah.'

'Go for it. You can use the phone,' said Toni, gesturing to the telephone sitting on the sideboard.

'Cheers,' said Valerie, having to look up the number for the hospital in the phone book before dialling and asking to be put through to intensive care. 'Hi,' she said nervously to the voice on the other end. 'Could you tell me how Sebastian Robertson is, please? I'm his Aunt Sarah.' She breathed a sigh of relief at the reply. 'Thank you so much, that's wonderful.' Valerie hung up and turned to the others with a smile. 'He had a good night and he's woken up.'

'Great news,' said Toni. 'See, things are already on the up and he will already have told his family that you didn't stab him.'

'I've just had a thought – the polis will be talking to him soon and it won't even occur to him to lie.'

'You need to get to him and tell him,' said Frankie, eyes sharpening into knives.

'His parents won't let me in.'

'Then we need to smuggle a message in to him.'

'There's your Uncle Martin,' said a voice.

They all turned to Moira, who they'd forgotten was there.

'He's a cleaner at Glasgow Royal,' she continued. 'He'll be able to give Seb a message.'

'Great idea, Maw,' said Frankie with pride in his eyes. 'I'll gi'e him a bell.'

Frankie snatched up the phone and dialled. Valerie thought he spoke to their uncle rather arrogantly, ordering him rather than asking, but Martin dabbled in the criminal underworld, so he'd probably already done some work for Frankie.

'He said he'd dae it,' said Frankie, returning the handset to its cradle. 'And he works on that floor, so no one will think twice about seeing him there.'

'And if Seb's only just woken up,' said Toni, 'then his doctor will probably still be keeping the polis away from him for a wee bit longer until he's stronger.'

'We can but hope,' said Valerie. 'And it will be one less thing to worry about.'

'I've got people out looking for Liam and Bill,' said Frankie. 'They'll be lying low but I will find them, drag them oot their hidey-holes and batter their fucking melons until they split, and by melons, I don't mean heids,' he snarled, left eye twitching.

'And I'll help you,' said Valerie. 'They've ruined everything.'

'Don't you worry, doll,' replied Frankie, mayhem shining in his eyes. 'We'll make them pay in buckets of blood for what they've done.'

'I can't wait,' she hissed, hands curling into fists.

Frankie and Toni smiled. Their cousin was back.

22

Uncle Martin managed to pass on the message that morning to Seb, who accepted it with weary resignation. Seb asked Martin to tell Valerie that he loved her and had asked to see her, so Valerie was determined to figure out a way to get into the hospital to see him.

She was forced to return home as word had spread about what had happened the previous night and her mother phoned Moira's house demanding answers.

Valerie gave them the same story she'd given the police and Seb's parents, and their eyes filled with disapproval. They knew she was lying but they didn't want to know the truth, so they didn't press her for answers. They were more concerned with Seb and were appalled when she told them his family had thought she'd stabbed him. They then launched into a lecture about how they'd warned her to stay away from Toni and Frankie, and Valerie stormed out of the house before they could finish their tirade. She needed comfort and reassurance, not censure.

Once outside, she had no idea where to go or what to do, so she just started walking, everything churning through her mind in confusion. She replayed the fight outside Frankie's house, Seb falling to the ground injured, his blood on the blade looking black in the moonlight, Liam's eyes shining with the desire to commit murder.

Valerie found herself making her way to Stevie Johnson's house. If you wanted to know what was going on, he was the one you spoke to.

She knocked on his door, which was pulled open by Stevie himself, who was surprisingly up and dressed.

'Valerie,' he said with surprise. 'And to what do I owe the honour of this visit?' His eyes filled with nervousness. 'Frankie's no' here, is he?'

'No, I'm alone. He doesn't even know I'm here. I really need to talk to you, Stevie. Can I come in?'

'Aye, course,' he said, opening the door wider.

Valerie stepped inside and he peered out nervously just to make sure no one else was there before closing it.

'I'm glad I didn't wake you up,' she told him as she stood in his neat front room.

'There's nae danger of that, I havenae been to bed yet.'

'I suppose you've heard about what happened last night?'

'Aye. The Thompsons attacked Frankie's house, the mad bastards that they are, but no one's supposed to know that. Frankie's told the polis he doesnae know who it was, which they don't believe for a moment.'

This confirmed her suspicions that Stevie had his own contacts in the police. Maybe he had friends or relatives on the inside?

'I'm not surprised,' she said. 'So you'll know that Liam Thompson stabbed my boyfriend?'

'I didnae know it was Liam who'd done it, I just knew it was a Thompson.' His eyes filled with sympathy. 'How is he?'

'Stable, but Liam was really determined to kill him and I don't understand why, he doesn't even know him and I refuse to believe it's because of Liam's crush on me. There's more going on than I know. As Seb's parents believe I stabbed their son...'

'What?' he exclaimed.

'Aye, I know. It's mental, they won't even let me see him, which is why I'm here. You know everything that goes on, so I thought you might be able to help me.'

'You're best letting sleeping dogs lie. Knowledge is power but it's also dangerous. I know that better than anyone.'

'So I'm right, you do know something. Please tell me.'

'I like you, Valerie, and you helped me out in the past, which is why I'm gonnae tell you this – let it go.'

'I can't. Surely you understand that?'

'I understand why you want to know, but it will hurt you.'

'If you're worried about Frankie finding out that you know something and kept it back from him, then don't be. I won't bring you into it.'

He shook his head.

'Please, Stevie. You owe me,' she added when he still appeared reluctant. 'I saved your life.'

He gazed into her pleading eyes and sighed. 'All right, but don't say I didnae warn you. Seb isn't who you think he is. I suppose he's told you he's some sweet innocent man who wants to do something harmless with his life – teach at a primary school, probably, or go to Romania and build shelters for orphans.'

'He said he's at uni studying Divinity and Philosophy and wants to be a minister in the Scottish church,' she replied.

Stevie laughed and shook his head.

'Why the fuck is that funny?' she demanded.

'Because he's a vicious bastard with a criminal record a mile long.'

'What are you on about? He's the gentlest man I've ever known.'

'Aye, that's what he wants you to believe, but he's got a long history of blood and mayhem behind him.'

'No,' she smiled, shaking her head. 'You've got the wrong person.'

'Sebastian Robertson? Mother Laura, father Jeffrey, sister Emily? Has a sweet old gran called Euphemia?'

'Aye, that's him,' she said slowly.

'He was arrested when he was fourteen for pushing his best friend down the stairs and severely injuring him. He said it was an accident and everyone believed him, until another friend of his almost drowned in a canal and another fell off the top of a garage. All his friends kept having mysterious accidents, until some of their other friends decided to go to the polis and finally tell them Sebastian had been responsible for all those incidents. It took them so long to say anything because they were all scared of him.'

'Then they were obviously lying and it was one of them and they threw Seb under the bus to protect themselves.'

'No charges were pressed because there was no evidence. Their word was not enough and the boys who were injured couldn't say for sure what had happened as their backs had been turned at the time, so it eventually blew over. Then Seb was done for shoplifting when he was sixteen, followed by vandalism...'

'So what? So have most of the people around here.'

'He assaulted a shop owner when he caught him stealing something from his shop, he then hit a security guard in some swanky department store and beat up a traffic warden. He got two years for that last one, but he was out in eight months.'

'No way,' she exclaimed. 'He's been nothing but sweet and kind to me.'

Stevie continued as though she hadn't spoken. 'It doesnae stop there. He made contacts in prison and when he came out, he was even worse. He's been dealing drugs for years and lately he's been encroaching on the Thompsons' patch...'

'This is fucking crazy,' she cried. 'His family's so kind and good, they're nothing like my family or the Thompsons. They're all normal and law-abiding.'

'Aye, they are, but he's no'. The problem is they go out of their way to protect him, and his maw's a bloody good solicitor. She's got him out of trouble plenty of times.'

'But they've said in front of me that he's studying at uni.'

'Maybe he is, but I can guarantee an evil bastard like that isnae studying Divinity and he certainly doesnae want to be a minister.'

'If he was a dealer then Frankie would know about him.'

'Seb deals to a lot of posh bastards, they move in different circles, so he's probably never even popped up on Frankie's radar. I know your cousin likes to make out that he knows all and sees all but he really doesn't, which is why he needs me.'

'Why didn't you say something sooner?'

'Because I'd no idea you were even dating Sebastian until I heard about what happened last night.'

'So much for you knowing everything,' she said scathingly.

He shrugged. 'I've had a lot on my plate lately what with trying no' to get murdered by Frankie or the Thompsons. When I heard what happened last night, I knew it was the same Sebastian.'

'But...' Valerie trailed off, feeling completely lost and confused. This revelation had floored her, and she found it all so hard to believe. The Sebastian he was describing was so at odds with the man she knew and loved. 'I want proof.'

Stevie nodded, retrieved a buff folder sitting on his coffee table, and held it out to her. She snatched it off him and flipped it open to be confronted by Seb's glowering mugshot. The photo was so different to the man she knew that it made her inhale sharply. His eyes were full of malevolence and hate when she'd only known them to be filled with kindness and love. Her hands shook as she flipped through his record, which was long and colourful and full of violence.

Tears blurred her eyes and the folder slipped from her hands, the papers fanning out on the floor, the mugshot landing on top, those evil eyes staring at her, as though the photograph was taunting her. 'This can't be right,' she rasped in a quiet, lost voice. 'He took me to a poetry reading, he knew the owner of the bookshop. He knows so much about literature, we've spoken about it for hours. He was working for Frankie to earn money for our future together.' There seemed no point in hiding it any more. Stevie probably already knew anyway.

'He was in Archaos last night. The two men he met with are his people. They want to take out Frankie and take over his patch. They've been after expanding out of their own territory for a while now and taking over somewhere away from the Thompsons. Frankie's territory is perfect as he's already got everything set up.'

'And he was using me to get close to Frankie?' she said, pain lancing through her.

'Probably.'

'I still can't believe Frankie wouldn't know about him and his friends.'

'They're very good at flying under the radar, thanks to the respectable front Sebastian puts on. I mean, who would believe someone called Sebastian could cause anyone any harm? He uses an alias, Harry Woodhouse, for his work. The Thompsons themselves have only just realised who they're really fighting as he's been encroaching on their territory a lot lately.'

'Seb's Harry Woodhouse?' she exclaimed.

'Aye. That's how I found all this out. Frankie wanted me to gather all the info I could on him. Harry Woodhouse is an alias for

Sebastian Robertson, which explains why Frankie's never been able to catch up with him before.'

'Jesus. Does Frankie know?'

'No' yet. I havenae been able to talk to him because he was hauled into the polis station.'

'Jeezo, he'll go demented about that. Harry Woodhouse was standing right in front of him and he didn't even realise. That also explains why Liam was so determined to kill Seb last night.'

Stevie nodded.

Valerie's expression hardened. 'How do I know you're not really working for the Thompsons and you've arranged all this crap to split up me and Seb?'

'What would be the point in that?'

'I know Liam would love it if I dumped Seb.'

'Maybe, but it seems like a waste of time when, in the scheme of things, your relationship with Sebastian is neither here nor there to them. If he hurts your feelings or worse, what would they care?'

Valerie had to admit that he had a point.

'If you'll take my advice,' said Stevie, 'you'll stay well away from Seb before he hurts you too, because he will. His previous girl-friends all ended up battered and bruised. Look through that folder and you'll see two of them took out restraining orders against him.'

Valerie dropped to her knees and frantically began sifting through the papers, the shaking of her hands uncontrollable. Her breath came out in heaving sobs as she saw her life and the future she'd envisaged with a good, gentle man falling away from her.

Taking pity on her, Stevie knelt down and found the paper she was looking for. Valerie snatched it from him and frantically scanned it.

'Samantha Jones,' she croaked. 'He told me she was arrested for shoplifting.'

'She was, and Seb was with her at the time.'

'And Libby Michaels for having a fight with another girl.'

'Aye, until she was released by the polis as they thought he was really responsible for beating up that woman, only it couldn't be proved. I reckon he's responsible for so much more that either couldn't be proved or no one knows about.'

'I have to talk to him about this and ask if it's true.'

'It is true,' he said gently. 'But please don't ask him because god knows what he'll do.'

'Christ,' she said, letting the paper she held flutter to the floor, wiping her eyes on the backs of her hands. 'Seb talks a lot about God. He was even starting to convince me that religion might be for me after all.'

'Just because he's a psycho doesnae mean he's wrong about that.'

Valerie's smile was impossibly sad. 'You're being so kind to me.'

'Fair's fair. You were kind to me.' He scooped up the papers and slipped them neatly back into the folder before holding it out to her. 'Take this and go through it properly, but don't do anything rash. This needs to be handled carefully. He's a proper loon, as are his friends. I'm working on getting their names too, so I'll let you know when I find anything else out.'

'Thank you,' said Valerie, wearily getting to her feet and taking the folder from him. 'I appreciate your help, Stevie.'

'Nae bother.'

Valerie left the house and wandered down the street, clutching the folder to her chest, blind to her surroundings as once again her mind whirled and spun. She kept seeing Seb's kind, gentle face overlaid by the evil mugshot.

'Jekyll and Hyde,' she whispered to herself.

This could all still be a trick, anyone could put together some papers and photographs could be faked. That would make more sense than Seb being a psychopath. If he was the lunatic Stevie had described, surely there should have been some sign, no matter how small?

In her mind, she went over the violence at Frankie's house and how well Seb had handled himself. Then there had been the time her cousin and his friend had attempted to mug them in the park. Seb had stood before her fearlessly, there hadn't been a flicker of uncertainty in his eyes.

Valerie aimlessly walked the streets, not a clue what to do or where to go. She was afraid to go to Frankie with this in case he had a knee-jerk reaction and decided to hurt Seb. Neither did she want to burden Toni with it because she would feel compelled to tell her brother. The person in the know seemed to be Liam Thompson, but she had no idea where he was and she couldn't get into the hospital to speak to Seb. He'd probably deny it anyway, even if it was true. Once she spoke to him, she knew she'd think it was all rubbish. He'd be his sweet, gentle self and she would decide to forget it all and continue as they were, which, if he was guilty, could be very dangerous. She had to confirm all this was true before confronting him about it, but she had no idea how.

Then it hit her.

'Euphemia,' she breathed.

Seb's grandmother might just talk to her. It was worth a try, anyway, and she knew where Euphemia lived because Seb had taken her to her home for a visit. Plus the old woman didn't leave her bungalow much because of her frail health, so there was a good chance she would be in.

Valerie caught the bus and alighted a few doors down from Euphemia's bungalow. It was small but very pretty with an eggshell-blue front door, a matching garden gate and a wishing well.

She rang the bell and waited, knowing it would take Euphemia a little while to reach the door.

It was pulled open and Valerie's heart ached when she looked into Euphemia's kind blue eyes that so reminded her of Seb's.

The old woman's smile faltered when she saw who was on her doorstep. 'Valerie, I wasn't expecting you,' she said, clearly uncomfortable.

'Can I come in, please? I really need to talk to you.'

'I'm sorry, I can't tell you anything about Seb. Laura and Jeffrey have given me strict instructions...'

Valerie thrust the mugshot into her face. 'I want to know if what I've been told about his extensive criminal record is true.'

Euphemia's eyes widened before she sighed in defeat. 'You'd better come in.'

'Thank you.'

Valerie followed her into the neat front room full of framed family photos. Many of them contained Seb's image and tears filled her eyes as she studied them.

'Are you okay, dear?' said Euphemia with concern.

'Fine,' she replied, blinking the tears away.

Euphemia gestured to the couch while she took the armchair. 'Please sit down.'

'Thank you.'

Euphemia patiently waited while Valerie got herself under control before speaking. She wanted to make sure she got this exactly right.

'A friend of mine who's good at finding things out gave me this folder,' said Valerie, indicating the buff folder on her lap. 'It details Seb's criminal record, which is longer than Al Capone's. Assault, robbery, shoplifting, drug dealing and even stalking. I want to know if it's true.'

Euphemia sighed wearily and rubbed her eyes as Valerie became increasingly uncomfortable. She'd wanted Euphemia to be outraged, to tell her it wasn't true and that he really was the sweet, gentle man she loved, but it seemed that wasn't going to happen.

'Please,' said Valerie when Euphemia remained silent. 'I have to know.' A tear slipped from the corner of her eye and slid down her cheek.

'Seb is a very troubled boy,' she began diplomatically.

'So it is true? He's a violent criminal.'

'That's not how Laura and Jeffrey would put it but yes, there's really no denying it. He's guilty of all those things.'

'Oh, god,' Valerie breathed, the tears starting to fall freely.

'It all began when he was ten. He fell and hit his head. He was in a coma for three days. When he woke, he wasn't the same sweet boy.'

'So it's not his fault,' said Valerie hopefully. 'It's because of a head injury?'

'Perhaps, but who knows for sure? Laura's used that same argument to get him out of trouble countless times but it's starting to wear a bit thin now. I don't know for how much longer she can get away with that excuse. Sometimes I think he does these things just because he enjoys them.'

'He told me he was studying Philosophy and Divinity at university and that he wants to become a church minister.'

'Aye, we know that's what he told you because he told us, but really he's studying Philosophy and Psychology and he almost got kicked out of university a few months ago for dealing drugs. It was only Laura's powers of persuasion that meant he was able to stay on and take his exams. Seb's a very smart boy with a genuine love of books and history. It's just a shame he enjoys violence and crime more.'

'Does he believe in God at all?'

'He's never discussed his beliefs with me, but I'm quite sure he isn't a strong enough believer to want to be a minister.'

'We'd envisaged this beautiful life of him being a minister and together we'd help the local community, and in the evenings we'd curl up together in front of the fire to discuss books and history and philosophy, but that's all destroyed now. He's not the man I fell in love with.'

'Perhaps, perhaps not.'

'What do you mean?'

'He's been different since you came along – happier, kinder. It's why the family didn't object too much to your hasty engagement.'

'Well, I'm not saddling myself with a violent man for the rest of my life.'

'Why don't you talk to him first? Honestly, you've no idea how much better he's been since you came into his life.'

'Oh, I want to talk to him, all right,' she said determinedly. 'But I certainly don't think it'll go the way you hope. How can I ever trust him again?'

'Come now, Valerie, you've been keeping a secret of your own. We know you're part of the McVay family.'

'How do you know that?'

'The polis let it slip when they went to speak to Laura and Jeffrey.'

'Great,' she sighed. What a time for that bombshell to drop. 'But I didn't lie to Seb about it. He knows exactly who I am and who my family is. My cousin Toni even introduced us, we met at a party at her house.'

'You lied to us about it, though.'

'Because I wanted you all to like me and I thought if you knew who my family was, you'd encourage Seb to dump me. He's the first man I've ever loved, and I wanted it to work.'

Euphemia's eyes filled with tenderness. 'You love him?'

'Of course I do. I could never agree to marry a man I didn't love, but it turns out I love an illusion because my Seb doesn't even exist.'

She broke off and buried her face in her hands, attempting to stifle the sobs, but they wouldn't be contained and her shoulders shook with the violence of her emotions.

Euphemia hauled herself out of her chair, shuffled over to the couch and plonked herself down beside Valerie, placing a thin, wrinkled hand on her shoulder.

'I'm so sorry you're in this pain,' she said softly. 'But there may be a chance for you yet. I really do encourage you to talk to Seb.'

'How can I when his parents won't let me near him? They think I stabbed him. As if I could ever hurt him.'

'Just you leave it with me, I'll speak to them and make sure they let you in to see him. Besides, he probably won't be in hospital for much longer. Laura called to say he had a good night and is recovering well. He's been moved off intensive care to a standard ward.'

'I'm glad. Despite the lies, I don't want anything bad to happen to him.'

'Because you're a good person. I saw that the moment we met. Your family's reputation doesn't define you, and I hope Seb's past deeds don't define him.'

'I'm sorry to burst your bubble, Euphemia, but your grandson's still up to his neck in crime. I've already had that confirmed.'

Distress filled Euphemia's eyes. 'What do you mean? What's he been doing now?'

'You should speak to him about that. Do you know who his friends are?'

'Er, there are a couple of girls. One's called Celia and the other Megan. And there's a boy named Archie.'

'I don't mean the people he uses to maintain his cover, I mean his real friends. It's only just struck me that he hasn't introduced me to any of his friends, other than the ones I met at my cousin's party. He's never even mentioned any. That should have been a red flag and I didn't pick up on it.'

'It's easy to miss these things when you're in love,' said Euphemia, her eyes filling with infinite pain.

Valerie recalled what Seb had said about Euphemia's husband being abusive and, if that was true, then she was probably reliving her own painful memories.

'Thank you for talking to me,' said Valerie. 'I wasn't sure if you would.'

'My son and daughter-in-law have yet to learn that people don't simply vanish if you ignore them.'

'What will Seb do now?'

'If I know that boy, he'll go straight after the person who stabbed him.'

'Which wasn't me,' she said firmly.

'I never believed it was, but if you know who did it, then they should be prepared. Seb is like a hurricane when enraged.'

'Has he ever got violent with the family?'

'He's struck his father a couple of times.'

'What? But they seem so close. He was putting on a show?'

Euphemia nodded. 'I love my grandson, really I do, and I miss the little boy he used to be, but I'm not so blind that I don't recognise how dangerous he is, so please, take my advice – be careful. I think there is some element of the man you love within him but don't underestimate him. Laura told me that he's raging about being attacked and when he's angry, he's extremely unpredictable. Be on your guard.'

'I appreciate you being so frank with me.'

Euphemia patted her hand. 'Look after yourself. I don't think you deserve the situation you find yourself in.'

'I'm glad someone thinks so,' she sighed. Valerie spotted the small gold cross at Euphemia's throat. 'You're a believer?'

'I am,' she smiled, her hand going to the cross and stroking it. 'God has brought me great comfort, especially through the trials of my life. Without my faith, I wouldn't be here now.'

'I wish I had faith like that, but I've only ever relied on myself.'

'There is strength in that, but I'll keep you in my prayers.'

'Thanks,' said Valerie uncertainly. 'Seb said his grandda was a church minister, he didn't say which grandda, though, and that he was a kind and gentle man.'

'I'm afraid that was a lie too. Jeffrey's father was a bus conductor and my husband was an idle drunkard who never did a stroke of work in his entire life. Neither were kind or gentle.'

Valerie sighed as something else she'd loved about Seb fell away, leaving her feeling like a gullible fool.

23

Valerie got off the bus outside the hospital and stared up at the building uncertainly. This conversation would change her life, whichever way it went. After hearing what Seb was capable of, especially from his own gran, she was anxious about confronting him. She never thought she'd see the day she was nervous about seeing him.

Taking a deep breath, she stalked into the hospital and headed straight to the ward Seb had been moved to. She slipped onto the ward and was relieved when all the staff were far too busy to bother with her. It was visiting time, so she blended in with the other visitors.

Valerie walked past Seb's room and glanced inside as she went by. It was a relief to see there were no visitors. There was just Seb in his bed, head tilted to one side as he gazed out of the window. He wore a T-shirt and pyjama bottoms and his left arm was still held in a sling. His hair was tousled and he was unshaven but he looked even more gorgeous for it.

When Valerie felt herself softening towards him, being a McVay for once worked in her favour because she reminded herself of all the hard nuts and lunatics she was related to, and it gave her the confidence she needed to push that door open and walk inside.

'Valerie,' beamed Seb. 'Thank god. I've been asking to see you and my parents kept making crap excuses.' He held his hand out to her, his smile falling when she didn't take it and remained at the far side of the room by the door. 'What's wrong?' he said.

'First of all,' she said, forcing down the urge to fling herself at him, 'how are you feeling?'

'Good, thanks to you. You stopped the bleeding. If you hadn't done that, it would have been a lot worse. They've said I can go home tomorrow, if I have a good night tonight.'

'I'm glad you're recovering.'

'Aye, me too. Come here, I've missed you so much.' He frowned when she refused to budge. 'What's going on? What's that folder you're holding?'

Finally she approached the bed, produced the mugshot from inside the folder and tossed it onto his bed.

'Care to explain?' she said icily.

Valerie watched him carefully as he picked up the photograph with his good arm. The sweetness was gone. In fact, nothing was there at all. It was like he'd managed to completely erase his emotions from his eyes. The disconcerting impression lasted a few seconds before the warmth returned to his gaze and he looked to her with a smile.

'It's just a prank photo one of my pals took for Halloween.'

'Don't, Seb,' she sighed.

'Is this why you're upset, because of this photograph?'

'Not just that,' she said, dumping the folder on the bed too.

With a quizzical look, he flipped it open with his good hand and froze when confronted by his own criminal record. He didn't speak as he flicked through the papers. When he got to the end, he closed the folder and sighed.

'Well?' she said. 'I'm waiting, or are you going to say all that's a Halloween prank too?'

'How did you get hold of this?'

'It came from a concerned friend.'

'You mean Frankie?'

'No. He has no idea about any of this, fortunately for you. It was someone you don't know.'

'Their last name doesn't happen to be Thompson, does it?'

'Nope. I don't even know where Liam and his cronies are. They've gone to ground.'

'I'm not surprised.'

'Anyway, it doesn't matter who gave it to me. I want to know if it's true.'

'I think you've already made up your mind about that.'

Seb's voice had taken on a tone she'd never heard before, his demeanour cold and distant.

'So you are the violent person those documents detail?' said Valerie.

'Well, if it's written down on paper, it must be true,' he said sarcastically.

He'd never once spoken to her like that before and it was a shock. 'Are you saying it isn't?'

'What's the point?' he sighed, tossing the folder contemptuously to the bottom of the bed. 'You've already decided it is.'

'Why didn't you tell me about it?'

He shrugged. 'Would you have gone out with me if I had?'

'All my previous boyfriends had criminal records.'

'But I didn't want to be like that. I wanted to be the opposite for you.'

'So you could use me to get close to Frankie?' Inside Valerie was a raging mass of pain, but outwardly she managed to appear calm and in control.

'That was the idea, at first. You see, it was Toni I was trying to get close to, but it soon became clear I wasn't her type. Then she told me all about you and I switched my plan over to you instead. I thought play the sweet wannabe minister and I'd be something different, something you hadn't explored before, and you loved it.'

'I did,' she murmured. 'I really did. I'd never met anyone like you – or should I say him – before. But all that about literature must have been true. You know far too much.'

'It was. I've always loved books. They've been good companions in my darkest moments,' he said, a shadow settling over him as he relived some painful or violent memory. He shook himself out of it and his expression brightened slightly. 'And I really enjoyed discussing the subject with you. I've never met anyone I can talk to like that before. I didn't lie about everything.'

'Why did you propose to me? Was that to get close to Frankie too?'

'I did that because I wanted to. I do love you, Valerie,' he said more gently.

'How can I believe that's true when you used to me get close to my cousin and take the business he's building up? I know you're Harry Woodhouse and those men you were talking to in Archaos weren't Frankie's people, they were yours. You're a violent drug dealer who wants to increase his territory and you were going to use me to do it. I can't believe I fell for your lies, I feel such an idiot. I bet you had a good fucking laugh about how gullible I was.'

Valerie's voice increased a few decibels as the hurt and bewilderment morphed into rage.

He shrugged. 'You were after a certain type of man, so I became him. I can read you like a book, Valerie. I was deliberately late on our first date, there was no Dan. It was a test to see how much you liked me. If you weren't that bothered, you would have left when I'd kept you waiting, but you didn't. You waited half an hour,' he smirked. 'So I knew I'd already reeled you in.'

'You bastard,' she spat, tearing the engagement ring from her jacket pocket and hurling it at him. It hit him in the centre of the chest and dropped into his lap. Seb paid it no attention. 'You can take back that piece of crap,' she yelled, her tears now falling. 'The engagement's off.'

'Maybe you shouldn't be so hasty?' he said.

'What?'

'We're great together, and I still want to be with you.'

'Are you completely insane? Scratch that because, actually, I think you are.'

'I love you, Valerie.'

'You've no idea what love is,' she practically screamed at him.

The door burst open and a nurse charged in. 'I'm sorry, but we cannot have yelling on this ward.'

'Oh, piss off,' Valerie told her.

'Excuse me?' demanded the nurse, her eyes flashing with anger.

'Hello, Valerie,' said a deep voice.

They all looked to the door to see a large figure standing there.

'Not you again,' sighed Valerie.

Detective Sergeant Baillie entered the room with a knowing smile.

'And what merry hell are you causing?' he asked her.

'She told me to piss off,' the outraged nurse told him.

'So I heard, but she's upset. Why don't you gi'e me a few moments with her, eh, doll? I need to talk to her as part of my investigation.'

'Well, okay, but Sebastian needs his rest, so you can't be too long.'

'Understood.'

With one last glare at an oblivious Valerie, the nurse left the room.

'What's all this arguing about then?' said Baillie, addressing Valerie.

'I've just found out that my ex-fiancé is a violent, lying creep.'

Baillie's brow creased. 'You mean you didnae know?'

'Of course I didn't,' she exclaimed. 'I thought he was sweet and kind and wanted to be a church minister.'

Baillie spluttered with laughter. 'Sebastian Robertson wants to be a minister? Oh, god, that's the best thing I've heard all year.'

Valerie's eyes flashed. 'It's not funny.'

'If you knew this lad like I do, then it would be hilarious.'

Valerie desperately fought the urge to punch Baillie right in the middle of his smug, chubby face. 'Why didn't you mention what he was like when you interviewed me?' she said.

'Because I thought you already knew. You mean you really had no idea?' Baillie grinned and shook his head. 'You might be a vicious bastard, Sebastian, but you've got a great sense of humour, minister indeed.'

'Do not call me Sebastian,' Seb glowered, radiating menace.

'I came here to tell him that we're over,' Valerie told Baillie. 'I don't want to be engaged to a bastard like him.'

'I don't know why you're getting so uppity,' said Baillie. 'Most of the men in your family are like him.'

'Which is why I wanted someone kind and gentle.'

Baillie threw back his head and roared with laughter.

'Aye, well, that's a shame, but better you find out now what this shitebag's really like than after the wedding.'

'That's a very good point,' she said, glaring at Seb, who just reclined back in his bed, looking completely unconcerned. 'Anyway,' she continued, looking back at Baillie. 'I hope you've finally realised that I didn't hurt him?'

'I knew that from the get-go. I was just hoping to get some information about his activities from you. Now it's clear you don't have a clue.'

'No, I do not. Can I leave now?'

'Aye, away you go. I want to talk to Sebastian in private.'

'You're not going,' Seb told her. 'I love you and want to be with you, so we're no' splitting up. We're right together, Valerie, and you know it,' pressed Seb.

'I know that you're a psycho and I want nothing more to do with you.' Valerie paused before continuing, wanting her voice to be completely steady because this was tearing her apart. 'Goodbye, Sebastian,' she said before leaving.

Valerie closed the door behind her and hurried away. Tears blinded her as she ran out of the ward, not stopping until she'd left the hospital and was back on the street. The future she'd longed for and had been preparing for was well and truly gone. No Aberdeenshire, no living in the countryside with a good man, helping people and absorbing themselves in history and books. It was back to being a McVay, mistrusted and feared by everyone. It was all gone, and she didn't have a clue what to do.

A car pulled up at the kerb beside her and the rear door was pushed open. 'Get in,' called a voice.

She was shocked to see Liam Thompson in the backseat of the old Volvo. 'Fuck off,' she told him. 'I want to be alone.'

'Get in. I have so much to tell you.'

'Do you think I'm crazy enough to get in there after you abducted me?'

With that, she hurriedly walked on.

To her surprise, Liam hopped out and the car pulled back into the flow of traffic and drove off.

'Valerie, wait,' he called, hurrying to catch up.

Her hand went to her pepper spray, but she didn't pull it out, she just kept hold of it, ready to use if necessary.

'Aren't you supposed to be in hiding?' she asked him when he caught up with her.

'Aye, I was, but I have to talk to you. There's so much you don't know.'

'I think I know now – Seb is a violent, drug-dealing bastard and he's lied to me our entire relationship.'

'Oh, so you do know, then.'

'I've just been to see him at the hospital and thrown his ring back in his face. He was so cold, I've never seen him like that before. It was such a shock. Dammit,' she huffed, furious with herself when the tears rolled down her face again. She'd not cried so much in her entire life and she was getting sick of it.

'Let's go in there,' said Liam, pointing to a café further down the road. 'You could do with a sit down and something hot inside you. I meant a cup of tea,' he hastily added when her eyes flashed with anger.

'That café isn't owned by your family, is it? I won't be dragged into a back room, tied up and tortured?'

'Course not.'

'Oh, fine,' she sighed, lacking the energy to argue.

The café was quiet and they both automatically took a table away from the windows but far enough from the counter, so they could talk without being overheard. They ordered a cup of tea each and Liam a doughnut. He encouraged Valerie to eat something, but she had no appetite. Liam didn't press her, although he thought eating something would help her. He'd realised trying to push Valerie Brown into anything was futile.

'Right, you,' she told him. 'Talk.'

'Me and my whole family just assumed you knew who Seb was. It didnae occur to us that you wouldn't.'

'Well, I didn't,' she said wearily. 'And I feel like a bloody idiot. And before you ask, Frankie had no idea either.' A thought occurred to her. 'Or maybe he did and he was playing Seb, just as Seb was trying to play him? Oh, my god, that could be exactly what was going on and there was me in the middle, clueless.'

'I wouldnae put it past Frankie to use you to get his own way.'

'Course he would. Maybe that's why he was so friendly to Seb? He invited him on a family outing to Largs.'

'If Seb had gone, he might not have come back alive.'

'Maybe, or maybe Frankie really didn't know. Seb had purposefully flown under his radar and he was using an alias for his dealing.'

'It's possible. My family's had trouble with Seb and his pals for years. We only found out a few days ago that he and Harry Woodhouse were the same person.'

'You were determined to kill him that night,' she said, voice dropping to a whisper.

'Aye, I was. I lost it when I saw him because I think he killed my younger brother,' he whispered back.

'Leighton?'

He nodded, eyes full of sadness.

'But your family blamed mine for that, even though he died of an overdose.'

'Because we assumed it was your lot at first. Leighton was dealing on Frankie's territory. He'd got heavily addicted to heroin, it was slowly killing him and he'd dae anything for a fix. Then I found out recently it was Seb who'd roped him into working for him and got him hooked. The hit that killed him was laced with all sorts of nasty shit, purposefully, the polis thought.'

This fresh revelation that Seb could do something so evil and cruel sent a fresh wave of pain through her. 'God, I'm sorry. That's awful.'

Liam nodded, eyes flashing with his own deep pain. 'I didn't know Seb would be at Frankie's when we attacked, and when I saw him, I couldnae control myself.' His fierce expression softened. 'But I still couldnae bring myself to go through you to get to him.'

'I'm very glad you didn't. At the time, I hated you, I couldn't understand why you'd do something so awful to someone so innocent. Now I wish I'd stood back and let you go to town on the bastard.'

'I don't think you would, even now you know what he's really like.'

'Maybe,' she shrugged, taking another sip of tea. 'I left him at the hospital with Detective Sergeant Baillie. That's one sarky polis, he burst out laughing when I told him what Seb had done, but it's not funny to me,' she said earnestly. 'That's the man I fell in love with, but it was all a big joke. He said he saw what sort of man I wanted, so he became him, he read me that easily and that is fucking frightening.' Valerie had no idea why she was opening up to a man who had recently abducted her, but she just had to get all this out. She didn't want to discuss it with her parents because she'd only get a lecture or they'd somehow make it her fault and she wasn't sure how Frankie would react when he found out she'd brought a viper into the nest.

'If it makes you feel better,' said Liam, 'that is a talent of Seb's and he's pulled it on a lot of people, including people who are older and a lot more experienced than you. It's one reason why he's got away with it for so long, that and his maw.'

'I was angry at Laura at first for protecting him, but now I just feel sorry for her. I can dump Seb, but she's stuck with him for the rest of her life. She can never escape.'

'And that is her punishment.'

'Just so you know, no one's told the polis it was you who stabbed him, although they probably have their suspicions.'

'I didnae think any of you would grass, but thanks anyway.'

'Wow, this is weird – a McVay and a Thompson being polite to each other.'

'Miracles do happen,' he said wryly. 'You're the only McVay I've ever liked.'

'I suppose I wouldn't think you were too bad either, if you hadn't kidnapped me and helped your uncle try to get information out of me.'

'How can you be angry about that when you escaped and I got savaged by a couple of dogs?'

'I admit, that does take the sting out of it,' she grinned. 'Did they hurt you?'

'My legs are covered in bite marks but Bill got them off me pretty quickly, so there was minimal damage.'

Valerie was surprised to find that she was rather glad about that, but she wasn't about to tell him. 'I want to know everything you can tell me about Seb because I don't think he's done with me. I broke it off with him, but he says he loves me and still wants to be with me.'

'You're no' gonnae get back with him, are you?'

'God, no, but forewarned is forearmed.'

'I can only tell you about what's gone on between him and my family. He started encroaching on our patch a couple of years ago with the help of his two pals, Gregor and Simon. They're a pair of major twats, by the way. They're violent and vicious but no' as bad as Seb, he's the worst one. They like to hook people on drugs to make them blindly obedient to them. Desperate addicts will do anything for their next fix,' he said bitterly as he thought of his brother. 'They're the ones who take all the risks while Seb and his pals rake in the cash and if their names are brought up, who cares, because no one would believe an addict over the son of a respected solicitor. Despite his record, it took the polis a while to click onto what was happening. By the time Seb tried to take over our patch, he was well and truly on the polis's radar. They knew what he was up to, they've just never had any proof, apart from the word of a few druggies who a jury would never believe, especially not when Seb can present himself so well.'

'Aye, that's true,' she muttered as she pictured a jury finding a sweet, gentle, wide-eyed Seb innocent of any wrongdoing. No one would believe he could hurt a fly, never mind be capable of all the terrible things he would be accused of.

'So he's got away with all sorts for years,' continued Liam. 'You need to be really careful because he is violent and has hurt plenty of people in the past, often for very little or no reason at all.'

Valerie's eyes widened as she made a connection. 'He attacked William Lundy, the shopkeeper?'

'Aye.'

'But why?'

'I reckon he was trying to get to Frankie. He got one of his addict pals to point the finger at you and Toni.'

'Which is why he invited me to his grandma's birthday party, so I'd have a strong alibi.'

'Probably, but he was banking on Toni no' having one. If she'd been arrested, Frankie would have been angry and distracted and while he was distracted...'

'Seb could have swooped in and taken over his turf, only Toni did have an alibi, so it didnae work. Oh, god, I told him Toni's maw was going to a friend's birthday party and that she'd be alone. I was going to stay over to keep her company, only Moira's plans got cancelled. He invited me to the party so Toni would be alone.'

Liam nodded.

'The twisted, scheming bastard. I could kill him myself.'

'Do yourself a favour and stay away from him. He's dangerous and even you might not be able to stand up to him.'

'I've no intention of going anywhere near him ever again.'

'But he might come to you. Maybe it would be best if you went away for a bit and let this blow over?'

The prospect of getting out of Glasgow for a while was tempting. 'That's no' a bad idea, actually.'

'Do you want any company?'

'Do you mean you?'

'Aye,' he said, leaning into her. 'I dae. You deserve far better than that creep.'

'You're right, I do, but I don't think that person's you.'

'Charming.'

'Sorry, but our families would lose their minds. Anyway, I think I'll be off men for quite a while. I don't know how I'll trust anyone ever again.'

'You could always get Stevie to do a background check on them,' he said knowingly.

'That's not a bad idea. Right, I'm off. Thanks for setting a few things straight for me. At least now I know what I'm up against.' As she got up to leave, she hesitated. 'Can I ask you something?'

'Anything,' he replied, pleased to have her company for just a little longer.

'How did you get that scar?'

'Why do you want to know?'

'Because every scar is a story.'

He smiled. That was such a Valerie Brown thing to say. 'My da did it to me when I was eight. He was whacking me with his belt because I cried when I fell over while playing outside and the buckle caught me under the eye and got dragged down my face.'

'Oh, god, I'm sorry,' she said.

'Don't worry about it. The cunt died a slow, painful death from liver failure because he was a raging alcoholic, so I like to think he was paid back for what he did.'

'Good,' she said before getting up to leave. 'See you around, Liam.'

'Aye, you definitely will,' he replied, watching her go with a smile.

24

Valerie caught the bus back to Springburn and to home, when she realised that she was supposed to work that day and hadn't even called in. Taking her phone out of her jacket, she saw she had missed calls from her mum, Frankie, Toni, Aunty Mima and the petrol station. She called work first and told the outraged manager that her boyfriend had been stabbed the night before and she'd been at the hospital with him. The manager immediately stammered an apology for shouting and told her to take all the time she needed. Valerie thanked her and hung up, relieved that at least she hadn't lost her job. Now she wasn't going to Aberdeenshire, she needed it. She decided to ignore the calls from Frankie, Mima and her mum and rang Toni instead.

'Val, thank god,' said her cousin's husky voice in her ear. 'I've been so worried, no one's been able to get hold of you. I even asked Aunty Mima to call because I thought you'd pick up for her.'

'Sorry, I had my phone on silent. It's been one hell of a day.'

'Are you okay? Has anyone hurt you?' Toni said anxiously.

'I'm fine physically.'

'What do you mean? What's going on?'

'Where are you?'

'Just leaving the nail bar, I've worked a shift.'

'I'll meet you in the pub around the corner. I really need to talk to you, Toni.'

Twenty minutes later, Valerie walked into the quiet, respectable pub. She ordered herself a glass of white wine from the beaming landlady and joined her cousin in one of the booths. Toni was nursing a glass of red wine.

'You look like shite, Val,' commented Toni.

'That's because I feel it. I've got so much to tell you about Seb.'

'Is he all right?' said Toni with concern.

'Aye, he'll be fine. Jesus, I don't know where to start.'

Toni patiently waited for her cousin to begin, her eyes so full of concern Valerie wanted to cry. Taking a deep breath, she laid it all out for Toni. She even told her about her conversation with Liam. She felt Toni should know everything. Her cousin's eyes grew wider with each word.

When Valerie had finished explaining, Toni sagged back in her seat, looking pale. 'Jesus Christ, I can't believe it. I feel so bad.'

'Why do you feel bad?'

'Because I introduced you to him. I thought he was sweet and kind and all the time he was plotting to take everything from Frankie. I can't believe he fooled me.' Toni's eyes narrowed. 'No one fools me.'

'You're not the only one he's taken in over the years, it's why he keeps getting away with it.'

'Well, the bastard's going to pay. Let's go and tell Frankie.'

'What if he already knows?'

'He can't possibly know. If he had, he wouldn't have let Seb anywhere near either of us.'

'He might have been playing the long game, lulling Seb into a false sense of security.'

'No, I don't believe that. He would have just lopped his head off. I'm no' sure Frankie's got the patience for long games.'

Valerie thought of her cousin containing his formidable temper and the urge to hurt Seb, which must have been intense if her theory was correct. She then considered how genuinely affable he'd been to Seb at Toni's party and wondered if she was barking up the wrong tree. She sighed and shook her head. 'All this is giving me a headache.'

'I'm not surprised. What are you going to do?'

'I might take Liam's advice and go away for a while. Work owe me a few holidays.'

'You're best checking with Frankie first.'

'I don't need his permission. If I want to go away for a holiday, I will. In fact, I might not come back.'

'Don't say that, please, Val. You're my best pal. I need you.'

Valerie's anger softened. 'You're my best friend too, but I refuse to live under Frankie's thumb and if I stay here, I'll have to and he's only going to get worse.'

Toni's eyes flickered but she didn't reply because she knew her cousin was right. 'At least talk to him first. Frankie has to know what's going on and he'll deal with Seb for you.'

'Okay, but he has to be careful because the polis are all over Seb. They've spotted their chance to finally bring him down. I'll go and tell Frankie, but will you come with me? He'll take it better if you're there.'

'Course I will,' said Toni, relieved that Valerie was doing the sensible thing.

* * *

Frankie was at home, snarling at the workmen fixing the damage to his house. Although these men were twenty years Frankie's senior, he had them terrified, and they jumped at his every command. Paul and Jamesie were, as usual, by his side, chuckling as he barked orders at the workmen.

'There you fucking are,' exclaimed Frankie when Paul escorted Valerie into his home, accompanied by Toni. 'I've been calling and calling and nothing. No one ignores me,' he hissed.

'I wasn't ignoring you, Frankie,' sighed Valerie. 'I was busy. I've had the day from hell.'

'Oh, I do apologise,' he said sarcastically. 'Perhaps you should get a secretary and I could book an appointment, so you can fit me into your busy schedule?'

'We need to talk,' said Valerie before nodding at the two workmen, who were plastering the dents in his walls.

'You two,' snarled Frankie, causing the men to jump. 'Go and wait in the backyard.' He rolled his eyes when they stared at him in surprise. 'Do it now before I kick you both right up the arse.'

His yelling made them dump their tools on the floor and rush through the house to the back door.

'Make sure they stay there while we talk,' Frankie told Jamesie, who nodded and followed them out. 'Are all workmen such fannies or is it just that pair?' he said to no one in particular.

'They might work better if you didn't keep them in a state of perpetual fear,' said Valerie.

'Shite. Fear makes people work harder. There's nothing like a good dose of terror to make people obey you,' he grinned maniacally. 'Now, what have you got to tell me?'

'You won't like it.'

'I don't like anything, so you may as well spit it out.'

Valerie laid it all out for Frankie, although she didn't tell him that she went to a café with Liam as he would see that as fraternising with the enemy. Instead, she pretended that he'd been waiting for her outside the hospital.

When she'd finished, Frankie just stared at her, unblinking.

'You're telling me that big, soft pudding is Harry fucking Wood-house?' he eventually exploded.

'Aye. You really didn't know?'

'If I had, I would have chopped off his baws and put them in my trophy room by now.' His demeanour turned aggressive. 'You brought that dangerous cunt into our family, you let him be around Toni.'

'Er, blame me for that,' said Toni. 'I was the one who introduced him to Val, not the other way round.'

'Aye, but...' Frankie turned purple when he couldn't think of a reply to that. 'That's no' the point. Why didnae you realise who he was?'

'Why didn't you realise who he was?' retorted Valerie. 'You're the one in the know around here, not me.'

'Val,' said Toni. 'Take it easy.'

'I will not,' she retorted. 'I've had the crappiest day of my entire life. The man I was going to marry isn't real and is in fact a dangerous lunatic.' Valerie thought how strange it was that truth outraged her when her own cousin was equally if not more dangerous. 'He lied to me and the life I thought I was going to have with him is gone, so don't start on me, Frankie, because I'm not in the fucking mood.'

To everyone's surprise, he threw back his head and brayed with maniacal laughter before slapping Paul so hard on the shoulder he almost fell over. 'You see that, pal? Val's so tough she only comes back harder.' He looked back at his cousin. 'I'm glad to see the arsehole hasnae broken your spirit, doll.'

'It takes a lot more than a prick like that to get to me.'

Toni once again marvelled at how Valerie was able to get away with so much with Frankie that no one else could, not even herself. Could it be that he actually respected her?

'The important thing is we now know the truth about him,' said Valerie. 'So he can't carry out his plan any more.'

'Aye, you're right,' said Frankie. 'And we can get busy planning what we're gonnae dae to him,' he added, eyes glimmering with numerous violent possibilities.

'Good luck with that. I'm going away for a bit.'

Frankie scowled. 'Why the hell would you want to dae that when things are about to get interesting? Besides, I need your help.'

'I'm in so much pain, Frankie, and I can't think straight. I'd be a liability to you.'

'That's bollocks. You take all that anger and you use it as a weapon to hurt the bastard and believe me when I say I'm gonnae gi'e him a world of pain.'

'I don't want to get involved. I still love the Seb I thought he was, so I won't be able to hurt him. I know I said I wanted to kill him, but I was hurt and angry.'

Frankie's gaze turned dark, lips drawing back over his teeth. Valerie forced herself not to flinch as he leaned in to whisper in her ear.

'Don't tell me you don't want to make him hurt bad for how he used you, to see him bleed and hear his cries of pain?' He leaned back slightly to meet her hard gaze and his bizarre grin widened. 'Aye, course you dae. It's the only thing that will help you heal.'

'Do what you like to him because I don't care.'

'Are you sure? You'll be missing out.'

'I'm sure. I'm so tired, Frankie. I need a wee break.'

'Fine, go away then. I'll sort it all out and when you come home it'll be like the bastard never existed.'

'Thanks, Frankie,' she said, pleased he'd acquiesced so quickly. She decided not to mention that she might not come back.

* * *

The manager at the petrol station was happy to give Valerie a couple of weeks off, so she decided to book a holiday to the island of Bute. She'd gone there on holiday a few years ago with her parents and thought it would be a great place to heal and get over recent events.

When Valerie broke the news about Seb to her parents, they claimed they'd realised there was something shifty about him and had never liked him, which Valerie knew was an absolute lie. She avoided them as much as possible because they kept giving her lectures about how she'd never find a decent man and would only attract losers if she didn't stop hanging around with Toni, who they'd decided to blame for the entire thing as she was the one who'd introduced their daughter to Seb.

Despite this, Valerie spent most of her time with Toni, who was counselling her and distracting her from her darkest thoughts. Most people thought Toni was as bad as her brother and was another flourishing psycho, but Valerie saw the kind-hearted woman beneath who hid from the world that had hurt her so much.

All Valerie had to do was get through the next few days without anything happening before she could escape. Her bags were packed and waiting under her bed. She'd packed extra clothes just in case she decided to stay for longer. Her plan was to enquire about work and homes to rent while she was on holiday. She wanted to escape Seb and all the pain of that doomed relationship but Frankie too, who would attempt to get increasing control over her.

She had to get out.

* * *

Although Chris Cathcart had fled the area to escape the Thompsons' wrath, Valerie wasn't taking any chances and still always ensured she had her pepper spray on her and checked her surroundings before leaving work.

She got safely onto the bus and breathed a sigh of relief. No one bothered her on the journey and she alighted just a couple of streets from her home. It was six o'clock in the evening, so there was some traffic about and a few passers-by, but as it was a residential area, it was pretty quiet, everyone having returned home from work and school.

Everything was normal but unease still rippled up and down her spine. As she picked up the pace, Valerie kept looking over her shoulder, expecting an attack.

She reached home safely and breathed a sigh of relief as she unlocked the front door and stepped inside, locking it behind her. Her parents were out, her father working and her mother at a friend's birthday party.

After slipping off her shoes and jacket, Valerie walked into the front room and was astonished to find Seb perched on the couch.

'What the hell?' she exclaimed.

'Hello, Valerie,' he smiled. He looked fit and healthy and not like a man who had just been discharged from hospital. He'd even discarded the sling. 'You look great.'

'What the fuck do you think you're doing, you mad bastard? How did you get in?'

'I made an impression of your front door key. It was a simple thing to have it cut.'

'You actually have a key to my house?'

He nodded.

'Get out right now before I call the polis.'

'I don't think so. We've got things to discuss. Sit down.'

'There's nothing to discuss. We're over, end of.'

'No,' he said, his gaze growing angry. 'I said sit down,' he said more firmly.

'My dad will be back from work any minute.'

'Actually, he won't. I made a call and he's currently driving to Falkirk to collect a fare, so we have plenty of time.'

Valerie bolted for the front door, snatching up her keys from the stand in the hallway. As she slid the key into the lock, an arm snaked around her waist and dragged her back into the front room.

'Get off me,' she yelled.

'I won't hurt you, I just want to talk. I don't think so,' he said, wrenching the pepper spray from her hand when she pulled it from her jeans pocket. 'Don't make me use this on you,' he bellowed in her ear.

Valerie's head rang with the volume of his voice. If he pepper sprayed her, she'd be completely helpless and that she couldn't allow. Hopefully he'd just talk and then leave. Angering him wouldn't help. This man was far more dangerous than Leo.

'All right, let's talk,' she sighed.

'That's better,' he said, his grip on her relaxing. 'I really don't want to hurt you,' he murmured, pressing his face into her hair.

To Valerie's relief, he released her and gestured to the couch for her to sit.

'I want to explain properly,' he began, sitting beside her. 'I didn't get the chance at the hospital.'

'Okay. Off you go then,' said Valerie, who was actually curious to hear what he had to say.

'When we first started dating, yes, I wanted to use you to get close to Frankie. I hoped he'd recruit me and I could start working in his operation. That way, I could bring it down from the inside and take it over. But I'd no idea you were trying to protect me from that.'

'Because I thought you were so good and innocent,' she said flatly. 'More fool me.'

'Still, he did recruit me, although the bloody Thompsons attacked before I could really get a feel for his business or find out who his contacts are. But I developed real feelings for you, Valerie. I've never been able to talk to anyone like I can you. Yes, I've done bad things, but my love of literature is genuine. I've never had such fascinating conversations in my life, they were so fulfilling. I meant it when I said I love you and I meant it when I asked you to marry me. My friends said I was crazy, but I know you're the woman for me. I want you back and I'll do whatever it takes to make that happen.'

Gently he took her hand in his own. Valerie made no move to pull away, even though the feel of his skin on her own now made her shudder.

'Why don't you understand that I can never trust you again?' she said. 'I fell in love with someone else, not you.'

Seb's eyes flickered as he dealt with emotions she was guessing he'd never felt before. 'No, you didn't, it was me you loved.'

'Maybe the part who loves literature and history, but I fell for the sweet, kind man who never hurt anyone in his life. That's who I want and, god, I miss him so much.'

'He's here, inside me,' he said, pressing her hand to his chest. 'And I can bring him back, I know it.'

'But he won't be you, he'll just be some character you created to play a part. I can't live like that.'

'Can't you give the real me a chance? You might like me more than him.'

'You can't give me the life I want, which is away from all the violence and gang warfare. I've been around it my entire life and I'm sick of it. I want that good, decent life with Seb the minister,' she said, voice cracking.

'He's here, look,' he said earnestly.

Valerie watched in horror as all the hardness vanished from his eyes and filled with the softness and kindness she'd come to love. It wasn't just his eyes that changed, it was his entire body. When he was being his real self, his muscles pumped up with aggression, making him appear larger and more imposing, but now he looked completely non-threatening. That darling innocence filled his eyes and he reached out to stroke her face in that gentle, familiar way. It was disturbing but at the same time stoked all the love she had for Seb.

'Don't do this,' she whispered, a tear sliding down her cheek. 'Please.'

'I'm still here, Valerie,' said *her* Seb. 'You can have me whenever you want. Just be with me again.'

'My god, you're actually ill, you must be. Jekyll and Hyde.'

'Jekyll was the real man,' pressed Seb. 'Hyde was just a creation of his and that's how it is with me.'

She shook her head, sending more tears spilling down her cheeks. 'No, you're the other way around. Hyde is the real man and Jekyll the creation.'

He placed the pepper spray in his lap and took her face in his hands. 'We both exist,' he breathed, leaning in closer. 'And we both love you.'

Gently he kissed her and Valerie moaned with longing, aching for this man she still loved with her entire being.

The kiss deepened and she wrapped her arms around his neck, sliding her fingers through his hair. Valerie allowed him to press her back into the couch as their movements became more frantic.

He pulled her jumper off over her head, kissing her breasts, moving down to her bare stomach.

'You're the most beautiful woman I ever saw,' he murmured into her skin. 'And by far the best in bed.'

'You're the best I ever had too,' she smiled up at him.

He beamed down at her and kissed her, groaning when she pulled open his shirt and ran her hands down his body. God, she'd forgotten just how hot that body was. He went rigid with anticipation as her hand cupped his crotch before starting to unfasten his jeans.

Valerie grabbed the pepper spray, which had landed on her right thigh when he'd pressed her backwards, flicked it open with her thumb, closed her eyes and sprayed. His cries filled the air.

Seb sat bolt upright, hands clamped to his eyes. Valerie slid out from under him, grabbed her jumper and pulled it on over her head before racing out of the room towards the front door.

'Get back here, you fucking bitch,' she heard Seb roar. This was followed by a groan as he walked into something in his attempt to find the door through his blurred vision.

Valerie snatched up her keys, unlocked the front door and yanked it open. She paused to grab her boots, jacket and handbag before tearing down the street in her stockinged feet, not daring to stop until she was around the corner where she pulled on her boots, pulled her phone out of her pocket and continued to run as she called Frankie.

'Seb's here, at my house,' she panted into the handset. 'I pepper sprayed him so I could escape but you need to get over to my house right now.'

'On my fucking way,' he exclaimed, the joy of battle audible in his voice before he hung up.

Valerie wondered where she should go because no doubt Seb would come after her once he could see again.

She saw a bus coming down the road, heading in the direction of the city centre, and she managed to make it to the stop in time. Valerie paid and took a seat near the driver with a sigh of relief. Maybe she should just keep going and head to Bute early? She could buy what she needed there, but the guilt of letting down her manager when she'd been so good to her was too much. Also, Bute was only a couple of hours away and suddenly that didn't seem far enough. She should have booked John O'Groats instead. But if Frankie did get hold of Seb, there wouldn't be anything to worry about. She had to trust her cousin to sort it all out.

Just as the bus reached the city centre, she received a text message. Her stomach dropped when she saw it was from Seb.

You had your chance but I only ever give one. You're dead, bitch.

Unable to help herself, she replied:

So, you can see again then?

He responded with a furious message full of threats and Valerie sighed and shoved the phone back into her handbag. It seemed Frankie hadn't managed to get hold of Seb after all.

25

Frankie picked Valerie up from a bar in the city centre and she was pleased that he'd brought Toni with him.

As he drove them back to Springburn, Valerie explained what had happened, Toni becoming increasingly furious with each word.

'Can you believe his bloody cheek, having a copy of your key made?' she exclaimed. 'You have to get the locks changed.'

'I already called someone about that, but they can't come until tomorrow. My maw and da won't be impressed.'

'They'll have to fucking deal with it,' scowled Frankie, who had no love for his aunt and uncle.

'I take it he was gone before you arrived?'

'Aye. The place was a bit messed up, like someone had been pepper sprayed right in the eyeballs and then tripped over everything,' he grinned.

'Any idea where he could be?'

'Naw, but I'll find him.' Frankie frowned at her through the rear-view mirror. 'You do know what I'll have to do to the walloper when I finally get my hands on him?'

Valerie slowly nodded, knowing he meant he'd have to kill him. Although Seb was a psychopath intent on killing her, she didn't want him to die, but there was no choice. He would always be a danger to her and her family.

* * *

Janet and Charlie were not impressed about Seb's foray into their home or the fact that they now had to change the locks. They demanded Valerie pay for it, and they seemed more upset about the minor damage done to the house than the danger their daughter was in.

Frankie set a couple of his men to watch the house and let him know if Seb showed his face there again, but Valerie knew he wouldn't. He was far too cautious a man to make the same move twice, it was how he'd flown under everyone's radar for so long, but she still felt vulnerable, jumping at every sound.

It was Toni who came up with the idea that Valerie should stay at the second cottage the family owned in the middle of nowhere until she could leave for good. She was at Toni's house and Frankie was there, along with Caesar, who had been set to watch over Toni at all times. Frankie was worried Seb would use her to get to Valerie.

'But he knows about the cottage at Lochwinnoch,' said Valerie.

'I'm talking about the one at Slamannan,' replied Toni.

'Oh, aye,' smiled Valerie. 'God, I haven't been there in years. We had some good times at that house.'

'Aye, we did,' Toni smiled back. 'Remember when we nicked Uncle Barry's wig and hid it in the garden?'

'He went pure mental trying to find it, running around with his baldy heid,' grinned Valerie.

'Which got burnt in the sun,' laughed Toni.

'If you've quite finished taking the piss out of Uncle Barry's baldy heid,' said Frankie, 'we've got plans to put in place.'

'Give over, Frankie,' said Toni. 'You were laughing harder than anyone when Aunty Jean had to rub aftersun lotion into his scalp.'

'Aye,' he grinned. 'That was pretty fucking funny. Although it wasn't for Aunty Jean, having to share a bed with him when he started to peel.' He threw back his head and treated them to more of his manic laughter.

'So what do you think, Val?' Toni asked her. 'Do you want to stay at the cottage?'

'Aye, it's a good idea. Seb doesn't know about it. I've cancelled the booking for Bute because it's not far enough from Glasgow. I wouldn't be able to relax wondering if he'd track me there, so I've booked a cottage in Caithness, but I can't leave for another three days because of work, so I can stay at the cottage until it's time to go.'

'What about work?'

'It's only a half hour drive from Slamannan, if I can get someone to give me a lift.'

'Caesar won't mind,' smiled Toni.

'Sounds like a plan,' said Frankie. 'We might have even sorted the bastard out by then.'

* * *

The cottage at Slamannan was even prettier than the one at Lochwinnoch, and it was larger too, with four bedrooms. It sat in an acre of its own land, a long, winding driveway leading up to it. Frankie drove Valerie and Toni up there, the latter insisting on accompanying her cousin. Valerie hadn't been to this cottage since she was fifteen years old and she remembered the garden bursting with beautiful blooms of all colours and varieties, as well as a large koi pond with a little bridge arching over it and a greenhouse. As she got out of the car, she was disappointed to see that the garden had been reclaimed by nature, the pond was now a boggy marsh and the greenhouse had collapsed. Still, the building itself looked as lovely as ever, the light brown stone warm to the touch after absorbing the rays of the sun all day.

Frankie waited in the cottage while the two women hauled their bags inside. The cottage had been cleaned and aired in anticipation of their arrival and felt cosy and inviting.

'I havenae been here for years,' said Frankie, studying the lounge with a smile. 'Brings back memories.'

'Aye, it does,' smiled Toni. Frankie rarely got sentimental, so this was special.

'I remember our dippy cousin, Alan, lopping off half his middle finger when he was trying to cut carrots. There was blood everywhere. His da had to run him to hospital.'

'Oh, aye, I remember that,' said Toni, not surprised that Frankie's fond memory was a bloody one. 'They tried to find the end to sew back on but couldn't.'

'Because I threw it in the bin,' chuckled Frankie. 'That taught the bastard no' to play with my He-Man.'

'But you hated He-Man, you said he was a poof. You wanted Skeletor instead and you got really pissed off when you didn't get one.'

'I don't care, it was still mine and no one touches my stuff. Right, I need to get back and carry on looking for Sebastian dead man Robertson. If you see anything suspicious, call me immediately.'

'Will do, Frankie,' said Valerie.

'Caesar got a lead about where I can find him, so hopefully this will soon be over and you can both come home.' He had intended to send Caesar with them as a bodyguard, but that idea went up in smoke when his newest employee caught Seb's scent. Still, Frankie thought it safe to leave Toni and Valerie here alone because no one outside the family knew about this cottage and even if you did know, it was still hard to find.

'We'll be fine,' said Toni. 'We've got chocolate and wine and plenty of videos.'

'Aye, that's great,' he muttered. 'And don't leave the cottage grounds, whatever you do.'

'We won't.'

Frankie just nodded and stomped out, muttering something unintelligible to himself. It was driving him mad that he hadn't got his hands on Sebastian yet.

Toni was relieved to see her brother's car heading down the drive. When it had disappeared altogether, she smiled. It would be good to have a break from his ever-present shadow. 'Let's crack open the wine,' she told Valerie.

'Hadn't we better check the house is secure first?' replied Valerie.

'Aye, all right,' she sighed. 'Then it's wine and Brad Pitt on the telly.'

They checked the cottage together, heading from the lounge into the spacious kitchen with an island and cold slate tiles on the floor. Across the hall from the kitchen was a second sitting room. Three of the bedrooms were on this floor and the fourth was in the loft, which had been converted and was accessed by a pull-down ladder. Toni claimed the master bedroom with the en suite, leaving Valerie with the smaller second bedroom, not that she minded. She was just glad of the company. Being alone all the way out here would have been a little intimidating, especially as the nearest neighbour was a quarter of a mile away and there were no street lights. This cottage was beautiful during the day, but only now did Valerie recall the absolute darkness at night that had scared her when she was a child. Back then the house had been filled with family, so she'd been able to close her curtains against that darkness and forget it was there. Now, even though she could still draw the curtains, she would still be conscious of the impenetrable blackness surrounding the cottage, like a living, conscious thing that would loom over her until the rising sun chased it away. This sensation would only be heightened by the fact that Seb was hunting her so he could hurt her.

Valerie gazed out of the window into the overgrown garden, the bushes and trees all twisted together creating plenty of hiding places for a stalker to crouch, watching and waiting for their moment.

'I've got the wine,' exclaimed a voice.

'Jesus,' cried Valerie. 'You made me jump out of my bloody skin.'

'Sorry. Are you coming, then?' said Toni, waggling the open bottle of wine enticingly. 'Mr Pitt is waiting.' She'd already changed into white pyjama bottoms with large red flowers, and a matching camisole top that barely contained her bosom and a floaty white robe.

'I prefer Tom Cruise,' replied Valerie.

'He's too short. Come on then, I've opened the box of chocolates too. Let's get pissed and fat.'

'Sounds good,' smiled Valerie, the chill her morbid thoughts had left her with dissipating.

* * *

Stevie just wanted a quiet night in to catch up on some telly and rest. Life had been a nightmare lately, but finally everything seemed to be settling down. Frankie seemed to have forgiven him and had decided he didn't want to hack bits off him any more, especially as he'd finally discovered Harry Woodhouse's real identity. It also seemed the Thompson family had decided they had bigger fish to fry and were leaving him alone too. Everything had worked out for the best.

He happily got up to answer the knock at the door, assuming it was the pizza he'd ordered, so Stevie was appalled when he pulled open the door to reveal Sebastian Robertson.

'Holy shit,' he exclaimed, attempting to slam the door shut.

Seb kicked the door and it hit Stevie in the face, knocking him to the floor. Seb stalked in, closed the door behind him and drew a huge knife.

'I believe you're the one to come to for information,' began Seb, with a smile that froze the blood in Stevie's veins. 'I want to know where Valerie Brown is. She's not at home or work. My spies tell me she was seen leaving her house with a suitcase and her cousins. Her family's hiding her somewhere and I want to know where.'

'They havenae told me,' blurted Stevie, who was still on the floor.

'Maybe, but Valerie told me Roddy McVay had a few bolt holes in the countryside to run to when he wanted to disappear. I know she won't be at the one at Lochwinnoch. I want to know the location of his other hidey-holes and if you don't tell me, what I'll do to you will make Frankie McVay look like Esther Rantzen. He likes cutting bits off people but I'm different. I prefer cutting them open and pulling things out of them.'

A gasp of fear was all Stevie was capable of as Seb loomed over him with the terrifying weapon.

* * *

'God, he's just so hot,' said Toni, lusting over Brad Pitt as they watched *Interview with the Vampire*.

'That's the fifth time you've said that and the film's not been on long,' said Valerie.

'But he's bloody beautiful. Look at him.'

'Aye, he is pretty gorgeous. I'm not sure Caesar would be happy to hear you talking like this.'

'Caesar's great, but we're not dating or anything.'

'Really, why not?'

'Frankie's forbidden it,' she muttered. 'He wants Caesar to be my bodyguard.'

'Why does that mean you can't date?'

'Because he's worried if we break up, I won't want Caesar anywhere near me. That's not stopped us sleeping together, though, and by Christ, he's very gifted in many ways, if you know what I mean?' winked Toni.

'Aye, I get it.'

'I think Frankie's got a good point, though. You know how I am with men – after a couple of weeks, I start to get bored. I really like Caesar and I want him to stick around and that won't happen if we become a couple. So we're going to be friends and just have sex when the opportunity arises.'

'Sounds a good idea,' said Valerie, thinking Toni could do with a genuine friend and not just another boyfriend to be discarded when she got bored.

'I think so. Best of both worlds. Ooh, look. Brad's about to bite the sexy slave girl.'

While Toni watched, enraptured, Valerie topped up their wine glasses. She was drinking a little faster than she normally would, but she felt restless and uneasy. She was finding it difficult to concentrate on the film, even though it was one of her favourites.

Valerie got up and headed to the window. Twilight had set in, making it difficult to see clearly as definite shapes began to morph into vague shadows. The darkness was creeping through the garden, slowly claiming everything, innocent objects turned into something sinister that could possibly conceal a stalker.

'What are you doing?' Toni asked her.

'I don't know, I just feel uneasy. I think I'll check the doors again.'

'You don't need to because they're locked, the windows too. We checked them ourselves. It's only natural you're on edge. Come and sit down and let the beautiful Mr Pitt take your mind off it.'

Valerie retook her seat, attempting to keep her mind on the film. The slaves were rejoicing in front of the plantation house as it burned, but she only saw it briefly before lapsing back into her thoughts. Seb had no idea where she was. She was safe and she should be taking this time to lick her wounds and recover from the ordeal she'd been through, not fretting.

The pitter-patter of rain against the glass drew her attention back to the window. The wind was also getting up, causing the trees and bushes to wave wildly. All the movement outside only increased her anxiety, making her imagine an intruder was heading towards the house.

Toni could see exactly what was running through her cousin's mind, so she got up and yanked the curtains shut.

'There,' she said, returning to her seat. 'No weather to freak you out.'

'Sorry,' said a sheepish Valerie.

'You'll feel better in the morning, when it's daylight.'

'Probably. I always did get a bit freaked out here at night when I was a wean. I thought I wouldn't feel like that any more.'

'You might not if you didn't have a split personality psycho after you.'

Valerie regarded her with an incredulous look.

'Sorry,' said Toni. 'Chocolate?'

Valerie took a fudge delight from the box of very expensive

chocolates but she barely noticed the taste, her eyes continually flicking to the window, which somehow seemed even more menacing now the curtains were drawn.

When Antonio Banderas made his debut as the beautiful Armand, Valerie's attention was finally claimed by the film and she managed to forget her woes just for a little while.

As the credits started to run, accompanied by the haunting music, one of the doors leading from the living room slowly swung open with a creak worthy of a Hammer Horror film to reveal nothing but the darkness of the hallway beyond. The wind suddenly picked up and howled around the house, rattling the windows, as though something was trying to get in.

'Jeezo,' said Toni. 'I expected a loon in a hockey mask to burst in then.'

'A draught probably pushed it open,' replied Valerie.

The two women stared at the dark, yawning doorway.

'We should shut it,' said Valerie.

'I'm not going anywhere near it,' replied Toni.

'Is the redoubtable Toni McVay actually scared?' smiled Valerie.

Toni's eyes flashed. 'I am never scared.'

'Go and close the door then,' she said, amused.

'I'm too comfortable to get up.'

'Fine, I'll go,' said Valerie, getting to her feet.

Slowly she approached the door, her eyes riveted to that black void.

'Aren't you going to move a little faster?' said Toni, raising an eyebrow.

'What's the rush?'

'I'm going to put on the next film – *Goodfellas*.'

'So you can drool over Ray Liotta?'

'Aye, and his beautiful blue eyes, so hurry up.'

Valerie decided to stop being a wuss and get it done. She rushed up to the door, slammed it shut and returned to the couch while Toni swapped over the videos.

As they settled back onto the couch, the door leading from the lounge into the kitchen burst open just as a fresh gust of wind raged around the cottage. Once again, they were confronted by an impenetrable blackness.

'This is getting fucking creepy,' said Toni.

'It's your turn,' said Valerie.

'Fair's fair, I suppose.'

Toni placed her wine glass on the coffee table and got to her feet. She stalked over to the door and just as she reached it, the door leading into the hallway burst open again.

Valerie gasped and leapt to her feet when Seb stalked in, looking beautiful and insane.

'Toni, run,' cried Valerie.

She turned and made for the door leading into the kitchen, which Toni had already gone through. Before she could reach it, Seb grabbed Valerie by the arm and dragged her backwards.

'Missed you, sexy,' he growled in her ear, pressing his face into her hair before throwing her to the floor.

Toni backed into the living room, Seb's friends Gregor and Simon stalking in after her, the smirks on their faces enraging her.

'How did you find this place?' demanded Valerie, getting back to her feet.

'Stevie gave me the address, after some persuasion,' said Seb. 'I remembered you telling me he's the one to go to if you want to know something.'

'What did you do to him, you total bastard?' she yelled.

'He'll be fine,' shrugged Seb. 'After a bit of surgery, anyway.'

Furious, Valerie snatched up one of the wine glasses and hurled it at him. He ducked and it hit the wall behind him with a smash, splattering red wine everywhere. She glanced at Toni, who was still being backed up into the room by Seb's two friends, her gaze riveted to them, not a flicker of fear in her eyes. Seb ignored them, entirely focused on Valerie.

Gregor and Simon were a little nonplussed when Toni reached into her cleavage, their eyes widening when she pulled out a small flick knife, which she hurled at them, the blade sinking into Simon's left shoulder.

'Argh, you bitch,' he cried, gaping at the weapon sticking out of his body.

When Gregor made a move on her, Toni produced a second knife from the pocket of her robe, which caused him to back off, having seen how skilled she was with a blade.

'The next arsehole who comes near me will get this in their baws,' Toni snarled at them, her fierce glare daring them to attack her.

The men glowered at her but advanced no further.

Valerie threw a vase then the empty wine bottle at Seb. The vase missed but the bottle caught him in the stomach, doubling him over.

'Toni, go,' Valerie yelled as she dodged around Seb and ran for the door.

Toni charged into the darkened hallway and Valerie ran after her. A large shadow appeared between them and the door. Valerie cried out in surprise when she was shoved in the chest and hit the wall with such force her vision blurred. As she recovered, she saw the glint of Toni's blade. There was a grunt of pain and the door was yanked open, the sound of Toni running outside in her slippers making Valerie smile. Toni knew the overgrown garden a lot better than the intruders and she could easily lose them in it, especially in the dark.

Just as Valerie recovered from hitting the wall, she was grabbed by her hair and yanked to her feet, making her grimace.

'Get off her, you fucking idiot,' yelled Seb.

The hallway lights burst into life, making Valerie squint. The man who'd thrown her into the wall was enormous, standing at six foot four with a rectangular head, mean dark eyes, thin lips and a scowl. He had a scar down one side of his face that made Liam's scar look like a paper cut. His body was very muscular, and Valerie thought she'd got off lightly. He looked like he could have sent her through the wall.

The giant released her on Seb's order.

'I told you not to hurt her, Freddy,' Seb told him.

'Appropriate name for someone who looks like a fucking nightmare,' commented Valerie.

'I didn't want you escaping again,' Seb told her.

'Your tame beast didn't stop Toni, though, did he?' she retorted, noting the blood trickling down Freddy's left arm.

'I don't care about her. It's you I want.'

'Right now, she'll be getting help. Frankie and his men will turn up very soon with all their instruments of torture.'

'Nice try, but both your mobile phones are on the table in the lounge and you don't have a car. It'll take her ages just to reach civilisation. By the time she gets back with help, it'll be too late.'

A chill crept down Valerie's spine. 'What do you mean by that?'

'Let's talk in private,' Seb said, grabbing her by the arm. 'Gregor, get out there and look for that daft cow. I would prefer to have her under control.'

Gregor nodded and rushed out to obey.

'Freddy, Simon, go and clean yourselves up,' he added before shoving Valerie into a bedroom. He smiled as he locked the door. 'Alone at last.'

26

'How did you get in?' Valerie demanded of Seb. 'All the doors and windows were locked.'

'I picked the lock on the front door,' he replied. 'It was easy enough.'

'What the hell do you think this is going to achieve?' she exclaimed.

'We have unfinished business and I do like to tie up loose ends.'

'So I'm a loose end now? We broke up. Why can't you just leave it at that and let me get on with my life?'

He loomed over her, the shadows cast by the trees outside the window being shaken by the wind moving across his face, making him look diabolical.

'Because we're meant to be together. Surely you've realised that?'

'Why can't you get it into your head that I don't want you?' she yelled back at him. 'You tricked me and used me, and I hate you.'

'No, you don't. You still love me. I can see it in your eyes.'

'I am in love with someone but it's not you. It's the fake you. Anyway, your message said you never give second chances.'

'Usually I don't, but I'm willing to break that rule for you, but only this once. Last chance.'

'And if I say no?'

'Then you'll provoke Mr Hyde,' he said with a wicked smile.

'Seb, you can't blackmail me into restarting our relationship with the threat of violence. It'll never work.'

'All I'm asking is for you to give the real me a chance. I've seen what you can do. Together we can get rid of Frankie and take over his patch.'

'You want me to betray my own blood?'

'Why not? Do you think family loyalty would stop him from using you to get what he wanted?'

'Probably not, but that doesn't mean I'm willing to do the same.'

Gently he took her by the shoulders. 'Just think of what we could do together. We could be the real king and queen of Glasgow.'

Seb smiled inwardly when he saw an involuntary spark ignite in Valerie's eyes. She was a McVay, after all.

'I don't want that life,' she replied. 'And what about your poor family? Your maw's used all her influence to keep you out of prison.'

He shrugged. 'More fool her.'

'You don't give a shite about her or any of your family, do you? All that was a pretence too.'

'They're all right, I suppose, but they do nag me a lot. It really gets on my tits.'

'Because they love you and they're trying to stop you from going down a bad path. You're so lucky to have them and you don't appreciate them at all.'

'Families hold you back.'

'They also hold you up.'

'How poetic,' he smiled sardonically. 'Anyway, this isn't about them, it's about us. So, how about we take over the fucking city?'

'No, thanks. I'm moving away from you and Frankie and all the endless violence. I'm so sick of it.'

She expected Seb to rage, perhaps lash out and strike her, but he just continued to stare at her icily.

'And what will you do then?' he asked her after a few moments of creepy silence.

'Anything I can.'

'There's no need to cry,' he said softly when tears of exhaustion and sadness began to slide down her face. Seb wrapped his arms around her waist and pulled her close. 'We can still have a great life together.'

Valerie sighed heavily and turned to face the window. Seb kept his arms wrapped tightly around her and rested his chin on her shoulder. She closed her eyes and took a moment to enjoy the feel of him, imagining he was the man she fell in love with and they were still going to live their beautiful life together.

Inhale.

Exhale.

Valerie opened her eyes.

'It's over,' she told him.

Seb gave a heavy sigh and a chill enveloped her as he released her and took a step back. She turned to face him. His blue eyes had turned to hard, narrow shards, a waving tree branch outside throwing erratic shadows across his face.

'I really hoped you wouldn't say that,' he said. 'You've left me no choice.'

'What are you going to do?'

He pulled a knife from the back of his jeans. The menace in his eyes said it all.

'It doesn't have to be this way,' said Valerie, although she realised for him it did. That was why he'd attacked all his previous girlfriends. It was because they'd tried to leave him.

'It'll be quick,' he said. 'I don't want you to suffer. Much.'

'I don't understand why you can't just let me go.'

'Because I can't bear the thought of you being in the world and not being with me, of some other man touching you, making love to you. It would drive me out of my mind.'

'I think that happened long ago,' she retorted. 'You're just like your grandda.'

His eyes flickered. 'What do you mean?'

'You're an abuser, like he was. You know how much he made Euphemia suffer and you're doing exactly the same thing.'

'No, I'm not,' he growled.

'Aye, you are.'

'I am not like him,' he snarled.

'I bet he wouldn't let her leave either and threatened to kill her if she tried. But you don't have to be like him, Seb.' She pressed her hand to his cheek and he closed his eyes with pleasure, turning his head to kiss her palm. 'You were my first love, and you always will be.'

Seb pressed his forehead to hers and they remained locked together like this, Valerie all the time conscious of the knife he still held, which he'd lowered to his side. Any moment he could thrust it up into her abdomen, but she had to try to win him over with tenderness because the last thing she wanted to do was fight him physically.

There was an almighty crash as something burst through the window, shattering it. Valerie and Seb instinctively reeled back from it, avoiding the flying glass. The howl of the wind as it tore through the void filled their ears.

Valerie didn't stop to think as her hair was whipped about her face. She leapt through the hole created by the bricks that had shattered the window and landed on the soft ground outside. A ghostly figure shimmered in the darkness, and it took Valerie a moment to realise it was Toni in her pyjamas.

'Well, don't just sit there, move,' her cousin yelled at her.

Valerie shot to her feet and ran towards her cousin, who grabbed her hand and together they disappeared into the blackness of the garden.

'I hope you know where you're going,' said Valerie as they ran. 'We don't want to end up falling and hurting ourselves.'

'Relax, I know this place like the back of my hand.'

Toni pulled her to a tree and they crouched behind it to watch the house.

'Are you okay?' Toni asked her, having to talk quite loudly to be heard over the shriek of the wind. Valerie didn't have a coat on and she was cold but Toni, who was just in pyjama bottoms, camisole top and a skimpy robe, appeared unaffected, as usual.

'Aye,' replied Valerie. 'He didn't hurt me. You?'

'I chipped a couple of nails, for which they will all pay. One of his friends came out to look for me but he got lost, so god only knows where he is.'

'That just leaves Seb and another two men. One of them is fucking massive.'

'Aye, I caught a glimpse of that big boy.'

'We need to avoid him if we can.'

'Shite. The bigger they are, the harder they fall.'

'If he falls, he'll cause an earthquake. I don't know how we're going to fight him and Seb.'

'We don't need to. All we need to do is stay away from them

until Caesar gets here. I called him and he's on his way. He was going to let Frankie know what's happened.'

'How did you get hold of him? Your phone's in the house.'

'Caesar gave me a phone just to call him on. I had it in the pocket of my robe, just in case.'

'You're a bloody genius, Toni. Do you know that?'

'Of course I do,' Toni said with a self-assured smile.

'I hope he's not long. I'm freezing.'

Valerie's mind was taken off her discomfort when the front door of the cottage was pulled open and Seb stormed out looking very pissed off, still holding the knife. His eyes scanned the darkness and the women hunkered down even further behind the tree. Thanks to the wild weather, even his sharp eyes were unable to spot them in the huge overgrown garden. Freddy the giant joined him in the doorway and Valerie and Toni watched them, Seb frantically gesturing with his arms. With that, the two men disappeared back inside, Freddy closing the door behind them.

'I thought they would have come out looking for us,' said Valerie.

'Seb obviously knows it would be impossible to find us in this jungle in the dark,' replied Toni.

'True, but I can't see them giving up so easily. Their car's over there,' said Valerie, nodding at the blue Ford Escort. 'If we could get hold of the keys...'

'I think we should just sit tight and wait for Caesar and Frankie to arrive.'

'Have you still got your knife?'

'It's right here,' said Toni, patting the right pocket of her robe.

They went silent when the front door opened again and Seb and his giant stalked out of the house and towards the car.

'Are they leaving?' said Toni.

'Seb would never give up that easily,' replied Valerie.

They watched Seb open the boot and the giant delved inside and hauled out a bound, struggling figure.

'Jeezo, they've got a hostage,' said Toni.

'I wonder if it's Stevie,' said Valerie.

'It's not Stevie, they're too tall,' said Toni. 'It's Liam Thompson.'

'Oh, Christ,' gasped Valerie. 'Seb's a mad bastard. He's already got Frankie on his tail and now he's going to have the entire Thompson family out for his blood. This will be his revenge for Liam stabbing him.'

Freddy held Liam before him. Liam was a big man, tall and broad, but he looked tiny compared to the giant.

'I know you can hear me, Valerie,' Seb yelled into the darkness, the wind picking up his voice and hurling it towards the two women, amplifying it. 'If you don't want to watch him have his throat cut, then you'll come out right now.'

'Don't you fucking dare,' Toni told her cousin, knowing she had a powerful selfless streak.

'I can't just sit here and watch them kill him.'

'Course you can. He's only a Thompson.'

'He's also a human being.'

'Are you forgetting that he kidnapped us and was going to cut off my hand?'

'But he didn't and we both managed to escape. He doesn't deserve this.'

'We are not putting ourselves in danger to save Liam bloody Thompson.'

'It's me Seb wants. You can cause a distraction so me and Liam can escape.'

'Don't tell me you have a thing for Liam now?'

'Course not, but I won't sit here and watch him be murdered because of me.'

'But what distraction?' said Toni, looking anxious.

'I'm sure that clever brain of yours will come up with something. Don't let them see you,' said Valerie before leaving her hiding place. 'All right, I'm here,' she called to Seb, holding up her hands as she walked back to the house. 'You don't need to hurt him.'

'See, Freddy,' smirked Seb. 'I told you he'd be useful. Get him inside.'

Freddy nodded and dragged Liam, who looked limp and disorientated, along with him.

Seb held his hand out to Valerie. 'Let's get out of this wind. It's freezing.'

Valerie ignored the offered hand and walked into the house, Seb closely following. She was relieved to be back in the warmth, even though she was trapped with a bunch of psychos. Liam didn't look too good, he was battered, bruised and semi-conscious. If it hadn't been for Freddy's thick arm around his waist, he would have collapsed to the floor.

'Where's Toni?' Seb demanded of her.

'No idea. We got split up in the darkness. Where are your other friends?'

'Gregor's not come back from his hunt for Toni and Simon's still tending to his wound.'

'Oh, dear,' she smirked.

'They don't really matter because Freddy's worth ten of them, aren't you, pal?'

The giant smiled proudly while continuing to hold Liam, seemingly barely conscious of his weight.

'So now we can get back to completing our unfinished business,' Seb told Valerie, the blade still in his hand.

Valerie knew she just had to keep him talking until Caesar and Frankie arrived. If she could do that, then everything would be okay. 'Do you really want to do that in front of Freddy and Liam? Surely this should be a private conversation?'

'So you can escape through a window again? I don't think so.'

'Aww, you need your friend to help keep me in line,' said Valerie, hoping to shame him into ordering Freddy to leave. 'That doesn't fit in with the image of the dangerous man I've heard so much about.'

'Normally it wouldn't be an issue, but I know you, Valerie, and I've seen you in action. You're no ordinary woman and you've already escaped from me once. I'm making damn sure that won't happen again.'

'Liam,' she called. 'Are you okay?'

He didn't reply, remaining slumped in Freddy's arms.

'You've half-killed him,' she told Seb.

'In revenge for stabbing me and kidnapping you.'

'Why are you doing this when you know DS Baillie's keeping a close eye on you? Kidnapping and assault will send you to prison.'

He shrugged. 'My maw will get me off any charge. With her working on my behalf, I'm practically untouchable.'

'And that's why you've turned into such a nightmare, because you've never really faced any consequences for your actions. I understand Laura wanting to protect her son but all she's done is make you think you're untouchable, but you're not, Seb. No one is. You can end this now before it goes too far. All you've done is smash a window, there's no need to bother reporting that to anyone and if you get Liam to a hospital, I'm sure he'll be fine.' Valerie tentatively reached out to take Seb's hand, not sure what sort of reaction she would get. His expression remained stony, but he allowed her to touch him. 'Only you can stop this madness. If you turn from this bad path you're on, then maybe one day in the future we can get back together and lead the good, decent life we talked about.'

His eyes filled with mockery.

'What you obviously don't understand about me is that I don't want to lead a decent life. It's fucking boring and we both know that even if I do release you unharmed, Frankie will still come for me, it's in his DNA, and you know what? I can respect that. I'd do the same, so I want you and Liam dealt with before he gets here. Then I'll get rid of him too and take over his business.'

Seb lunged for her but Valerie dodged. She ran around him, aiming for the door.

'Get her,' snarled Seb.

Freddy let Liam drop, and he hit the floor with a thud and remained there, crumpled in a heap. In one massive stride, Freddy managed to grab Valerie's right arm and held her tightly. Valerie pounded her fist against his arm but to no avail. He barely seemed to notice her efforts to free herself.

'Nice grab, Freddy,' said Seb, causing him to smile proudly again.

Seb knelt by Liam's side.

'This is how it's going to work,' he told Valerie. 'Every time you do something wrong, he will pay for it.'

Valerie looked on in appalled horror as Seb splayed Liam's left hand out on the floor and stamped on it. There was a loud crack as a bone in his hand snapped. The pain jolted Liam back to his senses and he groaned in agony.

'You sick bastard,' cried Valerie.

'I don't know why you care after what he did to you.' Anger caused his eyes to blaze. 'Unless you two got close while he had you tied up and helpless?'

'Don't be ridiculous.'

Seb slapped her hard across the face, knocking her into Freddy.

'Is that what happened, you dirty slag? Have you been shagging him too?'

It took Valerie a moment to reply as she was dazed from the blow. 'No, I haven't,' she mumbled, tongue thick in her mouth. 'I was thinking about you the whole time because I was going demented with worry for you.'

'I don't believe you,' he glowered.

Valerie sighed. Her life seemed to be full of men who refused to believe her. 'Tough because it's true. I never would have cheated on the Seb I loved.'

He struck her again full in the face with his fist, knocking her off her feet as Freddy released her. Valerie landed on the floor close to Liam, who now seemed to be entirely unconscious. The blow almost knocked her out and all she could do was lie there, her head pounding with pain.

'You're a lying bitch,' roared Seb.

Gregor burst into the room, panting. His clothes and shoes were covered in mud, leaves were stuck in his tangled hair and there was a scratch on his left cheek. 'Seb,' he cried.

'What is it?' he snapped back.

'The car's been vandalised. All the tyres have been slashed, the windows are smashed and the engine won't start.'

Valerie, who was still lying on the floor, smiled.

'Call Dennis and get him to come up here with his car. We've got all the time in the world. No one else knows we're here.'

'Aye, good idea,' said Gregor, taking out his phone and dialling. 'Crap.'

'What is it now?' demanded Seb.

'I havenae got a signal.'

'Then try outside.'

'Oh, okay,' said Gregor before leaving the room, reluctant to go back out into the fierce weather.

Seb glanced at Liam to make sure he wasn't going to give him any bother, but he was out cold on the floor. 'So,' he casually asked Valerie, 'have you seen Leo lately?'

This statement caused her blood to run cold. 'No. Why?' she mumbled, one side of her face rapidly swelling.

He nodded. 'Toni took one of his eyes.'

'You're lying, she wouldn't do that.'

'Aye, she would, because she's just as much of a lunatic as her brother. She popped his left eye right out of his head. The creepy thing is, no one could find the eye, I reckon she kept it.'

Valerie turned cold. She'd known of Toni's disturbing predilection, but it was still a surprise that she'd finally given in to the impulse. 'At least she let him keep one.'

Seb shrugged. 'True.'

'How do you know about this?'

'I made it my business to know. Naturally he hasn't grassed on her and he probably never will.'

'Where's Leo now?'

'I gave him seven grand to piss off and leave Glasgow forever. It was the most money he's ever seen in his life.'

Valerie kept in mind that Seb could just be trying to drive a wedge between her and Toni. Divide and conquer, it was a classic tactic. But what would that matter if he was going to kill her?

Just as she was attempting to puzzle this out, there was a crash from the direction of the kitchen, followed by a cry.

'Watch them,' Seb told Freddy before rushing to the kitchen door and pulling it open.

He found the large kitchen window had been smashed too, the wind that wailed inside now accompanied by rain. A large damp rock sat in the middle of the floor alongside an unconscious Simon, who it had crashed into. Seb rushed to the window and peered out but could see nothing but the mad swaying of the trees.

'I know it's you, Toni,' he yelled, his words immediately snatched from his mouth by the wind.

With a growl of annoyance, he strode through the kitchen, intending to take his displeasure out on Valerie, when something struck him in the back of the head.

'Ow,' he frowned.

Looking down, he saw a small rock on the floor. As he turned back to the window, another projectile soared through the window and struck him in the centre of the forehead. He managed to glimpse a figure in white and heard a husky bark of laughter before the figure vanished.

'You bitch,' he roared, leaping up onto the kitchen unit and jumping out of the window, determined to make that cow suffer. He would take her back to the house and make Valerie watch him rip her apart.

Up ahead, he saw the ghostly figure, the gown blowing in the wind. Seb raced forward and leapt at Toni, reaching out his arms to grab her. His hands slid down the silk of the gown before he plunged into a deep pool of water.

Seb broke the surface of the pond, coughing and wiping the green slime that coated the neglected pool from his eyes. He'd lost his knife in the water. It was then he saw the gown had been hung from a small tree and Toni was nowhere in sight.

27

Toni chuckled to herself as Seb's enraged howl echoed across the garden. It should take him a few minutes to get out of that lot. With a bit of luck, he'd get entangled in the weeds and be dragged down.

She ran up to the house in just her thin silk camisole top and pyjama bottoms. Seb and his friend were outside but that meant another two were still in there with Valerie.

She sidled up to the window and peered in.

'Thank god,' she breathed when she saw her cousin was still alive, although it looked like she'd taken a good whack. Liam was out cold on the floor, but who gave a shite about him? The big freaky giant was watching over them. He appeared to be unarmed but she couldn't be certain. He looked big and clumsy. It would be easy to outrun him. She just needed to get him looking the other way so Valerie could get herself out of there.

'Distraction, distraction,' Toni muttered to herself.

She looked around for inspiration, but none was forthcoming.

'It looks like it's all down to you, girls,' she said, looking down at her chest.

Toni knocked on the window, drawing Freddy and Valerie's

attention. The light pouring through the window lit up Toni like a lantern as she pulled her camisole top off over her head and stood before the glass, bare-breasted.

Freddy's eyes popped out on stalks as he stared at her in astonishment. Valerie seized the moment and leapt to her feet, intending to run, until she looked at Liam. She couldn't just leave him, Freddy would probably pull his arms off. She grabbed a vase and smashed it across the back of Freddy's head. The giant just turned to her with a frown.

'Oh, shit,' she said.

He attempted to grab her but she jumped backwards, stumbling over Liam and falling backwards onto her hands. She stared up at Freddy as he loomed over her, an evil smile lighting up his face.

The giant's eyes widened when a pair of arms wrapped around his legs and he toppled forwards like a felled oak. As he hit the floor with his face, his nose burst.

'Run, Valerie,' rasped Liam.

'Get your arse up and we'll both go.'

'I can't.'

'Oh, yes, you can.'

Valerie snatched up the lamp, tore the flex from the base and looped it around Freddy's thick neck before tying the other end to the leg of the armchair and forming a complicated knot.

'What are you doing?' said Liam.

'The more he struggles, the tighter the knot will get,' she replied.

'You are fucking amazing,' said Liam, managing to lift the left corner of his mouth, which felt to be the only part of his body that wasn't injured, into a smile. 'How do you know how to do that?'

'Frankie. It's one of his favourite torture techniques.'

'I should have guessed.'

Toni raced in, her top back on, although it didn't do much to conceal her assets. 'Hurry up, will you?' she told her cousin.

'Just making sure this freak can't come after us,' said Valerie, getting to her feet.

Freddy looked up at her, face set into a snarl, blood trickling from his busted nose. His eyes widened when the knot around his neck tightened and he hastily lowered his head again.

'Let's move,' said Valerie, helping Liam to his feet.

'Leave him behind.'

'Charming,' winced Liam as pain shot through his body.

'We're all leaving,' Valerie told her cousin firmly.

'Fine,' sighed Toni, slinging one of Liam's arms over her shoulder while Valerie took the other and the three of them staggered towards the door.

'Jesus, you're heavy,' commented Toni. 'Why don't you go on a diet, you fat bastard?'

'It's muscle, no' fat,' mumbled Liam.

They were a few steps from the front door, which Toni had left open, when a figure covered from head to toe in mud, green slime and pond weed appeared, blocking their exit.

'Bloody hell,' said Toni. 'It's Swamp Thing.'

With a cry of rage, Seb charged at them and the two women were forced to release Liam in order to defend themselves and he dropped to the floor. Toni drew the short, stubby knife from her pyjama pocket but before she could use it, Seb's fist connected with her jaw and she fell back against the wall, out cold.

Valerie attempted to punch him but he dodged and kicked her in the stomach. As she fell backwards to the floor, he leapt on her, wrapping his hands around her throat. Panic consumed Valerie as her air supply was immediately cut off. She tried to prise his arms away from her neck, but he was far too strong and he looked demented in his rage.

Seb's grip on her throat tightened, squeezing tears from her eyes. Valerie spotted the glint of Toni's blade lying just off to her right and she frantically groped for it. Her fingers grasped the hilt of the knife and in one last burst of energy, she rammed it into his stomach. Seb's eyes widened and his jaw fell open, a groan of pain emanating from his mouth. His grip loosened slightly, allowing her to talk.

'Please stop,' she rasped.

Purpose filled his eyes and he started to strangle her even harder. Valerie plunged the knife into his body again and again but he only seemed to squeeze harder despite his wounds. The blade was so short it was only piercing his skin and failing to do any serious damage. Spots danced before her eyes and she felt herself weakening. In seconds, she would lose consciousness and he would win.

'Seb,' she murmured, his name a mere breath on the air. 'Don't...'

He squeezed even harder. Pain erupted in Valerie's neck, and it felt like he was going to crack her throat. She drove the blade into his right wrist, twisting it, and blood started to pour from the ragged wound. This forced him to release her and Valerie gasped with relief, although her neck ached horribly. But he was still determined to finish the job. While Valerie attempted to recover from being half-strangled, he tore off a piece of his jumper and wrapped it tightly around the wound, stemming the blood flow. Furious, he wrenched the knife from her limp hand and raised it above his head, ready to bring down on her.

Valerie snatched the pepper spray from her pocket and sprayed it in his face. As he cried out, she tore the blade from his grip but he managed to knock her hand before she could stab him with it. Valerie was unable to maintain her grip on the knife and she dropped it.

Valerie started to cry when he snaked his hands around her throat again, frantically blinking because of the pain in his hellish, bloodshot eyes. She tried to plead for her life, but he throttled the words away.

With tears of agony rolling down her face, she slid her shaking hand into her jeans pocket and produced her house key, ramming it into his left eye. As Seb released her and arched his back, bellowing in pain, Valerie grabbed the knife and thrust it up into his heart.

This time, the knife pierced its target. Seb's eyes bulged, the ruined orb looking grotesque. He gazed down at her, raising his right hand to touch her face. The wound in his wrist was still bleeding and the blood dripped down his fingers and landed on her cheek. He released a long exhale and at last the light in his eyes died.

Something hit him in the left side of the head, knocking him off Valerie, and he landed on the floor beside her, unmoving.

'You loosened some of my teeth, you bastard,' yelled Toni, dropping the heavy umbrella stand she'd used to hit Seb. She threw herself down by Valerie's side. 'Val, are you okay?'

'Seb?' she managed to croak.

'Never mind that twat. Are you hurt?'

'Just my neck,' she replied, grimacing at the pain. 'Check Seb.'

Toni pressed her fingertips to his throat. 'He's dead,' she said as gently as she could.

Despite everything he'd done, a deep well of anguish bubbled up inside Valerie and she started to cry.

'It wasn't you who did it,' Toni hastened to assure her. 'It was me. That umbrella stand's made of heavy wood. I cracked his skull. You didn't kill him, Val.'

But Valerie knew that she had. She'd watched the life die in his eyes before Toni had hit him.

Toni stared at Seb's ruined eye in fascination before tearing her attention off it and onto her cousin. 'Can you get up?' she asked her.

Valerie slowly nodded and held out her hands to Toni, who took them and helped her to her feet. Valerie stood swaying, feeling like she could fall over at any moment. The pain in her neck didn't seem to be abating and it felt like Seb still had his hands wrapped around her throat. Her eyes widened when she saw a figure stealthily creeping up on Toni from behind. She raised her hand and tried to shout a warning, but all she could manage was a weak croak.

'What is it?' frowned Toni.

She turned to see Simon, blood trickling from the side of his head, staggering out of the kitchen towards her with a large knife and murder in his eyes. Toni had no other weapons and there wasn't time for her to dodge out of the way.

Alarm filled Simon's eyes and he toppled forward. Liam, who had tripped him, frantically clambered on top of him and wrapped one arm around his neck. He gave a quick jerk, there was a snap and he let Simon drop, dead, his neck broken.

'Well,' purred Toni, 'perhaps you aren't such a prick after all. That was very impressive.'

'Aye, great,' sighed Liam before flopping back onto the carpet. 'Valerie, are you okay?'

'No. You?' she replied, her voice barely audible.

'Nope. I feel like shite.'

'That makes two of us.'

The cousins regarded each other with alarm when there was a terrific crashing sound from the direction of the living room. Freddy rushed into the hall, the cord still around his neck. It appeared he'd smashed off the leg of the armchair to escape, the other end of the cord hanging loosely, making it look like he wore a lead.

'Oh, shite, the monster's escaped,' exclaimed Toni.

The front door burst open and Frankie and Caesar stormed in, wielding guns.

'Fuck me, what's that?' exclaimed Frankie, aiming the gun at the giant.

'Freddy fucking Krueger,' replied Toni.

When the giant sprang at Toni, the two men fired, Freddy jumping as bullets riddled his torso. When the gunfire ended, Freddy was still on his feet, blood pouring from his wounds.

'Christ,' said Caesar.

He and Frankie looked at each other before looking back at the staggering giant, who was still reaching for Toni, even though she had stepped well out of his grasp.

'Die, you fucking yeti,' said Frankie before firing again, striking Freddy in the centre of the forehead and pitching him onto his back. 'Jeezo, look at the shot,' he exclaimed with glee. 'That's fucking perfect. I'm getting good at this.'

'Are you two okay?' Caesar asked the women.

'I'm fine,' said Toni. 'But Valerie's got a sore neck.'

'Why, what happened?'

'Seb tried to strangle her.'

The two men peered at the marks on her neck and judging by the way they grimaced, Valerie assumed they looked bad. She turned to Seb, dead on the floor, lying on his side, his undamaged eye open and staring vacantly. Valerie dropped to her knees beside him, grief welling up inside her as she recalled the man she'd loved. She was convinced he'd existed in there, somewhere, trapped inside all the madness.

When she buried her face in her hands and started to cry, Toni knelt beside her and hugged her. Valerie clung onto her as she continued to sob.

'Who's that walloper?' said Frankie, gesturing to the dead Simon.

'One of Seb's men,' replied Toni while continuing to comfort her cousin. 'Liam killed him.'

'Liam?' Frankie's ginger eyebrows shot up. 'Liam Thompson?'

'Aye.'

'Is that who that is? I couldnae tell through all the bruises. Bastard,' he spat, aiming his gun at him.

Valerie shot to her feet and put herself between her cousin and Liam.

'What are you doing?' Frankie snapped at her. 'Get out of the way.' He rolled his eyes when she attempted to talk, her voice an inaudible squeak. 'I cannae hear what you're saying,' he exclaimed.

'I don't think she wants you to shoot him,' commented Caesar.

'Liam wasn't in on this,' explained Toni. 'He was beaten and kidnapped by Seb. In fact, he saved my life. He killed Simon when he was sneaking up on me from behind with a knife.'

The mayhem in Frankie's eyes died a little. 'Oh, aye? Well, maybe I shouldnae kill him just yet.' He was always grateful to anyone who protected his little sister.

'That's a wise idea, Frankie,' said Toni.

'Besides, we're gonnae need him if we're gonnae hush this up.'

'How will we do that?' Valerie managed to croak before wincing with pain.

'We'll bury the bodies up here. No one will ever find them. Roddy didnae just use this place as a bolthole, he used it to hide the evidence.'

'You mean there are already bodies buried up here?' said Toni.

'Aye, a few. There's some at the Lochwinnoch cottage too.'

Valerie sighed. Something else that had been special to her had been tainted by violence and death.

'There's another of Seb's men in the garden somewhere,' said Toni.

'We caught him running down the drive. Looked like he was abandoning his pals. Tam, Paul and Jamesie are sorting him out.'

'Good. That's all of them, then. We need to get Val to a hospital.'

Frankie and Valerie objected at once, the former by exclaiming, 'We cannae dae that,' and the latter by frantically shaking her head.

'The hospital staff will see she's been strangled and will want to report it to the polis,' added Frankie. 'And thanks to that nosy bastard Baillie, they'll realise there's one prime suspect and he'll want to talk to Seb about it. It's best if they think Val dumped him and never saw him again.'

'But she could have some serious damage,' said Toni. 'He squeezed her neck really hard.'

'I'm fine,' rasped Valerie through her pain. 'Honestly.'

'Do you really think we can keep all this quiet?' said Toni, gesturing to the dead bodies.

'Aye, I dae,' said Frankie. 'No one comes up to this cottage any more. We'll bury them deep and clean up and we'll never mention it again.'

'Fine by me,' said Toni. 'But how can Liam help?'

'He'll tell the polis Seb battered the shite out of him and a warrant will be issued for his arrest.'

'The Thompsons don't go to the polis any more than we do.'

'If he doesn't do it then he'll be buried up here with these twats. I'm only offering him this because he saved your life.'

'I'll do it,' said Liam's weak, tired voice. 'I just want to get out of here.'

'Good.' Frankie turned to the women. 'Caesar will take you both home and drop Liam off at the hospital. We'll sort everything out.'

'And when the polis come calling, asking if we've seen Seb?'

'You'll tell him you've no' seen him. They'll think he's done a runner because there's a warrant out for his arrest.'

'Why should he do a runner now when he's never done one before?'

'Look, it's all arranged,' snapped Frankie. 'So just do it, eh, doll?'

Toni nodded. 'Whatever you say, Frankie.'

'Thank Christ for that. You'd better get going before the yeti comes back from the dead. If this was a film, that's what would happen,' he replied, following this bizarre statement up with a bark of laughter. As he spoke, his eyes remained riveted to Toni's exposed cleavage, making her shift uncomfortably.

'We need to pack our stuff,' said Toni.

'Get on with it then and do it quickly.'

Caesar had to help Liam to his feet and hauled him out the door to the car while Toni assisted Valerie into her bedroom to pack.

'You sit there and I'll pack,' Toni told her.

Valerie just nodded as she sank onto the bed, feeling dislocated from reality. Surely this charnel house was just a bad dream? This cottage had always held a special place in her heart, full of warm family memories, which was a rarity in itself. Now it was tainted. In her mind, it would forever be a tomb.

There wasn't much to pack and Toni made Valerie shower and change her clothes, which she gave to Frankie to dispose of because they were covered in Seb's blood. Toni then led her outside to Caesar's car. The wind had died down to just a gentle breeze. She seated Valerie in the back with Liam, who was slumped in the corner, while she got into the front with Caesar. Valerie was happy to leave everything in the hands of her very capable cousins because she was still trying to accept the fact that she'd killed Seb, the man she'd loved. Even though it had been self-defence and he would have murdered her if she hadn't killed him first, the guilt was bearing down on her like an unbearable weight. She looked down at her hands and although they'd been washed, she was sure she could still see blood on them. How had this happened? Only recently she'd been attempting to escape all the violence and start a good, clean life and now she was a murderer.

Silent tears slid down her cheeks and she felt a hand on her arm. It was Liam, whose eyes were bright with concern through the swollen mess of his face. Valerie gave him a sad smile and patted his hand, this small comfort from an enemy meaning a lot to her.

Liam kept his hand on her arm the entire journey, even though Valerie knew his kind gesture was causing him physical pain. On arrival at the hospital, Caesar stopped outside A & E, opened the back door and helped him out of the car. Valerie's heart went out to Liam when Caesar abandoned him at the door and returned to the car, leaving him to stagger inside before crumpling to the floor. The car had already set off by the time someone came to assist Liam, Valerie watching through the back window until she could see him no more.

'Do you want to come back to mine, Val?' Toni asked her from the front seat.

'Aye, please,' she replied, the gratitude clear in her croaky voice. She couldn't bear to go home. Her parents would ask questions and she was quite sure she would crumble and confess everything, she felt so fragile.

Caesar dropped them off and set off back to the cottage to

assist Frankie and the others. Thankfully Moira was in bed, so it was just Valerie and Toni.

Toni poured her a brandy and pressed the glass into her shaking hands. 'Drink. It'll help.'

She then poured herself one and sat on the couch beside her cousin.

'I... I can't believe,' began Valerie before stopping to wince at the pain in her neck.

'No, neither can I,' sighed Toni. 'God, I feel so guilty for introducing you to him.'

Valerie clasped her hand in her own and shook her head. 'Not your fault,' she whispered as that was slightly less painful than attempting to talk at full volume.

'Don't you dare feel guilty about what happened,' Toni told her. 'He wouldn't have stopped until you were dead, Seb gave you no choice.'

'I know, but it still hurts,' said Valerie, starting to cry. 'I can't stop thinking about his family.' She could just imagine them all getting worried and then frantic when Seb never came home. They would have to live with the agony of never knowing what had happened to him and she couldn't bear it.

28

The next few days passed in a haze for Valerie. She kept to her room most of the time, unable to find the will to get out of bed. She told her parents she was unwell, but they put it down to depression after her split with Seb. They'd no idea he was dead at their daughter's hands and Valerie had no intention of them ever finding out. The bruise on her face she explained away as fainting and falling because she was unwell. They didn't bother to question this explanation. As she'd already booked the time off with work to go on holiday, Valerie didn't have to bother making up excuses to her manager about her absence, which was an enormous relief. The thought of going back to the petrol station and carrying on as normal seemed beyond her. Every time she handed someone their change, she'd see blood on her hands. She would feel like she was tainting every person she came into contact with. Everything had changed, her entire world turned upside down, and she didn't know how she would carry on.

DS Baillie turned up on her doorstep four days after the terrible events at the Slamannan cottage. Fortunately her parents were out at work when he made an appearance. Valerie was curled up in bed, her mind torturing her with thoughts of Seb's last moments. When she heard the knock at the door, she determined to ignore it, until a voice called out that it was the polis and if they didn't open up, they'd batter the door down.

Valerie sighed, dragged herself out of bed, pulled on a roll neck jumper over her pyjamas to hide the bruises on her throat and ambled downstairs. The bruise on her face had turned a livid yellow so there was nothing she could do about that.

Baillie frowned as she pulled the door open. 'Jeezo, you look like deep-fried shite.'

'Thanks,' she muttered. Her voice had almost returned to normal, it was just slightly hoarse. 'What do you want?'

'Can I come in? I don't want to talk on the doorstep.'

She nodded, retreated into the living room and sank onto the couch, leaving him to close the door and follow. He placed his bulk in the armchair usually occupied by her father.

'So what's wrong?' he asked her. 'You ill or something?'

Valerie nodded. 'Aye, I've got some sort of bug. Throwing up and that, so don't get too close, I don't want to infect you.'

'You won't. I've never had a day's illness in my life. And the bruise on your face?'

'I passed out and fell.'

Valerie held her breath as his sharp eyes assessed her.

'In that case, I won't keep you long,' he eventually said, seemingly accepting her explanation. 'Have you seen Sebastian Robertson lately?'

Valerie ached at the mention of his name but once again her talent for putting up a calm front came to her rescue. 'No, not since that time in the hospital. I don't want to see the lying pig ever again. What's he done now?'

'Beat Liam Thompson to a pulp. You know Liam Thompson?'

'Not really. I know of him.'

'Course you do. His family's been fighting yours for decades.'

'Is he okay?'

'He's in a lot of pain, with plenty of broken bones, but he'll recover. His left hand's in a bad way, most of the bones were shattered. He'll never regain full use of it.'

'Jesus. And you say Seb did that to him?'

'According to Liam. Seb must have got wind that a warrant was issued for his arrest because we cannae find him anywhere.'

'And you think I might know where he is? Well, I don't.'

'Did he ever mention anywhere to you that he might have gone to hide?'

'Not that I can think of and even if he did, it wouldn't be any use because everything he told me about himself was a lie. I never even knew him,' she said miserably. 'I know my family are the black sheep of Glasgow, but we don't know the identity of every scumbag in the city. We had absolutely no idea Seb wasn't who he said he was.'

'All right, take it easy,' said Baillie, holding up his hands.

Valerie just scowled back at him.

'If you see or hear from him then please let me know immediately,' he said, placing his card on the coffee table. 'I can't stress how dangerous he is.'

'I'll let you know, but I doubt I will. He didn't seem to give a shite that he hurt me. I was just another in a long line.'

'If you ask me, he's realised his maw cannae get him off this charge, the procurator fiscal's determined to send him to Bar-L this time. And the Thompson clan are out for his blood. If they get hold of him, they will kill him, they're so furious. So Seb will be lying low somewhere.'

'Probably, like the snake he is.'

'Aye. Well, I'll leave you to it. I hope you feel better soon. Don't get up, I'll see myself out.'

Valerie breathed a sigh of relief when he'd gone. She'd thought it would be harder to get rid of him than that. The mad impulse to confess to the sergeant came into her mind. Being punished for what she'd done would be the only way to alleviate her guilt, which she wasn't sure she could live with. If she said it was self-defence, she might not even serve that long in prison. But an investigation at the cottage would uncover the other bodies hidden up there, old as well as new, and no one would believe she took down all four men alone. Her cousins would be dragged into it and she couldn't bear the thought of Toni being flung into prison for defending her. The prospect of the same thing happening to Frankie didn't cause her as much pain, as that could only be for the good of the local community. But Tam, Paul, Jamesie and Liam would be dragged into it too and Valerie knew Frankie would find a way to silence her before the case even got to court. No doubt his good friend Duncan Blackwood would be able to pull that one off. No, confessing to the police would cause her family too much damage. But how else could she cope with what she'd done?

* * *

A full week passed and the emotional pain only deepened for Valerie, depression cloaking her like a black pall. She refused to leave the house or see any visitors. After ignoring Toni's calls, her redoubtable cousin came to the house, stormed upstairs and banged on her bedroom door, demanding to be let in, but Valerie had already locked it and refused to open it, leaving Toni no choice but to leave. Janet and Charlie told their daughter she was stupid for allowing herself to wallow in pity over a man, that Seb was probably seeing other women and she should snap out of it and find someone else. They lost patience with her refusal to get out of bed and their reprimands only made things worse.

Her parents did manage to have one positive effect, though – they got her out of the house, or rather drove her out in her desperation to escape their condemnation.

For the first time in days, Valerie wandered the streets, the hood of her coat pulled up to disguise her face, wanting to avoid everyone she knew, so she caught the bus into the city centre. Not even the bustle of a vibrant city could lift her out of her fugue. Her surroundings were mere background noise, her head entirely taken up with thoughts of Seb and the moment she'd taken his life. She hadn't been able to stop thinking about it since it had happened and, rather than become accustomed to its horror, it only tightened its grip on her crumbling psyche. It felt like it would never leave her, that she would forever be tormented by the memories, and she didn't know how she would live with it.

Valerie found herself eyeing up every tower block she passed, wondering if she could get to the top unhindered because the fall would definitely be enough to kill her. She passed Charing Cross train station and considered what it would be like to throw herself in front of a passing train. Would it be a quick death, or would there be enormous pain first? Whenever a bus passed her on the road, she was tempted to throw herself under its enormous wheels. It was only the thought of the trauma or possible injury she would cause other people that held her back. She just wanted the pain to go, she couldn't live the rest of her life like this. If it didn't kill her, it would turn her into a monster like Seb and that she refused to become.

The one mercy was that the Robertson family hadn't contacted her to ask if she knew where Seb was. They too had accepted that he'd done a runner to escape arrest, so they left her alone. Looking into their anxious faces would have been too much for her.

Valerie hesitated outside a pharmacy. Of course, here was the best solution – she could buy a load of paracetamol, take the lot and quietly slip away. New laws restricting the purchase of paracetamol had recently come into force, but she could go to different shops to get what she needed.

Just as she'd decided to enter the pharmacy, something urged her to turn around and she found herself staring up at a church. It was an old leviathan of a building made of red sandstone with a spire that once would have dominated the landscape but had been overshadowed by the rise of the tower blocks. The last time she'd been in a church had been for a family wedding. The groom's ex had burst in just as the vicar had asked if anyone had any objections and said she and the groom had slept together just the night before. Her cousin had punched her husband-to-be in the face and burst into tears while the majority of the family had leapt on him and battered him to a pulp at the feet of the horrified vicar. That had been two years ago, and she hadn't been in one since. She winced as it occurred to her that Seb, despite telling her he was a big believer in God, had never taken her to a church or even mentioned going to one. Another red flag she'd completely missed because she'd been in love.

Valerie glanced back over her shoulder at the pharmacy, but something about the church was inviting. She jogged across the road and pushed at the door, half-relieved and half-disappointed to find it unlocked. Now she had no choice but to follow the mad urging inside her.

She sneaked inside, quietly closing the heavy oak door behind her. The church was empty, although the atmosphere was heavy, as though a rapt congregation had just exited, leaving behind the passion of their prayers.

Her boots clicked off the stone flags as she walked to the nearest wooden pew and took a seat. The vaulted ceiling towered above her. The stained-glass windows were beautiful, depicting images of figures she didn't recognise, although she did spot Archangel Michael with his flaming sword.

Valerie slowly exhaled, hung her head and closed her eyes. The frantic thoughts that had tormented her outside this building suddenly eased, giving her a modicum of relief. Everything inside her settled down as she drank in the peace that hung in the heavy silence. She realised it had been so long since she'd experienced perfect silence, the thick stone of the building keeping the outside world at bay. It was a relief to her aching heart.

The image of the moment Seb had died once again popped into her head and she jumped, eyes flying open. She was a little shocked to see a tall man wearing the long black robes and the white collar of a minister staring down at her with a friendly, welcoming smile. He was middle-aged, short dark hair just starting to turn grey. His hazel eyes were bright and reflected the light as beautifully as the stained glass. She wouldn't say he was handsome, but there was something about him that was captivating.

He took the seat beside her and smiled, being careful to leave a little space between them. 'My name's Michael,' he opened.

'Like the archangel?' she said, nodding at the glorious image in the window, lit up by the sunlight streaming through it.

'Aye,' he smiled. 'My mother was always very fond of him, so it was only natural she named me after him. Would you like to talk or would you rather I left you in peace?'

It was Valerie's instinct to tell him to leave her alone, but perhaps this man could help her? 'I... I lost someone very dear to me recently and... I'm not coping.' A blush stole across her cheeks. 'Sorry, I'm not used to doing this.'

'Coming to church or opening up about your feelings?'

'Both. This is the first time I've come to church, actually, other than for a wedding or funeral. I've not even been christened.'

'That doesn't matter. My door is open to everyone,' he kindly replied. 'And you're here to seek comfort?'

'I don't know, to be honest. I just saw the church and something urged me to come inside.'

There was a gentle knowing in his eyes as he smiled. 'You did the right thing listening to that urging, for that is how the divine communicates with us. Many people call it instinct, but it's something far higher.'

'Right,' she said slowly.

He stared deep into her eyes and Valerie felt he was examining her grief. It was soothing, as though he were taking some of her burden from her.

'You are in so much pain,' he said gently. 'And you feel no one understands?'

Valerie nodded, a tear slipping down her cheek. 'I feel like I'm drowning in it and I can't escape.'

'Grief is one of the most powerful emotions we can experience but its grasp on us does start to weaken.'

'How do I keep my head above the water until it does?'

'I think you're feeling more than just grief. You have guilt too?'

'Yes,' she replied, the word choked in her throat as she fought against the torrent of tears. 'I'm going to hell.'

'Do you believe in hell?'

'I didn't, until I started feeling like this. I feel like I've been abandoned and will never feel or experience anything good ever again. I'm being punished.'

Michael's smile was gentle. 'God doesn't punish. The only ones who punish us are ourselves.' Mischief filled his eyes. 'And between you and me, I don't believe in hell either.'

'Isn't that a cornerstone of your faith?'

'It is for others, but not for me. My God is unconditional love. He doesn't judge or punish. Whatever you feel guilty about, He still loves you and will never abandon you, that's why He led you here today. You've cloaked yourself in these emotions to cut yourself off from Him. Cast them off and you will find Him again.'

'That's the problem, I never really believed in Him, that was until I met someone who started to convince me that He does exist. Then it turned out he was playing a cruel trick on me, that he never really believed. I thought I was getting an angel, but he was a demon,' she said, starting to cry. 'Sorry,' she croaked through her tears.

'Please don't apologise,' he softly replied. 'The only way for you to move through these emotions is to release them.'

Valerie buried her face in her hands and cried her heart out with Michael sitting quietly and patiently beside her. He made no comment and was just a strong, silent presence supporting her in quiet solidarity. Eventually her tears slowed before calming down altogether and when she raised her head, she found herself looking into his gentle, smiling face. He seemed to be the essence of the man she thought she'd fallen in love with, *her* Seb. But there was no danger of her falling in love with him, she didn't think she'd ever love a man again after what she'd been through.

'Thank you,' she said. 'I feel a little better.'

'You certainly look lighter. I run a group here for the bereaved. You don't have to go into details if you're not comfortable. Sometimes the presence of others who are going through a similar experience can be of immeasurable comfort. We have tea and excellent homemade cakes too. The next meeting is this evening. You're more than welcome to come along, if you like?'

'You know what? I think I will.' Even if the group wasn't any good, just being in this peaceful place was helping her no end.

'Excellent. It starts at six o'clock. I must warn you, if you're late, I might not be able to guarantee you a cake. They do go very fast.'

Valerie laughed for the first time since Seb's death. 'I won't be late.'

* * *

Valerie joined the bereavement group and found it to be made up of kind, gentle and very supportive people. Some of them had suffered their bereavement years ago but still came to the group to counsel the newer members. It helped Valerie to know she wasn't the only one suffering from guilt, although none of the other members had actually killed the person they were grieving for. One man was supposed to stop at a shop on his way home from work for some supplies, but he forgot because he was tired, so his wife went instead and ended up dying in a car crash. A woman dismissed her young son's symptoms as a heavy cold when in fact it was the meningitis that took his life. These people had contemplated thoughts of suicide too but were slowly working through their emotions and were learning to live with their pain with the help of the group. Valerie naturally couldn't give out any details and no one pressed her to, but just confessing her feelings to them and basking in their warm words of support began to help her heal.

She went to the group faithfully each week and joined in other activities at the church – helping out at craft fairs and jumble sales to raise money for repairs, as well as charity nights, not just for the church but for other good causes. It wasn't long before she started attending the services. At first, she found listening to Michael preach rather painful as he reminded her of the man she'd loved and of the future she'd thought she would have. When the pain inside her started to swell, somehow Michael's gaze always found hers and just that connection was enough to soothe it. She became a regular at the church and Michael became a firm friend, although it was purely platonic, and it was a relief to Valerie to have a friend not connected with the city's underbelly. He was so kind and good, and it helped her to know that such people really did exist.

Valerie started to cut herself off from all the bad influences in her life. When she wasn't working, she was at the church, helping out or attending services. Her parents were appalled to learn that their daughter had joined an organised religion and denigrated her new beliefs at every opportunity, but Valerie was strong enough to refuse to allow them to ruin the peace she'd found. The memories of Seb no longer tortured her and she looked to the future with happy optimism. Frankie was too caught up in cementing his new position to bother with her. With Seb out of the way, he took over his territory and expanded his power base. Toni didn't like the change in her cousin and sensed she was slipping away from her, which did pain Valerie, but she recognised Toni was on a dark path and she refused to follow her down it. Her own path had finally been revealed to her. She could still live the beautiful life she'd envisioned, only she would live it alone.

Valerie asked Michael how she would go about training to be a minister in the Scottish church, and he was delighted to hear this was what she wanted to do. She'd already confided in him that she was a McVay but he didn't anticipate this would cause her any problems and said he'd put in a good word for her. She would have to get a Bachelor's in Divinity, which would mean studying at university. Valerie worried how she would afford it, until Michael informed her that he would be able to help her get a grant.

* * *

Valerie decided to study for her degree at Aberdeen University. Glasgow University ran the course she wanted to do but if she was going to be successful in her new life, she had to escape her old one. Michael's friends helped her find somewhere to stay and only once Valerie had arranged a flat to rent in Aberdeen and her manager at the petrol station had got her a transfer to a station close by did she break the news to her family. Aunty Mima was the first person she confided in, and she was incredibly supportive and seemed all for her escaping Frankie and his insatiable lust for power. After leaving Mima's, Valerie thought it only right she tell her parents next, and they became stone-faced and sniffy, listening to her big news in icy silence.

'I can't believe I spawned a God-botherer,' were her father's only words before retreating to his shed in the garden.

'I hope you're happy, you've upset your da,' snapped her mother before storming upstairs and slamming her bedroom door shut.

Valerie had been feeling a little guilty about moving away but their reaction eliminated that feeling in an instant. She got the sense that from now on she would only see her parents at Christmas and that was fine by her. There was a new serenity about her that meant the outside world could no longer affect her as much as it had.

She left her house to go to Toni's. It was only fair her best friend was the next to be told.

'Well, well, well,' said Toni when she opened the door to her, eyes flashing. 'Look what the cat dragged in.'

'Hi, Toni. Can I come in? I've got some news.'

Toni merely sniffed, turned on her heel and stalked back into the house. Valerie followed her into the living room. To her surprise, no one else was there.

'Where's Aunty Moira?' she asked Toni.

'She has a hospital appointment, Frankie's taken her. Why, did you want to tell them your news?'

'No, it's okay. You're the important one here.'

'Naturally,' said Toni in a tone worthy of a grand empress.

'I came to tell you that I'm moving to Aberdeen. I'm taking a degree in Divinity so I can become a minister.'

Toni gaped at her. 'What?' she shrieked. 'I thought all that church shite was just you getting over Seb and that you'd snap out of it eventually.'

'It's what I want to do with my life. I've found the perfect way to help people as well as myself.'

'You do know you have to be a believer to be a minister?'

'I do and I am.'

Toni snorted. 'Valerie Brown, the terror of Glasgow, believes in God?'

'I really do, and I've never felt better. Finally I'm at peace and I hope you can be happy for me.'

Toni took her by the shoulders. 'Listen to me, Val – Frankie's power's increasing by the day and he still wants you working for him.'

'Toni,' sighed Valerie.

'No, please, listen. He's left you alone hoping you'll snap out of this church stuff you've lost yourself in, but he won't stand for this. He won't let you go.'

'Let me go? This is my life and I'll do what I want with it. I'm leaving for Aberdeen in three days, and I hope you can be happy for me.'

'Happy for you? You're abandoning your family and friends.'

'To start a new life. This is what I want to do.'

'Why can't you do it in Glasgow? There's a university here. Oh, I see,' said Toni. 'It's us you want to escape, isn't it?'

'If I don't, Frankie will drag me into his world and I'll never be able to do what I want. I have to get away if I'm going to succeed at this and I really hope you'll support me.' The hurt that flashed in Toni's eyes pained Valerie, but she would not live her life for other people any more. It was time to do what she wanted, for once.

'I will not support you abandoning this family, you traitor.'

'I'm not a traitor and I never will be. I love you, Toni, you're my best friend but I can't do this any more. Seb's death nearly destroyed me and it was God who brought me back from the brink. I was thinking about killing myself until I walked into that church.'

Toni's eyes widened. 'You were?'

'Aye. I was about to go into a pharmacy to buy some paracetamol to overdose on. Then I saw the church and decided to go in there instead. If I hadn't, I would be dead now.'

Toni released her and turned her back while she regained control over her emotions. 'Then I'm truly glad you did walk into the church,' she said, husky voice full of pain. She took a deep breath and turned back round to face her, eyes full of imperiousness. 'But you're talking about abandoning the family and that is treason.'

'I'm not abandoning you, I can still be a part of this family in Aberdeen. Other family members have moved away and they're not called traitors.'

'Because they weren't involved in the family business. Just think, Val, if you stay, we could work together and Frankie will make us rich. We can buy big houses and flash cars and anything we want.'

'I already have what I want – peace – and that's something money can't buy.'

Toni huffed with annoyance. 'You're being really stupid, Val.'

'Perhaps, but I have to do this and I want you to understand.'

Toni took a step back from her, gaze cold. 'I don't understand how anyone can abandon their own family.'

Toni's expression turned to stone. Already she was distancing herself from her. This caused Valerie much more anguish than the distance that had been created between herself and her parents.

'Aunty Mima's arranging a leaving do for me in The Admiral tomorrow night,' said Valerie. 'I hope you'll be there.'

'I won't be, and I doubt anyone else will be either. You turn your back on us, we turn our backs on you.'

'I'm not turning my back on you and one day I hope you'll come to realise that. I fear for you, Toni, really I do. I know you took Leo's eye.'

Toni merely shrugged. 'And?'

'He didn't deserve that.'

'Of course he did, he hurt you.'

'What did you do with it?'

'I keep it in a glasses case,' she said proudly. 'Appropriate, don't you think?'

Valerie sighed heavily. There was no saving her cousin now she was taking her own trophies, her course was set. She kissed Toni's cheek. It was like kissing ice. 'I love you, Toni,' she said before turning and leaving, blinking back tears.

Toni watched her best friend leave with a lump in her throat, which she determinedly swallowed down. Emotions made you weak and she refused to succumb to them. She was moving into another stage in her own life and sentiment had no place in it. Toni would harden her heart until nothing could permeate it.

Valerie felt even more dejected as she left Toni's. The only one who was supporting her new life was Aunty Mima. She imagined her farewell party would be very small.

There was one other person she wanted to see, even though if Frankie found out he'd be furious, but fuck him. As she was constantly reminding everyone, this was her life.

Liam was back in hospital. He'd been discharged after recovering from the beating he'd taken from Seb, but he'd had to go back in for surgery on his hand. He looked pretty miserable, lying on a bed in a room on a ward with three other men, his hand encased in plaster. His eyes lit up when he saw who his visitor was.

'Valerie,' he beamed. 'I wasn't expecting to see you.'

'I felt I had to come,' she replied, pulling the curtain around his bed for some privacy and taking the chair at his side. 'How's the hand?'

'Fucking painful. The surgery was successful and has given me a bit more movement, but it'll never be the same.'

'I'm sorry to hear that.'

'It could be worse. I'm still alive, thanks to you.'

'And Toni's alive, thanks to you. Have you heard anything from DS Baillie?'

'They're still looking for Seb. Baillie's got it into his head that he's hiding out in Wales.'

'Let's hope he keeps thinking that. I came here to say goodbye.'

'Why, where are you going?'

'This might sound crazy to you but I'm going to Aberdeen University to study for a degree in Divinity. I want to be a minister.'

His eyebrows shot up. 'Seriously?'

'Aye.'

'Oh, well, if that's what you want, then you should go for it.'

'Thank you,' she smiled. 'I wish my own family would say the same.'

'They're not supportive?'

'Only Aunty Mima. My parents have practically disowned me, and Toni thinks I'm mad.'

'I don't blame you for wanting to get away, to be honest, after everything that's happened. When my hand's better, I'm moving away too. I'm sick of it. Nearly getting killed was a big wake-up call. I've got a pal in Dumfries with his own garage, selling cars. He said he'd gi'e me a job. I love motors, so it'll be good being around them all day. A lot safer too.'

'That's great. I'm so glad you're getting out. If you stay around here...'

'I'll probably be killed.'

'We both will.'

'Aye. You could come with me, if you like? They have churches down there too.'

'I appreciate the offer,' she smiled. 'But everything's ready and waiting for me in Aberdeen.'

'Shame. I think we'd be pretty good together.'

'Maybe, although Frankie would follow us down there and kill us both slowly and painfully.'

'You're right, he wouldn't be able to swallow that. We'd be like Romeo and Juliet, star-crossed lovers from rival families. See, I do know a bit about Shakespeare.'

'I'm impressed,' she laughed. 'I hope you get out of here soon and that your hand heals well. Have a nice life.'

Liam's eyes widened with surprise when she leaned over to press a kiss to his lips. He snaked his good hand around the back of her head and gently pulled her closer, the kiss deepening.

'Are you sure you don't want to come to Dumfries?' he breathed when the kiss ended. 'That was hot.'

'It certainly was, but I'm sure. I'll never forget you, Liam.'

'Me too, Valerie.'

He smiled as he watched her pull back the curtain and leave. She hesitated at the door to look back over her shoulder at him. Then she was gone.

Liam sighed and sank back into the pillows, still tingling from that kiss. He got the feeling he'd just let something wonderful walk out of his life, but he knew there was no stopping Valerie Brown.

29

TWENTY-THREE YEARS LATER

Valerie spoke from the pulpit to her congregation in Fraserburgh on the north-east coast. They hadn't been too certain about a female minister at first, but they'd quickly come to like her. Valerie was always there for her flock when they needed her, whether it be day or night. Her devotion had quickly endeared her to them and they had welcomed her into their community. It was Sunday service on a warm July day and her sermon was about forgiveness, something she knew a lot about, when the door clicked open at the back of the room. A latecomer was sneaking in, which wasn't unusual. Valerie didn't look their way because she didn't want to embarrass them. It was the click-clack of high heels that convinced her to look up. Valerie's gaze connected with a pair of black eyes before she returned to her sermon. This unexpected arrival had disconcerted her, but she had a job to do.

When she'd finished, she waited at the main doors to say goodbye to her congregation, avoiding those black eyes that followed her every movement.

The latecomer remained in a pew, waiting for her to return.

When the last member of her flock had gone, Valerie returned to the church and closed the door.

'Finally we're alone, Reverend,' said a husky voice.

'It's good to see you, Toni,' said Valerie, sitting beside her. 'I see you've got the fur coat you always wanted.' She thought her cousin looked wonderful, she'd hardly aged. Her black curls were arranged into a sophisticated updo and diamonds hung from her ears. There was a self-assurance about her that she hadn't possessed before.

'Only the finest mink. I have four of them, actually,' Toni sniffed. 'I came to tell you that Frankie's dead.'

Valerie sighed and shook her head. 'His end was violent, I suppose?'

'Of course.'

'It's so sad but inevitable. When's the funeral?'

'There isn't one. He went to Manchester to help out some contacts of ours and he never came back. No doubt he's resting in a shallow grave in some desolate place in the north-west of England.'

'Poor Frankie. And who are these *contacts*?'

'It's best you don't know. They're not people who like their secrets being revealed. I suspect Frankie tried to pressure them into doing something they didn't want to do.'

'That does sound like him.'

'So I'm head of the family now,' said Toni, tilting back her head proudly. 'And I want you to come back to Glasgow with me. You've spent too long stuck out here. It's time to come home.'

'I'm happy here.'

'How can you possibly be happy being stuck in this draughty old church all day? Don't you miss the bustling big city?'

'Occasionally, but I enjoy my life here. It's peaceful and I'm happy.'

'I want to shake up the family a bit, do things differently. I intend to be a subtler leader than Frankie, who doesn't maim someone for nothing, for whom violence is only a last resort, and you can help me do that. Hang up the dog collar and come and work for me.'

'I appreciate the offer, Toni, but sorry, I'm very content with my life. Since I've been here, I've only known peace.'

'And I can help you know so much more – excitement, thrills, money, adventure.'

'Serenity is far more important to me than those things.'

'Serenity?' chuckled Toni humourlessly. 'What use is that?'

'If you'd ever experienced it, then you'd know its value. When peace rules your heart, the trials of this life can no longer touch you.'

Toni's look was withering. 'You're full of shite, Reverend.'

Valerie just shrugged.

It annoyed Toni that her cousin's serene expression didn't so much as slip. 'So you refuse to come back to Glasgow with me?'

'I do. I can't be a part of your world, especially not now, because I'm guessing you're not going to lead the family down a more legitimate path?'

'You guess right. Frankie built a good foundation for the business but I'm going to steer it in a new and more profitable direction. Frankie let his temper and lust for blood rule him. I'll be more subtle and will only court trouble when I have no other choice, although I'll make damn sure everyone in Glasgow fears me. Now I'm older, I want a quieter life, to enjoy the fruits of my labours in a gossamer blanket of luxury, being pleasured whenever I want by beautiful men and women. Doesn't that sound much nicer than preaching to a bunch of people with terrible dress sense and even worse haircuts in a musty old church?'

'No,' replied Valerie steadily. 'I've found the perfect life for me.

Maybe one day I will return to Glasgow, but if I do, it will be as a minister of the church. I will never rejoin the family business.'

Toni's expression was stony. 'Does this life of yours stop you feeling guilty?'

'I have no guilt.'

'I don't believe that for a moment. You're hoping this goody-goody life of yours will cleanse you of what you did at the cottage at Slamannan. Do all those hideous parishioners of yours know their good reverend has blood on her hands?'

'That's all in the past.'

'No, it's not. I can see it in your eyes. It's never left you and it never will.'

'You're right, Toni, but that's because I have a conscience. You did once, but it seems to have deserted you.'

'It was holding me back. Now I live my life unfettered. That is real peace, not hiding away from the world here. I can't stay, I've got a business meeting with a multi-millionaire. I'm about to close on a very important deal that will make me a ton of money.'

'Although I might not agree with the life you're living, I'm glad you've found what you were looking for.'

'I miss Frankie, but his death did set me free, and I had the strength to keep everything together and prevent our enemies from taking over. I saw Liam Thompson the other day, by the way. He still lives in Dumfries but he was visiting family. He's gone fat and bald and his wife looks like a hippo. He also has a brood of hideous children. He asked after you and I swear the life returned to his eyes at the mention of your name.'

'That's nice. Does this mean you've brokered a truce with the Thompson family?'

'Call it an uneasy truce. One day, they will give me trouble again, but for now, they're behaving themselves.'

'I wish you could stay longer. I have missed you, Toni.'

'And you, Val, but I think we're just too different now. We're a long way from the girls we used to be.'

'I miss those girls,' said Valerie with a twinge of nostalgia.

Toni's black eyes softened. 'Me, too.' With that she got to her feet. 'Must go, I can't keep Caesar waiting.'

'He's still around, is he?'

'He never left. He's my bodyguard and I trust him with my life.'

'That's nice. I'm glad you have that with someone.'

'Tam's here too. He's waiting in the car, he refused to come into a church. He says they creep him out. He's my second-in-command.'

'Tam? But he was always a huge misogynist. I can't imagine him taking orders from a woman, especially one younger than him.'

'Well, he is,' snapped Toni.

'Watch your back with him, he can be sneaky and dangerous.'

'Believe it or not, I do know what I'm doing.' Toni took one last look around, nose crinkled with disdain. 'I'm leaving now. The smell of damp is intensely irritating.'

'I'll see you out.'

'So kind, Reverend,' said Toni sarcastically.

Valerie saw her cousin to the door. 'It really has been wonderful seeing you again and I hope to see you again soon.'

'Perhaps you will.'

Valerie looked to the gleaming black Mercedes parked at the kerb outside her church. Caesar stood beside it in an immaculate and very expensive grey suit, a Rolex on his wrist. His hair was still long and black, although it was slicked back off his face and he wore designer sunglasses. Valerie waved to him, and he nodded back.

The rear window was wound down and Tam's egg-shaped head popped out. 'You all right, doll?' he called to her.

'Aye, no' bad, Uncle Tam. How about you?'

'Great, sweetheart, just great.'

With that, he popped his head back inside the car and closed the window.

'You will keep a close eye on him, won't you?' Valerie anxiously asked her cousin.

'Don't worry,' replied Toni. 'I keep him on a tight leash. Well, goodbye, Reverend. Enjoy your boring, quiet life up here, won't you?'

'I certainly will,' said Valerie serenely.

She watched Toni sashay down the steps and smile flirtatiously at Caesar as he opened the rear door for her to get in before gently closing it behind her.

The car drove off, Valerie unable to see its occupants as the windows were blacked out, and she experienced a painful pang. It had been good to see Toni again, albeit briefly. Toni had had no choice but to harden herself to the world in order to fulfil the duties of her new position, but Valerie got the feeling some of the kindness she'd once possessed still dwelt inside her, it was just buried deep.

Valerie returned inside the church, shut the door and sank into a pew, looking at the spot where Toni had sat. Perhaps she should return to Glasgow? If she did, she knew she would inevitably be pulled into Toni's world, but maybe she could perform some good down there? Her cousin was right, she had been hiding away up here, away from her demons, when the only way to truly vanquish them was to confront them. She would wait and see if a parish became available down there just far enough from Toni to avoid getting caught up in her world.

Gang violence and knife crime were on the rise in her home city, especially in some of the neglected areas of greater Glasgow. Bored young men with a thirst to improve their lives and with no job prospects getting caught up in dangerous situations with no way out. Perhaps she could work with them to improve their lot? Yes, she would mention to the Church's main administration office in Edinburgh that she wanted to return to Glasgow and hopefully she would save some young souls from turning into her cousin. A position would open up for her one day, when her help was needed the most. It might take years as she would have to wait for a colleague to leave their parish, but return she would, on that she swore to almighty God.

MORE FROM HEATHER ATKINSON

We hope you enjoyed reading *Wicked Girls*. If you did, please leave a review.

If you'd like to gift a copy, this book is also available as an ebook, digital audio download and audiobook CD.

Sign up to Heather Atkinson's mailing list for news, competitions and updates on future books.

http://bit.ly/HeatherAtkinsonNewsletter

Why not explore the best selling Gallowburn Series,

ABOUT THE AUTHOR

Heather Atkinson is the author of over fifty books - predominantly in the crime fiction genre. Although Lancashire born and bred she now lives with her family, including twin teenage daughters, on the beautiful west coast of Scotland. Her new gangland series for Boldwood, set on the fictional Gallowburn estate in Glasgow began with *Blood Brothers* which was published in December 2020.

Visit Heather's website:
https://www.heatheratkinsonbooks.com/

Follow Heather on social media:

 twitter.com/HeatherAtkinso1

 instagram.com/heathercrimeauthor

 bookbub.com/authors/heather-atkinson

 facebook.com/booksofheatheratkinson

PEAKY READERS

GANG LOYALTIES. DARK SECRETS.
BLOODY REVENGE.

A READER COMMUNITY FOR
GANGLAND CRIME THRILLER FANS!

DISCOVER PAGE-TURNING NOVELS
FROM YOUR FAVOURITE AUTHORS
AND MEET NEW FRIENDS.

JOIN OUR BOOK CLUB
FACEBOOK GROUP

BIT.LY/PEAKYREADERSFB

SIGN UP TO OUR
NEWSLETTER

BIT.LY/PEAKYREADERSNEWS

Boldw⚭d

Boldwood Books is an award-winning fiction publishing company seeking out the best stories from around the world.

Find out more at www.boldwoodbooks.com

Join our reader community for brilliant books, competitions and offers!

Follow us
@BoldwoodBooks
@BookandTonic

Sign up to our weekly deals newsletter

https://bit.ly/BoldwoodBNewsletter

Printed in Great Britain
by Amazon

13243755R00208